I0698961

BELTANE

MIDSUMMER
BOOK FOUR

JENA DOYLE

DIRTY WORDS PUBLISHING LLC

Copyright © 2025 by Jena Doyle

All rights reserved.

No part of this book may be reproduced in any form or by any electronic or mechanical means, including information storage and retrieval systems, without written permission from the author, except for the use of brief quotations in a book review.

Line Editing: Misha at Verity Ink Editorial

Proofreading: Kimberly at Revision Division

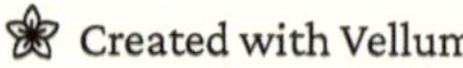 Created with Vellum

For my main girl, Freya.
Thank you for saving my life.
I'm still trying not to fuck it up.
I love you most of all, you know.

READER DISCRETION ADVISED

While some parts of the Midsummer series touched on sensitive themes, none have hit the point where I felt I needed to warn my readers. This one, however, does require a notice. Your mental health is important. Please take care of yourselves. I understand if you can't finish the story because of the below. Be well, my friends.

Beltane contains references to sexual assault and self-harm that happen off the page. It is described briefly in exposition and memories, and I've tried to keep it as non-triggering as possible.

If you're still here, thank you for reading.

Until the End.

PROLOGUE
MIRI

AFTER THE END

It was not a sham marriage.

We were in love, all of us, together. We were always meant to be a four.

The world looked at our relationship and judged us for it, but I no longer cared what they thought. I couldn't, not when my wife brought out my inner fire, not when one of my husbands lived in the darkness with me and the other was as blinding as endless sunshine.

"Are you sure about this?" Ivy asked, wrapping her fingers in mine as we walked through the woods. The pads of my bare feet sank into the wet undergrowth, but I barely felt it.

Once, long ago, the trees would have whispered to me of their secret schemes. They would have told me if this was a good idea or if I should turn back, but I hadn't heard them in years...not since the end. Not since that night in Killwater when we'd lost so much and gained much more in return.

"I'm sure," I said, more confident than I'd ever been about anything. I'd been dreaming about this for months. The woods had been calling me, reaching out however they could. So many times, I had ventured here and shoved my fingers into the dirt, praying I'd vibrate with that same vitality the plants had once used to communicate. I'd close my eyes and unfurl my senses to dead air.

Ivy was no longer able to get inside our minds. Lex tried to get the truth out of his clients, but the words held no magic. Carter's luck had finally run out.

A part of me, perhaps the part that had always had a special connection to the trees, lamented what we'd lost...what we'd given up so we could win. But in my darkest moments, I'd admit I'd do it all again if it brought the same results. I'd go through the tears, the heartache, the threat of a terrible, irreversible loss only to know unimaginable joy.

Until the end, we once promised. *Until the end* had been branded on our hands for four years.

The end had come and gone and we'd survived. All of us. All four of us. Here to bring in the new day.

"If I thought we could get it back," Lex said, catching up to me on the side opposite Ivy. "I would have suggested this after we rescued you from—"

"I'm certain," I cut him off, refusing to even think about the memory he mentioned. Those were dark days, indeed, and now that we were on the other side, I refused to relive them. I had made mistakes. I had loved them dearly, only to disappoint them when it mattered most.

I was unworthy of their forgiveness, and yet, they had offered it anyway.

"Yes, but how?" Lex said as he brushed his dark hair out of his mesmerizing eyes, no less beautiful for the years between now and when I'd first met him.

"I just know," I said.

"Are you hearing the trees again, Juliet?" Carter asked, grabbing my shoulders with a loving squeeze.

"No," I said, "but this is the right thing to do, regardless."

"It *is* Midsummer," Ivy said. "We made the original vow on Midsummer."

"Yeah, on the grounds of a sacred ruin in Faerie," Lex added with a scoff and a roll of his eyes. "Don't tell me you've found another veil for us to slip through."

"Goodness, no," I said. "But this land is sacred."

Lex looked unconvinced but Carter wrapped his arms around my prince's shoulders and tucked his head into the crease of his neck. "C'mon, DC. Give her a chance."

"I don't take chances," Lex said. "Not anymore."

"Regardless of whether we get our gifts back, we need to renew our vow," Ivy said, bringing my hand to her mouth to kiss my knuckles.

"Hmm." Lex curled his lips into a devilish grin. "Didn't I just make you do that last night when I had my cock in your a—"

"Our *actual* vow, Lucifer." Ivy laughed, and it pleased me to be a witness to their interactions these days. They still bickered like they hated each other, but now I understood that was their dynamic. They loved as much as they fought, and in that turmoil, they sated a side of their personalities that could only be soothed by the other person. I loved their love, just as they adored the affection I had for Carter. There could only ever be one Ivy for Lex, and only one Romeo for my Juliet, and around and around the earth spun.

"Here," I said, stopping inside the clearing I'd found two weeks ago on one of my walks. The meadow formed a perfect circle with the trees, naturally made considering this was too far away from the cabin for anyone to have done it purposely. It thrummed with an otherworldly energy, something I sensed even without my fairy gift.

"Oh," Carter said, breaking away from us to walk ahead and glance around. The trees had grown tall on all sides, and despite the natural cover, wildflowers bloomed in the center. It was beautiful, idyllic, reminding me of the meadow outside the ruins in Killwater. "This is perfect, Juliet."

I smiled and walked toward him to grab his neck and pull him down for a kiss. "I don't care if we never get our gifts back. I want you to know I still love you...that I still want to be married to you."

"Well, you do crawl into our bed every night," Lex said, grinning as he snaked an arm around my waist to tug me away from our husband.

"I can't explain how I know it will work," I said. "I just know."

"What if the lust hits us again?" Ivy said. "What if we get stuck out here for the next few days?"

"We're not expected anywhere," I said. "It'll be okay."

Ivy took a deep breath and nodded, sinking to her knees in the grass before opening the bag we'd brought with us. Ivy grabbed the candles and put them on the ground as I sat down next to her to light them. I used scissors to cut off a piece of my long white dress before handing them to Carter to do the same to his white T-shirt. Lex cut off a strip of his matching shirt and handed it to me as Ivy sliced through her dress for a scrap of the same.

Once I had the four pieces of linen, I tied them together into a tight knot and held my hand out in the middle, overtop of the open flame. I grabbed the ceremonial knife that had been cleaned and sanitized before coming out here and made a tiny incision in the palm of my hand, right where the words had once shined bright against my alabaster skin. Crimson blood bubbled over the cut, and I watched as my spouses did the same to their hands before placing them over mine. Ivy gripped my palm and Carter laid his on top of hers. Lex went under me, holding us up with his indomitable strength, truly the king of our world, the gravity holding us together.

I wrapped the fabric around our combined embrace, over and under and over again until Ivy helped me knot it on top.

Blood dripped from Carter and Ivy over my hand and down onto Lex's, combining each of us, mixing our life force. Ivy's fire soothed

Lex's ice and emboldened Carter's autumn chill. Each of them complemented the sunny frost of my springtime spirit. We were always meant to be a four, and after everything that had happened, I thanked God that had not changed.

"Okay," I said, glancing at each one of them before returning my attention to our embrace. "Here goes nothing."

ACT I

Sickness is catching: O, were favour so,
Yours would I catch, fair Hermia, ere I go;
My ear should catch your voice, my eye your eye,
My tongue should catch your tongue's sweet melody.
-Helena, Act I, Scene I

I

MIRI

THE BEGINNING OF THE END

I gasped as I stared at the television in the safety of my private apartments in Kensington.

"Ivy and Lex are missing." The newscaster touched his ear and glanced at his fellow reporters, hoping to get a clue. "As are Katherine and Jon Washington. Half the bridal party's gone."

This had to have been the fairy king. It couldn't have been anyone else. Icy-cold fear shot straight through me, the memories of how he'd manipulated my mind squeezing my chest. If he'd gotten to Ivy and Lex, I was next.

"What the bloody hell?" My cousin, Edward, crossed his arms and stood next to me. He'd been surprisingly helpful these last few months, staying at Aberdeen to make sure I wasn't a complete invalid. If I didn't know any better, I'd suspect Gran had sent him to force me to take care of myself. But he hardly qualified as a life coach seeing as he'd fucked half of the Commonwealth by now.

The wedding guests talked among themselves in the background, and even though there were no obvious signs the king had returned, only one thing could have stopped today from happening.

My phone buzzed in my hand, Carter's name flashing across the top. I'd called him a few minutes ago but I no longer had privacy. Maybe it didn't matter anymore. Maybe he was right and I needed to play my part in this. I couldn't hide anymore. Hiding never quite did me any good anyway, and it certainly hadn't made anyone safer.

Before I could answer, shadows played across the light streaming in from the windows, a powerful force hitting me in the gut, nearly bringing me to my knees. Tingles cascaded over my skin, echoing down my spine and the back of my legs. The worst had happened. The king was here.

"Edward, run." I grabbed his arm, trying to yank him to the door, but it was too late. Obsidian spirals slammed against the windows, spilling to either side, darkening the space like an eclipse in the middle of the day, casting everything in gray shadows.

"What is that?" Edward froze, transfixed by the display of paranormal power. When it coalesced into a human form on the front yard, I pushed my cousin behind me, realizing we were too late. Alberich was already here, and judging by the scowl between his dark eyebrows, he was furious.

"Oh, my dear Little Thistle," the king called, stepping closer. His dark coat dusted the grass, emphasizing his matching clothes and long hair. Magic radiated out of him in such magnificence, I wanted to wilt. Instead, I stood taller, jutting my chin out, reminding him I was the one who kept him out last time, and I'd figure out a way to do it again.

"Alberich," I said.

"Do you know him?" Edward turned to the guards in the room. "Get security." When they didn't move, he went to investigate. I focused on the king, waiting for his next play, wondering why he hadn't just blown a hole in the wall.

"Let me in, my dear." He held his arms out to either side, a tempting gesture of solidarity. "We have much to discuss."

"Go away," I said. "You and I have nothing between us."

Even from the third story, I saw a smirk mar his perfect lips. The king was beautiful in the way of all majestic things. He was tall and proportionate, and the sharp edges of his cheekbones and jaw would make Michelangelo weep.

"We have a debt to settle." His gaze echoed with amusement, like he was messing with me. "A life for a life."

"I never asked you to save me." It might have been better if I'd died in the car accident with my parents, but the king had reached in and grabbed me at the last second, sparing me but forcing me to live my life without them.

"Miri, what are you saying? What's going on?" Edward tried to break me from the spell, grabbing my shoulders to maneuver me so I had to look at him. But I couldn't lose focus. I stared at Alberich, daring him to do anything spectacular. The hum of the surrounding trees echoed in my blood, though we were far from any real forest. But I'd gotten so weak in my separation from my beloveds. I doubted I could muster much, even if I was prepared to do anything to protect my family.

"Would you have preferred I let you die?" Alberich raised an eyebrow.

"We'll never know now."

He chuckled, the sound echoing around the room despite the thick stone and glass between us. "Miriam, this story has always ended this way. There's no stopping it. You might as well...*submit.*" The word weighed on my shoulders, tightening the tension in the room to the point where I could pop it with a pin. It rang through me, shaking my joints, willing me to give in to his commands.

But...

Something was different about him, even in this display of his prowess. His energy had dampened, that radiance that had once made him so terrifying in Faerie now reduced to a blip. Why *hadn't* he burst into my room like a juggernaut monster? Why hadn't he brought his army of fairies with him?

"I'd sooner slit my own throat."

"Be careful what you wish for." The fairy king twisted his lips, obsidian spirals emanating out of his body, writhing as they descended on Kensington once more, shrouding my castle in his hatred.

I reached out using my gift, searching for my plant allies on this side of the realm. Kensington didn't have a huge garden, but the nearby park supplied more than enough. Now that I needed their assistance, the energy in them reciprocated with hearty agreement.

Grow, I commanded, sensing my magic shudder as I attempted to use it.

Yes, they replied, seeking my presence, reaching out for me. But I wasn't as strong as I used to be, my body too frail from having been isolated for so long. Somewhere deep down inside, I knew the reason the king had been able to get out was because I had failed to hold on to that energy. Whatever he'd done to me that night in Monaco, whatever I'd allowed him to do, it had caused this.

"Edward," I shouted, backing away from the glass. We'd have to hide somewhere safe, somewhere I could control the plants and keep the king from hurting us. "Edward, let's go."

I turned to look for my cousin, but he was gone. The guards that stood sentry at the doors stared at the ceiling with their eyes hazed over in dark spirals, seemingly entranced by something only they could see.

"Edward?" I raced into the hallway but pulled up short at the sight from the other end. My cousin stood with his green eyes wide and his mouth open in a silent scream. Poppy had appeared next to him, one hand wrapped around his, the other grasping Lizzie, Carter's sister.

"Poppy, what are you doing?" I took a step closer, but the changeling shook her head.

"Miri, I'm sorry. I really am." Tears streaked her blushed cheeks, her hair in wild blond curls around her head.

"You don't have to do this," I told her, holding out a hand. "Come with me. We'll go to Lex and Ivy. We'll tell them what you've done, and they'll fix it."

Alberich's spirals pricked at the windows like rain on a tin roof, sending pinpoint screeches through the entire building. My pulse raced and I clenched my hands into fists, preparing to lunge at her if I had to.

"It's too late to fix it." Poppy sighed and held them tighter. "I wish things could have been different."

"Poppy, stop that," I barked. "You are in control of yourself. Remember who we're fighting. Remember who the real enemy is."

"I know." Poppy sobbed, wiping her eyes on her shoulder before taking a deep breath and righting herself. "That's why I have to do this. Don't you see? If I don't, I'll never see her again."

"Who?" I furrowed my brows. "Ivy? We can go to her right now."

"No." Poppy regained her composure and held on to my cousin tighter, his look of horror intensifying. "No, it has to be this way."

Tick, tick, tick. Alberich's magic pressed on the walls, suffocating me, pulling my focus from protecting us. If I thought dealing with watching two loves of my life marry each other was terrible, add in Alberich and Poppy, and I wanted to crawl into a hole and never come out again. My gut churned and the hot sting of panic squeezed my lungs harder.

"Tell Lex I'm sorry. Tell Ivy...Tell them all. I'm just so"—Poppy sucked in a ragged breath—"so sorry."

I scrambled to reach for them, to stop her from disappearing or maybe attach myself to wherever they ended up. Just as I brushed a fine yellow curl, they vanished, leaving me shocked and standing in the hallway.

The chaos outside erupted, the dark spirals banging harder on the glass, the king's torment now furious for how long I'd been denying him. I ran into my room, only to see him still standing outside, his tendrils of majestic power stifling the magic in my plants. They tried to overpower him, to wrap around his arms and legs, but no matter what they did, he broke them to pieces.

"*Little Thistle,*" he hissed, his voice seeming to boom from every direction all at once. "*I will break through these walls, and when I do, I will have you.*"

"No," I snarled, desperate for a way to escape. I'd been hiding here for months, certain staying away from my beloveds would protect them. He could get inside my mind, manipulate my memories, and make me do things I didn't remember. But in doing so, I'd put my family at risk.

Who the bloody hell knew where Poppy had taken Edward? And if I stayed, the king might hurt my grandparents or the staff. Was there no place safe?

I had to get out. I had to get to Carter as soon as I could.

He was still in London. I'd just talked to him less than an hour ago, so when I pressed call on my phone, he picked up after the second ring.

"Are you okay?" he asked, his voice coming out in a rushed panic.

"The king is here," I whispered as I raced through the palace, running down to my grandmother's rooms. But she, too, had been transfixed.

"Come to me, Little Thistle." The king's voice bounced off the walls in a threatening display of horror.

"Poppy, too," I said to Carter, ignoring the king's exacting demands. "She took Edward. She has Lizzie."

"I'm coming to you," Carter said.

"No," I cut in. "No, stay there. He's done something to my family. He has to be stopped."

"Miri," Carter said, exasperated. "We have to get back to Ivy and Lex. We're stronger together."

Tears streamed down my face as scalding shame reverberated through my body. I'd been vulnerable; I still was. Going to them would put them at risk, but what other choice did I have? I couldn't stay here. Any second, the king would break through the walls and grab me. Then what?

"Okay," I said to Carter. "Okay. Meet me at the airport."

"I have a private charter," he said. "It can take us home to DC."

"Are you trying to run, Little Thistle?" Alberich made an indignant tsking sound with his teeth, as if to suggest that was the most idiotic idea I'd come up with. "Where will you go? Back to them? What will they do with you now?"

"Carter," I said, trying to block out the sound of the king's voice. "I love you. Be careful."

"I love you," he told me. "See you soon."

I hung up and closed my eyes, searching for the plants or whatever trees had decided to help me. My power was weak, but they were surely there, growing and seeking out the source of my terror.

"Help me," I called to them. *"Help me."*

"Oh, come now," Alberich said as I ran through the palace, my heart pumping and my legs nearly unable to carry me. "Don't you remember how much fun we had?"

No. No, don't think about it. Don't focus on it. Just get to Carter. Get to the airport.

I burst through the entrance and out into the evening air, certain Alberich's tendrils would wrap around me and yank me into oblivion. I froze, my knees locking into place when I finally met his gaze a hundred yards ahead. Dark and intimidating, his threatening aura held the weight of the terrible things he could do to me. But rather than seek me out, he tilted his head to the side and smirked.

"Are you planning to run back to them?" he said, and even though he was so far away, I heard the words as if he were right next to me. "Are you going to try to escape me? How adorable."

Fight him. You are stronger than this.

But I didn't feel like it. I'd been separated from my spouses for months, telling myself it would protect them, that I was the weak link. And here was the proof. He held me in his terrible clutches, and I could barely access my gifts. Even if I could fend him off, how would I get away? Everyone around me, my family and the staff, they were under his spell...transfixed into some kind of dream state.

"What do you want, Alberich?" I said, standing tall, forcing myself to maintain a sense of confidence I didn't feel.

"I *want* my wife," he said, taking a slow step toward me. "I will make you a deal...the same deal I offered to Ivette and Alexei. I will remove this so-called *gift.* In exchange, you will deliver the queen to me."

I took a deep breath and shifted my gaze to the impending threat behind the king. Finally, my earthly allies had caught up, their vines and roots twisting through the atmosphere like a tsunami wall of vegetation.

Devour him, I commanded, and they were all too willing to comply. They descended upon his body, snaking around his legs and arms, seemingly intent on bringing him down.

"Have you forgotten who I am?" he taunted, pulling his lips back into a sneer. With one simple jut of his chin, the ropes of ivy closest to him turned black and charred, crumbling away as they disintegrated to ash. A stab went through my midsection at their loss, and I dropped to my knees in agony, instinctively wrapping my arms around myself. I gasped, struggling to inhale even the slightest bit of air.

"Give up this tedious charade," Alberich said, his footsteps coming closer. "There is nowhere for you to run. Where will you go? Back to your beloveds?" He tutted and shook his head, squatting down so he was eye level with me. "Will they even have you after what you did?"

I narrowed my gaze, choking back a sob as more tears ran down my cheeks. *What did he mean?* I focused on that memory from Monaco, the one with the shimmer around it, the one where I'd been certain something had been done to me...but what? It had only been a dream, right? A terribly realistic dream?

No, no, no.

"You were always meant to end up here, my darling," he said, grabbing my chin, his fingers surprisingly gentle despite our altercation. He tilted my head up so I had to look him in the eye. "This is where it ends. You and me, forever in this dance of wills."

I hated him, and I hated what he'd done, whatever it was. I hated that he could manipulate my memories, make it so I couldn't trust my mind. Was any of this real? Or was I like my family, standing in my room somewhere with obsidian eyes, locked inside my mind with whatever visions he decided to give to me?

"Let me go," I whimpered, the words sounding pathetically weak to even my own ears.

"That, I'm afraid, I cannot do." The king shook his head, his features softening as if he were taking pity on poor pathetic me. "Come now. It is not so bad. I will take care of you...if you take care of me."

"No." I couldn't...I wouldn't. Bleeding Christ, I had been such a fool. How could I ever think I could protect anyone? I could barely protect myself. A wave of anguish rose in me, so desperate and over-whelming that it had nowhere else to go. I couldn't hold on to it. I couldn't contain it. I dug my fingers into the grass, gripping it for dear life.

This was a fairy tale cut from my worst nightmares, and I had no idea how the princess would save herself in this one.

I stared up at him, willing the energy to coalesce around me. The branches from my plants regrew, spiraling toward us, wrapping around his neck and body, yanking his limbs back faster than he could defeat them. I poured myself into them, sucking in air as hot, sticky liquid dripped from my nose, over my lips, and down my chin.

"Grow," I said, holding my hands out to reach for them, to give them whatever I had left...which admittedly wasn't much. "Grow!"

He burned through them as quickly as I could get them around his body, and just when he'd gotten free, just when he was about to go for me again, a big black blur slammed into him from the right, catapulting him to the left with a sickening crunch.

I blinked, gaze rooted to the spot where he'd once been as I focused on the dark SUV in front of me.

"Miri!" called Carter's voice as the back door opened. "Get in!"

Carter danced his fingers through my hair as he sat on the sofa in the chartered jet with my head in his lap. He'd called Ivy and Lex to let them know we were coming and explained he had hit the king with a Range Rover.

"Knowing that piece of shit, he'll be after us again no matter what." Carter had told them. "I've only bought us some time."

"*Come home,*" I heard Ivy say. "*We need to regroup and figure out our next steps.*"

"How did you know to come for me?" I asked him once he'd gotten off the call.

"My luck told me you wouldn't make it to the airport," he said. "I was supposed to come rescue you."

"I'm glad you did," I said. "I nearly exhausted myself trying to get away from him."

Because of Carter's newfound fame and connections, he had spared no expense on his publicity tour. Now, his agent, who also happened to be my cousin, was on the phone in the back, doing damage control to his career while we passed the eight-hour flight to DC watching the newest season of a Scottish television show about a woman who goes back in time through a set of stones.

Honestly, even with the chaos that had ensued, I would have given anything to fall into a big rock and wake up in the arms of some six-foot-six ginger who had no idea who I was or where I came from.

"I'm sorry for staying away," I said, glancing up at Carter. "Please forgive me."

"Don't be sorry," he said, his features soft and adoring. "And there's nothing to forgive, Miri. I love you."

"Are they properly upset with me?" I murmured, a small tremor shooting through my nerves at the thought of seeing Ivy and Lex again. Ever since we spent the summer in California together, Carter had become a safe haven for me—my best friend and confidant. The love between us didn't simmer like it did with Ivy, nor did it slice sharply inside me like Lex. But that was what made my relationship with Carter so unique. Lex and Ivy were a force unto themselves, and loving them often came with a harsh smack of reality. Carter was the only other person on this earth who knew that as well as me.

He sighed and glanced down at me, brushing away a tear that had trickled over the side of my face.

"They're worried about you," he said. "We all are."

I swallowed my shame, admitting my isolation tactic had perhaps been ill-advised at best. I thought I was protecting them. I thought staying away would keep us safe. I'd ruined everything because of it.

"Miri," Carter said, gently brushing his fingers against my scalp, massaging certain areas to make me more relaxed. "Yesterday, when I met you in the closet at Danae, you said we weren't safe with you, not anymore."

I tensed, recalling my breakdown. In the fluster of trying to get him to leave before he got caught, I'd overstepped my own boundaries.

"I said a lot of things I didn't mean." I'd told him I was tired of coming in third, that Ivy would end up with either him or Lex, and I'd get screwed in the end. But those were lies. I'd only said them to get him to go, to protect him from whatever the king had done to me.

"You're not third, Miri." He swallowed hard and shook his head. "I'm sorry if we ever made you feel that way."

"You didn't." Damn my poor pathetic heart. I couldn't have him blaming himself, especially not when I'd been the dishonorable one. "I've..." Clearing my throat, I clenched my hands together and sighed, deciding enough was enough. Of the four of us, Carter had always been the more empathetic, the one who would grab a strange child from the queen of fairies to protect her. If I were going to come clean to anyone first, it helped that it was him. "Something's wrong with me." The words came out in a whisper, as if speaking them any louder might make the damage worse.

He furrowed his eyebrows, straightening upright so he could turn to face me. "Whatever it is, it's not as bad as you think."

"This is all my fault, Carter." My throat scratched like I'd swallowed an entire beach. I had to tell *someone*, but maybe it was better to wait until I could tell them all together. I believed something happened to me that night in Monaco. I'd woken up sure that I'd had intercourse the night before. But I didn't remember having anyone in my bed. The same glimmer existed on that memory as the one with my parents. The king did something to me; I knew it. He'd get to me again. "If you hadn't come for me...if you hadn't hit him when he wasn't suspecting it..." I didn't dare look at Carter, knowing I would see anger and disappointment in his stare. "Don't you see?" I turned to face him, my vision blurring as water welled in the corners of my eyes. "I'm the easy target. I'm the liability."

"No, you're not," he said. "But fault doesn't matter. You're alive, and you're here with me, and that's all we need."

I sucked in a deep, desperate breath. "Is this real?"

Carter's features broke, his chest sagging like he couldn't believe I'd had to ask. More tears streamed over his cheeks, and this time, I wiped them away. I didn't like that he had to cry for me. I didn't like that I had become something worth crying over.

He turned me around in his lap, putting my legs to either side of his hips so I straddled his thighs. He leaned me on his massive chest and held me in his strong arms, his steady heartbeat a soothing metronome to the chaos inside my mind.

"Yes, it's real, Juliet."

"How can you be sure?" I closed my eyes, letting his scent and his energy coax me into relaxing.

"I'll tell you when it's not, okay?" He kissed my temple, holding me tighter. "Just ask me, and I'll tell you."

"Okay," I said, tucking farther under his chin like a kitten might to a new owner. The relief his promise brought me evaporated some of the tension in my chest. "Thank you."

It spoke volumes about our relationship that Carter didn't immediately try to fix me. He didn't try to tell me things would be okay or that he'd get some demented toxic revenge for my honor. He didn't make me feel lesser, and for that, I owed him my eternal gratitude.

Exhausted from the battle with the king and the separation from my source of strength, I closed my eyes and let unconsciousness take me.

I stared up at the two-story cabin and took a deep breath, squeezing Carter's hand tighter. The last time I'd escaped from my family and ran to the States, we'd been in the middle of a terrible lust. I had craved their connection the way a dying plant prayed for rain, knowing if I didn't get it, I would wilt away to dust.

Not much was different this time except for the possibility it was more likely they'd turn me away. I hadn't been gone quite as long, certainly not long enough to draw out the lust again, but once they learned how vulnerable I was, they might not want me anymore.

"Will they even have you now?" The king's voice haunted me.

I was still a threat, a sleeper cell wearing their lover's costume. I simply could not be trusted.

Carter gave me a wink and soft smile before climbing the porch steps to the sliding glass doors and pushing one aside. My heart in my throat, my blood on fire, I ascended the stairs and wrapped my arms around my ribs, turning the corner to come face-to-face with my spouses.

Lex pushed to his feet from the sofa, a cigarette between two fingers, his dark hair sticking out at odd angles. Ivy paced behind him, her soft ginger plait hanging down the side of her body, one of Carter's old college hoodies swallowing her Amazonian frame. My stomach dropped to my ankles, the weight of the time between us choking the words in my throat.

At my entrance, they both froze.

"Fuck," Lex said. I expected as much from my prince of darkness, but Ivy didn't say anything. Her face turned a bright shade of pink, the X on her neck standing out against the rest of her porcelain skin. Dark bags hung under her eyes, hinting at recent sleepless nights, and she'd lost at least twenty pounds since February. Her once muscular frame now seemed almost as frail and lifeless as mine. We were a matching set. Objectively, I looked worse than her, but Carter had been right. The few months apart had not been kind to either of us.

Carter closed the door and stepped next to me, taking my hand again, reminding me he'd rescued me and brought me to them. I wasn't alone. In some twisted way, it reminded me of when I'd absconded with him to Malibu.

All we have is us.

"Look at you." Lex raised an eyebrow. "Like death warmed over."

"Lex," Carter cut in, giving him a *cut-her-some-slack* expression, but I squeezed his hand to let him know it was okay. I deserved this.

"Fuck that." Lex shifted his glare from Carter to me. "Poppy's gone, the fucking fairy king has Jon and Kit, the queen's mind is fried, and here you are." He chuckled incredulously, rubbing his thumb over his eyebrow before inhaling deep on his cigarette and stabbing it out. "Well? What do you have to say for yourself?"

"Lex, knock it off." Carter's curt tone slapped with righteous justice.

I opened my mouth, knowing I should spill my guts. "I, uh…" I cleared my throat and straightened my shoulders, staring them dead in the eye as I said, "I know my absence has been challenging, and I apologize for any inconvenience."

"Inconvenience." Lex's features dropped, all pretense gone. "This is a goddamn nightmare."

Ivy stepped toward me, her gray eyes going from accusatory to curious. She touched Lex's arm, giving him a glance that made him clench his jaw and shift his shoulders.

"C'mon, Princess," he continued. "You owe us an explanation."

"What happened to you, Miri?" she murmured, her features so

calm and welcoming despite all I'd put her through, all the world had put her through.

Excuses flipped through my mind faster than I could rationalize them, but in the end, I only dropped my head and murmured, "I don't know, and I'm scared."

Ivy nodded and closed the rest of the distance between us to pull me into her arms, tucking her head into my neck so she could inhale me deeply. God, how I had missed her. Her vanilla-sugar scent wrapped around me, reminding me of what it was like to love her, to truly be hers in every way that mattered. It took me back to that dorm room at boarding school, just her and me and our secret kisses between us. I wrapped my arms around her chest and held her so tight, I thought I might break her in two. Ivy had always been tall and statuesque, but now the hard edges of her bones dug into my skin when we touched. We were two skeletons, holding each other up. We needed rest. We needed a break.

We needed each other.

Stinging tears poured down my cheeks when she stepped away and cupped my face, bringing her soft lips to mine for a wet, loving kiss.

"I missed you," Ivy said. "I'm so mad at you, but I love you and I missed you."

"Please forgive me." My chest cracked in two at the broken words, seaming itself back together again at the same time. I had longed for the rest of them as much as I had for Ivy, but there was something about my wife that set her apart. "I have so much to tell you. I just..." My heart broke, and I didn't have the strength to say it all, even as I knew they deserved the truth.

"I forgive you," Ivy said, kissing me again. "Whatever it is, whatever happened to you, I forgive you." She said it over and over, kissing my nose and my cheeks, wiping away my tears with her thumbs. A weight lifted off my chest, one she didn't even know existed, but it made me love her infinitely more. "You're home now. That's all that matters. I'll take you any way I can have you."

I choked on the guilt that came with that because I knew, even as I nodded and leaned in to kiss her again, that I was greedy for wanting a life with them. I didn't deserve them, and my very presence put them in danger. We needed to defeat the fairy king, break this curse, and get our family back, but after that? Would they ever be safe with me here? If I were gone, they could live their lives in peace, and nothing like the scandal that had erupted when pictures of Ivy and me hit the press would happen again.

I didn't tell Ivy that. I let her pull me into her arms and run her fingers through my hair, brushing it back from my face.

"Isn't this a fucking picture-perfect moment?" Lex snapped, forcing Ivy to take a step away from me so she could face him. "Should I run upstairs and grab my Nokia? Or do you remember that the rest of us have been dealing with this mess *by ourselves* for the last three months?" His hazel eyes pierced me with his icy cruelty, holding me in my spot.

I understood what this was. I had scared him, and now, he wanted to punish me to make sure I knew, *really knew,* how it had impacted him. This time, my absence had done more than break his heart. I had allowed Ivy to waste away, and whether it was because we were so connected or because this would have happened anyway, I had put us in danger.

Worst of all, I'd left *him*. Him, who had picked me up eight years ago after I returned home from boarding school, brokenhearted from leaving Ivy in the first place. Him, who had loved me and accepted me the way I was, no questions asked.

In college, Lex and I had a tumultuous relationship. We were together as much as we were broken up, which meant we'd seen the worst of each other. I called him my prince of darkness because when he got angry, he burned so cold, it hurt to be near him. He thrived in the shadows, but I, too, had a foot in the frost. I'd once reveled in his darkness with him, and when he lost his way, it was always me there leading him back to himself.

"What do you suppose I've been dealing with?" I couldn't help the tremble in my voice and the shake in my limbs as the truth spilled out of me before I could stop it. I had wanted to ease into this confession, but even before his fairy gift, Lex always had a way of getting me to spill the beans. "The king is messing with my mind, and if he can do that, who knows what else he can do? There is no place safe. You should get as far away from me as you can."

Ivy balked and recoiled while Lex raised an eyebrow. "Now we're getting somewhere."

"You don't always have to be a dick to get what you want." Carter shoved at Lex's shoulder, but Lex only refocused on me and shook his head, accusation in his stare.

I opened my mouth to tell him to sod off, but a loud thump from upstairs stole my attention, and I glanced at Ivy with a raised eyebrow.

"Ah, shit," Lex said, heading toward the second floor.

2

MIRI

While we walked upstairs, Ivy filled me in on everything that had happened since I last saw her, including the meeting with the fairy who had given us the gift, Siobhan, and the subsequent attack by the fairy king. She had told me most of this already via voicemails over the last few weeks. Then, she explained what happened at the wedding. After suspecting Poppy knew where the queen was, Lex had called his uncle to look for her. Dmitri found the queen roaming his property and captured her to bring her to Lex. That was before the king crashed their party and took Ivy's siblings.

"I don't know how I did it," Ivy said, walking down the hallway to the room at the back. "I told him to leave and he did."

"You claimed the city," Lex said, reaching the closed door that led into Ivy's office.

"I don't think the rules work like that." Ivy shook her head. "Either way, now that he has our family, we need to create a game plan."

"And we need to figure out what to do with her." Lex opened the door to reveal the queen sitting on Ivy's desk, leaning back on her arms with her legs crossed. Her long blond hair hung around her shoulders, just as beautiful as the last time I saw it, but she'd lost that vibrance that once made me wilt in her presence. Dressed in Ivy's powder-blue silk evening gown, she looked like a ghost of her former self, her cheeks sunken, her skin a pale, translucent gray.

What had that monster done to her?

Two guards stood sentry on either side of the desk, their hands behind their backs, stern expressions between their brows. I took a step forward, but the one closest to me straightened.

The queen uncrossed her legs and stood, putting a hand on the guard's shoulder and muttering something in a language I didn't understand. He backed down, and the queen smiled, moving toward me. She cupped my cheeks and leaned in, pressing our foreheads together, muttering more confusing syllables.

"Right." I turned to Ivy. "What's wrong with her?"

"Alberich did something to her after we took off with Poppy at Samhain." Ivy rubbed her neck, a neurotic habit she'd had as long as I'd known her. "He blew some kind of ruby dust in her face, whatever that is. Now, she speaks in tongues and touches us like we're her best friends."

The queen twirled over to Lex, the skirt of her dress spiraling out around her, and brushed a piece behind his ear. He jerked his head away and gave her a look, but she didn't react to him, just danced over to Carter and grabbed his hands. She lifted them above her head and ducked under them, giving him a dreamy smile.

"Siobhan and her commander, Finn, told us it was a powerful spell," Carter said. "But this is…"

"Duneh aburgus!" The queen giggled before twirling around again to face me. She stopped and eyed me like I was a naughty child, tsking through her teeth as she walked closer and mumbled. When she touched me, I froze. My gut clenched and my heart ached, the electrifying reaction so sudden and overwhelming, I nearly folded in on myself.

I had experienced something similar to this before with dying plants, but never this intense. The diseased energy latched on to me like a prisoner reaching out from between iron bars, attempting to yank me into the cell with them. Perhaps, if I let it, I could help her. I'd never heard of ruby dust before, but there had to be a reason why Lex and Ivy couldn't sense this about her and I could.

The queen stared into my eyes, squeezing my wrist tighter until it pinched. There was something there, and if I focused hard enough, if I stared deep enough, I could access it. It felt like *her*—the way she was the last time I'd seen her.

"Miri!" Ivy grabbed the queen's fingers to tug them away, but when she connected with the queen, intelligence sparked behind those mesmerizing eyes—there for a heartbeat and gone as soon as my connection broke, but I saw it.

Diana spun away, continuing her song as she pranced over to the guards and coaxed one into holding her hand.

"What was that?" Ivy asked, furrowing her brows.

"I don't know." I took a deep breath and shook my head, rubbing the nail imprints on my arm. The rest of my energy seeped out of me, that moment with the queen stealing it away. My head pounded, my eyelids weighed a ton, and my knees almost buckled.

"Did she hurt you?" Carter stepped closer, glancing down at the marks, but they weren't anything serious.

"No, it's just..." I hesitated because I didn't trust myself anymore, not with this. I hadn't been able to keep the thistles up. I couldn't keep the king out of my memories. I didn't know what I was talking about anymore.

"I felt it," Ivy said. "It was like"—she shook her head as she struggled to put it into words—"her."

"Her?" Lex raised his eyebrows. "The queen?"

Ivy nodded.

"Fuck, do it again." Lex nudged me forward, but I stopped. Those few milliseconds were draining enough. I didn't have the strength. I needed to sleep for about a month and eat for another six before I'd try to take her on. There was no time for that.

"We need to take a second to regroup," Ivy said. "Think through our options."

"Burgh a come jurgan!" the queen said, giggling and falling back on the couch, kicking her feet up in the air. Clearly, she found herself hilarious.

"Exactly," I added. "I've missed a lot, and I'd like a bath to freshen up."

"Me too." Ivy nodded toward the door to the bathroom.

"Oh." I cleared my throat and glanced at Lex and Carter before dropping my gaze to the ground. "I meant a-a-alone." I couldn't let them see me naked, not anymore. If they did, they'd know what I'd done. If they did, they'd guess at the sickness lurking deep inside me.

"There's no fucking way that's happening," Lex said, stripping off his shirt as he walked toward the bathroom. "It's time the four of us had a talk—a real one."

Carter gave me a sympathetic glance before nodding toward the door, suggesting he thought it was time I told them everything. From the sounds of it, they had a lot to tell me, too. Carter followed Lex into the other room, leaving me alone with Ivy, the epitome of American nobility. My heart pounded, echoing in my head, and my throat felt like I'd swallowed an entire ocean.

"Miri," she said, her footsteps stopping in front of me.

I stared down at the ground, visions of what little memory I had dancing just behind my eyes. I clenched them shut against the burning sobs that almost barreled out of my throat.

Take a deep breath. Inhale...Exhale...

I tried to follow my own directions, willing the bile and shame back down into that dark corner of my soul.

"Miri, my love." Ivy slowly reached out to grab my fingers, lifting them to her lips, kissing my knuckles with tender touches. "Miri, please let us back in. We love you no matter what's happened."

I wanted to believe that. I really did, but I couldn't. The threat of losing her forever wasn't nearly as bad as what would happen when she learned the king had been inside my head, twisting and squirming and who knew what else. They weren't safe around me. Hell, I couldn't even protect myself. I couldn't protect this realm. I was useless.

What was I doing there? I should have packed up and returned to London. They didn't need me. They—

Ivy's warm mouth broke my chain of thoughts, pressing against mine with a tenderness I hadn't felt in so long. My knees shook and my stomach flipped over, and for a second, I let myself believe that I could have her again, that I could be worthy of them again. With that thought, I mentally slapped myself and stepped away, touching my lips as they burned where she'd been.

"Don't do that," I hissed.

She winced and cleared her throat. "Okay."

"Okay." I shook my head, jutting my chin out as I blinked back my blurry vision. Even hurt, Ivy was incredibly mesmerizing and beautiful. She reminded me of a Goddess come to life, some ancient warrior gifted with wisdom, strength, and compassion. I wanted to fall to her feet and pray for redemption, pray for forgiveness, pray for any empathy she'd grant me.

"If you can't tell us, I can just—" She reached out, but I moved away.

"No," I snapped. "Just...give me some space."

Perhaps I expected her to retreat at my outburst, but she didn't. Ivy nodded and dropped her arms to her sides, anguish and frustration echoing behind her steel gaze. That made me feel worse. Despite what I'd done to her, despite what had happened to me, I loved her. I never wanted to upset her.

I memorized the slope of her neck as it became her collarbone, now more pronounced and rigid since the last time I'd seen her. We both looked horrid, and I swallowed down the panicked guilt that came with the realization I'd caused this.

The four of us were connected in our own ways. Lex and I softened each other like no one else could. Carter was my best friend and star-crossed lover. But Ivy was my emotional tether. She was the glue that held me together, truly my first love in all the ways that mattered.

If I weren't me and she weren't her, I would have proposed we run away together after boarding school and never venture into high society again. She would have been enough for me, if only we had been enough for the world.

"We can bathe together," I said, moving past her to the bathroom. "But don't get too close, okay?"

Ivy swallowed and smiled, following me without saying anything else.

I FELT Ivy's eyes on me while I stripped, her blistering stare even more intense for how long I'd ached to have it on me again. Carter leaned over the enormous Jacuzzi tub, swirling his fingers in the water while it filled, and Lex had already gotten in, leaning back against a corner with his head relaxed and his eyes closed. I ignored Ivy's scrutiny and pushed my trousers down to my ankles, stepping out of them before yanking my blouse over my head. I was just about to climb into the tub when I caught her gaze and paused.

She ran the length of me, and I immediately covered the scars on my thighs with my hands, the ones I'd picked at until they bled, the ones I'd done to myself. But that was a psychological door I didn't want to open tonight. They didn't need to know, not yet.

"I'm happy we're home," Carter said, holding out a hand to help me step into the water. I refused it, grabbing onto the porcelain sides to ease myself in. The steamy pool soothed my tired muscles, and when I finally relaxed against the sloped wall farthest away from the others, some of the tension from the last few months slipped away.

"It's not safe for me to be here," I said. "I should go back to England as soon as we figure out how to break this curse." I wanted to stay. I'd always want to stay. But I was dangerous to them, and I might always be. I had ruined Ivy's reputation and my own with it. What more damage could I do?

"Hmm." Lex didn't bother to pick his head up, just grunted a sardonic noise that said he didn't believe me.

"I'm serious," I snapped as Ivy sank into the water next to me, unraveling her long, shiny hair so it hung in thick waves down her back.

"I'm sure you think so." Lex raised an eyebrow, his gaze scrutinizing every inch of me.

"Don't gaslight me," I said, more bite in my tone than I'd meant. Sure, Lex had reason to be upset. I'd broken his heart and cut him off, something I'd sworn I'd never do. We were married, after all. I'd made an oath to the three of them. It was written right there on my hand.

Until the end.

The end hadn't come yet.

"I'm not gaslighting anyone," Lex said, finally deigning to look at me. "I don't need to. You know what happens when we're apart." He shook his head, his features softening for the first time since I'd been home, like he'd finally decided to take pity on me. "You know we can't break the curse."

My chest caved in on itself. Yes, Siobhan had told them that when they met up with her and her lovers. They'd talked about the *Fianna,* about Siobhan admitting she couldn't take it back, even if she wanted to.

"There are some other things you should know, things we didn't get a chance to explain." Ivy talked about her connection to the king's mind and Lex training Poppy to go back in time. In the end, none of it worked. The king still took Ivy's siblings and Poppy had done God knew what with my cousin and Lizzie.

"I don't know what we'll do now," Ivy said. "I don't think he'll hurt anyone we love, not until he has the queen." She rubbed at her temples and laughed. "I can feel him squirming around in here, but it's like...a nightmare I can't forget."

I blinked back tears and swallowed, wondering what this could mean for my secret. "So you're connected to his mind?"

She shrugged. "I don't know. He's always been able to get inside my head, planting nightmares, scaring the hell out of me. It's more like I'm inside his now."

It was all so complicated and strange, but perhaps she'd be able to figure out what he'd done to me. What would she do when she found out? Worry because she wasn't there to protect me? Go off after the king like an imbecile, hell-bent on avenging my virtue? I gave a small laugh and sighed.

"Miri," Ivy said, pushing through the water so she stopped right in front of me. "We can't help you if you don't let us in."

I wanted to tell them, I did, but perhaps I still felt ashamed that I could be so fragile, so vulnerable to attack. Perhaps there was a small part of me that had been grateful he'd come after me instead of them, and what did that say about me? I was a wretched beast, truly.

"I'm your wife, and I love you more than anything else in this world. If I can help you, I will." She kissed the tip of my nose in a move so tender, I almost started crying again. Ivy wrapped her arms around me and pulled me into her lap, tucking my head into her neck. "Talk to us, my love. Tell us what you're going through."

"The king...he did something to me..." I sputtered, agony spearing my chest. "I don't know."

She leaned back and put her hand under my chin, forcing me to look her in the eyes. "Then show us."

Suddenly, I had grown so very tired of carrying this weight alone. I didn't relish the thought of anyone else in my mind, not after whatever Alberich had done to me, but if it was Ivy, if it was them, perhaps it wouldn't be so bad. I nodded and closed my eyes, intertwining my fingers with hers, giving her permission. When I felt her presence knocking at the mental barrier between us, I submitted to her dominance, allowing her feminine strength to infiltrate every secret part of me. Lex's icy aura joined next, quickly followed by Carter's warmth and empathy. Once we were all connected, she found it quickly, wasting no time before going to the most guarded area of my memory. It played like a movie, the events going backward and forward before reorganizing into the correct sequence.

I'd had dinner with Reginald, then gone to bed, where I'd had an intense sexual dream about Carter. He took me rougher than usual, but gentle enough that it was realistic. When I woke up the next morning, there had been blood on the sheets, but I assumed it was my period. A person knew when they'd been penetrated, the soreness almost unmistakable. But I believed I'd been alone all night, so what other conclusion could I draw?

In the weeks after the photo leak, my body tried to remind me that something else had happened, some violation I needed to reconcile. Combined with the distance from my spouses, I had no other way to cope. Scratching the insides of my thighs became the avenue to deal with the loss of both my memory and my dearest companions, a self-soothing mechanism that made the emotional pain physical and therefore bearable.

We watched as I dragged the razor along the inside of my leg, hissing against the pearl of blood as it trailed down the inside, relaxing into the sharp bite of release that came with it. No one else knew this about me, no one except them.

"Are we having fun yet, Little Thistle?" The king's antagonizing voice cut through it all, vanishing my self harm in a misty fog. *"Bring me the child. Bring me my wife. Then, I'll give you what you seek."*

Startled, Ivy retreated, pulling out of my mind so quickly, the absence stung. When I opened my eyes, she stared at me with shock and fury rising behind hers, the normal steel color now a molten fiery metal. It wasn't directed at me; she'd reacted exactly as I predicted. The king had done something to me, and she wanted his heart on a silver platter.

Tears streamed down Carter's face and he wiped them away, swallowing whatever he truly wanted to say. Sympathy radiated off him in thick, debilitating waves, and it was that more than anything that made me realize why I'd stayed away. I didn't want them to see how feeble I was, how disgusting and vile. I didn't want them to feel sorry for me.

Me and my stupid pride.

In the end, it was Lex who spoke first. "Why did you think you couldn't come to us with this?"

"I'm the weakest," I muttered, sounding small and shattered. "He can mess with me because it's easier. You and Ivy have each other, and Carter's luck protects him." When Lex still looked unconvinced, I steeled my jaw and kept going. "Don't you see? He can get to you through me."

"You're not weak, and you're not putting anyone at risk," Carter said, his tone more gentle than I deserved.

"He's inside my head, even now," I tried to counter.

"He's inside mine, too." Ivy cupped my jaw so she could rest her forehead on mine. "Miri, I am so sorry this happened to you. I promise, we'll figure out the truth."

"I don't need your pity, Ivy." I tried to break free, to get some space.

She wouldn't let me, holding on to me tighter. "I don't pity you." She kissed me, a soft, tender peck that reminded me of why I'd loved her to begin with. "You've been so strong. I wish you'd told me sooner. I wish I could've carried this pain with you."

"I can't sleep," I admitted. "I can't eat. I can't stop to think about it because when I do, I never want to move again. It's me he wants. I'm the reason all of this happened. Who knows what he can make me do, what he can make me forget? I could hurt you and not even know it." I was exasperated by the end, pouring my heart out to the people who had loved me the most.

"So self-sacrificing, aren't we, Princess?" Lex let out a disbelieving laugh, burning my cheeks and making me feel small and silly. "Ivy has been having nightmares for years, the king and the queen and Siobhan and who the fuck knows who else getting inside her head. Carter has to drink himself to sleep every night without you, and me—" He cut off, his voice having risen to the point where it echoed off the walls. Lex paused to collect himself before calmly saying, "I've been holding it all together by my fucking fingernails. Siobhan said it was the four of us in this...*four,* Miri."

"I'm here now." I matched his ire with my own, the months of stress finally catching up to me as I glared right back at him. Ivy had always been the one to go head to head with Lex, and normally, I didn't see the point in fighting with him. Now, perhaps I was looking for someone to be mad at, someone to take the blame for what I'd lived through, what I had allowed to happen.

"You're here now." He repeated the words like they meant nothing. In his mind, what was the point of showing up after the battle had already been lost? The damage was done, and we might never be the same. "I needed you three months ago. *We* needed you three months ago."

"Lex," Carter cut in, "c'mon. Take it easy."

"Easy?" Lex made an incredulous laughing noise just as Ivy grabbed my hand in solidarity. "She'd be lucky to get easy from me."

"Don't be a dick," Ivy said, but that just caused him to direct his wrath to her. "I can't imagine going through these last few months alone."

"She was alone by her own volition." Lex cleared his throat to try to stay calm, but a thick wall of ice grew behind his eyes.

"I was protecting you," I said, my voice carrying now, steaming-hot tears sliding down my face.

"And who was protecting you, Miri?" Lex slammed his hand down on the water, dousing us with a sobering splash. All this time, I'd thought he was mad at me because I'd broken his heart, broken Ivy's. But that was only a small part of it. He was most upset that I'd put myself in danger, and it widened the chasm in my heart. He'd been afraid of what could happen to me while I was gone, and lo and behold, his worst fears had come true. Now, all that energy came out as visceral anger.

My cheeks burned as I stared at him. God, he could be so cruel when he wanted to, but I understood him better than anyone ever had. Lex lashed out when he got scared. That had been the reason he treated Ivy the way he had his whole life. I suspected it had to do with losing his brother at such a young age. Bleeding hell, it might have gone back even further than that. When it came to something he really cared about, Lex would rather destroy it himself than see someone else take it from him.

"You broke his spell before, Princess," Lex said, moving toward me with an intimidating glare in his hazel eyes. "Why don't you try harder? Or maybe we can throw you in front of the king like we did last time. Perhaps you can be useful and grow a wall of thistles around the fucking world."

"Stop it." Carter moved at the same time Ivy did. He had one hand on Lex's shoulder while Ivy pushed him back.

"What did you do to your legs, huh?" Lex went on, his scowl hardening, his lips twisted with anger. "You think no one saw the way you sliced yourself up like a Christmas ham?"

"Lex!" Ivy let go of me to give him a hard shove in the chest, but I'd already had enough.

Magic licked at my fingertips, every plant in a fifty-mile radius responding to Lex's threat. Ivy had been nursing a tender pothos in her bedroom, and now, I willed it closer to me. Vines crept over the walls like thick green spiderwebs, twisting as they came closer, wrapping around Lex's wrists and neck.

"Stop it," he said, yanking at them, but I didn't. I coiled them tighter, wrapping them around his waist and legs, confining him until he'd stop threatening me. Rage boiled my blood and tears blurred my vision, the anguish of Lex's words mixing with the fact I had so little control over my own life. "Miri, what are you doing, stop it." He writhed, trying to get away. "Stop it. *Tell me the truth! What happened to you?*"

"I don't know!" My scream echoed off the walls, sending a shock wave through the room, exploding in every direction. Water flew up around us like a tsunami, hanging in the air, weightless, like gravity had ceased to exist. Time stopped. The world stopped. And for one brief moment, I heard the king's voice again, barely a faint whisper... *"There's a good girl. Come for me."*

The tenderness in his voice sliced me in two, and the pain brought me back to reality. I crashed into Carter as my knees gave way. The water slammed into the tub with a loud *swoosh,* time restarting like a punch to the gut.

We flew to either side of the bath, my back slamming into the porcelain so hard, it radiated pain down my legs and up my neck to my skull. My hands trembled from the magnitude of the magic I'd just put out, and it rolled around in my gut like acid. I had terrified them...fuck, I'd terrified myself. Where had that come from?

"There's a good girl. Come for me."

Oh, God...*No, no, no, don't think about that. Put that away. File that in the darkest part of your heart.*

Closing my eyes, I did. I swallowed it and forced myself to forget the moans I'd made while Alberich whispered in my ear, his voice deep and soothing, coaxing me to relax while he took what he wanted.

None of us said anything for a long moment, just staring at each other as we independently debated what had happened and what to do next.

"I think that's enough for one night," Carter said.

I didn't wait around for more. Wiping tears from my cheeks, I got out of the bath, wrapped a towel around myself, and walked into Ivy's room. The sound of my wife's wet feet padded behind me until she shut the door, enclosing us there together.

"Don't listen to him," Ivy said. "He was scared for you. He doesn't always know the best way to—"

"I know," I said, shaking my head while I yanked on a pair of Ivy's shorts and one of her tank tops. "I'm exhausted, and I don't have the strength to talk about it more tonight. Can we just...can we just go to sleep?"

She nodded and wrapped me in her arms before leading me to her bed, scooting in behind me. I was asleep moments after my head hit the pillow, and I vaguely recalled Carter and Lex making their way to the same bed sometime later, but I hardly woke up. In that small moment of intimacy, I found the first bit of peace I'd had in months and slept with little fear of what would await me when I woke.

3

CARTER

"Lizzie's fine," my mother said when I called her later that evening, her tone more lighthearted than what I would have expected from someone whose youngest child had been abducted by a changeling. "She's busy with finals. I talked to her a few hours ago."

Despite what she thought she remembered, that wasn't true. Lizzie had been taken during Lex and Ivy's wedding, and no matter how many times I tried to reach out to Poppy, I got no answer. Ivy and Miri hadn't gotten out of bed yet, and Lex sat at the dining room table with a pile of books open in front of him, chain-smoking cigarettes down to the filter.

"Promise me you'll keep an eye on Sophie and Charlie." My other sisters went to college, but both had randomly been home this week.

"Of course," Mom said. "Are you sure you're okay? It couldn't have been easy, watching all that on TV." She knew how I felt about Ivy, and perhaps she even suspected how I felt about Lex. A self-described mystic and Reiki healer, she had always seen with more than just her eyes. She'd been a sympathetic ear my entire life, no matter what my issue may have been.

"They didn't go through with it," I said, avoiding Lex's intrigued gaze. There were more important things to deal with, like finding our abducted family members and pushing the fairy king back into his own realm. But I'd admit, it was a small victory that Lex and Ivy hadn't gone all the way. Some selfish part of me still saw her as mine, even if I shared her with two others, and if she ever married anyone legally in this realm, I wanted it to be me.

"Good news for you, then." Mom gave me a small laugh, and when I didn't return it, she sighed. "Carter—"

"Just...stay at your house, okay? Promise me you'll be safe."

"Come home, my baby boy," she said. "You're scaring me. I need to see you."

"I will soon." I had to finish this, but then I'd be on the first flight back to Chicago.

We said our goodbyes and I thanked my lucky stars that my mother and my other sisters had been out of town when the king attacked. He didn't know where to find them, if he'd even gone looking for them, and by the time they returned, he'd already gone back into hiding, seemingly to lick his wounds. Siobhan had put a ward on their houses, but if Poppy had gotten to Lizzie, I figured she could get to any of them anytime she wanted.

"She's okay," Lex said, bringing my gaze to his. He stood and walked closer, pinching his cigarette between his index finger and thumb to place it between my lips. "Even if Poppy takes her to him, he won't hurt her until he gets what he wants from us."

"He could be hurting Lizzie right now, all of them. Poppy, too." I blinked back tears and forced myself to inhale deeply on the smoke before stabbing it out. I loved all my sisters, but Lizzie and I were the closest. Maybe being the oldest and the youngest set us apart from the middle two.

"That won't happen either." Lex dropped to his knees in front of me, his hips between my thighs. "He thinks too highly of his grand plans. He'll want to make sure we know he's hurting them, and until he lures us out of hiding, they'll be safe."

Lex could be incredibly convincing when he wanted to, and in this case, I yearned to believe him. His calm stoicism soothed the anxious side of me that wanted to give in to the panic, especially after what Miri had done yesterday. Things were getting more daunting the longer we waited to do anything about it. Lex grabbed me, palm to palm, and pulled me down so I leaned my forehead against his.

"We're going to fix this, Chicago," he murmured. "We're going to save our family and the whole fucking world, so help me God."

"How?"

He stood and shook his head, going back to his side. "Not sure yet."

I pursed my lips, debating whether I should say what was on my mind. The king had done something irreparable to Miri, and it made me so fucking pissed, I could burn down the world just to get my vengeance. I wanted to hold her and protect her and keep her with me for the rest of her life, just so I'd know that whatever came for her would have to go through me first.

"It's not safe for me to be here," Miri had said last night. *"I should go back to England as soon as we figure out how to break this curse."*

That hurt most of all. Even if we could end this connection between us, I didn't think I'd want to. We had something unique and profound, and the rest of the world would never understand it. The idea of Miri not being with us pricked at this imaginary future I'd built where we all grew old together and reveled in our gifts until the end of time.

"What are we going to do about Miri?"

Lex narrowed his gaze and shook his head. "What about her?"

"The king is screwing with her mind, Lex." I pointed to the stack of books between us. "Just like all those messed-up fairy tales. He lured her into a deep sleep, and what do you suppose he did after that?" I raised my eyebrows. She couldn't remember, but it didn't take a genius to guess. The lore was filled with stories of the fairy king drugging his human consorts and having his perverted rapey way with them.

Lex went eerily still, which wasn't a good sign. When he got that villainous look in his eye, he wouldn't stop until he got what he wanted. In this case, it was mutual: the king's decapitated corpse.

"You can't blame her for keeping it to herself," I continued. "For thinking it was better to stay away to try to protect us."

"I can blame her for whatever the fuck I want."

"You need to apologize to her, make it up to her somehow."

"I will," he said. At my scowl, he cleared his throat and rubbed a thumb over his eyebrow. "Besides, Miri is one of the strongest people I know. We'll figure it out, Chicago."

"What about the king?" I raised an eyebrow. "What about how we can't get in touch with Poppy?" I met his gaze, remembering he'd been teaching the changeling how to travel back in time. "Don't tell me you didn't plan for this."

He made a noise and gave me a look like I'd lost my mind before adding, "Of course I did. We just have to fix her."

The puzzle pieces fell together. "The queen? That's your big move?"

Lex leaned forward over his books, eyeing me with that piercing stare. "Remember when we were in Faerie and I tried to use my gift on her?"

"Yeah." The memory seemed comical now, considering all we knew. Lex had been arrogant and naive, and we were damn lucky she hadn't ripped his head off, especially after she threatened to.

"She told me she was older than anything I'd ever seen, that she was the Great Source. All of it, everything, it lived inside her."

I remembered that, too. Her power had been overwhelming and intimidating. It lured me in and frightened me at the same time. I thought she'd kill all of us as a show of strength. She hadn't. Then the king had attacked, she'd shoved Poppy in my arms, and we escaped.

Lex pursed his lips, going back to his books. "The Great Source of what, I wonder. Fairy magic? Gifts? And just *how* old is she? Old enough to remember how the fairies trapped the king the first time?"

Good lord, he was right. I sat up straight, my mind racing faster than I could speak. "She must have been there. Siobhan said the king and queen were equals, that one could not exist without the other."

"When he got trapped in Faerie, so did she," Lex continued.

"When she got loose, he followed her." They were linked by more than we could ever understand, but it seemed similar to what the four of us experienced. We couldn't be apart. What affected one of us impacted the rest.

"This can't be the first time a fairy's mind has gotten fried." Lex went back to flipping through his books. "There's got to be lore about it. I saw everything from sacrifices to changeling children to getting stuck in Faerie forever."

"Sacrifices?" My mind danced with images of medieval rituals and bloody still-beating hearts.

"Yeah," he said, rubbing a hand back through his hair. "But who the hell knows what's real and what's fake. It could all be bullshit."

I watched him while he talked, taking a moment to revel in our reconnection. I had missed him so much. I always did, but the ability to leave him was getting harder every time I had to go. I stood and moved around the dining room table, keeping his gaze as his eyes tracked me. I stopped right in front of him, taking the cigarette from between his fingers so I could have a drag before stabbing it out. Inhaling a deep breath, I ran the length of my disheveled king. Dark circles lined the bags under his eyes, and the crease between his eyebrows had grown more pronounced. And was that a gray hair by his temple?

"No one looks at me like that and gets away with it, Chicago." He licked his lips and smirked, mischief floating just behind his gaze.

"By God, don't start now." I kneeled between his knees, mirroring his pose moments ago, and ran my palms up his thighs to the button on his jeans. He didn't say anything, just watched as I pushed the metal through its hole and pulled the zipper down. Lex shifted his hips so I could yank his pants and boxers to his mid-thighs, freeing his beautiful half-erect cock. "You need to relax. We all do."

I spat on my hand and grabbed his shaft, giving the tip a good squeeze that had him groaning and sinking farther into the chair.

"There's a mad fairy king on the loose and you want to suck my dick." He rolled his eyes and playfully scoffed. "Typical."

"I think you'd move mountains if it meant you got your cock in my mouth." I leaned over his torso, bringing my lips to his neck so I could kiss my way over his pulse. He still smelled the same, like cigarettes and deodorant and him, and I wanted to bury myself in it. It reminded me of the first time we hooked up, all those years ago in London. I'd been so wide-eyed and carefree, and Lex had barreled over my innocence with his extravagant debauchery.

He grabbed the back of my neck and brought his lips to mine, biting inside my mouth until he could wrestle my tongue with his own. I loved him like this, rough and hard, all sharp edges looking to polish themselves against my rock-steady grace. He coasted his fingers higher up my head, tunneling into my hair so he could fist a handful and yank my head back.

I hissed as agony zigzagged through my skull.

"You want my cock that bad?" Lex shoved my head into his lap, forcing his dick into my mouth. "Fucking take it."

I did. I licked and sucked, a thrill shooting down my spine into my balls when he groaned and dropped his head back against the chair. He tightened his fingers, gripping me so he could angle me the way he wanted it.

I let him use me. It had been a stressful week resulting from a stressful four years. Even though it felt like it was all coming to a head now, we still had the worst of it yet to survive. These precious moments, these few hours when we could take our pleasure freely, they might be our last. And damn it, I was going to enjoy it.

"Fuck, Chicago," Lex murmured, making me feel like a God. Look at how willing and pliant this monster became once I had my skin on his. When I gripped his balls and teased a finger farther back, he shifted his hips and spread his legs wider, urging me on.

I chuckled, and he must have liked the sensation because he hissed in a breath, his hazy eyes squinting as he watched me. I was about to venture lower down, but he yanked my head back and leaned down, bringing his face inches from mine.

"Stand up, pull down your pants, and bend over the table."

I gave him a lazy grin and licked my lips, swallowing his lingering taste. "No."

Oh, the look he gave me then—his jaw so tight, the muscle by his ear twitched, his eyes shooting daggers right through my heart. I would bet Lex had only been told no a handful of times in his life, and probably only by me and Weeds. How I lived to make him submit to me for a change. Lex ran his gaze over me, trying to decipher if I was drawing a hard limit or if I was playing the great game.

I let him see the truth, that I wanted him to let out some steam, and the only way he was going to do that was by opening the valve with me. He and Weeds had their own brand of roughhousing, one that had been there since they were children. But Lex and I were nearly the same height, and even though I'd put on some muscle for my job, he didn't have to hold back with me. More importantly, I didn't have to hold back with him.

"No?" Lex raised an eyebrow, his smirk indicating he had realized I wanted to play the role where he owned my body and I let him. "Carter Scott, get on your fucking feet." He stood, dragging me with him to my full height. Even though he only had an inch on me, he filled the room with power, the proverbial Titan in a world full of peasants. "Pull down your pants." Lex growled the words, sending a submissive shock down my legs. My knees trembled as I unbuttoned my jeans, tugging down the zipper before digging my thumbs under the waistband of my boxers. I intentionally moved slowly, trying to draw out the anticipation, but he'd had it. Lex shoved his fingers under the fabric and dragged it down, scratching the skin near my belly button with a satisfying burn.

My cock sprang free, throbbing and sticking straight out between us in an embarrassing display of arousal. Sucking Lex off always turned me on, and he knew it. So when he glanced down at the precum dripping off the tip, I swallowed my humiliation as he laughed and shook his head.

"Such a fucking slut for me, huh?" He grabbed my cock and I buckled at the hips, falling into his chest. That made him laugh harder, but in a cruel, sinister way that shamed me for being so damn in love with him that making him hard riled me up.

"I'm not the one so hot and bothered that I've forgotten about foreplay." I pushed my hips forward, jerking myself in his fist. "I thought you were a gentleman."

That made him almost break character, and he licked his lips and smiled. "When did you get so desperate for my mouth?"

I leaned in to taste the skin between his pulse and his clavicle, and then it was his turn to shake. He tried to hide it, but I felt it, and he shoved me against the table, my ass hitting the edge before he pushed my shoulders back and positioned my hands above my head.

"Don't fucking move." He leaned down to kiss me, covering my body with his before kissing his way down my neck and shoving my shirt up so he could drag his tongue over my chest. Last Solstice, I'd caught an early flight home and come here to spend the winter holiday with them. I'd walked in on Ivy tied to this very table, blindfolded and gagged. Lex had edged her for an hour beforehand, so when I touched her, she jumped. Every inch of her skin had been so sensitive that I thought I'd make her come just by ghosting the tips of my fingers over her arms.

Now that I found myself in her position, I didn't know how she didn't. Lex hadn't even touched my dick yet and I was about to bust all over the place. Then, he looked up at me from between my legs and put a hand on my stomach to hold me down while he took me.

Fucking hell, my hips fought him on their own, seeking more of him, more of the slick warmth inside his mouth. He flicked his tongue over my cockhead, circling down and sucking back the way that made me tremble. He tightened his grip on my shaft as he worked me, and I threw my head back and closed my eyes, relishing in the euphoria cascading over my body.

"Fuck, DC," I said, resisting the urge to run my fingers through his head of thick dark hair. Lex had been the first guy to ever do this to me, and if that eighteen-year-old boy could see me now, he'd be impressed with how long I could hold my load. I'd come in about a minute the first time, the temptation of Lex's magnificence far too irresistible. Who wouldn't want to shove their cock into the mouth of a man this powerful? That he was equally obsessed with me fueled a sick part of my ego, and I sometimes wondered if that made me a piece of shit. Maybe I'd stopped caring a long time ago.

When he'd had his fill, he let me go with a loud *pop* and stepped back, grinning like a thief who'd stolen the crown jewels and gotten away with it. He ran his hands over my abs and my chest, running them up my shoulders to my arms.

"Such a fucking meathead," he said before flipping me over and slamming my torso back down on the hardwood. I winced at the sharp jolt that went through me, but that added to the pressure building in my balls. I loved him like this, and I loved to be used like this. And he knew it, which made it even more intense and overwhelming.

He stepped away, a cool rush of air taking his place as the sound of a drawer opening and shutting brought me back to reality. The click of a bottle lid echoed through the room, and Lex took his spot behind me again, his hard thighs pressed up against the back of mine. My cock was trapped between my stomach and the table, but even that felt like heaven when his fingers slid against my ass. I sighed and melted into the touch.

"There he is," Lex murmured, "my pliant knight. So defeated now that I've got my fingers in your ass, huh?" He nudged inside me, his forefinger slick and hot. I pushed back against him, welcoming the touch, needing him deeper inside. Tingles shot down my legs when he hit the spot that drove me wild and I sighed, a soft moan echoing from deep in my chest. "Imagine how good my cock will feel."

"So fucking good." The words tripped over my lips, coming from a place only he drew out of me. I wanted to give in, to let him have his way, but I'd started this for a reason. I couldn't lose my intention now. "But do you think you deserve that?"

"Deserve." He repeated the word, not so much to question as to make sure he'd heard it right. "I took care of your precious Weeds the way you wanted. I held down the fort while you went off to play soldier on some soft-core porn TV show." He leaned over me, his chest to my back, one finger becoming two inside of me. "I think I deserve quite a bit."

Visions of a hot dorm room in Killwater came to the forefront of my mind. Me—holding him down by the throat as I fucked him into being nice to Ivy. Him—fighting how he felt about her the whole time but willing to do anything for my tongue on his cock. Not much had changed since then.

Once upon a time, he'd made me promise to come home to him and Ivy, that once I'd had my fill of Hollywood, I'd spend the rest of my life with them. I'd sworn my devotion at the time, but I thought I'd have decades until I'd have to pay up. It had only taken four years.

The long nights of filming for months on end had caught up to me. I hadn't told them yet, but this tour was my last. I had negotiated a change in script that would allow my character to return home earlier in the story than planned. While they weren't killing me off, I would only be needed for a few episodes in the next two seasons. It wasn't over, but it was a reprieve, and that was what I needed.

"You were a prick to our princess," I said. "Such a nasty fucker until she put you in your place. I should edge you all day to teach you a lesson."

He snarled and yanked my hair, forcing me to stand upright, his body pressed so firmly against mine. "She put herself in danger."

"She was scared," I said, "and trying to protect you."

"She hurt you," he whispered, barely loud enough for me to hear, but the words broke when he said them. He snaked one arm around my torso, holding me tighter, as if clinging to me for strength. "Watching Ivy waste away nearly killed me. It doesn't matter what he did to Miri. I'm..." He paused and let out a ragged breath. "I'm gonna gut him for fucking with her...for tormenting all of us."

"It's okay, DC," I told him, grabbing his hand on my stomach to give him comfort. "We need each other. She's home now. She's safe."

He pressed his forehead to the back of my neck and nodded, inhaling me deeply and gripping my fingers tighter. He kissed me, soft and sweet, before digging his teeth into the meat between my neck and my shoulder, half branding, half resuming our game. I groaned and sagged into the pain before he shoved me down on the table, gripping the back of my neck with one hand while he lined his cock up at my ass with the other.

"You fucking come before I tell you and I'll make this last all night," he said, squeezing more lube on his dick and down my entrance before sliding inside. The sensation of him filling me would never get old, and when he put a hand on my hip to hold me steady, I thought I'd never want to get up again. My dick squeezed between me and the hardwood, agonizing yet fueling my desire. I wanted it rougher, so I pushed back against Lex, who slapped my ass so hard Ivy and Miri had to have heard it upstairs. The sting sent a surge of lust up my spine and through my balls, propelling a laugh over my mouth.

"Jesus Christ," I said.

"Nope," Lex added, spanking the other side this time, thrusting to the hilt. "Just me, but he fucking wishes, right?"

Lex had taken me hundreds of times, thousands probably, but this felt more magical than any before it. It was a reclaiming, a recon-nection, a grounding in ourselves. I reminded him to nurture our relationships, and he reminded me to fight for them. Together, we created balance.

It didn't take long for me to come. A few thrusts and some dirty words had me nutting on our dining room table like a teenager. Every muscle in my body tightened with the release, at once mind-splintering and all-consuming. Euphoria and ecstasy skated through my blood, coating my insides with warmth and adoration.

Lex laughed in that sick, twisted way of his and said, "Look at the fucking mess you made." He tsked his teeth, gripping my hips harder as he pulled out the slightest bit and spit on our connection. I vaguely heard the cap of the lube open again and more cool liquid hit my ass, but I'd been launched so far into another universe, I couldn't do anything except lie there and shiver and take it.

"I've always loved fucking you, Chicago." He spanked me again, harder this time, and I moaned as the vibrations went through my body. The sounds echoing off the wall were perverse and filthy, but I reveled in that, too. Lex always could turn me to mush.

Who knew how long he fucked me. Time had ceased to be real when this started. I came again and again, and he rutted harder inside me, stopping every so often to stroke my cock or tease my balls. Whatever frustration he'd been building inside himself at Miri's absence, he took it out on me. I let him.

When he finally found his release, his teeth deep in my neck, his cock buried in my body, he collapsed on top of me, a heaving, sweaty mess, and sighed. I held him there, bearing his weight for both of us.

"I love you, Chicago," he softly murmured. "Thank you."

"I love you, DC," I found the strength to say.

4

MIRI

I woke to the sounds of Lex and Carter downstairs. They weren't being terribly quiet, and the visions that went through my mind made me smile. A loud spank echoed through the house, followed by Carter's muffled grunt, and I rolled toward Ivy. She was already awake, staring at the ceiling.

At my movement, she glanced at me. "I could tell them to knock it off if you need me to."

I shook my head and smiled. "Let them have their fun. Lex needs the outlet."

Ivy sighed before scooting down the bed next to me. She curled on her side and grabbed my hand, bringing my knuckles to her lips. She was always so beautiful in the moonlight, her steel eyes even more silver, her ginger hair a darker, more mysterious shade of cherry.

Lex moaned, and the sound sent an involuntary tremble through my body, an automatic reflex from the years spent pulling that noise out of him myself. I bit my lip and eyed my wife, a hot sting of arousal sizzling my veins for the first time in months. Perhaps I needed someone to touch me with affection. Perhaps I wanted to reclaim my own body and mind by giving them to someone who loved me, who adored me unconditionally.

Ivy and Lex may have been together since birth, but it was me and Ivy first. I'd fallen in love with her at boarding school and I'd loved her every day since. Right then, I needed her in ways only she could understand. She brought me back to myself, reminded me why I let anyone close in the first place.

Perhaps she read this in my eyes, or maybe she needed the same thing from me.

She scooted closer and pressed her lips to mine, a soft, reserved kiss to test the waters. When I returned it with a fiery one of my own, pushing my tongue in between her lips, she moaned and rolled on top of me, positioning her hips in between my thighs. I opened eagerly for her, hoping she wanted this as much as I did.

Her forearms framed my head, and compared to her long limbs, I felt small and delicate under her.

"What do you need from me?" she whispered, brushing her nose against mine.

"Just love me," I murmured. "Please love me like you used to."

"Miri," she said, running her fingers over my face, brushing the hair out of my eyes. "I never stopped loving you."

It broke my heart. She should have. She had every reason to hate me. I would have hated me. I had disappeared for months with hardly a good explanation as to why. For all that she raged and burned hot, Ivy had endless forgiveness, especially when it came to me. When I thought about that night with the fairy king, I wasn't sure I ever wanted to know. Did that make me terrible? For so long, I had been desperate for more information, but now...now I didn't want that memory. It was better if I never had to live it at all.

"There's a good girl. Come for me."

"Who will want you now?"

No, no, no. Go away.

I blinked back his voice and kissed her again, harder, more desperate than before.

"Let me touch you, Miri." Ivy kissed her way down my neck, grabbing my hands so her fingers could intertwine with mine. I thought back to the girl she'd been when I met her, so innocent and terrified when it came to sex. It was all I could do to resist her that entire year, and when I finally gained the courage to kiss her, she'd trembled so hard, I thought she might fall apart. The first night between us, when I'd drunkenly taken what I wanted, she'd been nervous about doing it wrong. My, how the tables had turned.

"Yes, please," I told her.

She hummed in approval, liking the sound of that, before sliding her hands down my torso and dipping them under the tank top. Pushing the fabric over my head, she threw it to the side and returned her attention to my body. I watched as Ivy dragged her tongue down my sternum, lapping at one nipple while caressing the other with her thumb, sending sparks over my skin and between my legs.

"You are so amazing, Miri," she said, sucking the tender flesh between her lips. A surge of wet heat hit me in the cunt, as if connected to that area of my body with electricity. I moaned and arched into the touch, dragging my fingers over her scalp as she went to the other breast to do the same thing. "I love how soft your skin is."

The compliment made me blush, the sensation twisting down my chest and into my gut. Ivy took her time working me up, kissing and tasting every inch of my skin like she could find the secret to life inside my soul. I closed my eyes and focused on the sensation, how her mouth was like sticking my hand in flames. It sizzled and crackled and I knew I should withdraw because when I got burned, it would hurt a million times worse for the time I spent ignoring the impending doom. But silly, stupid me, I never could keep myself out of trouble.

When her hand drifted to the inside of my thigh, I let it. When her knuckles brushed over the outside of my shorts, I moaned and spread my legs wider so she could slide them down my legs and off my feet. When she gave me one last chance to back out, looking up at me with a kiss to my knee before she said, "Tell me you love me, Miri."

"I love you," I murmured.

Her grin melted some of the frost around my heart. It reminded me of that eighteen-year-old version of her, so innocent and curious. I had loved her then, and I loved her still. Infinitely and indefinitely.

"Come for me, Little Thistle. Who will love you now? Will they still want you?"

Ivy sank her teeth into the skin where my leg met my pelvis, not enough to hurt, just enough to bring me back to the present—here, in this bedroom, with her.

"He's not welcome here," she whispered, running a gentle hand over the inside of my other leg. "It's just you and me, understand?"

I nodded and took a deep breath, focusing on the way her hot exhale coasted over my skin, a shocking contrast to the air in the room. It was a cool spring night in the Mid-Atlantic, the bite of winter still lingering in the air, refusing to give way to summer's greedy grip.

"Do you know how long I've ached to get you all to myself?" Ivy said, fluttering her tongue over my clit, staring up at me with those penetrating eyes. Wrapping her hands around my thighs, she tugged me closer to her, kissing and holding and loving me back to myself. "You're so beautiful and so soft and so...*mine.*"

I shivered at the word, knowing it rang true deep down in my heart. My feelings about Lex and Carter were so wrapped up in my feelings about Ivy that I'd never know where one stopped and the other began. We were meant to be a four, but this connection held its own special place in my heart.

Ivy licked me, sending a jolt of pleasure up my spine and down my legs. She intertwined her fingers with mine on one hand and used the other to hold me down so she could take me the way she wanted. I sagged into her embrace, wanting her harder, yearning for her deeper. I needed to feel her everywhere so that she could burn out the evil rotting away my soul.

There was no progress without destruction, and Ivy could set my heart ablaze like no other. She reached into my molecules and found the pieces that had been petrifying in our distance, incinerating the dead parts so that new life could begin. She sucked and moaned and pushed a finger inside me, rubbing at all the right places to have me melting into the mattress.

"Tell me you love it," she said. "Tell me you're still my good princess, my perfect wife."

"I'm your good princess," I said, urgency on my lips and in the nod of my head. I wanted her to keep going, to bring me to that special brink like only she could. The pressure built inside me as she lowered her head again, fucking me with her fingers and her face, reminding me why she had always owned me, heart and soul.

I clenched my fists in her hair, the euphoria reaching an apex, and she pulled back to rub my clit, spitting on it so she could go faster. Just when I thought I'd burst with sensation, she leaned down to suck me between her lips. I exploded. My entire world erupted into nothing and everything all at once. My nerves had been electrocuted, and every part of me that had been soiled by the unknown now rang with truth again.

I was meant to be with her. I was meant to be loved by her, by all of them.

She didn't let me have the aftermath very long. I was vaguely aware of her getting up and going to a dresser across the room, and when she came back, she had a rainbow-striped strap-on around her waist and a bottle of lube in her other hand. She crawled between my legs again as excitement laced through my bloodstream and into my gut. I loved when Ivy fucked me. Sure, the boys could find my G-spot well enough, but Ivy fucked like her soul was on fire.

Cool liquid hit my vulva, followed by Ivy's fingers smearing it in. She stroked the dildo a few times before lining up at my entrance and inching in, bit by bit. She covered my body with hers, a scalding blanket that comforted me and brought me back to my senses. Her soft breasts pressed against my rib cage, her heart a thunderous riot against my own. When she pressed her forehead to mine and surged the rest of the way in, I sagged in relief. I thought it might hurt. I thought it might bring up memories of whatever had happened to me.

But Ivy kissed my nose and eyes and cheeks, grounding me in the bed with her.

"Don't ever leave me again, Princess," Ivy said, rocking into me, finding her rhythm. "I made you a promise, and I won't be as patient next time."

A long time ago, I had made Ivy swear never to let me leave her again. If I'd been trapped by my family, she had promised to come rescue me. I never expected to push her away myself. I never expected to one day believe I was a danger to them, to all of them.

"Hey," she murmured, nuzzling her head against mine while sparks of ecstasy rattled my molecules. "You're mine. No one's going to hurt you again. I promise. I swear. You're mine. You're mine." She said it over and over again while she fucked me, as if by repeating it, she could brand it into my skin as a warning to whoever might think to touch me in the future.

I kissed her and met her thrust for thrust, willing myself closer to that edge of climax again. Perhaps I thought that would solve all my problems, that for one perfect moment here in our marital bed, everything else would go away—the king and the queen and what I would do once this was over.

Perhaps I could be strong again. Perhaps I would survive this after all.

5

IVY

I fucked Miri into a limp pile of mush, and then I ran my fingers through her hair until she fell asleep again. She'd asked to get me off, but she needed rest. I wanted to remind her why I loved her in the first place. She should have come to us with this from the beginning.

I understood her reasoning for staying away and going along with her grandmother's plan to put distance between us. She believed herself to be the weak link, the vulnerable one, thereby putting the rest of us at risk, especially after the king had repeatedly altered her memories.

I imagined she felt like she couldn't trust her own mind, and therefore, couldn't trust herself. I should have seen this coming. Out in the UK all by herself, she *was* vulnerable and alone. Even though she'd been the one to protect us by growing the thistles and keeping the king in Faerie, we were stronger together. Carter visited more often and lived closer, not to mention the luck on his side whenever he traveled.

Miri resided on the other side of the world, her highly visible role in the English royal family making it nearly impossible to get away as much as she wanted. The king had already proved he was capable of manipulating her memories. What more could he have done to her?

Part of me wanted to lower my walls to Alberich's mind and figure it out for myself. I didn't know exactly what had happened, but I could guess, and there had to be a reason. However, if I did that, I opened myself up to him, and I had no desire to have another one of our telepathic chats. Regardless, I would never forgive him for this. I would hunt that bastard down and tear his heart from his chest. Perhaps it was even better that he was immortal; I could torture him until the end of time.

I could still feel him there, crawling around in the back of my mind despite my mental shields between us, and when I closed my eyes, his voice called out to me from deep within.

"Are you watching, Ivy? Are you listening?"

When his telepathic claws threatened to dig into my boundaries, I reinforced them with more energy and opened my eyes again, gasping with relief to be back in my room.

I still didn't know how I'd managed to force him out of Mount Vernon at the wedding, and from what we could tell, he hadn't been back. Lex and I couldn't have possibly overwhelmed him. He had more power than we'd ever dream of, and we were the most effective when there were four of us. Down two, Lex and I shouldn't have been able to do anything, much less coax him into submission.

What did it mean? And more importantly...could we do it again?

I extracted myself from Miri's embrace and got out of bed to put on a robe so I could head downstairs to find our husbands. It was well after three in the afternoon by now, and my stomach reminded me of exactly how much stress I had been under these last few months without Miri.

I paused halfway, gripping the railing tighter as I met Lex's gaze. He sat in front of the fireplace, wearing nothing but his boxers, his bare chest streaked with pink welts and scratches. I was happy

Carter and Lex could be there for each other while I reacquainted myself with our wife.

Dark hazel eyes ran the length of me, coating my skin with the heavy weight of judgment and accusation. I crossed the room to stand in front of him, staring down from in between his knees. He'd always looked so beautiful like this, a king in repose, even if the weight of our crowns would destroy us. So much went unsaid between us, yet we were screaming at each other even in silence.

"How is she?" Lex murmured.

"Better."

He licked his lips and nodded, raising the whiskey glass so he could take a long sip. "Good."

I grabbed it from him, finished the rest of it in one burning gulp, and set the tumbler on the coffee table. "Where's Carter?"

"In the shower." Lex grinned and leaned his head back, the lion in him sated after the time alone with one of his favorite treats.

I climbed in his lap, my knees to either side of his hips, my cunt pressed up against his well-used cock. He smelled like sex and Carter, and the combination hit me deep in the gut. I had a lot to say to him, but there was a sick part of me that wanted to lick every ounce of one husband off the other. If I asked, Lex would let me. If I asked, Lex would *make* me.

"I've thought of something." I cupped his face so he had to stare at me. "I know how we can defeat the king."

"Uh-oh. Ivy Washington: the mastermind, hard at work. Go on." His cynicism used to frustrate the hell out of me. Now, it made me want to hold him down by the throat and ride his face until he couldn't breathe.

"Siobhan said only the four of us could do it," I explained. "That the four of us were the key piece of the puzzle."

Lex smoothed his palms over my hips, coasting his fingers up my ribs and back down again while he eye-fucked me. I let him, the hedonist glutton. "Uh-huh." He was only partially listening.

"It only took two of us to get him off Mount Vernon property, if that's really what we did." Jury's still out if it would be permanent. "What do you suppose the four of us could do?"

Lex's gaze snapped to mine, an eyebrow raised. "You've got my interest. Drive it home."

"Do you think, if the four of us attack him, we could force him back to his realm?"

"I want more than a shove back to Faerie," Lex said, leaning in so he could whisper. "I want his fucking blood."

I didn't disagree.

He pressed his lips to mine in a soft embrace I never would have thought him capable of ten years ago, contrasting the violent language he used. Now, I knew him as intimately as I knew myself. Lex and I were a partnership, a marriage of power and convenience, certainly, but no less real for its foundation in publicity. I loved him and I hated him and now we were so bound together, I didn't know how to live without him, not anymore.

I wrestled my tongue into his mouth, sucking the taste of Carter off his skin, biting him like I could devour the very best parts of their intimacy. When Lex reached between us and freed his cock, I tilted my hips to let him slide home. He hissed like he'd been well worn, and based on the sounds I'd heard earlier, I knew he had. I ran my fingers through his hair and held his head close, letting him bite and suck on my neck as hard as he wanted.

He forced my mouth back to his while he fucked me, licking my tongue and lips, moaning to himself.

"She still tastes the same," he murmured, thrusting into me harder, spearing me deeper. Hot, steamy lust shot through me as I rocked against him, wanting everything he'd give me, knowing he needed this reconnection as much as I did.

"So does he," I said, nuzzling my head into Lex's neck so I could inhale all that remained of Carter. He had showered since they fucked, the heat from the water still radiating from his skin, but that sandalwood and pine scent could only be from our husband, and when it mixed with Lex's manly pheromones, I went wild. It was an intoxicating blend, made just for me, and when it combined with what remained of Miri in my mouth, I sank into my perverse longing for three people at the same time. Lex dug his nails into one hip, holding my throat with the other hand, and I grabbed on to his shoulders like I might fall off any second.

Our sex was hard and quick, all pleasure in its sadistic, feral glory, and when I came, I sank my teeth into his pulse point to remind him he fucked Carter because I allowed it. He was mine, so was Carter, so was Miri.

Lex may be the axis around which we rotated, but I was the gravity. I was three months older than Lex, and therefore, he was made *for me*. Miri had come to live in *my* dorm room, she was *my* roommate, and Carter had been obsessed with *me* since we met.

Something territorial went through me, perhaps fueled by this need to remind him of who he belonged to. Lex gasped as I bit harder, clawing his nails into me deeper, and I pulled back so I could hold him by the windpipe as he reached his own climax.

"You're mine, Lucifer," I told him. "You're all mine, and I'll have you because I want to. Promise me you'll help me defeat him. Promise me you love me. Promise me this is real."

Lex and I had gotten primal in our time together, discovering a side of each other that had always been there but never made itself known. I'd never spoken to him like this, never claimed him so blatantly and dominantly. Maybe I wanted him to recognize the connection between us again, maybe I wanted him to come to terms with how I'd forgiven Miri, maybe I just needed to hear him say it.

"I'm yours," he said, moving my body against his own faster. "I'm yours until the end, X. I love you. I love you. This is real." He buried his head in my neck and groaned, release coming from deep inside him.

It echoed through our connection, seizing my molecules and thrusting me into outer space with him. This was how Lex and I found each other, through sweat and tears and come. We were equals, codependent and intertwined forever.

When we came back down to earth, he wrapped his arms around my torso and pulled me back against the couch, humming a deep sigh of approval. "We'll defeat him," he said. "We'll fix the queen and we'll find Siobhan."

"I know." I kissed him one more time before delivering my final blow. "One more thing."

He narrowed his eyes, clearly seeing my ulterior motive regardless of the amazing sex.

"Apologize to Miri," I said. "Whatever he did to her, it wasn't nice."

"It killed me to be without her...to watch you be without her." Lex cleared his throat and nodded, looking between us. "I was fucking pissed."

"Was..." The hope echoed in my tone.

"Well"—Lex met my gaze again and gave me one of those killer smiles—"she's a little terrifying, isn't she?"

More than a little.

6

CARTER

"Now that everyone's reacquainted"—Lex stood at the head of the breakfast table, his hands splayed out in front of him—"anyone have any ideas how to end this fucker?"

Ivy told us about commanding the king to get off Mount Vernon. "That had just been Lex and me. With the four of us?" She shrugged. "We're a lot more powerful."

"Remember when I tried to compel the queen at Samhain?" Lex told our spouses the same thing he'd said earlier that day about her claim to be the Great Source. "I wonder how many mysteries are waiting to be unearthed in that noggin of hers."

"You think if we fix her, we can get rid of the king?" Ivy pursed her lips, considering it.

"Maybe she knows how it was done the first time, how they banned him from our realm at the beginning." Lex shrugged, indicating he thought it was a good idea. "She might even know a better option—something more than sacrifices and blood oaths."

"Siobhan said they were equals, that one could not exist without the other. They create a balance." Ivy pinched her bottom lip while she paced and thought out loud. "At the wedding, Alberich looked wrecked, barely a version of his former self." She closed her eyes and squinted, like something was coming to her out of nowhere. "He tried to open the car door by the handle."

Lex furrowed his eyebrows, and I waited for her to continue.

"But he couldn't because it was locked." She looked up when she realized we were staring at her. "Why didn't he use magic to open it? Why was it just him and not his goons?"

"Are you saying he can't use his magic?" Lex asked.

She shrugged. "Siobhan's sister, Ashley, said they couldn't be apart from each other without consequences. What if they're like us?"

"Well, shit," I said, rubbing at the back of my head as all this information fell into place. "If they're like us, does that mean we're like them?" Three sets of eyes turned to me, as if that had just uncovered something profound. "What?"

"Siobhan said the magic mutated when we took the vow in those ruins." Ivy glanced at Lex. "She said when this all ends, it's the four of us left standing."

"What is that supposed to mean?" Miri scrubbed her face, clearly exhausted by everything that had happened and everything left to come.

I understood. My agent had to cut my tour short because of this family emergency, but both back to back had turned me into a zombie. I'd need to sleep for ten years after this was over.

"It means we defeat him," I said. "It means we were always supposed to do this."

"Alright, Mr. Toxic Positivity," Lex said. "We're still trying to figure that out."

"Siobhan said it was the four of us that ended this, right?" Miri asked.

"In the end, it's the four of us," I confirmed.

No one said anything for a long moment while we processed that. Could we bring him down? Could four measly humans do what had taken a powerful fairy to accomplish ages ago? Based on what we'd done thus far, we'd have better luck landing on the moon.

"Us being back together again means something, definitely," I said, "but if we're going to get rid of the king, we should start with the queen."

"I've tried to use my magic on her. So did Ivy. It doesn't work." Lex shook his head.

"I felt something when I touched her yesterday," Miri explained.

Ivy raised her eyebrows. "Felt what?"

Miri shrugged. "I don't quite know. But I got a glimpse...a hint of something. Should we try?" Miri glanced between us. "Should we go upstairs and put our hands on the queen to see what happens?"

As if summoned by talking about her, Diana coasted down the stairs with one hand on the banister, giving her an angelic ambiance. Power and decadence radiated off her in powerful waves, but nowhere near as strong as it had once been.

She smiled and asked us something in her strange language before twirling around the table and opening the fridge to retrieve a juice box we kept there for Poppy. She opened the straw and slammed it into the hole, glancing up when she noticed all of us staring. Inquisitive, she made a bright sound and walked over to the table. "Dune-shatcha-thee?"

Diana put a hand on Lex's shoulder, giving him a tender look that reminded me of the incredulous one she'd given us in Faerie the first time we met her. She'd mentioned cutting off his pretty head to hang on a spike in her tent if he tried to use his magic on her again. Even as she said the words, her eyes echoed with amusement and fascination. That same expression lingered there now, the one that was curious about Lex and wanted to know more.

"Are we doing this?" Ivy asked.

Lex answered that by giving the queen a gentle grin and taking her hand to bring her knuckles to his lips for a respectful kiss. I moved closer, putting my hand over his. Ivy and Miri did the same, and we stood in a circle next to the queen, all of us linked with her.

"Tell me the truth," Lex said. "Are you still in there?"

Tightness squirmed in my chest, creeping up my spine and over my scalp. It was the same kind of tingling that coated my skin anytime we crossed over into Faerie. *Magic.* It pulsed between us like an electric current, bright and sharp and potent. My knees almost buckled as the shock hit me in the gut.

"Fuck." I leaned over the table to hold myself up. A thunderous vibration shot down my legs, churning in my stomach, almost like when I let myself play poker, like luck was literally on my side, effervescent and overwhelming. I drank it in, pulling whatever it was over us, washing us with its majesty. We'd need it. We'd need all the help we could get. The bond between us burst open, pumping power through my veins and all around us like a hurricane. The queen moaned and tried to pull away, but Lex held her tighter.

"Let me in," Ivy said. "Just let me in."

"I can feel it," Miri said. "The sickness. The evil. Whatever he did to her, it's gripping her tight."

"Tell me," Lex bellowed again. "Are you in there?"

Diana shouted out in anguish and ripped her hand away, clutching it with her other fingers. Her guards rushed down the stairs at the sound of her scream. Where once they had worked for Lex, protecting her because his Uncle Dmitri had ordered them to, now they seemed like she had transfixed them. She spoke to them in her strange language, and they did her bidding, which suited us fine as long as they didn't turn on us.

Diana didn't say anything, just glanced between the four of us with narrowed eyes and pursed lips. She didn't seem mad, at least not now that she realized she was safe. She was more confused, her eyebrows furrowed and her lips slightly parted. Then, she turned on her heels and marched upstairs, muttering something low under her breath.

"Did it work?" I hissed, glancing at the other three, arguably the most powerful out of the four of us. "Did we fix her?"

Ivy grimaced and ran a hand over her neck. "I don't think so."

"Fuck," Lex snapped, rubbing his face.

"She's better," Miri said with a small nod. "We helped."

"How can you tell?" I didn't feel any different, and the queen hadn't suddenly returned to her old self.

Miri shrugged and said, "I can see it," before heading outside to the porch.

I looked at Ivy, who gave me a sympathetic pat on the shoulder before following our princess. Lex met my gaze with a cynical one of his own. It was true that Miri had some connection to their realm that we didn't understand. When we were in Faerie, she could tell who was fairy and who was human. She said the trees talked to her, told her things about her life that turned out to be true.

If she said we'd helped the queen, I believed her. But I also worried about our princess. I didn't know what strain this was putting on her, and I didn't want to lose her. Never again.

We ate dinner together and schemed the rest of the night. We needed to contact Siobhan, but we couldn't count on her being alive or still willing to assist. Ivy's siblings, Abigail and Henry, could be useful in keeping Ivy's mother distracted, but other than that, we didn't want them involved. We talked in circles until we couldn't see straight, but ultimately went to bed with nothing more than conjecture and a list of possibilities.

Without Siobhan and Poppy, we were on our own. Without the queen, we had nothing but each other.

Ivy and Miri curled up in the middle of the mattress with Lex on the other side, protecting our most valuable center. The four of us hadn't reconnected the way we used to, and the tension between Lex and Miri hadn't fully healed. I wasn't sure they'd even talked alone since their argument in the tub.

It could be good again, if we tried. If we defeated the king. If we still had our bond after all this was over. If we still loved each other.

The thought that this might end ached deep in my gut. I loved my spouses, each one in their own way, and I sure as hell liked being lucky. Maybe it wasn't as useful as being able to detect lies or as powerful as invading someone's mind, but I lived an easy life because of it. I liked having my gift, and I liked the people I shared it with.

I woke up around 3 a.m. parched, and I went downstairs for a glass of water where I found Miri out on the patio, her hands splayed out to either side of the railing, her skin glowing in the moonlight. She wore a floor-length lavender silk nightgown, mirroring her dark hair as both floated around her in the breeze.

For a moment, I paused to watch her, memorizing the slender slope of her neck as it became her shoulder and the way her spine rolled down the middle of her back in a delicate curve. She looked like a goddess, like the queen of the night come here to destroy us. She glanced over her shoulder and caught me staring, her eyes illuminated from within. In the months apart, she'd lost the fleshiness around her hips that had once made her soft and pliable. Now all hard edges and sharp corners, she seemed more evil than she was. But Persephone was the Goddess of springtime and the underworld for a reason. Both could be true.

"What are you doing awake?" I asked as I took a few steps closer.

She hummed and returned to admiring the cool night air, lifting her chin as the wind picked up the pieces of curly chestnut locks around her face. "Listening."

The trees rustled, whispering secrets only Miri could understand. Still, I closed my eyes anyway, hoping that I might get lucky, that I might be given a rare opportunity to see behind the curtain. An owl hooted in the distance, and the crunch of last autumn's leaves hinted at a larger animal moving close by—maybe a deer or a mountain lion.

"What are they saying?" I murmured.

"They're coming," she said.

I snapped my eyes open and looked at her, my heart rate starting to skyrocket. "Who's coming, Miri?"

She shrugged, but didn't seem bothered by whatever it was. "Don't be scared. They're not here to hurt us. The trees will protect us."

I thought about running back inside to wake up Lex and Ivy, but I wanted these few moments alone with her. I understood why she had pulled away, and I understood how she could believe she was a danger to us. Furrowing my eyebrows, I cleared my throat and stuffed my hands in my pockets, hoping she took what I said next with love and not accusation. "Why didn't you tell me...about your memory...about what you suspected? Why did you keep it from *me?*"

Miri didn't say anything, just looked back out to the woods and took a long, deep inhale. "What would you have done?"

"Something," I said. "Anything besides leave you alone all this time."

She made a sad laughing sound, shook her head, and wrapped her tiny, delicate hand around the inside of my elbow before leaning her head on my shoulder. "No, my darling. You couldn't have done anything at all."

"I would have tried. I would have..." Fuck, I didn't know. "I would have taken you on tour with me. We could have been safe together."

"Romeo." She gave me a soft smile and leaned in to kiss my cheek. "The same reasons we could never be together are still there. You're you, and I'm me, and that will never change."

Once upon a time, I'd been a lowly nobody from Chicago and she'd been HRH Princess Miriam, and we'd run away to California together with nothing but our heartbreak and a promise not to hurt each other. If we were ever going to give it a go, just the two of us, that would have been the time. Still, I fought it. If she had just told me what was going on, I would have insisted. I would have figured out how to delay filming or perhaps persuaded them to recast me altogether. I wouldn't have cared because we both would have been safe.

I took a step closer, pressing against her so I could wrap my arms around her from behind, pulling her closer to me. Resting my chin on the top of her head, I inhaled her deeply, devouring her flowery scent, letting it ease my nerves.

"All we have is us, Juliet," I said, kissing her crown.

She nodded and relaxed back against me, intertwining her fingers with mine. "I'll miss nights like this with you, Romeo." Her lips brushed my knuckles with a warm caress as she kissed each one individually. "When all this is over."

I thought again about what she'd said in the bath.

"It's not safe for me to be here. I should go back to England as soon as we figure out how to break this curse."

This was never going to be over. Siobhan had told us back in March. The bond we'd formed during this ordeal would never go away, not completely. I tried to imagine my life without her in it, without Ivy or Lex, and the thought made me so hollow, I wanted to curl into a ball and die.

I opened my mouth to respond, to tell her she'd never be able to get rid of me, no matter what her stupid grandmother tried to make her do, but something moved near the tree line, startling me enough to push Miri behind me.

"What is that?" I said. "Did you see that?"

She nodded and walked toward the stairs, despite my attempts to grab her arm and stop her. Miri descended a step before blinking up at me with owlish brown eyes and a devilish smile. "They're here."

A familiar figure finally stepped out of the shadows, holding up a hand in peace and solidarity.

Siobhan.

Her dark brown hair hung around her face in thick waves, much longer than the last time I'd seen her, and bruises marred her cheekbones and jaw. Her commander and lover, Finn, appeared next to her, his once short platinum hair now down to his shoulders. His face looked beat to hell as well, but he certainly seemed healthier than when he'd been stabbed through the chest by one of the *Fianna* a few months ago. Now, he stood upright with a huge round metal shield in one hand and an enormous axe in the other. Finally, Donnelly appeared on the other side of Finn, tall and lithe and quiet. His obsidian hair had also grown to his shoulders, a scowl between his eyebrows. Icy eyes peered at the two of us as he put one hand on the arrows in his quiver and the other on his bow.

"Miri?" Siobhan said, taking another hesitant step forward. "Is that you?"

Miri nodded. "That's right. It's me."

"Fucking hell." Siobhan took a long, deep inhale and let it out on a sigh. "It's about damn time. Do you know how long we've been waiting for you?"

"Her?" I cut in. "You're two days late."

"Yeah, yeah." Siobhan walked past Miri and climbed the stairs, her warrior lovers following her. "But we got what we needed."

"The *Fianna?* The battle maidens? You got them?" I looked between her, Finn, and Donnelly, trying to verify I understood what she meant. When they'd helped us plan to bring down the fairy king, they had taken the responsibility of getting reinforcements. The *Fianna* were the king's most loyal soldiers, his army of henchmen that had done whatever he'd asked for centuries. As commander of that army, Finn had their loyalty through a blood oath sworn to him before Alberich. Siobhan had also promised to find the queen's battle maidens, the ones who had dedicated their lives to protecting Diana.

Finn nodded in answer to my question, the lines of sweat and mud on his face indicating how far they'd traveled and how exhausted they must have been. "We got them."

I didn't see anyone behind them.

"They're waiting in Killwater," he explained. "They're ready when we are."

"Killwater?" I blew out a breath. "How the hell is that supposed to help us here?"

Footsteps from inside the house drew my attention to Weeds, wrapping a robe around herself as she blinked and stepped outside. Lex followed behind her, his features rumpled and puffy with sleep.

"Jesus Christ," Lex said, brushing his hair out of his face.

"I'm so happy you're okay." Ivy pulled Siobhan into a hug before going to Finn and Donnelly to do the same. "It's good to see you."

"It's good to see you, too, Ivy." Siobhan gave her a gentle smile. "You have no idea how much."

"Come on," Donnelly said, eyeing Miri suspiciously as he walked up the porch steps. "We've got a lot to catch up on."

ACT II

I'll met by moonlight, proud Titania.
-Oberon, Act II, Scene I

7

IVY

"It nearly killed us to retrieve them," Finn explained, rubbing a dirty palm over his face. We sat around the living room while they explained what happened, me and my spouses on the longer couch, Siobhan and her companions on the shorter one.

"We had to find a way to get the *Fianna* out without the king knowing." Siobhan leaned forward and put her elbows on her knees, the bags under her eyes indicating how war-torn she actually was. Whatever they'd done, it had taken them going somewhere dangerous to accomplish it. When we came up with the plan, Finn had chided that it wouldn't be getting in that would be hard, it would be getting out. "It was brutal and bloody. We lost good soldiers."

The three of them made identical hand gestures over their hearts, a swish of the thumb that must have indicated something important.

"We're here now," Donnelly added as his features slipped into that stoic hunter's calm that always unnerved me. "And we kept up our end of the bargain. What about you?"

A dark eyebrow went up his forehead as his cold eyes glanced between us. Lex sat forward and told them the story, how the king had shown up at our wedding and everything that had happened since then. I swallowed down my shame and anger when he mentioned Poppy abducting our family members.

"She turned on us?" Siobhan's eyes widened as she focused her gaze on Carter. "She turned on you?"

"She took Lizzie and Prince Edward." Carter's eyes reddened like he was remembering the memory in detail. I could only imagine how terrifying that must have been. "We don't know where she is or what she's done with them. She won't answer our calls."

"We believe the king has Jon and Kit," I added, remembering how Abigail had screamed. I never wanted to hear that sound again. "He took them before I pushed him out of Mount Vernon."

"How did you do that?" Finn's emerald-green gaze almost glowed with its intensity.

Lex and I looked at each other before I cleared my throat. "That night we met with you, I connected to the king's mind. I can see his memories, feel his emotions."

Donnelly snorted and shook his head. "I fucking knew it. I smelled him on you."

"What does that mean?" Lex asked, rubbing his eyes, clearly exhausted.

Donnelly's lips curled into a smirk, but he didn't answer the question.

"There's something else." I scratched my neck, composing myself and straightening to face our fairy friends. "Poppy can travel through time. She took Lex back to see his brother when he was still alive."

Siobhan didn't say anything, just pursed her lips and glanced at Finn. He met her gaze with some kind of wordless communication before glancing to Donnelly, who sat motionless, assessing me as I talked. Of the three, he intimidated me the most. Sure, Finn was huge and Siobhan probably knew how we all died, but Donnelly had an eerily stillness that told me he'd seen the worst of his realm and lived to talk about it. Whatever he had to do to get to the *Fianna*, I figured it was dark and dangerous, something he wouldn't talk about openly.

"I thought she could hone her skills and use them to our advantage," Lex confessed. "I only partially accounted for her stabbing us in the back."

"Well, she hasn't. Yet," Siobhan said. "We don't know why she took Lizzie and Edward. Did she seem upset?"

"Terribly," Miri said. "She was sobbing."

"She's playing her own game," Donnelly said. "She lied to us when we asked her what she knew."

That rubbed salt in the wound. I should have seen this coming. I should have listened to Lex when he told us to watch out for her, but I'd been blindsided by my love. Just like the king, Poppy had used my affection against me, and it picked at a scab I didn't want to examine. I'd spent most of my life protecting my siblings, the urge to provide and protect ran in my molecules. I wouldn't dampen who I was just because it could be perceived as a weakness.

"There's more." Miri shifted uncomfortably in her seat, crossing her arms over her chest. "Alberich tricked me. He's inside my head. He…" She took a deep breath and let it out slowly. "He's warping my memories, doing things to me and making me forget them."

Carter grabbed one of Miri's hands and I gripped the other, sending my love through our shared connection. We weren't complete without her. We needed her the way the sky needed the sun, and I wanted to make sure she knew that. There was no me without her, and there never would be.

Siobhan didn't say anything for a long moment, just hung her head and pressed her fingers into her eyes. Finn's hard expression turned even more stony as he cleared his throat and took a deep breath.

"I'm sorry that happened to you," he finally said. "The king is… mercurial and apparently, he's getting more aggressive. There's no sacred boundary he won't cross."

Siobhan leaned toward Miri, her deep brown eyes desperate for more information. "What do you mean when you say he's doing things to you and making you forget them? How so?"

Miri told them what she meant, how she knew that something had been altered because it reminded her of the way he'd tampered with her parents' deaths. "He can manipulate me, and I can't trust myself."

"I told you it needed to be the four of you." Siobhan sighed and pinched the bridge of her nose, obviously reeling from the information we'd dumped in her lap. "You were vulnerable because you were separated."

"We're together now," Lex said, his hazel eyes narrowing. "And we're all playing on the same team for once. Isn't that right?" He glanced at me before focusing on Miri, who nodded and curled her arms around herself again.

"What about Poppy?" I asked. "You once told us she was the key to everything. What exactly is she supposed to do?"

"Remember the prophecy, the one that started all this?" Siobhan looked between us as a conversation with her sister, Ashley, came to the forefront. Back when we'd gone to Faerie for Samhain, she had explained the reason Alberich feared Poppy so much had to do with a vision that their seer had about the changeling. According to them, she was the key, the one who would bring peace to the realms by reuniting the humans and the fairies. *"Which fairies? Which humans?"* Ashley had said, *"Prophecies are notoriously vague."* Alberich had thought it meant that she'd destroy the veil, and Faerie would be overwhelmed by humans intent on destroying them. Once he found out what she could do, he wanted her killed.

"It's coming true," Siobhan said. "If we reunite the king and the queen, and she contains him, we will have ended the war between them."

"Or he'll kill her outright and put our heads on spikes," Lex said.

"He can't," I said, recalling what else Ashley had told us that day. *"One cannot survive without the other. Where she is light, he is dark."* It confirmed what Finn had said about them. *"He'd never be able to kill the queen. They're equals in every way."* They needed each other for balance.

"If he kills her, he'll end himself, too," Carter said.

"He's too narcissistic to do that," I added.

A long time ago, he'd tried to escape the fairy realm and a powerful fae had cursed him to keep him in Faerie. Lex had believed the queen knew who had done it and perhaps had been there when it happened. After all, she had supposedly been impacted by the same curse, as tied together as they were. Whatever impacted him affected her.

"We need to find the queen," Siobhan said.

Fuck. In all the catching up, none of us had mentioned the best part. A creak in the stairs alerted us to her presence as Diana descended in a flowing white gown, looking more regal than she had in months. We hadn't seen her since we zapped her with our magic yesterday, but now she radiated with warmth and vitality. Her long pale hair no longer seemed dull and lifeless, and her cheeks had color to them, like she'd gotten a good night's sleep.

Finn and Siobhan pushed to their feet while Donnelly remained seated with that same suspicious smirk.

"Oh," Diana said, giving a warm smile when she came into the dining room before continuing to talk in her unintelligible language.

My heart dropped. I had hoped that whatever we'd done had worked, but other than putting some color back in her cheeks, she still couldn't communicate with us.

"My lady," Siobhan muttered, melting into a flabbergasted bow.

"You see," I said. "We can't understand her. It's all jumbled."

"No, that's..." Donnelly closed his eyes, shaking his head like he was trying to solve a riddle. "That's Faero-Gaelic. Old Faero-Gaelic."

"I haven't heard that in centuries," Finn said.

Donnelly grimaced and muttered a few sloppy syllables, wincing at the last bit. Diana's eyes widened as she gasped, jumping into Donnelly's arms with a squeal. I couldn't understand the words, but

I knew what she meant. For the first time since we'd found her, someone had said something she could comprehend.

"So, he reset her brain to default?" Lex looked between Finn and Donnelly, hoping for an answer.

"That ruby dust is some heavy-hitting shit," Siobhan said while Diana rambled at Donnelly, clinging to his arms and regaling her entire life story.

"What's she saying?" I asked.

"Uh…" Donnelly shook his head. "I don't understand most of it."

"She's explaining that she woke up in the snow and the little girl found her. Since then, she's been staying with her until the mean guy brought her here." Finn looked at Lex. "I assume that's you."

Lex laughed. "My uncle."

"She thanks you for your hospitality, but she needs to find the little girl."

"Is that Poppy?" Siobhan glanced at Carter.

He shrugged. "I guess so."

Siobhan turned her angry glare on me, her jaw clenched. "You should have led with this."

"Oh, I'm sorry so much happened while you were dragging your asses to get here," Lex snarled, jumping to my defense. "We forgot a few important details."

"Enough," Finn cut in, shooting Lex a piercing stare before turning to Siobhan. "We have the queen. This is a good thing."

"Not if she doesn't remember who she is," Donnelly murmured, an amused tilt to his lips. "Not if she can't remember the last two thousand years."

"We can fix her," Miri said. "We just need to rest and try again."

"Fix her?" Siobhan's gaze narrowed. "This is old magic, stronger than anything I know."

"So are we." I took a deep breath and straightened my shoulders. "You said the gift you gave us mutated into something ancient and powerful, that it was out of your control."

"Yes, but—"

"We already helped her," I continued. "Yesterday, she looked like death. Today, she's better. And now that Finn is here to translate—"

Diana cut in, saying something to Finn while she placed her delicate hand on his arm and took a hesitant step forward. She'd braided her hair and, in that one vulnerable moment, she reminded me of the panicked fairy that had shoved Poppy into Carter's arms on Samhain. I had seen true fear in her eyes that day, and now, I recognized the panic. Despite not being able to understand us, she seemed to know we'd been freaking out.

"She wants to know what's going on, what happened to her."

"Tell her," I said. "Maybe it'll help her remember."

Finn explained it to her, the language eloquent coming from his lips. Diana nodded along, glancing back and forth between us for a long moment, her eyebrows furrowed like she struggled to understand what the other fairy was saying.

"You are the great queen of the fairies. See these marks." Siobhan held up her arm to show Diana the tattoos winding up her elbow and bicep. "They are a symbol of your lineage." She matched them to the same marks on Diana's arm. "They mark my loyalty to you."

Finn translated while the queen shook her head, clearly not remembering.

"She wants to know about the girl. Where is she?" Finn glanced up at us, green gaze flickering between us.

"We haven't talked to her in days," I said. "She won't answer our calls."

Diana's smile widened and she linked her hands in front of her, glancing to me with an encouraging nod.

"Call her again. She'll answer this time," Finn said.

I raised an eyebrow and glanced at Carter, skeptical of listening to an ancient fairy queen with magical amnesia. But weirder things had happened, so he reached into his back pocket and retrieved his phone, pressing the number for Poppy's contact.

She answered on the second ring.

8

CARTER

A loud zap went through the atmosphere, and Poppy appeared in the living room.

"He made me do it," she said, a sob barreling out of her throat as she collapsed into a pile by the fireplace. "He made me do it, and he took them."

Her curly blond hair still frizzed around her head, the same as it had the night I'd met her. Her big brown eyes still took up a sizable portion of her face, making her seem innocent and unassuming. But I knew better now. She'd grown nearly half a foot. Now, all knees and elbows, she looked closer to the age she probably was, despite the infant-like chubbiness remaining in her cheeks.

Three days ago, I would have said she was the child I'd never had, the one given to Ivy and me when we couldn't have one of our own. Even though Lex didn't trust her and said she was lying, I wanted to believe she wouldn't betray us. Then, she'd stolen my sister and claimed she didn't have any other choice, that she'd had to do it. Now, she stood in front of me with red-rimmed eyes and tear-stained cheeks.

Despite her betrayal, the ache in my heart throbbed, both for my missing sister as well as the version of me that had loved Poppy blindly.

Diana rushed to the child, cooing and taking her in her arms like a mother would, rocking her while Poppy sobbed. Siobhan stood frozen across the table from me, Finn and Donnelly likewise stock-still. I watched the queen soothe the young human, the connection between them obvious. "Shh, shh, shh," Diana said, murmuring other nurturing tones.

"I'm so—" Poppy sucked in a deep breath and hiccuped. "I'm so stupid. I tried. I tried so hard, and he still won." She dug her palms into her eyes and shook her head. "I'm sorry. I'm so sorry."

Part of me longed for her. I wanted to drop to my knees and pull her into my arms the way Diana had, somehow yearning to be the one who held her while she cried. But I stayed where I was, willing myself to harden and remember what she'd done, who she was.

Her swollen eyes met mine from across the room and she broke more, curling into the queen to cry harder, and I couldn't handle it anymore. Betrayal or not, I still loved her. She was still mine to protect, mine to keep safe. I moved without consciously thinking about it, kneeling in front of the scene.

"Poppy," I said, gently reaching out to tug her arms away from her face. "Poppy, what happened? Where's Lizzie and Edward?"

"You were right," she murmured. "They're dead. They're all dead."

Ice plummeted down my spine into my gut. *Dead? What? No.* I glanced back at my spouses, making eye contact with Miri, whose hands covered her mouth while she braced to learn the fate of her cousin.

"Marcus. Prince Gerald. Princess Emma." Poppy went on, taking another ragged breath, shaking her head as she cried harder.

My stomach clenched, and I struggled to maintain my gentle hold on her shoulders. Marcus? Gerald and Emma? What did Lex's brother and Miri's parents have to do with anything? Unless... *Oh, God.*

"He found me. I tried hiding, but he found me, and he made me take Lizzie and Edward. He made me say those horrible things. He was going to kill me. I had to."

Part of me wanted to be furious, and perhaps I was. But the other part of me saw desperation in her actions. She wanted the only mother she'd ever known back. When Dmitri had taken Diana and brought her here, Poppy must have thought the worst. Now, it made sense. She'd been a victim of the king's coercion, trying to solve something she had no business being involved with in the first place.

Poppy shook her head and sobbed. "He didn't have my lady. He forced me to go back in time." Her gaze drifted from me to Lex and Ivy across the room, her tears streaking her cheeks as she whimpered. "I watched him do it. I watched him sink that boat with Marcus on it. I watched him crash the car with Miri inside. And you..." Poppy's brown eyes met mine. "He tried to kill your father. But the nurse saved him, the one he married." Poppy swallowed, her eyes so sullen and sad, it nearly crushed me. "The king's a monster."

He tried to kill your father.

I'd never had a good relationship with my father, but sometime around age sixteen, he'd gotten into a car accident and ended up at the hospital. There, he met a beautiful young nurse and the person that would eventually cause him to leave my mother. Now, Poppy put a new filter on that. It had been the king who had caused it, hoping to kill him instead.

Had I been lucky then? Had my luck extended to my family even if I didn't know it? He had survived, after all, and lived long enough to alienate the children he already had in exchange for creating a new family with his mistress.

I glanced over my shoulder again, watching as Ivy and Lex realized how much the king had manipulated our lives. Tears streaked down Ivy's cheeks as she hastily wiped them away. Lex's jaw clenched so hard, I thought he'd break a molar. It didn't start at Midsummer. The king had been screwing with us since we were kids.

"Poppy," Siobhan said, taking a few steps closer. "Are you saying you took the king to do these things?"

She nodded. "He said he wouldn't kill me if I helped him. I didn't think he'd kill other people. And after Marcus, I didn't know how to stop him." Poppy looked at Lex and Ivy, a deep sorrow echoing in her eyes. "I'm so sorry. I...I'm just so sorry."

"How did you escape?" Ivy asked. "How did you get here?"

"After your wedding, the rest of his army abandoned him, including the ones guarding me." Poppy glanced back up at Diana to hug her tighter. "I teleported somewhere safe to hide, and when I knew he wasn't following me, I came here."

I glanced at Siobhan, knowing she and Finn were the reason the *Fianna* abandoned him. Her features dropped as she said, "It's happening." The banshee looked at Diana before returning her focus to Ivy and Lex. "The end. All the pieces are falling into place. We don't have long now."

Diana muttered something and stood to walk back to Finn.

"Your Highness," Finn started, explaining the situation to her while her eyebrows furrowed. When she still couldn't understand it, she shook her head and returned her attention to a still weeping Poppy.

"She doesn't remember Alberich or Faerie," Finn explained. "She only remembers waking up and being with Poppy."

"I was trying to protect her," Poppy pleaded. "You have to believe me."

I didn't know what to tell her as she stared up at me with big, sad eyes. I wanted to forgive her. I wanted to tell her she'd done the best she could, but now my baby sister was in the custody of a mad fairy king from another realm who would use her against me. As much as my bleeding heart begged me to, the anger inside wouldn't let me.

The things he could be doing to Lizzie...the things he could be making her do to him...

"We have to get to them," I said, rising to walk over to my spouses. "Now."

"We will, Carter," Ivy said, reaching out to squeeze my hand. "We will."

Siobhan grimaced, but it was Finn who got serious. "Our queen wants to help us. We just have to tell her what to do."

"Not to be a dick," Lex cut in, "but how is involving the queen of forgotten fairy things going to help with anything? She has no idea who she is, and until she does, it's more advantageous to keep her a secret."

"Yesterday, we couldn't communicate with her, but whatever we did helped," Miri said, looking between Siobhan and Finn. "Give us more time. We can get her back to her old self."

I didn't know how I knew she was right, but it writhed in my gut the same way all my fairy gift instincts did. My magic told me it was a good idea, that I should keep pushing it until they agreed. "Miri's right. We're the ones left standing in the end, right?"

"We don't have time," Siobhan said, impatience in her tone. "The end is starting now. We're about to face the big boss."

"We need to get back to Killwater," Finn said. "The *Fianna* is patient, but restless. We need a plan."

"The battle maidens will want to make sure my lady is sound before they agree to help us any further," Siobhan added. "Getting everyone to Killwater is the right next step."

"The king is here," Lex said. "Going all the way to Ireland is a risk."

"The king will follow you," Donnelly added. "Especially if he knows we have the child and the queen."

"How are we supposed to do that?" Ivy said. "It's not like we can disappear now, not after the fiasco at the wedding."

"That's exactly what we've been doing," Lex said, his voice broken and scratchy, making my heart ache for him. He'd just learned the way he thought his brother had died had been a lie. He deserved a break; we all did. "Lying low. Minding our own business. You took the rest of the term off, didn't you? We're supposed to be on a four-week honeymoon."

"We didn't get married, Lex," Ivy countered. "My mother—"

"Your mother no longer has any right to dictate our lives." Lex's hazel eyes peered out at her with a mixture of retribution and vengeance burning behind them. I cleared my throat and crossed my arms, echoing that sentiment. After all she'd done to us, she should consider herself lucky enough to ever talk to Ivy again, much less have a say in what she does.

"Okay, you're right," Ivy finally said, nodding as she looked at Siobhan. "I'm in."

"Me too," I said.

"Of course," Miri agreed. "When do we leave?"

"As soon as we can," Finn said. "Once we're there, we'll regroup with my other captains and sort out the details."

At the mention of the other captains, a chill snaked down my spine and into my legs. This was real. There was an *army* of fairies waiting for us on the other side of the realm, one that was depending on us to defend the maniacal villain who had plagued their world for centuries. We were four pitiful humans who had been given a mutated fairy gift less than five years ago, and it all rested precariously on our shoulders. A wave of nausea followed that thought, reminding me of the first time I'd ever walked out on a stage.

"Be honest," Lex said, glancing at Siobhan. "What exactly do you know about what happens next?"

Siobhan glanced at Finn as she cleared her throat and grew still, a trained soldier preparing for something terrible. "The last time we spoke, I told you that I believed you would hate me once you knew the whole story."

Donnelly tensed, sitting up straighter. "Banshee..."

I remembered that as the nickname both he and Finn used for Siobhan.

"We have to get to Killwater because that's where it ends," she said, ignoring Donnelly's warning. "On Beltane, we'll slip through the veil and go to Faerie. After that..." Siobhan took a deep breath and looked at Ivy. "There will need to be a sacrifice. I don't know what, but before this war is over...your hearts will shatter. You will lose what you hold most dear."

My gut told me this was bullshit. There wouldn't need to be a sacrifice. We would all make it out alive. I didn't know how I knew that, but I did.

"I read about that in the lore." Lex let out an exhausted sigh, like he was tired of the riddles and the half-truths. "What does that actually mean?"

Siobhan shook her head. "I don't know. I wish I did."

"That sounds quite ominous, doesn't it?" Miri asked, playing with a piece of her hair.

"I've had enough of this fairy-tale bullshit." Lex launched to his feet, causing Donnelly to stand as well, seemingly prepared to defend Siobhan if needed. Lex narrowed his eyes at him, like the fairy had gotten the wrong impression, and paced toward the whiskey crystal to pour himself a drink.

Siobhan's features softened at Lex's frustration. "One thing at a time, mate. The queen is a powerful ally. If we heal her, that's a big step."

"I'm worried about entering the queen's mind if the king is so easily able to infiltrate mine." Ivy chewed on her bottom lip, watching Diana comfort Poppy while she continued to cry. "I don't want him hurting her anymore."

"Which is why the *four* of you will continue to work together," Siobhan said. "You are strongest when the gift is complete. As for the king"—she refocused her attention on Ivy—"try to keep him out of your head. We can use it to our advantage if you can control it."

"There are mental tricks I can teach you," Donnelly said. "We'll start working on them when we land in Dublin."

Ivy seemed to consider this for a moment before nodding.

"There's something inside him. I can feel it," she said. "It's like...a piece of himself that he's hidden. He's not entirely evil."

"Well, no one's entirely evil, are they?" Donnelly said. "He's been alive longer than anything I've ever known. I'm sure there are countless pieces of himself he's locked away over millions of years."

I couldn't even comprehend that length of time, much less consider who or what I'd be if I could live that long. But then again, time passed differently in Faerie. What would millions of years mean on that side of the realm? The entire concept hurt my brain to think about.

"No, this is different," Ivy said. "It's like...he's forgotten that he used to love Diana. He's forgotten that he used to be kind."

Finn narrowed his eyes, studying me with a grim set to his mouth. "He has grown cold since I first met him. The things he's done...the things he's made me do...and now that he's on this side of the realm, he's even more unstable. We don't have much time."

"His separation from the queen is making it worse," Siobhan said.

"Once we get to Killwater, what then?" Lex said. "Do you have a way to get into Faerie and take us with you?"

Siobhan smiled and held up her necklace, where a silver ring in the shape of ivy leaves dangled from the end. *The ring.*

"Christ, where did you get that?" Ivy held her hand out for it, and Siobhan took it off her neck and gave it to her. "I thought I'd lost it."

"You did," Siobhan said. "But that's my fault. You weren't supposed to go back to Faerie. I had no clue the gift would warp like this. When I created the ring, I enchanted it so that you wouldn't be able to take it with you on your way out. It would get you back to your realm, but it would stay behind until I could collect it."

"That explains it," Ivy said. "I'd been so careful to hold on to it last time. I couldn't remember letting go of it."

Siobhan nodded. "Two days from now is Beltane. The veil between the realms will be thinnest. We'll go into the woods then."

"Beltane," Donnelly spoke up. "Are you sure that's wise?"

Siobhan turned to face him. "You have a better idea?"

He shrugged. "The woods are going to be...rowdy."

She snorted. "I would have thought you'd be excited about a party before a battle."

He curled his lips into a smile. "I'm not saying that. It's just…" Donnelly glanced at me and my spouses before going back to the banshee. "Well, some of us didn't exactly keep a sober mind at the last fire festival."

I tried not to be insulted. We'd been drugged and cursed by Siobhan. We couldn't be held accountable for our actions.

"It doesn't matter," Siobhan said. "It might be the last time we get to make such a mistake." She glanced back at us with a somber smile. "Smoke 'em if you got 'em. And for goodness' sake, stay together, yeah?"

But my heart sank into my stomach.

It might be the last time we get to make such a mistake.

The question balanced on the tip of my tongue, poised to spill over. What was the likelihood of us walking out of this alive? What were the odds we make it out of Faerie ever again?

But in that split second, I decided I didn't want to know. My luck was telling me to have faith, to believe things would work out. And it hadn't steered me wrong this far.

"So?" Siobhan asked. "Anyone got a spare plane lying around?"

Ivy and Miri looked to Lex, who clenched his eyes shut and sighed.

9

LEX

Within two hours, Ivy and I had rented a charter to Dublin International. This time of night and this late in the game, the only thing available was the most expensive option. The fucking thing had once belonged to the emperor of some small shithole country with a GDP less than my trust fund. Housing four bedrooms, a kitchen, and a main cabin fit to host a goddamned ball, it had obviously cost a small fortune, but what's an inheritance compared to saving the world, am I right?

We strategized the entire ride to the airport, trying to figure out a countermove to anything we could encounter. Finn and Donnelly were masterminds, and with Siobhan and Carter's added gut feelings, we had a pretty good plan. It wasn't a *great* plan, but what the fuck did I know about bringing down a fairy king?

I'd tried and I'd failed, and I didn't know what I was talking about anymore.

Sometime around 2 a.m., everyone had gone to their rooms in the back of the plane, determined to get some rest before the final showdown. But I sat on a sofa in the luxurious main cabin, chain-smoking while I stared out at the stars in the vast darkness of space. They twinkled in the clear night sky, almost mocking me.

You thought you could have it all, they said. *What a selfish prick.*

I kept imagining the scream Ivy's sister, Abigail, let out when she realized Jon and Kit were gone. I replayed the sound of the king's smoky tendrils ticking against the glass windows at Mount Vernon, sending shivers through each of my nerve endings. I saw Miri's tearful gaze when she showed up on our doorstep, frail and broken and terrified. Whatever he'd done to her, it was the last straw.

He'd used our love against us, and for that, I would tear his heart out of his chest while he watched. I didn't care if the lore said he was immortal. I didn't care if it would kill the queen. This was the last time he'd fuck with any human whatsoever, and I'd find a way to make sure he knew it. Ivy and I alone had been able to force him out of Mount Vernon. She was right—what could we do when it was the four of us?

I didn't buy Siobhan's insistence that there would be a sacrifice. Like the prophecy about Poppy, Siobhan's banshee instincts were subjective, which meant they couldn't be trusted. I didn't believe in divination. I was in charge of my own life, and if I didn't want there to be a sacrifice, I would make sure there wasn't. We would all make it out of this, and I would get to have that fantasy future I'd been envisioning since Midsummer four years ago.

Inhaling deeply on my cigarette, I leaned my head back on my shoulders and let out the smoke on a sigh, wishing sleep could claim me as easily as it had my spouses. Things were awkward between us, even if we'd all made our apologies. I guessed that was my fault.

I knew Miri's separation would cause something terrible to happen. Lo and fucking behold, I was right. Again. Being that far away from us had created a vulnerability for Alberich to sneak through, and not that I blamed her for what he'd done to her, but I was furious she'd put herself in the position for it to happen.

If she'd just come home...if she'd just been with us...

But between me and these four walls, I understood that, too. I took another long drag on the smoke and recalled a younger version of myself, traumatized by a father that wished I'd died instead of my brother. It was easy to push people away because it meant they'd never hurt me. It took me a long time to realize I wasn't the problem. I imagined it might take Miri just as long.

But wishing for it never changed the past, did it? Not with Miri, and not with Marcus.

An enormous hole opened in my chest where my brother's memory had scarred over. I thought time traveling with Poppy to see him again was bad enough, but to learn it was Alberich's fault he'd died in the first place twisted agony through my gut and into my chest. I nearly doubled over from it.

If we hadn't gone to Killwater, if we hadn't built the wall of thistles, Marcus might still be alive.

His death is my fault, too.

"Hey," came a soft voice behind me before a warm palm settled between my shoulder blades. Miri's springtime scent hit me next, morning frost and daffodils. She sat next to me, pressing her silk-covered chest along my arm so she could snatch my box of cigarettes from my lap and light one for herself.

"Hey." I turned to face her, tracing the way the moonlight reflected off her cheekbones and forehead. She'd always been so beautiful, one of the loveliest people I'd ever seen.

"I couldn't sleep either," she said, wrapping her arms tight around herself. "I close my eyes and I just..." She pressed her lids together, squinting against the monster on the other side. "We need to defeat him, Lex."

"I know." I wrapped an arm over her shoulders and pulled her closer, pressing my lips to her temple. "We will."

"I'm sorry I stayed away so long. You were right."

"I'm sorry I was angry when you got here." I shook my head. "I'm sorry for the things I said. I missed you so much. We need you."

"You were right to be upset." She stuffed her face into my chest, reminding me of the girl I'd met so many years ago—heartbroken and vulnerable and delicate. "I was an idiot. I knew what would happen if I stayed away. I can't be surprised that it did."

"Enough now," I said, tilting her chin up so she had to look me in the eye. "Can we put the past behind us?"

She nodded and smiled, pushing up so she could kiss me, and I melted into the contact like a starved man. Christ, I didn't realize how much I'd craved her until she was back in my arms. Carter and I had a yearning that went back nearly a decade, and Ivy and I had only just discovered the burning thing between us. But Miri always felt like home. She was the safe place that remained constant all these years, somewhere to put the most tender side of me, the side no one else knew existed.

Miri brought it out. She made me want to protect her, to shield her from everything else in this world save for my own worst impulses. In a polycule that, admittedly, revolved around my former archnemesis, Miri was the first thing I'd ever claimed as mine. Maybe it made me a ravenous asshole, but part of me still felt that way. Carter got to have his Weeds, and Ivy adored Miri unconditionally, but she and I had seen the worst side of each other and embraced that darkness with no judgment.

"I love you, my prince," she said against my mouth, running her fingers up my neck and into my hair.

"I love you, my princess." I nearly groaned when she dragged her nails against my scalp, slamming all my fuck-yeah buttons. Without a second thought, I grabbed the back of her legs and shifted us so I was between them, laying her on the couch. Her ankles twisted behind my lower back, her heels digging into the waistband of my pants to shuck them down. God, how I wanted to give in to her impatience, to shove myself deep inside her and refuel the intimacy between us.

But I didn't. I cupped her jaw and devoured her mouth, relishing the way our tongues danced together. Her soft little moans had my dick jerking between us, and when I bit my way down her throat to her shoulder, she rocked her hips, brushing her beautiful, warm cunt up against me. I groaned and wilted, licking between her breasts while I stared up at her. I teased the hemline of her nightie, brushing my fingers over the tops of her thighs while I continued my descent.

Her deep honey-brown gaze held me the whole way, her bruised lips parted in that adorable O-shape. I couldn't help myself; I brushed my hands over her chest and up her neck, tracing one finger over her bottom lip. She sucked it into her warm, wet mouth, rolling her tongue around it the way she used to do to my dick.

Fuck.

"Tell me I can touch you." My balls clenched and I couldn't restrain myself anymore, tracing soft circles over her thighs with my thumbs. Even if all we did was kiss, that would be enough for me. I just wanted her, any way she'd let me have her.

She nodded, but her eyes shifted away, so I grabbed her chin, forcing her to look back at me.

"Tell me." I gave her a slow kiss. "Use your words, Princess. You know I love to hear how much you want me."

A soft chuckle greeted me before she smiled and darted her tongue out to brush against my mouth, reigniting that old flame in my heart. "Touch me, Lex. Please. I've missed you so much."

Fuck. Yeah.

I pushed her silk dress up and clamped my fingers on her knees, coaxing her legs farther apart. But then we both froze as my gaze dropped to the violet lines on the insides of her thighs, scars she'd carved into herself as a way to cope with the mental barrier in her memories. She tried to put a hand over them, but I shoved that away, taking my time to run my fingertips over each one.

My beautiful princess had survived, no matter what that monster had put her through. She was here, in front of me, and I'd been so ravenous for her all this time that I wouldn't let her hide anything from me, not anymore.

We couldn't go on like we had, all solitary schemes and plots. We needed to be open from here on out. And I wanted to make sure she really understood that.

IO

MIRI

Lex stared up at me from his knees, a smile spreading across his aristocratic features when I agreed. Normally, he was so good about hiding his emotions, locking all of it away so no one could tell what was going on in that brilliant, maniacal brain. But I knew him too well.

I'd seen the brief flash of fear that I might turn him away. After everything I'd been through, after all we'd seen together, he should have known that was the last thing I would have done. Silly boy. I had always loved him.

He looked again at the vibrant scars on the insides of my thighs, and I knew better than to try to hide them this time. He held my eyes with his penetrating hazel counterparts, keeping my thigh firmly in place while he leaned in and kissed the one farthest down. A spark of lust shot up my leg, ending with a hard throb at my clit. I gasped, watching as his pink tongue darted out and dragged up the next one, and that silky warmth radiated everywhere. A moan barreled over my lips, my fingers clenching the sofa for stability. My heart pounded and my muscles shook, especially the ones by his head. He must have felt it, must have known what he did to me, because he smirked and laughed and did it to the next scar. And the next one, each lick bringing us one step closer to each other. Then, he turned his head and did it to the other leg, kissing and sucking, his gaze firmly locked on mine.

The eye contact would have been uncomfortable with anyone else, but not with Lex, not like this. The intimacy between us could rival epic romances. There was nothing Lex and I hadn't shared, even other people, even other great love stories.

"Princess," he said once he'd had his fill of the last mark. "You will not do this to yourself again, do you understand?" His voice smacked with the authority of a king, of someone used to people doing what he told them the first time without question.

I couldn't tell if he meant the scratching or the separation, but ultimately decided on both. I nodded.

"Say it."

"I won't do it again," I told him.

He moaned an appreciative noise, his eyes closing in relief. I hadn't lied. We'd figure out a way to break this curse, despite what Siobhan said. And even if we couldn't, I'd find a way to get out of this engagement to Reginald, the prince of Monaco. I wanted to stay. I wouldn't put us through this again, not now that I knew better.

"You could never hide the darkest parts of yourself from me. I see you, all of you." He didn't let me respond before spearing his tongue through my most sensitive skin, drawing it out while he had his fill. "And I've loved you anyway."

"I know." His deep grumbling moan made me roll my head back on my shoulders, melting into the contact, remembering when Lex had taken me before. Hundreds, if not thousands, of times, and no two were the same. He had always been insatiable for me, just as I had always lusted after him like a lovesick puppy. Now, he held on to me like he was starved, like I'd been denying him a basic need for decades. When I tunneled my fingers through his silky-soft hair, he preened into the touch and glanced up, molten fire swirling in his irises. He let me go with a hard suck, sending a shock up my spine and down my toes.

"Don't do this to me again."

"Yes, of course I won't." I said the words, but they didn't give him the same relief as it did before. Now, he seemed suspicious.

"Hmm." He stood and licked at his glossy lips before leaning in to kiss me, pushing that velvet tongue into my mouth like he was trying to coat the inside with myself. "You taste that?" He did it again, and I sucked on it, swallowing down me and that minty, smoky flavor that had always been Lex Fairfax. It intoxicated me, making my head spin.

"I do," I said, when he finally leaned back to look down at me.

"That's what I do to you. *Me.*" He brushed his nose against mine and pressed his forehead along my temple. "You're *mine,* and I claimed you in a Scottish cottage when you were eighteen."

"I know," I said.

"Don't ever hurt yourself to protect me again, Miri," he said, leaning in to kiss me harder. My heart swelled and tears blurred my vision, sliding down my cheeks before I could wipe them away. He brushed his thumbs under my eyes, forcing me to look up at him. "I forbid it."

"You're not the boss of me."

The childish response elicited a brilliant smile from him, and I nearly froze to take it in. He liked the humor, certainly, but he also liked the opportunity to prove me wrong.

He groaned again, wrapping his hands around the backs of my thighs. "We'll see about that."

In one quick movement, he lifted me, and I hooked my ankles together at the base of his spine. I hung my arms over his shoulders, grinning like an idiot as I kissed him. He walked us to the back of the plane, depositing me in one of the free beds before shutting the door. I scooted into a more comfortable position while he leaned over me, the tips of his dark hair falling into his eyes.

"Tell me you're mine," he said, pressing his lips against me to draw the answer out of the depths of my soul.

"I'm yours," I said.

I shivered when Lex lowered his weight on top of me and settled his hips between mine, his body so warm and sturdy and safe. He slotted his dick right up against my clit, the thin fabric of his boxers the only thing separating us, and slid a hand over my neck to my throat. Being with him, being with all of them, had banished the fairy king to the furthest reaches of my consciousness, so dim that he became an afterthought. He wasn't allowed here with my true king, and never would be.

With his lips millimeters from mine, he whispered, "Say it again."

Hot breath coasted over my cheeks as a chill echoed down my body. He smiled and intertwined the fingers from his free hand into mine to bring it over my head. Our palms brushed up against each other, the thick curves of our matching scars lining up.

Until the end.

It was coming faster than either of us wanted to think about, but those were worries for another time. I needed this reconnection with my prince of darkness. I needed to know he still loved me.

He tucked his face into the space under my ear, biting my lobe as he chuckled softly to himself.

"C'mon, Princess." He kissed my cheek, my jaw, the corner of my mouth, taking his time to devour me as slowly as he ever had before. "Say it again."

"I'm yours, Lex. Always yours."

"That's right."

I absolutely loved when he took control, when he cared for me like I was the most precious thing in the world, rolling his pelvis into mine to tease me. Lex could be a cruel, arrogant prick. He'd once delighted in breaking Ivy's composure on purpose, and I'd seen the marks he left on Carter after their nights together. To watch such a powerful man bring himself to be tender just for me flipped a go switch in my libido—it always had.

Lex had never been as mean to me as he was to everyone else. Despite our on-again, off-again thing in college, he'd never done to me the things he reveled in doing to others. It had always made me feel special, unique in a way no one else could ever be. Lex Fairfax hated the world and everything in it...*except for me.*

Of course, that wasn't still true. Now, Lex admitted how much he loved Carter and Ivy, and that turned me on even more. I loved watching him with our spouses. It reminded me of how special our relationship was and how much love he had to give in general. For a boy who once wished it had been him that died instead of his brother, he now knew such profound affection he'd had no choice but sink into it like a hedonist.

I dragged my nails down his back, adding that spice of pain that got him off, and he moaned, arching into the touch before grinning and kissing me again. Holding himself up with one hand, he reached into my curls with the other, tugging my head back so he could nibble on my jaw.

"So greedy for me, huh?" he said.

I nodded and licked his bottom lip, relishing in my own delight when he hissed in a gasp and grumbled low in his chest.

"God, I fucking missed you."

A desperate yearning rose up inside of me, an emptiness that only he could set right. I needed Lex to reset my equilibrium, to remind me what it was to be with *him,* the one who had shaped me and molded me in a million different ways.

"Please, Lex," I whimpered.

"Please, what?" he said, brushing his nose over mine again. "Tell me what you need."

"I need you, please." I sounded desperate and needy, even to my own ears. My hands dropped to his hips, tugging him tighter against me, and I ground harder against him, tilting just right.

"I need you, too," he said, reaching between us so he could position himself at my entrance, and when he surged home, a wave of rightness crashed over me, pulling me in, reminding me of why I'd sworn a vow to him in the woods all those years ago. Lex was mine, plain and simple. And I was his. And we were theirs.

"Fuck," he murmured, falling forward onto his forearms, his torso trembling on top of me. "I missed this. I missed you."

"I missed you, too." I wrapped my arms around his chest, holding him as close as I could, and he kissed my neck and buried himself in my hair, breathing me in like he couldn't believe I was real...like any second, he might wake up and find himself alone in his bed. I, likewise, memorized everything about the present—his pine-forest scent and how he whimpered in my ear. I focused on the curve of his cheekbones, the way they sloped down and became his jaw, and how beautiful he was in the moonlight.

We fit together, and it had always felt right, so very right. He fucked me like he owned me, like I was the most expensive and decadent thing in the world. He lavished attention on all the bits he knew I liked the best, and when the pressure built in my nerves, when I begged him to speed up and go harder, he obliged. Lex knew how to take me, how to bring me right to the brink, until he finally pushed me off the edge. I floated into outer space.

He met me there a few moments later, panting and cursing his way through his climax. Eventually, he collapsed on top of me, and I kissed his temple, holding him tighter and running my fingers through his hair.

"I love you," I murmured one last time. "Until the end."

He didn't say it back, just lifted his head and gave me a slow, gentle kiss. "You better fucking mean that."

I did.

II

MIRI

The closer we got to Killwater, the more uneasy I became. Fear lined the inside of my stomach like lead, pulling me down into the watery depths of near hysteria. The last time we'd come here, the trees warned me we would find nothing but chaos in Faerie, and that was exactly what happened. We should have listened to them.

"Imagine a sanctuary," Donnelly said, bringing me back to the present. We were currently on the tail end of a three-hour drive from Dublin to Killwater, where the lieutenant had taken the opportunity to teach Ivy and me those mental barriers. "One surrounded by a shield only you can manipulate. It could be anything...a stone wall, a field of thistles, a deep body of water. It should be personal to you."

The thistles had worked to keep the king and the queen out for some time, until they didn't. A symbol of House Stuart, I'd always identified with the plant. It had thorns and grew so fast it was nearly untamable, but when it bloomed in bright magentas, maroons, and whites, it reminded me that even grumpy, spiky things could be beautiful. Even weeds had their purpose.

Today, I envisioned a stone tower sitting atop a seaside cliff, like the ones near Aberdeen, the ones where ancient kings put their forts so everyone who visited knew they held the highest position of power in the area. It looked out over the ocean so the only way to penetrate would be from the front. I'd see anyone coming days before they attacked.

The walls were solid stone, the kind my ancestors had used to build their immortal monuments to conquest. No one could get through, not without laying a siege that would last a lifetime.

"Focus on reinforcing those shields," Donnelly continued, his voice like honey as it washed over me. "Make this place as sacred to you as you can, so that you can come here whenever you feel him breaking through."

"Mental manipulation is about making that person think what you want them to think," Siobhan said. "If the king invades, go to your safe space. He won't be able to break through, and you won't have to worry about which memories you'll reveal to him."

"It's that simple, huh?" Ivy snorted out a disbelieving laugh. "I would have thought I'd be better at this after all these years."

"I've lived for centuries, and I'm still learning how to reinforce my mental walls," Finn said from the driver's seat.

I glanced in the third row to find Diana and Poppy huddled together. They hadn't said much since we got off the plane, but after everything they'd been through, I didn't expect them to be particularly loquacious.

"Again," Donnelly said, drawing my attention back to him. "The more unique and personal it is, the harder it will be for him to get in."

He drilled us the entire way, to the point that Lex and Carter joined in as well. They'd never had the same problem as Ivy and me. The king didn't seem to pay them much attention, choosing instead to focus his assaults on the two of us. I wondered what that could mean, but before I went down that mental pathway, the vehicle came to a stop.

"We're here," Finn said.

Well after midnight, I stepped out of the SUV to the same sense of foreboding I had at Samhain. The windows lining the cobblestone streets were dark, hinting how long ago its residents had gone to bed, and most of the shops were boarded over or painted with 'for sale' logos. If I didn't know any better, I'd say the place had been abandoned. Or worse.

"Help us," the trees hissed, sending a vibrant shock wave of desperation my way. It rattled through me, stirring my dinner and sending it up the back of my throat. I swallowed it and gasped, clenching my eyes shut as the trees sent another plume of magic toward me. *"Help us. Help us. Help us."*

I curled in on myself, the next bout of trepidation hitting me right in the chest. It sounded like the trees, true. But it also sounded like Lizzie and Kit. It reminded me that Jon and Edward were also missing, that the king had our loved ones and we needed to find them just as badly.

Lex glanced around. "This place has gone to hell."

"Miri?" Ivy said, wrapping an arm around me. "Are you okay?"

"It's the trees," I said, catching Siobhan's and Finn's attention. "They're..." My heart pounded against my rib cage. This was so much different from the last time we'd come here. Then, they had warned me to turn around and go home, to take my beloveds and keep them safe. We would only find danger if we took that route. Now, they beckoned me toward them like I held the key to eternal life, like I could lay my hands on their roots and cure them of whatever sickness had taken hold of their magic with such a fierce grip. "They're sick. They're rotting from the inside out."

Siobhan exchanged a worried glance with Finn and Donnelly, who both echoed her concern with furrowed brows and clenched jaws. "We need to hurry."

"What does that mean?" Carter asked, wrapping his arms around me and rubbing his hands soothingly over my upper arms.

"It means we're running out of time." Siobhan shook her head and ran her hands over her face.

"This place is very deeply connected to the magic in the woods," Finn explained. "The veil is thin between our world and yours. If the trees are rotting, then it's only a matter of time before it spreads."

When Diana and Poppy got out of the SUV, they both froze, as if immediately sensing the same thing I had. Whatever had infected this place ran deeper than the woods. It had taken the very essence of Killwater and warped it into a dark, vile monstrosity. I didn't want to stay here. I wanted to get back in the vehicle and run to safety. But if we didn't do what we'd come here to do, there would be no such place.

"I can sense him," Ivy said, bringing the attention to her as she gripped at a temple. "Siobhan, you were right. He's trying to break through my mental barriers. He's close...he followed us here."

At her words, I shivered and reinforced my stone tower, determined to keep him out.

"We need to find the *Fianna* and the battle maidens." Donnelly made eye contact with me before glancing to Ivy. "Wait here. Keep reinforcing what you've built. The more mental energy you put into it, the stronger it will be, the more it will keep him out."

"And try to heal the queen," Siobhan said, nodding. "If putting your hands on her helped her before, then try again."

Finn translated all of this to Diana, and she gave a hesitant nod of approval, her fearful eyes peering around at our dark surroundings with the same skepticism I felt brewing in my belly. This wasn't a good place, and everything about it warned us to stay away.

"We shouldn't be here," Poppy said, rubbing her swollen, tear-stained eyes as she clung to Diana's skirts. "It doesn't want us here."

"I hate to say I agree," Carter added. "It gives me the fucking creeps."

The atmosphere reminded me of an old horror movie where the protagonists leave town for a night, only to return and find it desolate and abandoned.

"Stay," Siobhan said, nodding toward the path that led toward the woods. "And if the world burns down, use the ring to get in touch with me."

Ivy glanced down at the metal decorating her right ring finger. "I can do that?"

Siobhan nodded and took off, her commander and lieutenant following on either side of her. I turned to my spouses, hugging myself as the foul, disgusting ache in my stomach writhed around my heart. We weren't meant to be here, and the sooner we did our business and left, the better it would be for everyone.

This would be the last time I ever stepped foot in this place, and once we defeated the king, I would make it a point to never come back. Even as a twenty-two-year-old senior in college, the old town had contained a mystical quality that separated it from the rest of the world. This far north, it had been sheltered by a lot of the politics that shaped the country. The residents of Killwater still believed in the old ways, and the fact we found the place entirely derelict hinted at the terrible things that must have happened to it.

"If their magic is so connected to Killwater, what do you think happened to make it look like this?" Carter asked, walking up the steps to the pub that had once been owned by Siobhan. By Samhain, an older couple named Bill and Keely had turned the upstairs into a bed-and-breakfast. However, Carter yanked on the doors and revealed a darkened interior with leaves and dust decorating the ground. The windows had been left open, exposing it to the elements, so the place had become overrun with insects and plant life.

"The king and queen are gone." Ivy glanced around, gesturing to a booth for Poppy and Diana to sit. Still unable to separate, they did, clinging to each other's hands with identical looks of confusion in their eyes. "Remember what Siobhan told us? Faerie can't survive them being absent for long, and our realm can't tolerate them being here."

"We've upset the balance." Lex whistled and glanced around, pursing his lips as he wiped a finger down the bar top and examined the inch of dust left behind. "We must pay the sacrifice." With an indignant snort, he rolled his eyes and shook his head. "Whatever the fuck that means."

I didn't like the sound of any of this, but I'd admit, it was difficult to focus over the warning hiss of the trees.

"Help, help, help," they cried, vibrating with a weak sort of help-lessness. *"Come quick!"*

I shivered against it and clenched my eyes shut, holding myself tighter, wishing I didn't know what they were saying. It wasn't a good thing they were so insistent we come closer, and I feared what-ever was polluting them would inevitably drag us down with it.

Diana whispered something to Poppy, drawing my attention back to her. This time, a faint shimmer twisted around her head, almost like...almost like a dust cloud had formed in dark crimson swirls.

"What do you think it means? The sacrifice?" Ivy slumped into the booth behind Diana and Poppy, and I followed her, sitting across the table while Carter and Lex raided the fridge behind the bar.

I focused on the shimmering spirals around Diana, now picking up speed as it continued circling the queen. Could no one else see this? Was I the only one?

"Nothing, obviously." Lex grabbed a few bottles of water and walked back to Ivy and me, handing one to each of us before opening his own and sitting down next to Ivy. "Prophecies are bullshit, or have we forgotten Poppy is supposed to be the almighty key that will reunite the fairies and the humans?"

She was, at least according to Ashley. But I wouldn't hitch my pony to that cart quite yet. Some chosen one Poppy had turned out to be. She'd hand delivered my cousin and extended family to the king, which in turn had led to the deaths of my parents, Lex's brother, and almost Carter's father. Lex told us we shouldn't have trusted her, and despite his involvement in honing her new ability, using it to our advantage had been a terrible mistake.

"I won't use my power again," Poppy said, shaking her head. "I don't care what he does. It was horrible...I was too upset to teleport. I wasn't sure I'd be able to get back." Diana hugged her tighter, murmuring something in Faero-Gaelic that sounded soothing and maternal. Poppy seemed to eat it up, but we all knew better. She played the part of a twelve-year-old, but those eyes told a different tale. I looked at her, and an old soul peered out.

"Are you sure about that?" Lex raised an eyebrow at the changeling, which got my attention. Of course, we shouldn't use her power again. Messing with time was never a good idea.

"What are you thinking?" Ivy asked, clearly already onto Lex's ulterior motive.

"What if she went back in time and asked the fairy queen how they kept the king out the first time?" Lex shrugged. "What if she asked her how to fix the ruby dust and where the king would keep our family members?"

I immediately hated the idea for reasons I couldn't explain. The dust around Diana's head spun faster, growing more frantic the longer we talked. The queen winced, grimacing through it, almost like she could sense the same thing I could.

"That feels like cheating," Carter said, rubbing a hand over the back of his head as he sat down next to me. "She might not tell us, even if she knew."

Lex looked at Diana, narrowing his gaze on the queen of fairies. "You've been awfully quiet since Finn told you what was going on."

She glanced down to the table between us, shaking her head like she didn't understand him. But something had changed in her since we touched her yesterday, and now that we were in Killwater, she had a glimmer to her eyes that almost reminded me of when she'd been at the height of her power.

"We should try to help her again," I said, squinting at the queen as I held my hand out. "I see what's wrong with her now."

Diana glanced down at it, biting her bottom lip before looking at Poppy. The young girl nodded and shrugged as if to say it couldn't hurt.

"What do you mean?" Carter stood and came closer, placing his hand in mine, palm up, his scars on display.

"I can see the ruby dust around her head." I told them what I suspected, how it felt similar to when I connected with the earth's energy. "I think...I think I can heal her."

"You can?" Poppy's eyes grew wider. "You have to help her. Please, Miri. Please."

"And why should we listen to you, huh?" Lex sneered, raising an eyebrow at her. "Didn't you run off to betray us at the first opportunity?"

"Lex, cut it out." Ivy stood and walked to stand next to Carter, putting her hand over his. "Poppy already feels bad enough."

There would be time to admonish the changeling for what she'd done. I understood her reasoning, even if I didn't agree with her choices. It didn't matter anymore. We were here, staring down the end on the horizon. We had to keep plowing forward; we didn't have a choice. Diana still hadn't moved, almost like she was apprehensive of joining in. Had it hurt last time? She'd yanked her hand away rather suddenly.

"For goodness' sake." Poppy grabbed Diana's arm and put her hand in Ivy's. "It'll be fine. Right, Carter?"

Carter nodded, but he had no way to know that. Of course, his fairy curse had made him the luckiest person on this side of the realm. So if anyone was going to give us a boost of confidence, it was him. Once the four of us were connected, Lex opened his mouth to speak, but I shushed him.

"Allow me," I said, closing my eyes while I let the energy of our connection flow through me. "*Heal.*" I sensed the sickness in her the same way I knew when a plant was dying or thirsty. It started in her heart, a decaying vibration that had spread to her brain and stomach. It picked away at her sense of self, removing her further from who she truly was every day it went untreated.

Ivy gasped, a visceral pulse shooting from her hand into the rest of us, combining with Lex's frigid ability to seek the truth. Carter radiated fortune, amplifying the warmth and light we'd need to find the darkest parts of Diana. The queen squirmed, groaning as I poured all of it into her, nearly trembling with the potency of our combined gift.

"*Heal,*" I said again, my voice deeper and more robotic. It sounded properly demonic, but it contained the strength to break through. The crimson particles swirled faster, the cloud around her growing more dense, so thick it became impossible to see her through it. My heart pounded and my hands grew sweaty, shaking as the rush of our power roared again.

Diana tried to pull away, her soft panting now more alarmed and terrified. But no, we were almost there. This was for her own good, for the good of the world, for all of fairydom and humanity. We needed the queen back. We needed her to help us fix this, to set everything right.

There. I saw it, deep down inside of her, a faint burst of light that hummed with the radiance I associated with her. It had been tucked away, hidden behind a cloud of impenetrable red magic. I went closer, making sure to hold on to my spouses while I did. Ivy and Carter mentally urged me on, and when I visualized them in my head, I saw the four of us standing in the woods at twilight. A soft peachy haze coated the sky, painting the world in soft blushes and violets.

A few feet in front of us stood an enormous white tent, like the one she'd occupied the first time we met her. Rustling inside got my attention, and I climbed the steps to the porch, taking a deep breath as I walked toward the entrance.

12

MIRI

"Diana?" I reached out to pull the canvas aside, but she suddenly appeared through the crack, a tall, statuesque example of power and poise. The queen emanated strength, all of the magic that resided deep inside her presence. Her long blond hair had been braided down the side of her body, decorated with flowers and shrubs, and her bright pale gaze pierced through me, down to my very soul.

"Miriam," she said before glancing behind me. "Ivette. Carter. Alexei. It is time. I have been waiting for centuries." She turned and walked inside the tent with a silent invitation for us to follow her.

Glancing over my shoulder, I raised my eyebrows at my spouses before proceeding.

From the outside, the tent looked like nothing more than a ten by ten white rectangle. But once we were inside, I understood it must have been charmed to appear smaller than it was. Decorative pillows and furry plush bedding lined the space on either side with enough room for an entire army to sleep comfortably. Big white rocks created a pathway down the middle, leading to the enormous platform at the back, where Diana sat on a raised mattress covered in stuffed animals, pillows, and cushioned blankets. She had created a nest for herself, tucked this deeply in her mind, and now we might have to drag her out by her fairy wings.

"You've been waiting centuries, huh?" Lex stepped in front of me, glancing around as he shoved his hands inside his pockets. "It must feel that way."

"Your Majesty," Ivy said, coming to stand next to him before giving Diana a bow. "We needed to reach you."

The queen tilted her chin up, the very essence of regal propriety and elitism. She stared down her nose while she made a small huff, like we hadn't done enough, like we hadn't worked as quickly as she wanted, which was total bollocks. Ivy and Lex had sheltered and clothed her after his uncle discovered her hiding space. We'd done nothing but treat her with respect. Didn't we deserve the same?

"We are long overdue for a talk." Diana gestured to the pillows at the end of her bed, indicating we should come and sit with her. I hesitantly took a step forward, pursing my lips as I considered whether she could hurt us in this place. We were mentally linked, and certainly she could do to us whatever the king had done to her. But I didn't think she would. She seemed just as apprehensive of us as we were of her. Besides, I believed Ivy was powerful enough to yank us back if she needed to.

I took the spot in the middle, followed by Carter and Ivy on either side of me. Lex stayed behind us, seemingly on edge. Not that I blamed him. The queen had always been terrifying.

"You've been taking care of Poppy since I gave her to you on Samhain." The queen narrowed her gaze as she spoke.

Carter nodded. "Yes. She is...remarkable."

Diana smiled and hummed appreciatively. "Yes. Remarkable."

That was one way to put it. I might use different adjectives...but to each their own. We just needed to get Diana to the surface again, physically, if necessary. She couldn't go on as the amnesiac fairy formerly known as the queen. We needed her power on our side.

"Your Highness," Ivy cut in, "the king is in the human realm. He's put a curse on you and abducted some of our family members. We need your help—"

"My help." Diana cut her off with a raised eyebrow, her spine straightening. "What makes you think I wish to return with you, much less assist you in such an endeavor?"

Ivy opened her mouth, but nothing came out. I had suspected this might be the case. Look at this cozy space. After suffering the embarrassment of being cursed and bewitched by her husband, why would she want to face anyone again? No one stopped him. No one helped her. No one except us.

"Quite arrogant to bust into my mind and make demands, do you not think?" The queen tsked her teeth a few times before zeroing her attention on Lex behind us. "Alexei, what do you have to say for yourself?"

He snorted. "I wanted to string Alberich up and gut him alive on national television, but something tells me you wouldn't be on board with that idea, either."

Her puffy ethereal lips quirked, almost pulling into a smile before she recovered her stoic facade. "No, I should think not."

"We didn't mean to assume," Carter said, bowing his head in deference. "We were simply hoping, and perhaps praying, you might answer a few questions. That's all."

Oh, sweet heartfelt Carter. He could charm the world into doing whatever he wanted. I truly believed that. Again, the queen hummed, this time in amusement. We must have seemed so insignificant to her, like nothing more than puny humans asking to be squashed like bugs.

"Fine," Diana finally said, her eyes narrowing on Lex again. "I will answer your questions. But in return, Alexei will answer mine." A twitch near her right eye sent a small tremor of fear down the center of my chest. "Privately."

"No bloody way—" I started at the same time Ivy burst out, "Absolutely not."

"Fine," Lex agreed with hardly any hesitation. I gasped, looking over my shoulder to get him to take it back, but his gaze was set on the queen, reminding everyone why he was the strongest of us. I remembered the first thing I'd ever learned about fairies—don't piss them off and don't make deals with them. What you asked for wasn't nearly as important as what you didn't.

"DC," Carter said, looking at Lex with a shake of his head.

"You want me alone? All you had to do was ask." Lex winked at the queen, but she showed no response, simply glared harder.

"Lex, knock it off," Ivy hissed.

"You may ask one question each, and then I shall consider your request fulfilled." Diana shifted in her seat, sitting up higher, making herself appear bigger and more refined. "Ivette, you may start."

Ivy looked flabbergasted, her cheeks red, a blush illuminating the X on her neck. "How do we get Alberich out of our realm?"

The queen pursed her lips, seeming to contemplate Ivy's answer for longer than I would have imagined necessary. Finally, she sighed and narrowed her eyes. "You will need ancient magic to cast him back into Faerie and keep him there."

"Yes, I know that," Ivy said. "What's the spell? Who can cast it?"

Diana sucked in air through her teeth again, a chiding headmistress disciplining the naughty ginger who couldn't follow rules. "One question per person. Carter, what is it you want to know?"

Carter sighed and shook his head, his eyes darting back and forth. I could almost see the wheels grinding gears as he thought through the most important questions to ask. "Who cast the spell to keep the king out the first time?"

The queen's cool facade finally cracked at that, her lips curling into a big grin, a high-pitched tinkling sound pouring out of her throat. *Is she...is she laughing?* Sweet heavens, Romeo had made the queen of fairies burst into hysterics.

"Why, my dear boy." She shook her head. "You have not figured it out by now?" Her brilliant gaze came to me milliseconds before she said it. "That, I'm afraid, was me."

My heart dropped into my gut at the realization.

Of course!

It could have only been her. The only one powerful enough to stand up to the king was his equal, the one person who had stood by him through the eternal expanse of time. They could not exist without the other, and in cursing him to his realm, Diana had made the ultimate sacrifice. She didn't have the same animosity toward humans that her husband did, and in protecting them, she had cast herself from our realm for all of eternity.

"Miriam." The queen turned her gaze to me, and I gulped. "What question do you have for me?"

Up until now, I had remained as quiet as I could. The queen frightened me, and I suspected she could pulverize all four of us with nothing but a wave of her hand. I should have asked about the upcoming battle and how we could defeat him, but a faint glint in Diana's gaze spoke to a more mischievous side. Even this deep inside her mind, I sensed the trees calling out to guide me.

In that moment, I empathized with the queen in a way I hadn't before. The king had screwed with both of our minds, hers more so than mine, but in that similarity, I found an ally. He had made me forget what was likely the worst night of my life. Twice. He'd been messing with Ivy for the whole year, tormenting and taunting her. But for Diana, he had wiped her entire existence. We were victims in his sick game, and based on that look in her eyes, I knew she'd help us no matter what.

She wanted to have a private conversation with Lex for some purpose, but regardless of what came from that, she'd deal with the king because it was her fate to do so. He was hers, and she was his, and whatever he'd done to her would not change that. Therefore, asking about how to stop it was a wasted effort. Whatever would happen would happen.

When I opened my mouth, out poured, "What should I do?"

About Reginald. About my spouses. About how I didn't know where to go once this was all over, once the king had been returned to his realm and our fairy curses had been broken. The conflict churned so deep inside me that I sensed myself being split in two. I wanted to stay with them, to have my cake and devour it whole, in every sense of that idiom. I wanted to have the Stuart fortune and live contentedly with my spouses. I wanted it all, but had no idea how to get it, and it was tearing me apart.

At that, the queen's calm demeanor broke, and she sucked in a quick pitying noise before rising from her bed and gliding toward me. She dropped to her knees so close they touched mine, and she cupped my jaw, leaning in so our foreheads touched.

"You will know when the time is right." Diana kissed the space between my eyebrows, making my skin tingle, both in my mind and in my physical body back at the pub. "Trust yourself and trust your beloveds."

My heart cracked, forcing a hot wave of desperation up my throat, straight to my eyes. I clenched them shut as tears slid down my cheeks, and when I opened them again, I was back in that dark, decrepit bar, with Carter and Ivy gasping beside me.

Lex, however, still held on to Diana with his eyes glazed over in white.

13

LEX

The last time I'd seen the queen at her full power, she'd threatened to tear my head off my shoulders and put it on a spike so she could kiss my pretty lips every morning. Of course, I'd tried to use my power on her, so maybe I deserved it. The Diana in the abandoned pub with us barely qualified as the same person, but the mental image in this tent? This was the queen of fairies I remembered. She damn near shimmered with subdued might, primed to make good on her previous threat.

When she asked to speak with me privately, I wanted to tell her to fuck right the hell off. Whatever she wanted to say to me would get relayed to my spouses no matter what, so it made no difference whether they were here or not. If the queen of fairies wanted to play chess, I would try my hand. I was older and smarter than the young man she'd met at Samhain. I wouldn't be so naive as to think I could take her down on my own. So I agreed.

But now that I was facing the error of my hubris, I would admit I had no fucking idea what I was doing. If Diana felt threatened, she'd get defensive, and then I'd never get her back. Hell, she could keep me trapped in her mind for days, weeks, long enough for my body to decay like that fucking town. I had to be careful. Strategic. I had to figure out what she wanted from me and utilize it to my advantage.

"Well, well, well," I said with a smirk, stepping over the pillows to move closer to her. "Alone at last."

She pursed her lips and eyed me from head to toe, seemingly unamused by whatever she found.

"What did you have in mind?" I raised my eyebrows and shoved one hand in my pocket. "Do I get a question, too? Or was that my question?" I feigned a gasp and put a finger to my lips. "Don't want to get cheated." The queen continued to stare, perhaps waiting for me to dig my grave deeper. "Why are we alone, Diana?"

She hissed in an insulted breath at her given name. Ivy had referred to her as *Your Majesty,* and Siobhan had always called her *My Lady.* Perhaps she had expected the same level of pomp and circumstance from me, but I'd had enough of this charade. In Faerie, she may be the queen, but in the human realm, I was Lex Fucking Fairfax, and that carried more weight.

I bowed to no one, not anymore.

"I wanted to speak to you about what's to come."

"Hmm." I glanced around, noticing some of the pillows had disappeared while we'd been talking. Her bed no longer looked as opulent, and the plush surroundings had started fading away to reveal the wooden planks underneath.

She held her head higher, her back straighter. "If I were to help you defeat the king, it would require a sacrifice."

"Yes, I know." I ran a finger over my eyebrow, another slice of uneasiness slithering down the center of my chest. "Siobhan told us we would need to give something up, something significant."

Fuck that.

But the scared look in Diana's eye told me she wasn't screwing around. If whatever she had to say terrified someone as powerful and fearsome as her, then it would be in my best interests to be at least hesitant about that same thing. This upcoming battle with the king would come with a hefty price, and until now, I hadn't truly considered what that might be.

Now, though...now, she had my attention.

"Cursing him to Faerie cost me that which I loved the most, my connection to the human realm." Her voice cracked, and she blinked back a single shimmering tear. I stood frozen because it was a miraculous sight to see. Spending the last few days with her rarest form had convinced me that, deep down, she was just another soul like everyone else. But now that I saw that glimpse of emotion from her powerful alter ego, I almost felt sorry for her.

Almost.

Let us not forget *she* was the one who shoved Poppy into Carter's arms. She was the one who had caused the rift with the king in the first place. This was all because she couldn't sort out her shit with her husband. Apparently, marriage was a fucking trap in *every* realm of existence.

"Are you prepared to make such a decision?" Diana raised her eyebrows higher on her head, circling me while she spoke, like a snake preparing to strike. "When it comes to your life or that of Ivette, or Miriam, or Carter...which choice will you make?"

That was easy. I would die a thousand times for any of them. To save my spouses from whatever the king might have tucked away in his magical hat of horrors, I would do a hell of a lot worse.

"What if you had to choose between them? What if you could only save Ivette, or Miriam, or Carter?" Diana's calculating gaze narrowed as she came to stand in front of me again.

My heartbeat sped up, but I took a deep breath to hide my reaction. If I could only save one of them, I would sacrifice myself to save them all. But then I thought back to what Carter had said yesterday. If they were like us, we were like them. We could not survive without each other.

"That wouldn't happen." I was so sure of it, the rightness settled in my gut as I said it. "The gift can't survive without us all. If one of us were to die, we would all die."

She pursed her lips. "Is that what you believe?"

"That's what Ashley and Siobhan told us."

"Hmm." Diana made a small laughing sound deep in her chest. "And yet you want to gut my husband alive and watch him bleed to death."

Yep. Sure did. "He abducted our family. He's been haunting Ivy for months. He did something to Miri." Likely raped her, or worse. He had erased it from her memory, wielding it over her like blackmail, as if she didn't have the right to her own sovereignty. "He's fucking with their minds."

She nodded. "Yes, he is."

"He deserves to pay for that."

"Yes, he does."

Confused, I furrowed my brows and shrugged. "I don't see what the problem is."

"If you kill him, you will kill me, too."

"And you speak of *my* sacrifice?" I let out an incredulous whistle. "Your Majesty, your worshipfulness, all due respect, but if it takes putting you down to get rid of him, that's what I'll fucking do."

She hissed again at my language, shaking her head as she eyed me. "You are lucky we are alone. If any in my court heard you say such things to me, they would have your tongue as an ornament."

"I was curious why you wanted to speak with me privately."

"Because you are the epicenter," she said. "You are my contrast. Just as Ivette is to Alberich. It's why he's taken such an interest in her. Miriam, too, of course. And I would be remiss if I did not mention how beautiful Carter has become. I suspect Alberich and I would fight over him, if it came down to it." She sighed and shook her head, obviously frustrated with how little we had figured out on our own. "But you...Oh, Alexei. I have been watching you for such a long time."

That made me pause and straighten my shoulders. What did she mean by that?

"You are the strongest of them. You are the one they look to for protection, for leadership. A king, perhaps, in your own way."

I thought over the last year, how Ivy and Miri had crumbled at the seams, how lost and clueless Carter had been to fix it...and me—the conductor of this circus, the one keeping the beat and making sure everyone hit their marks.

In the end, it came down to one thing: I considered them mine. Ivy may have been born first, but I was the possessive fuck that had the nerve to claim them, all of them, so completely. Was that not the epitome of a great king?

"At the end, it will be up to you to decide who or what to sacrifice," she continued, "and you are the only one who can make this decision, the only one *powerful* enough."

All the air whooshed out of me, my lungs suddenly the weight of anvils. I understood what she was saying as well as what she wasn't. Only moments ago, I was willing to sacrifice myself for my loved ones, and now, I needed to let that possibility settle in my gut. Like most of the stories we'd read pre-Christianity, this fairy tale didn't have a happy ending. The sooner I came to terms with that, the easier this was going to be.

I thought of my reason for all this, the one image that kept me going—a sunny afternoon at our cabin. Miri hunched over in her garden, her smile huge and timeless. Carter, graying around the temples, wrinkles in the corners of his eyes, tossing a football with our children, chasing them around the yard. Ivy, with that molten silver stare, still Amazonian and statuesque, none of it having diminished with time. I wanted so much to be a part of that picture, to be the one behind the lens...but what if I was only the one able to give it to them?

The realization hit me in the gut, nearly dropping me to my knees. If it came to it, I would lay down my crown and fall on my sword if it ensured my loved ones returned home again.

No. Fucking no.

I wouldn't let it happen. I just wouldn't. All of us were making it out of this alive, so help me God. I wouldn't let Alberich or Diana or any of these pricks take that away from me. I didn't believe in sacrifice. I didn't believe in predetermination. *Fuck that.*

If I'd learned anything in this disgusting fairy tale, it was that no one could predict the future, especially not Siobhan. She got "gut feelings" and "instincts," whatever that meant. Carter and Ivy would call it fate, but I refused to believe my destiny lay in the hands of a bunch of psychotic fairies.

I decided my life. I decided my destiny.

For so long, I had wished it was me who died on that boat instead of my brother. And now that I'd finally accepted it wasn't, these fuckers wouldn't take that away from me.

"Oh, Alexei," Diana said, cupping my jaw as she stuck out her lower lip in a pretend pout. "Do not look so furious. You have always believed you are in control of your own fate. None of this has any real power over you." Giving me a quick pat on the cheek, she winked and said, "Remember?"

ACT III

O, when she's angry, she is keen and shrewd.
She was a vixen when she went to school,
And though she be but little, she is fierce.
-Helena, Act III, Scene II

14

MIRI

Nearly three hours passed while Ivy and Carter tried to wake Lex and Diana. But it was futile. Whatever conversation the queen wanted to have with Lex wouldn't be interrupted until she finished with him.

I tried to ignore her advice to me. *You will know when the time is right. Trust yourself, and trust your beloveds.* She said nothing about Reginald or my crown. She said nothing about what would be the right thing to do, only that I would know. Her words clawed at my insides like razor blades.

You already know what to do, came a small voice from the back of my mind, flashing images of me throwing my engagement ring at my grandmother's feet and riding off into the sunset with my spouses.

But what did that mean? Was she suggesting I give up everything I'd ever known?

What would my father think if he knew I tossed it away for a silly thing like love?

I had to stay true to myself, and I loved my spouses more than anything. That was what Diana meant. Trust in them. I couldn't betray them like that. I would stay. I had to stay, no matter what my gran did to me, no matter what happened here.

"I'm telling you," Poppy said, crossing her arms over her chest. "Nothing you do will get their attention. I was sitting here for over a day, screaming and shaking all of you. They're really under."

Over a day.

It was hard to believe that could be true, especially given my muscles and joints didn't ache like I'd been sitting in one place for twenty-seven hours, but that had been the case. For us, we had blinked and returned to normal. For Poppy, she said she had stressed the entire time, especially when Siobhan and her lovers didn't return.

Now, going on hour thirty, we were running out of options. Today was Beltane. As much as I balked at the idea, we had to get into the woods so we could slip into Faerie. We had the ring and the right time of year. We couldn't wait any longer.

"It's like...she's blocking me." Ivy shook her head and sighed, trying to grab both Diana and Lex at the same time, perhaps hoping she'd be able to get inside and pull them out. So far, she'd been sorely unsuccessful. Her focus went to the ring, and she closed her fingers around it while clenching her eyes shut, attempting to reach out to Siobhan mentally. She'd been trying since we woke up, and it still hadn't worked. "Damn it. I'm just getting static from her, too."

I watched the crimson spirals swirl around the queen's head, the cloud now more dense than it had been before we reached her. It was like the poison had been pushed out of her body but hadn't left her orbit. Ivy drifted through it, disrupting the particles, but not picking up any herself. She had an impact on them, but seemed immune.

I wonder if I could...

I reached out and waved through the dust, changing the direction of the glittering swirls like a dirt plume under water.

"Miri?" Carter asked, furrowing his brows as he looked at me. "Are you okay?"

"Do you see the dust?"

Ivy and Poppy both shot their attention to me, sharing twin stares of concern.

"Dust?" Ivy asked. "Like...ruby dust?"

"I think so." I touched it again, my hand undulating through it, back and forth. It was almost like I could collect it, like I could syphon it into something if I wanted. "Do you have a bottle or a bag? Something I could put it in?"

Carter glanced around and brought me a plastic sandwich wrapper. It wasn't perfect, but it would work. I took it and held it out, gathering the particles as if I were holding a kite out to catch the air. I scooped it into the bag, using my hands to shove it inside, leaving not a single particle left. And once it didn't have a fairy queen to circle, it relaxed into a soft, heavy mixture resembling sand.

It vibrated in my hand, perhaps recognizing the magic inside me. Just when I'd started to reach inside to touch it, Diana and Lex inhaled desperate, sharp breaths at the same time, drawing my attention back to them.

"Thank God," Ivy said, pulling Lex into a hug. "We thought you were stuck."

Lex laughed and shook his head, standing up to throw his arms around Carter next.

"My lady?" Poppy softly asked, her big eyes terrified.

"Hello, my darling," the queen said, smiling as Poppy let out a cry and jumped in her arms.

I stood and held up the bag, showing Lex what I'd been able to collect while they were having their private conversation. He nodded, and now that I had it, Carter and Ivy narrowed their gazes on it as well. Perhaps it being in my possession had made it visible to the others.

"All right, my prince?" I murmured, kissing Lex.

"All right," he said, but I caught the glimpse of a twist near his eyes. It was small and quick, but I still saw it. When I wrapped him in my arms, his entire body trembled and his hold tightened, almost like he was clinging to me for dear life. Whatever happened after we'd been pushed out had rattled him, which could not be good news. Just as quickly, he relented, hiding it under his bravado.

"Yes, very well," the queen said, rising to her feet and grabbing Poppy's hand. "Where are Siobhan and the battle maidens? Where is Finn?"

"They went into the woods to find reinforcements." Ivy nodded in the general direction of the forest and stood straighter.

Now restored to her former self, the queen shimmered with a preternatural aura, physical energy sparkling and glowing all around her. Being in her presence nearly brought me to my knees again, the urge to bend to her will, to do whatever she wanted, overwhelmed me. Fairies were intoxicating creatures on their own, but the queen made the rest of them seem insignificant. They were individual stars, and she was the whole damn galaxy.

"And what day is today?"

"It's Beltane," I said. "We were with you for quite some time."

"Hmm." The queen pursed her lips and shook her head, walking through the pub to the door, pushing it open so she could step outside. I looked wordlessly at my spouses before following her, carrying the bag of ruby dust with me. We found Diana on her knees with her fingers dug into the dirt, her eyes closed, her head tilted like she was listening.

"*Help us,*" the trees said. "*Help us, help us, help us.*"

"*I hear you,*" Diana whispered back. "*Be patient.*"

I froze, watching the queen communicate with the forest effort-lessly. For me, it cost me a bit of my spirit, and after a full day in the garden, I fell into the best exhausted slumber. But she seemed reju-venated by the interaction, somehow urged on by the panic in their voice.

"We need to go," the queen said, heading off toward the trail leading to the woods, and ultimately, the college.

"Wait," Ivy said, holding up a hand. "You're helping us now?"

The queen didn't stop to answer her question, just barreled on with Poppy following closely behind her.

"Wait!" Ivy rushed to catch up with her, and Carter, of course, went after Ivy, leaving me alone with my prince of darkness, who at this moment fit that role entirely too well. His eyebrows furrowed together in a brooding mix of concern and hesitation, and I desperately wished I had Ivy's gift so I could hop behind those big hazel eyes and figure out what had him so perplexed.

"What did she say?" I asked.

Lex blinked and smirked, hiding away his displeasure as he threw an arm over my shoulder, pulling me in close so he could whisper in my ear. "She wanted to have a good fuck before she went back to her husband."

I narrowed my eyes and looked up at him, a jealous heat licking its way down my chest despite how much I didn't believe him. *He's screwing with me.*

"But I told her I'm a married man." Lex smiled against my ear and gave me a tender kiss. "And I wouldn't betray my princess like that."

Of course, the queen wouldn't want Lex, of all people, certainly not after the way he disrespected her twice. But he'd lied, and that intrigued me. What exactly was he covering for? I thought we were all on the same page now, no more hiding secrets from each other. What happened to that?

Siobhan's warning rattled around in my mind. We'd have to make a sacrifice. We still didn't know what that meant, but a sickening idea dripped down into my gut, souring and twisting until I didn't want to keep going. Lex would only lie to protect me...to protect us. If he thought he was doing that, then perhaps the sacrifice was more personal than we anticipated.

"Alexei," I murmured, turning to face him. "Please don't keep this from us. If there's something we need to know, something we need to plan for—"

He cut me off with a quick kiss. "C'mon, Princess. We've run out of time and we need to catch up." Lex grabbed my hand and tugged me along behind him, my mind spinning while we raced through the woods.

"Help us," the trees hissed. *"Help, help, help."*

I shook that off, grimacing at their pain while I tried not to trip over the undergrowth. Drums roared in the distance, louder and more intimidating than I'd ever heard them before. Memories of a hot Midsummer night drifted up from the depths of my mind, when a twenty-two-year-old version of me had wandered this same path with Lex. Trepidation had lanced my heart, then, too, but for very different reasons.

We had once thought all of this was over after we graduated from college, that we would go our separate ways and never see each other again. We had been such idiots.

My father used to say history didn't repeat itself, it rhymed, and I laughed to myself at the irony of that statement as we crested the hill and joined Ivy and Carter on top. Staring down into that valley, I went back to that first night at Midsummer. How long ago that seemed from today, despite only being four years. We had lived for ages since then, no longer the wide-eyed twenty-two-year-old versions of ourselves, so innocent and naive to the trials that lay ahead of us. If I could go back to that day and tell myself to run, would I?

For as much suffering as we'd been through, for all the terrible things I'd survived, I didn't think I would. I'd do it again if it meant I got to have my beloveds at the end. I knew then that I wouldn't leave them when this was over. I had to stay, Reginald and my grandparents and the royal family be damned. I wasn't the first or even the second to abdicate my title, and I likely wouldn't be the last.

I gripped the ruby dust harder in my pocket, making sure it was still there, and took a deep breath as my eyes adjusted to the sight in the valley. Four huge bonfires flickered in either corner, their flames licking into the night while crowds of people danced around them. A giant maypole stood in the center, bodies weaving back and forth while they screamed with laughter. Maybe a hundred people had filled the small space four years ago, but now the entire town participated in the festival. They had abandoned their lives for this. How long had they been here?

Bodies crammed the tiny area, moving like a sea of flesh, hypnotizing and horrifying at the same time. A tremble skated down my spine, matching the churning anxiety in my gut. I felt like an intruder, like we'd stumbled onto something ancient, sacred, and overpowering, something we barely understood and had no business trifling with.

When the queen nodded at the party with a giant smile, I glanced to Ivy and Lex to make sure I understood what she meant.

"What? Go down there?" I blinked back my incredulity.

"We need to find Siobhan, Finn, and the others." She looked at Lex before shifting her gaze to Ivy. "But beware of the magic. It is very...*intoxicating*...this time of year."

I sighed and tried to ignore the thrill in her piercing stare.

15

CARTER

Cool spring air nipped at my cheeks while we walked through the crowd, contrasting the sharp bite of flames as they licked off the nearby fire. Bodies surrounded me, dancing and writhing on either side. Most had painted their faces in various shades of pinks and purples, and I narrowed my gaze on someone who had an epic snake twisting down their cheek and around their neck.

It reminded me of Midsummer on steroids, everyone so deeply entrenched in the party that they seemingly forgot about the rest of the world. The heavy stink of fairy magic coated my tongue in thick, euphoric waves, rushing down my throat every time I inhaled. Diana said to beware of that sensation, and Good Lord, she was right. It went straight to my brain, making me dizzy and hyper in all the right ways.

Clenching my eyes shut, I shook my head for a moment, hoping for a reprieve when I opened them again, but the revelry remained. Half-naked people surrounded me, laughing and roaring with joy. Drums beat loudly into the night, matching my pounding heart, and when a cool hand slipped into mine, I was thankful for the jolt back to reality.

"You okay?" Weeds asked, smiling at me.

I nodded and leaned down to kiss her, relishing in the soft feel of her mouth opening up to me. I could have stayed there and devoured her for the rest of my life, but we had a banshee, a lieutenant, and a commander to find.

"You think they already went ahead to Faerie?" I winced at the thought and continued to move through the crowd, meeting eyes with Lex and Miri a few yards away as they continued their search.

"No." Ivy took a deep breath and ran a hand over her face. "They wouldn't have left us behind. They would have come back for us." She held up the ivy ring Siobhan had given her. "At the very least, she would have contacted me to let me know. They have to still be here."

"If they came through the party, I can see why they would have gotten stuck." Another wave of tantric power rushed through me, zinging my molecules awake. I suddenly wanted to grab Lex, Ivy, and Miri, find a private corner, and lick every inch of their skin until I had my fill. "It's uh...overwhelming."

A young woman wearing a thin white dress danced toward us, her hair braided back with flowers, her dark skin emanating warmth from the nearby fire. She smiled and placed a wreath of roses and ferns on my head before leaning in to kiss me on the cheek. I froze, knowing it was these same townspeople that had gotten us into trouble at Midsummer. They had shoved chalices and condoms in our hands, practically begging us to make bad life choices. It shouldn't have been a surprise when we'd woken up two days later, married to each other, with no memory of how or why it happened.

She did the same to Ivy before handing us both a bundle of condoms, rose petals, and heather, bound together with twine. Then she smiled and pranced away.

"This place is so fucking weird." Ivy laughed, squeezed my hand, and continued walking through the crowd.

According to the lore, Beltane was a fire festival marking the middle of spring and new life in all its variations. The world had survived the long death of winter, and now the people celebrated the return of the sun. Which, of course, came with all the joys of human procreation and massive orgies in every corner. A pile of bodies moved together on the grass a few yards to our right, barely visible behind the people in between. Their moans of ecstasy punctuated the drumming, and the light from the various fires cast them in terrible shadows. They had taken on a lifeform of their own, like some form of demented Beltane monster, here to devour everyone in its path.

"C'mon." Ivy pulled my hand, diverting my attention back to the crowd, and led me through the center part of the valley, her bright gaze searching for our allies. I was taller than most of the people here, so I had an advantage. I saw Miri up ahead with Lex, pointing to the left, just past another group of people enjoying the fairy wine and lowered inhibitions.

A platinum blond head peered over the rest of the crowd, green eyes practically glowing in the moonlight.

Finn.

"Miri found him," I said to Ivy, nodding toward the fairy's towering form.

She gripped my palm and tugged us in that direction, and I nodded at Lex when we emerged from the crowd at the same time. Siobhan and Donnelly lay on the ground in a heap, kissing and rubbing against each other while Finn watched with rapt fascination. I winced, thanking whatever luck was on our side that we'd gotten here before things went X-rated.

"Finn," I said, grabbing onto his arm, hoping to break him from this trance.

Big mistake.

The second my palm came into contact with his skin, a whoosh of relaxation went through me, like I'd swallowed a handful of Xanax with a fifth of Jack chaser. My knees melted, and comfortable happiness settled in my gut like warm cocoa. My worries faded away. Hell, I couldn't even remember why we were so freaked out to begin with.

Finn turned to me, his green eyes even more beautiful than I remembered, and he cupped my cheek, leaning down to press his lips to mine. They were soft and inviting, and so damn delicious, I couldn't stop consuming them. The commander swept his tongue out, wrestling with mine, tasting like wine and pure, undiluted sin.

I wanted more.

A hard shove at my side broke the kiss, and I narrowed my unfocused gaze on a glowering Lex, his hazel eyes angry and piercing.

"Stop that," he snarled, clapping in front of my face. "Snap out of it."

Snap out of what?

There was nothing to do, nowhere to be, not a damn care in the world.

A low giggle got my attention, where I found Ivy kneeling by Siobhan, leaning in to kiss the banshee. It looked so damned fun, I couldn't resist. I dropped down next to them, connecting my lips with Donnelly's. He was firmer and more solid than Finn, holding a silent dominance that spoke of the hunter inside him. But I loved it. His scent enveloped me, and when Ivy leaned back up to wrap her perfect fingers behind my neck, I let her pull me to her mouth so she could relish me any way she wanted.

Hands skated over my torso and down my waist, so many fingers touching and squeezing and taking. I couldn't tell whose was whose, and at this point, I didn't care. I hung my head back on my shoulders, focusing my attention on the way Finn captured Lex's lips. The fairy commander held DC's face in his massive palms, claiming his mouth the same way he'd done to mine. Miri fell to my side, wrapping an arm over my shoulders before leaning in to take my earlobe between her teeth.

Chills of rapture erupted down that side of my body as Siobhan kissed Ivy harder, deeper, and I ran my hands through Donnelly's hair, reveling in how soft and shiny it was in the firelight. I couldn't focus. Everything seemed so blurry around the edges, so drenched in dream light that I thought I would never wake up again.

And that was just finnneee.

Ivy curled her fingers against my scalp, drawing my face toward hers so she could lick my mouth, sucking the taste of Donnelly off my skin. Soft, feminine fingers traced down my shoulders before another tongue ghosted across the back of my neck, sending goose pimples down the center of my spine. My shirt floated over my head while someone else worked at my belt buckle, and I closed my eyes to languish in the sensation of skin against skin, pheromones mixing in the air, the bite of winter lingering as spring tried to take root.

I could have stayed there forever. I could have let Siobhan and her lovers have the four of us. Rolling my head to the side, I wished for this party to never end. No wonder the entire town had abandoned their lives for this. Who would ever want to leave?

Sensations coasted through me, more potent and vitalizing than the last time, and when I opened my eyes, I focused on a tall blond woman dancing around the closest fire. She looked vaguely familiar, wearing a long white dress that had seen better days and waving her arms above her head like she commanded the drums instead of the other way around. Beauty radiated off her in thick white tendrils, powerful and effervescent, and I soaked it up, willing more of it to collect inside me.

I rolled my head back farther to allow a mouth more access to my jawline, but narrowed my focus when something horrific came into view. Just beyond the fire pit, a group of people writhed against each other so desperately that they'd become a mass of limbs and skin... and blood. I squinted, not sure I was seeing what I thought I saw, but yes...they'd scratched each other so hard flesh hung from muscle and bone. Yet, they kept going, kept moaning, seemingly welcoming the agony.

Shock surged through me in a nauseating rush, and I shoved to my feet, digging my palms into my eyes to rub them before opening them again. But in that split moment, another crowd had moved in the way and I lost track of the scene that startled me.

What the fuck? Did I...Did I just see that?

The woman in white danced harder, waving her hands more forcefully, ghostly webs of energy shooting off them. I turned back to the sight in front of me, where Siobhan held on to Ivy's face while she bit and sucked at her mouth, growing more demanding with each swipe. Lex and Miri rolled against each other while Donnelly kissed and licked at both of their necks, occasionally sinking his teeth in long enough to make Lex moan. Finn stood watch over it all, his attention rapt while he licked his lips and took long, slow inhales.

But just beyond us, over by the tree line, a group of people were fucking so hard, they had rubbed themselves raw, damn near as terrible as the others. Their mouths and teeth were covered in crimson liquid, dripping from their lips in a grotesque display of passion and lust. Their arms were painted ruby red, their chests streaked with dirt and grime and...

Fuck. We're so fucked.

I shook my head harder, grimacing against the magic, taking long, deep inhales to try to clear it. None of it helped. The spell permeated the air, electrifying everything in its path. We were stuck in its web, and it looked like Diana was only feeding whatever psycho trip had ensnared the town.

We need to get out of here.

If the king stumbled upon us like this, we would be screwed.

Fighting the euphoria threatening to pull me under again, I grabbed Ivy and yanked her away from the group by her shirt.

"Nooooo," she whined, trying to get back.

"Weeds," I said, clapping two inches from her face in a desperate attempt to get her attention.

She started crying, tears streaking down her face as she physically fought me to get back to Siobhan. Miri and Donnelly grabbed her arms, tugging her down into the pile. But my disruption had gotten Finn's attention, and he turned toward me, his emerald eyes glittering with anger, his brows furrowed at my insolence.

He stuck a hand out and tried to wrap his fingers around the back of my neck, but I lunged away from him, ducking out of his hold.

"Chicago," Lex moaned. "Join us."

"Join us, Romeo," Miri said, holding a hand out to me. "Come back to me."

Their siren calls hit me low in the gut, nearly bending me at the knees, but I had to stay strong. For whatever reason, luck or disgust or terror, I'd broken the fairy trance. I'd come to my senses and remembered why the hell we were here. We had no time to lose, and certainly not enough to get wasted and fuck an entire town in the woods.

And I definitely didn't want to be here when the fairies decided we tasted good enough to consume or...whatever the fuck was going on over there.

Finn reached for me again, his massive palm nearly colliding with my face, but I spun away and picked up a nearby silver stein that had been forgotten on a log. I didn't want to make contact with him again, since that was what seemingly pulled me under the last time, but I needed him to get a hint. I needed them to come back to themselves now, even Diana.

Instinct had my fairy gift taking over, and I swung the tankard at his face, slamming it hard against his cheek. He whipped his head to the side, grabbing at the assault before freezing.

"Finn!" I shouted. "Commander of the *Fianna!* Wake up!"

He rolled his jaw and shook his head before straightening to look back at me, shifting his shoulders as the muscles near his ears twitched. My heart throbbed while I waited to see what he would do next. If it didn't work, he'd probably grab that big-ass hunting knife in his boot and ram the business-end into my heart. I took a step back, inhaling a long, deep breath and waiting for his reaction.

Finn narrowed his gaze on me before looking around, gaping

when he realized where we were and what was happening around us. When he refocused on me, his eyes sparkled with relief. "Carter?"

I sighed, my shoulders deflating. *Finally.* "Finn. Help me. Please."

He looked down at our entranced spouses, now in various states of nakedness as they grappled for each other.

"Fuck, I was worried this would happen." He ran his hands back through his hair before swiping them down his face. "The king and queen stabilize the magic here. Without both of them, it's gone off-balance." He looked around, his grimace deepening when he saw the townspeople gone to violent madness.

"How do we fix it?"

He growled when his focus landed on Diana. "I'll be right back."

I watched as he walked over to the queen, dodging out of her touch when she tried to pull him into whatever magic she was creating. He pointed to us and her gaze caught mine, holding it for a moment while recognition dawned. But she only shook her head and said something that had him ducking his chin in defeat. They continued arguing, but I could tell the conversation wasn't going the way he wanted.

I had broken out of this trance on my own. Perhaps we didn't need the queen. Perhaps I could reach my lovers without having to hit them in the face. I kneeled next to Lex, grabbing his wrists when he brought his hands to my cheeks, trying to lean in to kiss me.

"DC," I said, twisting out of the way. "Remember when I first met you."

"You were so fucking hot," he moaned, attempting to connect our mouths again, "and I wanted to fuck you so goddamned bad."

I ignored his compliment and held him still while I continued. "I need you to come back to me now."

He didn't seem to know what I was talking about, and instead, leaned in to lick my neck, sliding his tongue down my windpipe before nibbling on that spot he could always find, the one that made my toes curl.

Trying again, I shifted his hands in mine, wrapping my fingers around the backs of them, my thumbs swiping over his palms.

The ridges of his scars bubbled against the rest of his smooth skin, and I caressed them, remembering the night they'd been made. How his eyes had shimmered in the Midsummer twilight sky, how he'd tasted like shame and devotion, how much I had envied him for getting to marry Ivy while being jealous of Ivy for getting to have him as well. I dug my thumbnail into those jagged lines.

Until the end.

The end hadn't come yet. I still needed him.

"Wake up, DC."

He grimaced, trying to pull his hand away from mine, and when I wouldn't let him, he attempted to smack my cheek. I gripped his wrist millimeters away from my face to stop him, digging my nails into that skin, too.

"Ow, fuck!" Lex groaned and attempted to yank away from me again, but I pressed my thumb harder into his scars, my nail almost breaking the flesh.

"Come back to me, Alexei Fairfax. You promised me until the end, and I mean to hold you to that." My voice grew darker as it went on, seeming to come from some despicable part of my soul. "Come back to me."

Lex blinked, his jaw falling open, and he let out a sharp gasp.

"Fuck," he said, looking around. "Fuck, how long have we been out?"

"I don't know," I said. "But we need to get the others and get out of here. Now."

16

MIRI

I came back to reality with a start, homing in on a bright indigo stare.

"There she is," Carter said, holding me to his chest. "There's my Juliet."

Tears streaked down my cheeks as I clenched my eyes shut and gripped Carter tighter, praying that this was a nightmare, that I'd wake up back at our cabin on Solstice and remember none of this was real. When I opened them again, I focused on a woman and a man clawing at each other in a desperate frenzy, their nails dripping with each other's blood.

"Oh, God," I cried, closing my eyes again. "What the bloody hell is happening?"

"It's okay," Carter said, holding me tighter while Ivy tried to wake Siobhan by smacking her.

"Are they tearing each other to pieces?" I tried to keep my voice stable, but it trembled anyway.

"Yeah," Carter said. "Just...don't look."

Instead, I watched Ivy put her hands on Siobhan's head to enter her mind. A few moments later, the fairy blinked back to reality and

Donnelly soon followed. The weight of the magic in the air pressed in on me from all directions, coaxing me under its spell. I wanted to let it. I wanted to fall under and let it consume me, never to wake up again. I assumed that had to do with the fairy magic as well. Ambrosia had been designed by the Gods to make a person never want to leave Olympus.

I had to stay strong. My beloveds needed me. I had to see this through.

"Fuck," Siobhan groaned, clutching at her head. "What day is it?"

"Beltane," Ivy told her. "We need to move."

"Two days!" Donnelly groaned. "We lost two days?"

"This isn't normal magic," Siobhan said, glancing around. "It's been corrupted." Her stern brown gaze found Ivy's. "How did it go? Did you fix my lady?"

Ivy nodded, but ran a hand over her neck when she focused on Finn arguing with Diana in the distance. "She's back, but I wouldn't say she's on our side."

Siobhan and Donnelly turned in time to see Finn walking back with the queen, her hair as wild as the rest of the party, sticking out at all ends. She looked feral, as much a beast as anyone else here.

"I'm unable to break the spell," Diana said, gesturing around. "This is powerful magic, ancient. We best let it be."

"We have to help them." I swallowed down my disgust at the carnage, at how what had once been festive and joyous had turned so wretchedly violent and horrendous. Groans of ecstasy mixed with screams of pain, the sounds of tearing muscle and cracking bone mixing with the first stirrings of summer wildlife. "We can't let them destroy themselves."

"*Help us,*" the trees called again, stealing my attention from the queen's response. I glanced behind me, branches rustling in the wind, just barely audible over the crowd. "*He is coming. He is coming.*"

Trembles skated down my spine and up the back of my skull, and I hugged myself tighter, feeling the weight of the ruby dust in my pocket. Pressure sat on my chest, warring emotions bubbling up inside of me. But I sensed it, that dark presence over the crest of the valley. It rattled through me, an icy wind on the worst winter day, freezing my nerve endings.

Run, a part of me hissed.

Fight, cried the other.

The trees were wrong. "He's already here," I whispered, more to myself than anyone else, but Carter heard me.

"What?" He ducked down so he could be eye level with me. "Did you just say he's here?"

"*Little Thistle.*" Alberich's voice echoed through the bristling leaves like a monster calling out to its prey. "*Have you missed me?*"

I grimaced and grabbed my head, shaking it to get him out.

Imagine your fortress. Go to your tower.

I mentally stood inside the stone walls of my safe space, reinforcing the thick walls with my energy. He couldn't get me here. He couldn't—

"Little Thistle," his deep, wicked voice called from outside the cinderblock walls. "I can smell you. You can't run from me; you never could. And after we had so much fun together."

No.

He couldn't reach me here.

He's a monster, and I'm the princess who has to save herself.

Hands clamped around my cheeks, dragging me back to reality and forcing my gaze into Ivy's steel-gray counterparts.

"I hear him, too." She nodded, imploring me to stay strong. "You're not alone. Stay with me."

For one heartbreaking moment, I considered running. She was wrong; we weren't the same. He had pinpointed me for some reason. He had attacked *me.* Perhaps it had been because I was easy to attack; perhaps I would always be easy to attack.

"*Remember how strong we are together,*" Ivy whispered inside my head, suddenly standing next to me in my stone tower. Because we were soul mates, because we'd built this tower together, she could come and go as she pleased. I gave her permission. She wrapped her hand in mine, squeezing my fingers tighter, almost to the point where it hurt. But it was a painful reminder that I simply couldn't fight him alone. Not anymore. I never could. I needed them. *"Remember that I love you."*

She loved me, and I loved her...I loved them all. I would do anything to protect them.

Adding Ivy to my safe space warned him off, and his presence retreated, allowing me to focus on the present.

Diana eyed me warily, a deeper knowledge passing just behind her eyes. I would have given anything to be able to read that expression and know what she knew. Instead of explaining, she gave us a small, almost pitying smile and said, "I have sent Poppy ahead to Faerie, but I believe it's time we headed home as well." Then, she took off into the tree line, the same that had once led to the creek we bathed in on Midsummer.

Following the queen into her native realm hardly compared to the first two times we'd done it. At Midsummer, we had been so intoxicated on fairy wine and Siobhan's gift, we'd stumbled into a different realm without knowing it. At Samhain, we'd heard ghosts in the woods, voices from our dead loved ones that called us to the realm like sirens, beckoning us to what should have been our deaths. This time, Diana floated over the undergrowth, her white robes nearly glowing in the moonlight, her long golden hair alive and electrifying with magic.

The queen held her hands out as she walked, streaks of pale shimmering wisps cascading behind her, coating the forest floor with life and vitality. In response, what remained of the plant life perked to attention, soaking in her wild essence as if the very proximity could heal their wounds.

Perhaps it could. Diana had once called herself the Great Source. Everything and all of it existed within her. Carter's words then rushed back to me.

If we're like them, they're like us.

"My lady," Siobhan said, interrupting my train of thought as she rushed by me to get to Diana. "The battle maidens and the *Fianna* will be standing by in Faerie. We are all with you."

The queen turned to Siobhan and ran a hand down her cheek, tenderness in her eyes. "Thank you, Siobhan. Tell them to prepare. We will need a show of strength. I will need their energy."

The banshee straightened her spine, shifting her shoulders and nodding as the weight of the queen's words settled around her.

"He is alone." The queen kept walking, her magic continuing to pulse and swirl from her palms. It reminded me of the king's dark tendrils in the way that it moved like mist and engulfed anything it touched. But the king had always terrified me, his magic entrancing people, making them think and believe whatever he wanted.

The white light emanating from the queen's fingertips soothed me, reaching down inside to find the most rotten part, the piece that believed I shouldn't be here. It wrapped itself around the shattered remains and stitched it back together, throbbing as if giving me a spiritual hug.

"My dear girl." Diana's voice spoke inside my mind, her tone that of a mother soothing a child with a skinned knee. I glanced around, thinking she had said out loud, but she continued to talk to Siobhan like nothing else had happened, her attention remaining on her banshee soldier. *"Stay strong. It is almost the end."*

I swallowed and hugged my sweater tighter around myself, ignoring the way Lex walked quietly at my side, equally lost in his own thoughts. I hadn't forgotten how he'd lied when he'd come out of the conversation with Diana, and once we had a moment alone, I planned to let the others know. Whatever she said, he couldn't face this on his own. No more secrets.

"What do you think we're gonna find on the other side?" Carter whispered to Ivy as they walked a pace or two ahead of us.

"Utter fucking chaos?" Ivy said, shrugging. "An orgy full of bloody fairies?"

"How am I ever going to get that out of my head?" Carter rubbed at his temples, and I agreed.

"I can't believe we left them there," I said, grimacing as we kept walking.

"What were we supposed to do? Go around, smacking them all until they woke up?" Lex scowled, his frustration clearly getting the best of him.

"We don't have time for that," Ivy said, glancing at me. "Alberich is close. He's already in Killwater, if not in the woods."

The echo of his voice chilled me, sending another shiver down my spine. Focusing on the image of Ivy and me reinforcing the tower together, I psychically gripped her hand and sent another bout of energy to my mental fortress.

Diana seemed unperturbed by it. She said she couldn't fix it and we'd best let it be before wandering into the forest. To her, people desiring each other so much they *literally* tore themselves to pieces was no big deal.

One day in the future, I would probably look back on this night and wonder how I could live with myself. It wasn't like I had other options, and I certainly didn't want to get ripped apart myself. But shame burned up my neck and into my cheeks all the same.

What would my father think? What would my mother do?

Despite the horrors that would undoubtedly haunt me to the grave, I wanted to stay strong for Diana...for my spouses and Siobhan...for myself.

We reached what had once been a veil in front of a giant wall of thistles, nearly thirty stories high, wrapping kilometers around in either direction. Now, there was nothing, just scorched earth and a broken shimmer to the atmosphere.

The veil.

When we'd left on Samhain, it had been damaged from the king's magic, fragile and unpredictable, but certainly still intact. We weren't sure we'd make it back. It should have been imperceptible, only visible to those who were fairy or had been invited. Now, it appeared unstable, like any second it might cave in on itself. Its sharp edges shimmered with brilliant jaded magic in the shape of an oval several meters in diameter.

"Fuck," Finn said, drawing my attention. "The gateway is fraying."

He walked around us to stand next to Diana, reaching his hand out to the border, but the queen stopped him, tsking her teeth. "Do not touch that."

"Yes, my lady."

Diana eyed the opening, tilting her head to the side as she considered. Her face remained annoyingly stoic, revealing little of what she thought or determined about the unstable magic. Finally, she straightened and turned to the rest of us. "Come along. It will allow our entry."

She held her palm out, gesturing us to go ahead of her with Siobhan leading the way. Ivy went next, followed by Lex, Carter, and Donnelly. I held back, a sickening weight lining my stomach as dread crept up the back of my spine. I looked over my shoulder one last time, whispering a silent goodbye to the trees.

"Be careful," came their solemn reply. *"And fare well."*

Perhaps I knew, even then, it might be the last time I ever heard them answer back.

CROSSING into the realm of fairies always skated over my skin like being dropped into a warm tub of pure ecstasy. There existed no other feeling like it. Despite missing its queen and king for months, the air still buzzed with euphoric energy. I could stay here forever and never know another problem.

The great fairy village, however, looked entirely different. At Samhain, white tents had been set up in a grid pattern, forming a sprawling community that had stood for centuries. Now, it had expanded, stretching much farther in either direction.

Fairies stopped and stared when we walked by, Diana and Finn at the head of our small party, Siobhan and Donnelly bringing up the rear. And in the middle, four lowly humans looked around like we had any right to be here, like we were just another part of this conflict.

Did they know about our gifts? Did they know about the promise we made in their sacred ruins, how we'd taken their magic and mutated it without knowing how or why we'd done it?

Some grimaced. Some shot angry stares. Others dropped to their knees in recognition of the queen and her chosen court. Diana walked with her chin tilted up, her shoulders pulled back, her arms out to either side, wisps of her magic coasting behind her like a train on a wedding dress.

Siobhan suddenly broke away from the crowd and darted into the arms of another female fairy. *Ashley.* Her sister. When we'd come here last time, she had been the one to escort us around the village, the one who gave us her tent and her bed for the evening. She had the power to distort reality, to make people see whatever she wanted them to believe.

I wasn't sure if it was a good thing or a bad thing that she was here.

"It's been so long, sister," Siobhan said as I passed her.

"Don't leave me again." Ashley gave the banshee one last hug before Siobhan came back to our procession, falling in line behind us again.

When we reached the enormous platform in the center, Diana climbed the stairs and crossed in front of her giant canvas tent to the two thrones on the far end. Her eyes met ours, and she nodded, indicating we should join her on stage.

Heart pounding and hands shaking, I followed Ivy up the stairs, Lex and Carter behind me. We walked to her right, Finn, Siobhan, and Donnelly arriving on the other side. The valley extended as far as I could see, all the attention focused on us. Murmurs drifted up from the crowd, whispers of confusion or disgust mingling with anticipation and joy.

The queen took a step forward and raised her hands, quieting the thousands...*no*, hundreds of thousands that had gathered in support of her...in support of us.

"I know," Diana said. "I know."

The crowd waited for her to continue, every single fairy hanging on to the edge of their sanity while Diana paused for their attention.

"It has been a rough journey," she continued. "The last time I was on this stage, my beloved husband tricked us."

I clutched the plastic bag containing the ruby dust in my pocket, inhaling deeply to clear the trepidation in my lungs. Instinct had told me to collect it, to keep it safe in case we needed it. But I didn't know when or how to use it. I prayed I didn't need to.

"He has become needlessly violent," she continued. "And he will descend upon us by tomorrow morn."

Gasps echoed all around me, followed by hushed murmurs. The populace couldn't believe he would show his face again after all he'd done.

"To my battle maidens, I owe you my appreciation. You tried to protect me then, and you stand to protect me now." The queen smiled in the direction of a group of female fairies, tattoos stretching down their left arms in twisting ivy patterns that matched the ones on Siobhan. "To the *Fianna*..." She said something in a language I didn't understand, but it sounded like old Faero-Gaelic, like the language she had been uttering only a few days ago.

Finn walked forward, holding his hands up as half of the crowd shouted in unison, nearly deafening the entire valley. Metal swords beat on shields as screams of allegiance echoed from all around us. Siobhan had undersold the strength of the *Fianna*. Judging by the number of bodies praising Finn's presence, I'd say he controlled a military larger than some first-world countries combined.

"To my human friends," Diana turned to us, a soft smile on her face as she eyed each of us individually, her gaze ultimately landing and staying on Lex. "You kept me safe when I was at my lowest. For that, I will never be able to repay you. I owe you my thanks." Then she muttered something in Faero-Gaelic that none of us understood.

A hush fell on the crowd again, and when I ventured a glance in that direction, I noticed they had all placed their hands on their hearts. Every last fairy, human, changeling, and halfling in the crowd looked at us with affection and adoration. Evidently, it meant a great deal for the queen to personally offer a debt of gratitude.

I widened my eyes, glancing to Ivy next to me. She twisted her fingers in between mine, her palm trembling as she squeezed my hand tighter.

"Ivette Washington, Alexei Fairfax, Carter Scott, and Miriam Stuart will be treated like most honored guests while they remain on our lands. And if they should not, you will answer to me." With that, Diana turned back to her followers and raised her hands again. "We will show my beloved husband how strong we are when we are united, and we will make him see reason."

She smiled when Poppy emerged from the tent behind us, nearly a foot taller than when I'd seen her a few hours ago. How long had passed in Faerie while we were entranced in the woods? The changeling wrapped her arms around Diana's waist and hugged her close, and the queen reciprocated by tucking her under her arm like a mother protecting her child.

"Make no mistake," Diana continued. "He will try to gain your allegiance. He will play his mind games and make you believe things have happened when they have not." The queen's eyes cut to me when she said it, not long enough for anyone else to notice, but it still sent a chill through my veins. "Our noble king has always been mercurial." Diana twisted her lips into a rare smile, the glimmer in her eyes hinting at both a sadness and a desperation that only she could know. "But the time has come to put this argument to rest. Stay strong. Do not let him win."

Cheers and shouts of encouragement rose up from all around us, the battle maidens and the *Fianna* both in agreement. They were

done fighting each other. They were done being two separate enti-
ties. Finn had once explained that the two had lived as one unit for
centuries before this split. Regardless of whether their tattoos
marked them as belonging to the king or the queen, they were
members of Faerie first. Like the royals, they needed each other to
survive.

"I beg of you, stand by me tomorrow," Diana said. "Stand by me.
Lend me your energy, your reverence, and we shall know peace once
more."

The crowd's cries grew even louder, more pronounced in their
acceptance. They wanted it to end. They wanted to go back to the
way things were before the king grew too radical, before he threw
their entire existence into peril because of his outdated ideas about
humans.

"Be with your loved ones tonight," the queen said, eyeing the
four of us again. "Revel in what it means to be alive. We will need
that reminder come tomorrow."

With that, she gave the crowd a nod, turned to us with one final
smile, and retreated inside her tent. In the valley below, everyone
dispersed, their sneers no longer furious or contemptuous. Now,
they smiled when they passed us, making eye contact with conge-
niality. Siobhan walked closer, putting one hand on Ivy's shoulder
and the other on mine.

"Come with me," she said. "I'll show you where you can rest
tonight."

I hated the waiting. If we knew where the king was and when he
would attack, would it not make more sense to go after him before
he could get to us? Perhaps we could blindside him and detain him
before he hurt us. But whatever we proposed would get no support
from anyone else. The queen had already announced her plan, and
now it was time to pause. We would deal with the king tomorrow.

As we walked through the camp, I smiled at anyone who met my
eyes, but most were focused on their levity. I thought I spotted Smythe

and Victor in one tent, hugging each other while they drank from chalices, but I couldn't be sure, and I didn't want to interrupt. I remembered when Victor had helped us earlier this year, we had asked him if he would support us when the time came. He said he'd like to think he would, and it pleased me to see him here, back at home, back where they started. Smythe had been exiled for falling in love with one of the queen's ladies, but now, bygones had been put to rest.

By the size of the crowd, it appeared she had welcomed all the fairies and fairy sympathizers back into her fold. Siobhan and her lovers had spent a lot of time corralling everyone to support the queen, but now that we were here, something seemed off about it. Why *had* the queen openly welcomed everyone home? Had she gotten over Smythe's prior indiscretions?

I ignored my skepticism and followed Siobhan under the canvas folds of a tent much like the one we'd stayed in last time we were here, much like the one in Diana's mind. It looked small on the outside, but it opened up into a grand space. Off to our right sat a large dining table with a feast on top. The smell of fresh fruit and garlic-roasted turkey hit my nose, reminding me that I hadn't eaten since the plane ride here. A grumble echoed from my stomach next, making Carter turn to me and snicker.

"I'm starving, too, Juliet."

"Of course you are." The man was six-three and two hundred fifty pounds of muscle, requiring a high caloric intake. An enormous bed rested on a raised platform, furs and pillows decorating the top. To our left was a small kitchenette with more food spilling over the countertops and cupboards.

"Please feel free to make yourselves at home for the night," Siobhan said, her drawn features and the bags under her eyes hinting at her exhaustion. It echoed the same radiating from me.

The impending doom glowed on the horizon, reminding me that this was almost over, that on the other side of this lay heartbreak. We would have to make a sacrifice, whatever that was, and once the end came, all of this would truly be done. Lex likely knew more than he would tell us, and I aimed to rectify that.

"If we eat the food," Ivy said, "will we be stuck here?"

Siobhan forced a tight laugh and shook her head. "Has that happened before?"

"The wine makes us"—Carter cleared his throat and straightened his shoulders—"*different.*"

"I promise, should you survive the king's vengeance, you will be returned to your realm unscathed." Siobhan met eyes with me, lingering for a moment longer before returning to Carter. "You heard my lady, mates. You are honored guests. No one will harm you, not so long as you are under her protection. And mine." Siobhan gestured to the food. "Eat. Rest. We've been through a lot these last few days, and there is still much left to do."

"What did she mean?" Ivy said. "We will need this reminder tomorrow?"

Yes, I had latched on to that as well. The queen seemed determined and assured that we would beat the king, but she had ended on quite a somber note.

"Beltane raises the sensuality in our spirits. A lot of power can come from the energy of love. If I were you"—Siobhan took a deep breath and let it out through her nose—"I would spend tonight like it's my last in this world together. It might very well be."

"Do you hear yourself?" Carter balked, crossing his arms. "You just promised to escort us back to our world unharmed and then you tell us it might be our last night on earth?"

"Should we survive the king's vengeance," Lex cut in, letting the suggestion hang between us. I went back to my earlier suspicion, to the way he'd looked when he'd come back from that conversation with Diana, to the way the trees had bristled when I stepped through the veil. They knew then, and so did Lex.

I hung on Siobhan's exact phrasing. She had said, "last in this world *together.*" As if we wouldn't be together after this. This furthered my melancholy because I had the sinking suspicion Lex had gotten secret knowledge from the queen about *his* stakes in the final battle.

But I knew better. Ivy would never part with Lex, nor would Carter. He was our king, our leader, the sun around which we orbited. If there were an expendable one, well...hadn't these last few weeks proved it was me?

Lex didn't believe in silly things like fate or destiny, but I did. And the horrible truth settled in my gut like lead.

I was the sacrifice. *I* wouldn't be returning. I would make sure of it. I wouldn't let any of them do it in my stead. The thought weighed a ton on my heart, damn near yanking me down into the depths of despair. There was a part of me that wanted to let it.

Perhaps that would be better for me in the long run. I wouldn't have to marry Reginald and I wouldn't have to worry about the Stuart reputation. Things like joining the royal family seemed so trivial now by comparison.

Fine, then. Let it be me.

Siobhan gave us one final nod and murmured, "Have a nice night, my friends."

With that, she turned to leave us alone, but I'd come to a final resolution. If tonight was going to be the last I spent with my spouses, the last time I got to hold them and worship them and love them the way I wanted, then goddamn it, I was going to bloody well take it.

17

IVY

"*What's going on with you?*" I mentally asked, grabbing Lex's hand as I passed him to move toward the table. I hadn't eaten since we were stateside and now, my stomach ached with emptiness. The food here had always been delicious, and if what Siobhan said was true, I'd need my strength for whatever faced us tomorrow.

"*Stay out of my head,*" he snapped, glaring as he swatted my fingers away. But I froze. In that split second of connection, I saw a picture of the queen patting him on the cheek, whispering something about him not believing in fate. My heart pounded, and my attention snapped to his hazel eyes.

"Lucifer," I said, trying to grab his arm again. Miri had already sat down in one of the seats, her arms curled around herself while she inspected the food. Carter loaded up a plate, his head perking at the use of my nickname for my archnemesis turned fiancé turned lover. "What was that?"

"It's nothing to worry about, X." He ignored me and walked to the other side of the tent, stalking around to the head of the table so he could grab a dish and pile a thick, juicy turkey leg on top of it.

I didn't like that answer.

After standing in Miri's tower with her, holding her hand tightly as we fought off the king together, we'd formed a telepathic link. I still saw myself standing there, even now, holding her close. She had been terrified the king would get to her again, but our being together had chased him away, the same way it had when Lex and I grabbed hands at our wedding. I needed *all* of my spouses to do this, so Lex couldn't check out on me now.

I stalked closer to him, grabbing his plate out of his hand and placing it on the table next to the fruit.

He huffed a deep sigh and clenched his jaw. "I'm too tired for your shit right now."

"You said no more secrets," I hissed. "You've been keeping one since that conversation with the queen."

"What'd she say?" Carter sat down opposite Miri and scooped a grape into his mouth. "What'd she want?"

"According to our prince, she wanted to have a good shag before returning to reality." Miri huffed out a laugh and picked at her turkey. "I think she has better taste than a human who lies to his beloveds."

"I turned her down, of course," he said, giving me that trademark annoying smirk. "I am nothing if not loyal."

"I don't believe you," I said, crossing my arms and staring him down. He reminded me so much of his younger self in that moment, his hazel eyes ablaze with challenge, his jaw muscles twitching with rage just below the surface. It was the same look he gave me right before he pounced on me, holding me down to smack me around and take what he wanted. "You know I'll get it out of you one way or the other."

Lex shook his head and dropped his gaze to the ground, dark hair falling in his face. I reached out to brush it back, the touch so familiar. I'd held his face a million times before, a thousand before we could even admit that we loved each other.

"It was all bullshit, okay?" He sighed and looked up at me again. "She didn't have anything important to say."

"She's the queen of the fairies," Carter cut in. "Anything she says is important."

"I don't buy into it. I don't believe in fate, and I don't believe that Siobhan or Diana or anyone can decide our future."

"How can you say that?" I asked. "After everything we've been through? After the four of us found each other? After you and me?" I grabbed his cheeks with both hands now, forcing him to stare at me, imploring him to let me in, to let me see. "Lex, tell me what's going on."

"Please believe me, X. There's nothing to tell." He leaned down to kiss me, locking his mental shields tight. "We're all making it out of this shit show, understand? There will be no sacrifice."

A punch lanced through my heart at being shut out. "Lex, c'mon."

"No more." He lifted his chin to stare at me without an ounce of remorse. "For years, we've lived and breathed this bullshit. We've poured our blood and energy into this...and for what? If the four of us aren't together at the end of this, it will have been for nothing. So I refuse to believe it."

That hurt worse than anything he'd ever said to me. It was the first time I'd considered that we might not all survive, that I might have to face a life without one of them. I couldn't do it. I wouldn't. And if it was between that or not returning to our realm, then I'd have to get used to Faerie. I *would not* live in a world where the three of them did not exist—*all* three of them.

"What are you saying?" Carter put his elbows on either side of his food and leaned forward.

"I'm saying that we stop worrying about the king and queen and this fairy bullshit. We need to make our own plans." Lex sighed and rubbed his hands over his face, taking a step back from me so he could pile more strawberries on top of his dish. Then, he moved on to the potatoes and vegetables before taking his seat in between Carter and Miri at the head, gesturing to the spot opposite him. "What do you say, X? Can you let it rest?"

I thought of my siblings, my guilty conscience urging me forward. I couldn't stop now, not when I'd gotten so close. I'd already wasted enough time in the woods, damn near becoming a three-course meal myself. Everything in me wanted to march into the forest to confront the king and demand he take me to my family.

Maybe I could lower the shields between my mind and his, maybe for just a second, so I could find them myself. I could find out what he'd done to Miri. I could find out how he was planning to attack.

"No," Lex snapped, getting my attention. "Don't you dare reach out to Alberich. I know what that look means; I know what you're thinking. Don't do it."

"Are you seriously considering contacting him?" Carter raised his eyebrows.

I didn't answer because no matter what I said, Lex would know the truth.

"We have the queen, we have the entire fairy army." Lex bit into a berry and leaned back in his seat, smirking while he chewed. "If that fails, we need to figure out what else to do." His attention danced to Miri. "You have the ruby dust, right? Do you think you could wield it? Could you do to him what he did to Diana?"

Carter pursed his lips but nodded at the seat next to him. I glanced at Miri, who narrowed her gaze on our husbands.

"I do," she said. "I probably could. Ivy would need to figure out what incantation he put on her."

"Suffer in silence, suffer in solitude," I said. "Then you will know the pain you've caused."

"There we go," Lex said, biting into another strawberry. "Finally, something useful."

The whole thing felt off. Even if I could find out where the king was, it wasn't like I could go after him alone. Maybe Lex had a point.

Maybe we should come up with a few contingency plans, just in case.

I glanced at the tent entrance again before giving in and sitting down at the square table. Carter smiled and plopped a big piece of turkey from his plate onto mine, giving me a few of his potatoes before replenishing his own.

"We'll try to get the king alone, pin him down, and use the ruby dust on him," Lex said, "And whatever happens tomorrow, remember we're strongest together. We have each other. Until the end."

"Until the end," Miri and Carter echoed.

I stared at Lex, a sick finality landing in my stomach. He knew more than he said, and whatever he was keeping to himself, it wasn't good. Blinking back tears, I shoved it to a corner of my mind to dissect later and focused on the present.

The last time we'd sat in a fairy tent eating dinner, we'd spent the entire night reminiscing. Tonight was supposed to be about raising the sensual energy of our spirit, whatever that meant. Siobhan suggested we spend it like it was our last night together, and the thought ached so much, I couldn't stand it.

"Miri," Lex said, biting into a piece of turkey, "what is one thing you're looking forward to once this is over?"

Our princess cut her eyes to me for a moment before returning to her food, picking at a piece of fruit to bring it to her lips for a nibble. She shook her head and huffed out a laugh. "I suppose...the new season of *Hanging with the Hiltons*."

I chuckled at the simplicity of her answer. "I can't believe you watch that shit."

"Oh, it's absolutely deplorable." She bit her bottom lip, her cheeks turning a bright shade of blush. "But I can't help myself."

"Me neither," Carter said, smiling at everyone. "Last season was wild."

Lex grinned, eyeing me across the table with that wolfish expression. Since the beginning of all this, I hadn't had a moment to simply stop, to pause and consider what would happen once I didn't have this to worry about anymore. In the last week alone, I'd trashed my wedding, invaded my mother's mind, fought off a fairy king, traveled across the Atlantic, and healed the fairy queen. I'd survived...*we'd* survived.

"Carter," Lex said, cutting into a potato with his fork. "What about you? One thing you're looking forward to."

Carter brought the chalice to his lips to sip his wine while he considered, placing a finger over his lips and swallowing. "Retirement." He glanced at me, reaching out to take my hand. "Being Ivy's stay-at-home husband."

Lex barked out a laugh. "That role is already filled, I fear."

"Fine, then I can be Miri's stay-at-home companion." Carter winked at her, causing a blush to radiate up Miri's neck and into her cheeks.

"Hmm." Lex liked that answer. He drained the rest of his cup, poured another round for all of us from the bladder on the side of the table, and then sat back in his seat while he assessed me. "Ivy."

"I'd rather hear your answer." I stabbed a potato with my fork and brought it to my mouth, choking down the savory tuber.

Lex pursed his lips and tilted his head to the side, perhaps trying to figure out my angle. But, of course, my motives were always the same with him—search and destroy.

He leaned forward and put his elbows on the table, steepling his fingers over his cup. "I'm looking forward to having children."

I froze and stared at him, chalice halfway to my lips. We had talked about kids before, but never in any concrete sense. Not like this, not with fire in his eyes and determination in his voice.

"Yeah?" Carter's smile lit up his whole face.

"Yeah," Lex said with a sparkle in his hazel stare. "I have this vision in my head of what our future looks like. I want Miri in her garden and Carter chasing around our kids, and it doesn't fucking matter who gave birth to which ones because they're ours...all of them. They're all a bunch of little Stuart-Scott-Washington-Fairfaxes."

Miri made a sad laugh, wiping at an eye when a tear slipped out and slid down her cheek. I remembered this image, I'd seen it during our four-year fairy curse. It was Lex's true north, the deep-seated motivation that kept him going, that peeled him off the floor when he thought he had no more fight left in him. It was this imaginary future that had gotten us this far. He wanted a family with all of us, he wanted *his own* family.

"We could change our names," Carter said. "Pick something we all like."

"Move to the cabin, live in the woods." Miri took a drink of wine, her tone wistful and light. "Isn't that a pretty picture?"

"What's stopping us?" Lex asked, glancing between us.

Carter hung his head between his shoulders and sighed. "What exactly are you suggesting, DC? That Ivy quit Congress? That Miri run out on the prince of receding hairlines?"

"Don't be cruel." Miri hid her wince, pretending not to be hurt, but even I felt the sting on that one.

"You're quitting your sexy primetime television show," Lex said. "We can't do the same?"

"I want to leave the family." Miri kept her voice soft and low, but pain echoed in those words regardless. "I want to stay with you."

"I would love you to." Lex's brilliant gaze snapped to her. "We can use the media against them. Tell our story our way. You can be the duchess of Aberdeen and married to us."

"No, Lex. They'll disown—"

"Yes, Miri. Who the fuck says you can't?"

I cleared my throat at this, and all three of them stopped to look at me. "Have you forgotten our life? Have you forgotten who you are?" Lex Fairfax. Son of the president of the United States. Public icon. The definition of American royalty. Hell, there was an entire section of Virginia that had his last name stamped right across it. "Or is the fairy wine already catching up to you?"

Lex leaned back in his seat, the very image of a disappointed king addressing his pessimistic queen.

"I hate to be the bearer of reality, but on the other side of this battle, there's just more of the same." I looked between the three of them. "Miri can't leave the family for the same reason you and I will end up getting married on live television in some undoubtedly more ridiculous circus that has been rescheduled to the most opportune time politically." I sat up straighter. "If we survive tomorrow morning, this all ends, right? Tomorrow *is* the end."

I held up my hand, bearing the scars that proclaimed our undying fealty to each other.

Until the end.

"We promised each other so much that night...more than we had to give."

They fell silent for a moment, long enough for Lex to let out a drawn sigh. "What are you looking forward to, Ivy?"

I didn't know. I didn't have a good answer. None of the save-the-world initiatives I'd tried to push through Congress had worked. I'd spent the majority of the last few months on a fairy curse and a dying planet, and now, both were out of my control. I had worked so damned hard for an idea of a family that didn't exist. I'd done so much for my legacy, for my mother, for my name...and none of it made a difference. I tried to focus on the things I could fix, the things in my immediate future.

"Saving my siblings," I said. "Trying to live with you three for as long as I can, as much as I can."

"Oddly vague." Lex's eyes lit with challenge. "You don't think we could have it all?"

"I think you're being too optimistic for the Lex I've come to love and loathe." I crossed my arms and leaned back in my seat. "I think the queen told you something else, something you're not sharing with the rest of us."

Lex pushed back from his seat, clearly done with my shit, and grabbed the leather bladder, yanking out the cork with his teeth so he could swig back a large drink from the jug. He stalked closer, taking it one slow step at a time, his predator gaze narrowed on me, his hips swaying in a proprietary beat.

"I think you're being needlessly argumentative." Lex dragged a finger over Carter's shoulders, who pursed his lips and narrowed his indigo stare on my former archnemesis while Lex trained his gaze on me. "I think you don't know how to have a last night on earth party, and you're too ashamed to show it."

Heat rose up the sides of my neck and into my cheeks, zigzagging across my skin in that telltale X that always gave me away. I gripped the armrests to keep from reaching up to cover it with my hand. Lex would see it anyway. I had to focus on remaining calm, on resisting the bait. He wanted to get a rise out of me, and if this was our last night on earth, I expected nothing less from Alexei "Lucifer" Fairfax, king of demons and things that go bump in the night.

"Did she tell you what the sacrifice was?" I raised an eyebrow, analyzing the almost skip in his step and the tremble in his fingers. "Is that why you're being sentimental? Because you know what we have to give up?"

There it is. The muscle around his eye twitched as he twisted his lips into a trademark smirk. Maybe he could tell I was lying with my X, but after all these years, Lex's hazel stare still gave him away.

He kicked the leg of my chair hard enough to scoot me back from the table and twist me around to face him, where he leaned down until we were eye level, his hands gripping my wrists over the armrests.

"X, I'm about two seconds from forcing Carter to his knees so he can blow me while Miri stuffs her pussy in my face." His words created a visual that sent a jolt of lust between my legs so hard, I had to squirm to keep myself from moaning. "If you don't drop this, I'm going to tie you to that bed and play with you last."

He reeked of fairy wine and bonfire smoke and a two-hour trek through the forest, but *fuck,* I couldn't resist the tremble that went through me when he gave me that look. He *dared* me to disobey him, to open my mouth and say something that would give him an excuse to do exactly what he promised.

We had agreed that we wouldn't play like this with the others around. I didn't want them to know how much I loved the fight, how much I had always loved it, but if this was truly our last night together...well...fuck it.

I took a deep breath, steeled my gaze, and opened my mouth to say, "Did you make a deal with her?"

That was all it took. Lex curled his lips into that cruel smile, recognizing that I'd given my consent, and then he attacked.

18

LEX

Fucking Ivy.

She'd always been able to read me better than anyone, and this was far too close to the truth for me to let it continue.

I grabbed her out of her seat by her waist, throwing her over my shoulder—fireman style. Sure, she was tall for a woman, but I still had eight inches on her and nearly a hundred pounds.

"Lex, damn it!" She squirmed in my hold, wiggling to get free, and when I slammed her down on the mattress, she bounced and tried to right herself.

"DC, maybe you should go easy." Carter walked to stand next to me, but I focused only on stripping my belt off my pants and wrapping it around my fist so I could approach Ivy.

"Shut the fuck up, Chicago, or you're next." I shot him a glare as I fought off Ivy's attempts to get free, grabbing her wrists and shoving them over her head so I could loop the leather over her forearms.

"Damn it, Lucifer, let me go." Ivy writhed against me, struggling hard enough that one of her hands slipped through mine and slapped me against the cheek hard enough to sting. I winced and dug my nails into her skin, making her grimace as I tied the belt harder. She knew the safeword; she knew how to stop me. When she didn't call for mercy, she'd given consent.

"Oh, yeah, fight me, X." I growled, standing up so I could unbuckle Carter's belt, resisting the urge to smile as he grumbled something about not bringing him into this. Once I had the leather thing off him, I grabbed Ivy's ankle and stretched it out so I could latch it onto the bedpost, relishing in her flushed skin and aggravated growl. "The night before the big battle and you're tied to a fucking bedpost." She looked so hot like that, so flushed and harried and easily tamable. "Do you have anything to say for yourself?"

"Fuck off, you monster." She yanked at the straps, but they wouldn't budge, and she threw her head back in a huff.

"Gladly." I chuffed out a laugh, stood, and patted Carter on the chest, nodding back toward the table. But he seemed resistant, looking at his Weeds with desperation and longing in his stare. "Don't worry about her. She likes it."

I recalled a snowy day at our cabin when Carter had walked in on a similar scene between Ivy and me, her strapped to the dining room table, me edging her until she sobbed for release.

Carter pinched his eyebrows together, but he didn't argue or try to save his beloved Weeds. He turned from her while she whined and groaned for help, and he followed me back to the table where I held a hand out to Miri, hoping she'd take it and stand to appease my threat to Ivy.

She looked at me skeptically before flicking her mahogany gaze over to our wife, who still struggled on the bed.

"What are you up to, my prince?" Miri raised an eyebrow, clearly seeing through me almost as much as X.

"Why don't you come with me to find out?"

She sighed, popped one last strawberry in her mouth, and took my hand, allowing me to pull her to her feet. When she stood in front of me, I kneeled to slide my hands up her legs and under her skirt, twisting my fingers around the waistband of her panties before shucking them down to her ankles. Looking up at her, I helped her step out of them, letting her use my shoulders for balance as she wiggled her shoes through the holes. Then I walked back to Ivy, who still protested the entire thing.

"Let me go, Lucifer," Ivy said. "This is some sick way for you to avoid—" She froze when I straddled her chest, crumpling Miri's panties in my fist before grabbing her jaw with the other hand.

"Open up, X."

She glared at me, steeling her jaw before glancing at the underwear in question.

Yeah, maybe I was asking too much, being too demanding when all Ivy wanted was to connect. I'd promised them the truth, no more lies, no more secrets. But this one? Well, this one would ruin the whole night. I didn't want them spinning on something that wouldn't happen anyway.

There would be no sacrifice. I would make sure of that.

I control my life. I control my fate.

End of story. So there was no sense talking about it or wasting our time together. If tomorrow was the face-off with the king, I wanted to have them like this. We could plan until our hearts exploded, and it still might not make a difference. Fucking them was the only pure bliss I'd ever known, and hell, I just wanted one nice thing for myself.

Ivy pursed her lips before slowly dropping her jaw, allowing me to slide Miri's panties over her tongue. I stuck two fingers under her chin to close her mouth again.

"If you spit those out before I tell you to, I'll turn your ass purple in front of our knight and princess." I wasn't kidding. I hoped she did spit them out. I hoped she fought me the whole goddamned time so I could show Carter and Miri what it really was between us. I wanted them to know that truth, to remember why Ivy and I brought out the worst in each other.

Carter had once made me swear to be nice to her, to put her back together when she was broken, but that wasn't what she needed from me. It never was. It was this. It was the king to her queen, her counterpart, her equal.

When Ivy nodded, I swung my leg off her and returned my attention to Carter and Miri, who stood next to the table with their heads bent toward each other, foreheads touching, whispers on their lips.

"Not keeping secrets, are we?" I tsked my teeth as I walked closer, eyeing Carter from head to toe. "Ivy's not the only one who likes a purple ass before I fuck it."

Carter had the nerve to blush, the little slut, but I didn't miss the hint of a grin. He wanted this. They both did.

"We think you're the one that should be tied up," Carter said, causing a muffled laugh from the bed. He crossed his massive arms, tilting his head to the side as he narrowed his beautiful eyes on me. "We think you're keeping secrets again."

I opened my mouth to reply, but Miri shook her head and stepped forward, running her hands over my chest and up to my shoulders. I stood, bewildered and curious, waiting to see where this went. Most of the time, when the four of us played, I took the lead. Occasionally I let Carter fuck me, but even then, I was the dominant. I liked to be fucked almost as much as I liked doing the fucking, but to see the two of them eyeing me like this, it sent a surge of lust straight down my spine, into my balls.

Fuck.

Miri unbuttoned my shirt, taking time to press tiny kisses to my chest as she did. I was so focused on her, I didn't notice Carter moving in behind me, not until Miri shucked my shirt over my arms, forcing me to put them together behind my back so she could pull it off. But Carter took advantage of my being entangled and twisted the fabric around my wrists before yanking it up, so my elbows were bent at my lower back. I arched into him, his chest between my shoulder blades, his mouth at my ear. I had an inch on him, but he'd come to outweigh me by at least fifty pounds of muscle.

"Such a fucking meathead," I murmured, but Carter put a giant palm over my mouth to silence me, leaning my head back on his shoulder.

"Shut the fuck up, DC," he said, mocking my earlier tone. "You like it."

I chuckled low in my chest, my knees damn near wilting at how hot he was when he teased me. Miri had that look in her eye, the one that meant she'd make me work for whatever she wanted, and in this case, they wanted me to tell them what the queen said.

I should have been honest. I should have just been out with it.

"Now that you're at our mercy," Miri said while she ran her nails down the center of my chest, ducking them under the waistband of my trousers before yanking my hips closer to her, "tell us what the queen said. Do not lie to me, Alexei Fairfax."

Fuuuccckkk. When Miri used my full name, I turned to butter. It rolled off her lips in such a delicate display of syllables and consonants that the first time she'd ever said it, I almost came in my pants like a goddamned virgin.

"She said I'm the sacrifice," I mumbled behind Carter's hand, forcing him to remove it so I could continue. "But I never believed in any of this horseshit. Fate, destiny, fairy tales, none of it is real."

They went silent for a moment, some kind of telepathic communication happening between them as they looked over my shoulder at each other. Both of them turned to Ivy, who gave a stiff nod, as if they should continue. Miri looked at Carter for one more moment before returning her soft, gentle stare to me.

But I knew better than to believe those pretty doe eyes. Miri had always lived in the frost. Like me, she had a darkness, a side she only brought out when she was trying to match my own. Those eyes glittered with that coldness now.

"It feels pretty real," Carter said, biting my earlobe hard enough to hurt. I hissed in a breath, but my cock ached for attention. Who knew mutiny would turn me on so much?

"If one of us dies, we all die," I said. "That's why it's bullshit. That's why it doesn't matter what the queen says. Because I'm the one keeping us together, so if I go, we all go." I curled my lips into a cruel smile. "How about it, Princess? You once promised me forever. Ready to die by your word?"

My heart pounded in my chest while I waited for a reaction, but she didn't give me the one I was looking for. I had hoped she'd haul off and smack me or perhaps call off her guard dog so I could make good on my threat to fuck them all like they belonged to me. Instead, she grabbed the back of my head, twisted her fingers into my hair, and yanked my face forward. Our lips collided, and I took my time to devour her mouth, sucking down anything she gave me. Her tongue explored mine while Carter held me tighter, adjusting his stance so his cock rubbed up against my ass. I arched into him, stifling a laugh when he gasped and clenched his hand harder around my wrists.

Miri reached between us to grab my dick, giving it a squeeze that had me sucking back a sharp inhale. She tightened her fingers against my scalp, tugging my head away from her while she bit down on my lower lip hard enough to hurt before letting it go with a snap.

"How dare you keep that from us, Alexei?" She snarled, shooting daggers at me from behind her brown gaze. She nodded to Carter, who hauled me over to the bed, snickering in my ear as we walked.

"You're in trouble now," he murmured, making sure to give me one last kiss before twisting my arms around so they were above my head. Then he pushed me down on the mattress next to Ivy, who eyed me with a tantalizing mix of fiery anger and amused mirth. Her steel eyes sparkled in the candlelight, making her seem ethereal like some archangel of retribution here to smite me for my many crimes. Carter straddled my chest and tied my hands to the headboard the way I'd done to Ivy.

He smirked at my fiancée and went for her pants, unbuttoning them and lowering the zipper before shucking the linen down to her ankles. Without a second's thought, he yanked her underwear from her body, ripping the sides of them so he could get them off without untying her.

"Open up, DC." He nodded as he fisted the fabric into a ball, focusing on my mouth until I complied. The delight in his eyes blended with the brilliance of his smile, and I found myself unable to resist.

Diana had said it herself. I was the vortex that had sucked these three phenomenal people into my orbit. It should be me controlling this scene. I had wanted it to be at the start. But leave it to Romeo and Juliet to take the spotlight, even from royal American shitheads such as X and myself.

My lips parted, and Carter stuck Ivy's expensive silk underwear into my mouth, closing my jaw the same way I'd done to her.

"If you spit those out before I tell you to"—Carter leaned down to whisper the words against my lips—"I'll turn your dick purple before I even start to get you off. There's no saying I'll stop. I'll suck you all night, DC, and that's not a promise. That's a threat."

19

CARTER

When Lex said he was the sacrifice, he cut somewhere deep down inside my chest, and after the words left his lips, I couldn't hold myself back anymore. Because I knew it wouldn't come to that. My luck told me it wouldn't. Unlike him, I did believe in fate. I did believe in destiny. After four years of this fairy gift, how could I not? I'd learned to trust my gut and right now, it said there would be no sacrifice. I knew that in my bones. It was the way my gift worked. It was how I knew which cards to play in poker, or how I'd gotten us to safety with my eyes closed the last time the king attacked. The luck ran in my blood, and if it came to it, I would put myself in the line of fire before I'd let any of them do it.

Aren't we a bunch of martyrs?

But this was my show now, my scene, and I wanted him to shut the fuck up.

After I dismounted Lex, I walked to stand next to Miri at the foot of the bed, eyeing our two spouses like we'd stumbled on the holy grail of riches. To be fair, we'd come pretty damned close.

Ivy Washington and Lex Fairfax: tied to a bed next to each other, underwear stuffed in their mouths, nearly disrobed and disheveled beyond all reason. It was the stuff of fantasies. It was what I had ached for since I was a freshman in college.

"My, my, what a sight?" Miri tapped her chin as she leaned her head on my shoulder. "Whatever shall we do with such spoils?"

Lex shifted his hips, bucking his arousal forward, clearly indicating what he wanted to happen. Weeds let out a loud sigh, scooting closer to Lex, perhaps so they could talk telepathically.

That shit used to hurt, but not tonight. If they wanted to communicate while I put them in their place, fine. So be it. After Lex tied Ivy up and stuffed Miri's panties in her mouth, I suggested to Miri that we do the same to him.

"Let's remind them why they married us," I'd said. She had agreed.

Now, I turned to Miri, wrapping my arms around her waist while hers came around my neck, relishing in the softness of her lips and the way she molded to me. It reminded me of California, when it had just been her and me and the heartbreak between us. Melancholy tightened in my chest, reiterating that we had no idea what tomorrow would bring.

I kissed Miri deeper, tugging the zipper of her dress down to her waist so I could drag the fabric over her arms and drop it to the floor at her feet. I lowered to my knees, helping her out of her shoes before taking the dress and throwing it on the chair behind me. I looked up at her, this Goddess of delicate energy, such devotion and sincerity radiating out of her gaze. Trembling and trying to hide it, I ran my hands up the sides of her thighs, memorizing how soft her skin was. She truly was so very beautiful, and I loved her as much as I loved the others.

All we have is us.

Perhaps I knew that more in that moment than I ever had before. Lex and Ivy lived to tear into each other: they always had, they always would. But Miri and I had always been on the same side:

about the two of them, about California and Poppy, about needing to check both of our spouses tonight of all nights.

"I love you," I told her.

She smiled and ran the back of her knuckles down the side of my face. "I love you."

For all that we had suffered, Miri and I wanted to take this moment to remind Lex and Ivy what we were together and why we loved each other.

There had been times when I'd held Lex down and taken what I'd wanted from him. Even Ivy and I liked to play a certain dynamic between us. But this wasn't about that...this was about taking care of them, all of them, on this trepidatious eve. I didn't know what we'd face in the morning, but the last few weeks had been traumatizing enough without Ivy and Lex biting at each other's throats.

Maybe the queen had told Lex he would be the sacrifice, or maybe the whole thing was a farce like he suspected. I didn't care. My luck didn't care. I had to fuck Miri, and that was it. After that, I'd fuck Lex until he couldn't stand, and I'd set Miri on Ivy to do whatever she pleased. Once they couldn't remember their names, only then would I let myself come. Only then would I let the magic of the night have me.

I'd witnessed horrors not even an hour ago, things that would surely come back to haunt me once I let myself think about them. But under the influence of Faerie and the fairy wine and the intoxicating scent of Miri's pheromones, I couldn't be bothered to care.

"Take me, Romeo," Miri whispered, and a moan came from Lex's side of the bed.

Hiding a smile, I kissed the inside of one thigh, slowly dragging my mouth up her body to her beautiful cunt, and when I slid my tongue through her skin, I hummed to myself at how wet she already was. I spread her open, latching on to her clit the way I knew she liked. I had spent hours between her thighs, even more watching Ivy and Lex do the same.

She rocked against me, spearing her fingers through my hair, holding me while I took from her.

"You both have forgotten why we're in this mess," Miri said, her words no more than breathy sighs as I lapped at her, swallowing down her arousal and her delectable energy like it could revitalize the broken parts of me. "And if tomorrow is to be the end, then I won't spend my last night listening to my prince lie to me while my favorite girl vibrates with fury."

I chuckled at her turn of phrase, scooting myself closer so I could press a finger at her entrance. Miri spread her legs farther, allowing the access, and when I eased inside her tight pussy, the thighs on either side of my head shook. She was so turned on and eager, I almost couldn't resist bending her over and taking her rough and quick. But I wanted to make this last, and I knew she did, too.

"I want to ride my Romeo's face so hard, his jaw hurts in the morning." She threw her head back, her dark curls falling down her shoulders, her neck arched in a glowing display of skin. I bet Lex ached to dig his teeth in it. I bet Ivy couldn't wait to lick across her pulse. I bet they itched with anticipation. "I want to make my wife come so hard, she doesn't remember why we're here. And I want my prince to watch it all, to make me kneel for him the way only he can."

The visual sent me skyrocketing, my cock jerking behind my jeans, aching with desperation for all that she described. Miri tightened her hold on my head, using my mouth however she wanted, and I kept finger-fucking her, relishing just how joyous I was in that moment. If I could freeze time, I would never leave this tent with them. I loved watching her fall apart, and when she made those breathy little moans, I felt like the king of the fucking world. Miri came on my face, rocking and making good on her threat to strain my jaw. But even the ache pleased me, and when she stepped back to glance down with that tenderness in her eyes, I fell even more in love with her.

Then, I set my sights on Weeds and DC, who had both turned a shade of blush while they waited. Lex's cock bulged behind his trousers, his desire apparent in the way he stared at me with that burning cold hazel gaze. Ivy, on the other hand, panted through her nose in deep huffs, her thighs clenched together like she was trying to alleviate the tension building there.

"My poor Weeds," I said, pushing to my feet. My dick pulsed at the two of them looking so disheveled and pitiful tied to the bed. "Do you need some attention?"

She only glared at me, fiery gray eyes drilling holes into my soul. It delighted me how much she always wanted us, how much she thrived when the four of us were together. Miri may be my one and only Juliet, my star-crossed lover, my best friend and confidante, but Ivy was my first love, my first favorite girl, the one who opened my heart for the others. She and I knew a side of each other that few would ever experience.

"What do you think, Juliet?" I put an arm over Miri's shoulders and leaned down to kiss her softly, grabbing the tip of my dick through my pants to soothe some of the hunger careening in my veins. An impulsive side of me wanted to take them both hard and fast, to devour whatever I could as soon as I could. But I held that piece back, knowing it would be better if I savored it, if we took our time. "Should I tend to our queen while you take care of our king?"

She hummed and smiled, leaning up to give me one more gentle kiss. "I believe he said something about you sucking his cock while I stuff my pussy in his face."

The reminder made me chuckle. "And playing with Ivy last."

Miri tsked her teeth, looking at Lex with a hint of devilish mischief behind her eyes. "Such arrogance."

"The audacity," I added.

Miri climbed onto the bed, straddling Ivy's legs so she could scoot herself up her torso, positioning herself on the redhead's chest. My princess leaned back so she could spear her fingers through Ivy's cunt, making Weeds groan and arch into the touch.

"My, my, she's so wet. We must have put on quite the show." Miri laughed and returned her attention to Ivy, holding out the other hand and wiggling her fingers so Ivy knew to spit out her panties. She did, and Miri quickly tossed them back to me, where I stuffed them in my back pocket for...uh...*souvenir* purposes. Lex stayed transfixed on our wives, and I watched him regard them as Miri spread herself open and placed her vulva right on Ivy's mouth.

Weeds wasted no time, licking and sucking at Miri like she was a starved woman. After all these months away from our wife, she likely was. I had missed Miri with a sick hollowness that almost drowned me. For Ivy, it had been unbearable.

Now that we were back together, Ivy let Miri do whatever she wanted to her. And I stared at Lex while I unhooked Ivy's leg from the bed frame. He caught the movement, trailing his attention over my body while I did. When she was free, I took her pants off and climbed onto the mattress between her knees, using my shoulders to spread them wider.

I may have played with Ivy's cunt a million times, but it never stopped being amazing. I loved the sounds she made against Miri when I kissed the inside of her thigh. When I dug my teeth into a sensitive part, she bucked and squirmed, and her beautiful pussy clenched so nicely. I wanted to be balls deep inside her and make her do that again. But I settled on fucking her with my face and my fingers until her thighs clamped down on my ears and she arched her hips every time I slid deep inside her.

"Yes, just like that," Miri groaned. "You have such a great mouth. I've always loved your tongue. Fuck, that's so good."

I couldn't stand it any longer. Miri's words combined with Ivy's squirms and Lex's hot stare, and I needed to be inside her. I dropped my jeans to my ankles, kicking them off with my feet before kneeling between Ivy's legs and lining the tip of my cock up with her scorching hot entrance.

Good Lord, sinking inside her always felt like heaven, like coming home, like she was made for me. Miri rose to turn around, now riding Ivy's face in my direction, and she leaned in to kiss me. Our mouths connected, and I swallowed one of her groans of ecstasy, where it settled deep down in my chest, amplifying my own. We were magic together, the four of us, and even though Lex hadn't been allowed to touch us yet, he was still very much a part of this.

His eyes never left our show, and the thrill of taking the ones I loved while the one that loved us watched made me feel invincible. The fairy king could try his best to separate us tomorrow, and I wouldn't give a shit because we had this...we would always have this.

The surety of that radiated so deep inside me that nothing could shake it. We would make it through this together, all four of us.

I hoisted Ivy's legs to my shoulders, turning my head so I could bite the inside of her calf while I fucked her. She moaned harder, and Miri leaned forward to rub at Ivy's clit while she writhed on her face until she fell apart again, her forehead pressed against mine, her desperate pants searing my cheeks and lips. Miri was so beautiful when she came.

Once she'd had her fill, Miri climbed off Ivy to finally tend to her prince of darkness, our proverbial king, the one who bore the weight of the crown so we didn't have to.

"Should I finally take you?" Miri raised her eyebrow as she teased a finger over the waist of Lex's pants, his stomach muscles trembling as she licked her lips.

"He deserves to be edged for hours," Ivy said, her voice croaky and harsh for how long she'd been gagged. Even in the throes of euphoria, she couldn't resist needling her former nemesis.

Lex groaned and rolled his eyes, sinking into the little contact that Miri gave him. I slowed my thrusts, drawing out the sensations like I'd never get to feel them again. I kissed Ivy's ankles and spread her legs farther so they fell to my hips. I leaned over her, dropping down to my elbows by her ribs, so we touched from chest to pelvis.

"Are you okay?" she asked mentally, drawing my attention from Lex and Miri.

"Just fine, Miss Washington." I kissed her gently, stuffing myself

deep inside her, making a deliberate display of connection. *"Are you okay?"*

She sighed and ducked her head into my neck, licking and sucking at my pulse point. Fuck, that felt so damned good, and I picked up my pace.

"Don't leave me, Carter," she said. *"Please. Whatever happens tomorrow. Don't leave me."*

"I won't," I pressed my forehead to hers, forcing her mouth back to mine. She tasted like Miri and wine and her, and it was such an intoxicating blend that I couldn't resist sticking my tongue deeper into her mouth for more. Always more. Forever more. Always with her. *"I promise I won't. You have me until we die, Weeds. Forever."*

"I love you," she whispered, low but loud enough for the others to hear.

"I love you," I repeated. "I've always loved you."

"Do you hear that, my prince?" Miri said, bringing my focus back to her. She had stripped Lex completely naked and now kneeled between his legs, flicking her tongue over the tip of his cock in featherlight caresses that drove Lex wild. He surged his hips up to her, trying to get more contact, but she only grinned and tormented him. "Weeds and Romeo are so in love. Do you love me like that? Are you jealous of what they have?"

He threw his head back, his eyes clenched in frustration, his lips struggling to hold in Ivy's underwear. It shouldn't thrill me as much as it did to see him in such a state of distress, but twisted amusement and arousal hit me low in the gut, making me rut into Ivy harder. Lex had always been beautiful in a haunting sort of way. His cheekbones could cut glass and the permanent scowl set between his eyebrows hinted at the darkness he put up as a front to the whole world. It had protected him his entire life, and now that we were so intertwined in it, that darkness had done the same for us. Because of it, he had been suspicious of Poppy when no one else was. He had been able to read the king and the queen in a way we never could. And now, his darkness would see us through the end.

I did believe in fate. I believed all of this had happened for a reason, that we were meant to meet and meant to be a four. We were meant to be together, or this would have happened to four other idiots.

No, we were chosen. It could have only been us.

And here was the proof—I was fucking his fiancée while he fucked the princess of England and after I was done with her, I planned to roll him over and remind him of the promises he made to me four years ago. We belonged to each other. That strengthened us, and it would see us through the other side of this fairy-tale nightmare.

"Good God," I groaned when the sensations became overwhelming. The scalding heat of Ivy's cunt combined with the way her body rolled under me and the sight of Miri sucking Lex off, and I nearly came. Lightheaded, I pushed myself up and sat back on my haunches, running my hands over my face and through my hair. "This is too good."

It didn't feel real, like I would wake up any second and realize I was freezing my dick off in some Romanian shithole while my costars bickered about who was blocking whose light. I'd been such a dumbass to think I needed the fame to be with my spouses. I should have stayed to see it through after college. I should have done so many things differently.

"Please, Carter," Ivy said on a sigh. "Please, make me come."

"Hmm." I turned to Miri, who sat up and stroked Lex's cock while she leaned over and kissed me. "Do you think it's time?"

Miri chuckled and shrugged. "You might as well go easy on her. She tries to be so tough, but she is such a delicate thing."

Ivy curled into herself and ducked her face into her arm, her cheeks turning a darker shade of pink as I picked up my pace, fucking her hard and rough, hitting the spot inside her that I knew would get her there. Suddenly, she wasn't the twenty-six-year-old congresswoman in front of me. She had become that eighteen-year-old girl I met at college: fearful of everyone she didn't know, refusing to let anyone touch her. I had been the first guy between these legacy legs, and after nearly eight years, I could say with complete certainty that I would never get tired of it.

I was so proud of her, of both of us, for everything we'd accomplished, for everything we survived. I poured all of those emotions into the way I took her, groaning when her cunt clenched around me so hard, I almost couldn't hold myself from spilling deep inside her. Her eyes rolled back in her head and breathy moans fell from her lips, chanting, "Yes, yes, yes."

I loved fucking Ivy Washington, but watching her climax had to be my most favorite thing in the world. To know that I, a mere no one from the Chicago suburbs, could unravel her so completely inflated my ego to epic proportions.

But I wouldn't let myself go completely. My climax wasn't for her. I had a bone to pick with my husband, and I wanted to make sure he understood the implications of his actions tonight.

I wouldn't allow him to keep things to himself. If this was our last night together, then I would demand his complete honesty. What would it take for him to understand we needed him just as much as he needed us?

Miri leaned in to kiss me again, grabbing Lex's cock with one hand and his balls with the other, squeezing so that Lex let out a deliciously agonized groan.

"That looks like fun, Juliet," I said, leaning over to kiss her temple.

"Care to have a turn?" She glanced up at me and grinned, pure joy radiating out of her gaze. I hadn't seen her look so happy since Solstice. I would do anything to make Miri grin like that for the rest of our lives.

"You're entirely too generous." I gave her one last kiss as we switched places, and she scooted in between Ivy's legs, leaning over her body to plant a kiss on her lips. I focused my attention on Lex, who stared up at me with icy fury behind his gaze.

I had ruined his plans, and sure, he could have gotten out of that button-down if he wanted to. He could have called for mercy and we would have granted it. But he stayed where I put him and endured Miri's oral torture, probably in anticipation of this exact moment when I revealed my true intentions.

I smiled like a kid that had been given free rein in a cookie factory and ran my hands up his long legs to his hips, purposely ignoring the beautiful cock that jutted straight up in the air. If I happened to give it a quick peck on my way up to his mouth, well, how could anyone blame me for that? Every part of Lex was beautiful, all hard edges and selective blue blood breeding—especially his dick. I licked a trail up his chest, relishing the salt of his sweat as it mixed with the sweet sugar of his natural taste, and stopped at his neck, where I nudged his head to the side so I could lick that, too.

He obliged, tilting his chin toward his other bicep, and when I sank my teeth into his pulse point, he jolted his hips off the bed and collided with mine. Chuckling to myself, I continued up to his ear, pressing my torso down on him, pinning him to the bed.

"Remember that time in Russia?" I whispered so low, only he would hear me. This was for him alone. The girls hadn't been there with us when I'd held Lex by the mouth and forced myself inside his hot body. "Remember how much you loved getting fucked like *my* little slut?"

He laughed out a deep moan, rolling his head back to look at me, Ivy's underwear sticking out from between his lips. Finally taking mercy on him, I reached up to pull it out, gleefully watching as he flexed his jaw and licked his lips.

"You're a wicked man, Carter Scott." Lex pushed his face forward to kiss me, and I allowed the touch for a moment before biting his bottom lip hard enough to make him squirm. I didn't break the skin though, just pinched and pulled and chuckled while he whined.

"Do you remember our promise?" I sat back, glancing over to Miri while she hitched Ivy's leg onto her shoulder, positioning their cunts together so she could gently rock into Ivy. I took a deep breath and returned to Lex, grabbing his cock with a tight grip. "Do you remember how you made me swear to come home to you?"

Lex groaned and rutted into my fist, seeking that desperate release that we'd been holding back from him.

"Yes, I remember," he breathed, his voice scratchy in that sexy way only he could accomplish.

"Good," I said, pushing up on my knees so I could get a good grip on Lex's hips. Then, I flipped him, hoisting his body up so his legs were under him, his ass up in the air. I reached inside my back pocket where I'd stashed a few packets of lube from the Beltane festival, and I ripped open the foil, spreading the cool liquid over my fingers and his ass, making sure to smear it in.

Lex arched his hips into me, moaning at the touch while I pushed a finger inside.

This wasn't the first time I'd fucked Lex, and judging by Ivy's toy collection, I suspected she pegged him on occasion. He normally liked to take the lead, preferring to run the show and fuck everyone his way. But even kings should be taken care of sometimes, and tonight, he needed the reminder that we were the ones who did that for him. He could rely on us for this. He could be vulnerable with us in a way he couldn't with anyone else.

One finger became two, and I studied his reactions, warm delight slithering down my chest and into my balls when he rocked back against me, his cock leaking precum under his body. Good lord, it went to my head.

I opened another packet of lube and rubbed it over my cock, mixing with the remnants of Ivy's arousal, and when I lined the tip up at Lex's entrance, he groaned and shoved back on me harder than I'd intended to go. I wasn't prepared for the sudden sheathing, and my stomach clenched so hard, I almost embarrassed myself.

"Fuuucck," I groaned, falling forward onto my hands.

Lex let out a dark laugh. "What was that about being a little slut? Looks like you can't even keep yourself upright."

"Oh, fuck you," I said through deep pants, using his back to push myself up again.

"What do you think, Princess?" Ivy whispered, reaching to wrap her fingers around Miri's neck and pulling her back down. Miri must have unbound her, and now they rubbed their clits together and moaned against each other in a glorious display of love and adoration. "Should we join our husbands?"

Miri laughed softly and nodded, rearing back so Ivy could scoot herself under Lex's massive body. He lined himself up at her cunt, and I used my hips to shove him deep inside her, nearly collapsing at how tight he became around me once he was fully seated inside our wife. Miri climbed on top of Ivy's mouth, facing us, and together, the four of us chased our combined pleasure.

Lex rocked in between me and Ivy, pressing tender kisses to Miri's lips while she ground down on Ivy's face, her head thrown back in displays of rapture. In that moment of affection, the atmosphere began to shift. What once had been sexual and overwhelming had now become suffocated by the complete awareness of *them.*

Ivy's scalding energy coursed through me, fiery and incinerating, combining with Lex's icy avalanche and Miri's grounded earthy presence to create a powerful vitality that seemed to be a part of us and separate from us at the same time.

"Do you feel that?" Ivy whispered inside my head, inside *all* of our heads.

"Yes," I said as Lex and Miri replied with the same word. The word rang in stereo, like it was coming from inside me and all around me.

"It's us." Miri grabbed my hand on Lex's hip, pressing her mouth to his, writhing against our wife, and that was what set me off. One simple touch had me thrusting into my husband like a wild beast, determined to see where this connection went. The vibrancy of our love for each other became a physical tension between us,

extraordinary and ethereal, a glimmering green mist that connected at our chests.

Was this what Siobhan meant by raising the sensual spirituality of the place? I didn't know, but the more I touched the three of them, the stronger I felt. I could face the king tomorrow. I could take on the entire fairy world if I had to. As long as I had my spouses at my side, I could do anything.

The barriers between us disappeared. I could no longer tell where I ended and where Lex began, and beyond that, Ivy and Miri. We were one soul, one body, one heartbeat, and I could have sworn our pulses synced up. Their blood raced in my veins, and mine thundered through theirs until we finally hit a crescendo.

Sparks of euphoria skated across my skin, and I clenched my muscles while my climax took me over, pushing into Lex a few more times before freezing to empty deep inside him. His cock kicked inside Ivy. I felt his inner muscles pulsing with his orgasm. Miri moaned and Ivy's toes curled, and for one blinding second, that brilliant emerald connection between us exploded, escalating every sensation in my body.

I didn't just disintegrate under my pleasure, but I shattered with the weight of theirs...*ours.*

"It's us," Miri had said, and the absolute magnitude of that raw power confirmed what everyone had been saying all along. We were better together. The strength we had as a foursome could topple entire kingdoms.

In the aftermath, Lex and I fell to one side of Ivy, and Miri lay down on the other, each of us lost in our own comedown while we panted away our hormones.

When I had the strength, I laughed out a quiet noise and murmured, "That was incredible."

To which Lex agreed with a chuckle of his own.

"Rest up, all of you," he said. "Because we're going to do that again."

He made good on that promise at least four more times. After that, I lost count. We took each other and raised that forest-green vibrance to the point where it hovered in the air around us like a fog, like a tangible thing we could control and move around.

"It's beautiful," Miri said, waving her hand through it long after Ivy and Lex had passed out. It was just the two of us for the last little while now. We had lost track of time a million years ago. Who the hell knew? I took another deep breath and let it out on a soft sigh.

"Do you think it's tomorrow?" I asked through my pheromone-induced haze.

She shrugged. "Perhaps."

"I don't want this to end."

Miri rolled on her side to face me, the sounds of Lex and Ivy's soft breathing coming from the other side of her. "Me neither."

"Make me a promise."

She narrowed her eyes. "Okay."

"Whatever happens tomorrow, you'll stay with us."

Miri froze and blinked owlishly at me. "Romeo."

"I'm serious," I said. "I won't let you leave us again. You saw what happened to you and Ivy when you were gone. If we all don't leave Faerie tomorrow, then none of us leave."

Miri closed her eyes and tears streamed down her cheeks. She opened her mouth to say something, but closed it again before she could, ultimately deciding to give me a small nod instead. "Yeah, Romeo. Okay."

ACT IV

Are you sure
That we are awake? It seems to me
That yet we sleep, we dream.
-Demetrius, Act IV, Scene II

20

MIRI

Shouting woke me. I snapped my eyes open to a face full of beautiful ginger hair and Ivy's sugar cookie scent deep in my lungs. I had my arm draped over her waist, my fingers intertwined with Lex's on the other side. Carter curled behind me, my back to his chest, his leg in between my knees, and for a moment, I didn't have a care in the world.

We'd taken each other so many times, my body ached in the best way, but I had also been rejuvenated. When I glanced down at my naked form, I was no longer a skeleton wearing a Miri costume. My body had a certain vibrance to it, as if I was glowing from the inside out. Carter, likewise, seemed more effervescent than he had before, and when I glanced at Ivy and Lex, I realized we made a matched set.

The four of us were shining, lit from within, and I remembered what happened when we all came together last night. A beautiful emerald energy had filled the space between us, coating us in ancient magic that we had no hope of understanding. I could still feel it there, thrumming just under my skin. It was no longer physical, but instinct told me it still existed inside us.

The screams got my attention again, and I looked at the tent

flaps where more fairies ran by the opening with gasps of excitement...or terror.

Just as I was about to disentangle myself from my lovers'
embrace, Siobhan shoved inside the entry with Ashley, Donnelly, and
Finn on her heels.

"Holy shit," she murmured, putting her hand over her
mouth.

Ashley's jaw dropped, and Finn's eyebrows went halfway up his
forehead.

"What happened to you four?" Siobhan glanced between us
while I pulled the covers up to my chest, trying to protect what little
dignity I had left. Carter groaned to sit up. Lex mumbled something
about them fucking off, but he didn't bother to appease them with
his attention.

"We don't have time to figure it out," Ashley said, her dark brown
eyes taking us in. "The king's here. It's time."

A blinding slice of panic shot down the center of my body like a
hot poker, and I shoved Carter harder. "C'mon. Get up."

"Fuck." He grumbled and rolled out of bed, grabbing his pants to
slide them up his legs. I yanked my dress up my body and zipped it
closed before slipping on my shoes. Once we dressed, we followed
the fairies outside, where the rest of Faerie had erupted into chaos.
Bodies bustled around me, wide, horrified eyes meeting mine before
refocusing on the center platform. They congregated by the queen's
tent, preparing themselves for whatever they needed to do to
survive.

"*Little Thistle,*" hissed a sinister voice deep inside my head. I
winced and assessed my mental barrier, watching as the stones of
my tower crumbled more quickly than I could repair them. "*Do you
feel me? Do you see how futile it is to resist? Come to me.*"

Ivy and Lex followed the crowd toward the queen, but I stopped
to look behind me, searching for his dark tendrils. He sounded different, weaker perhaps, or more agitated—almost like he couldn't
believe it had escalated this far. He had expected me to fold at Kens-

ington, and now that we'd held out this long, we'd rattled his confidence.

Images of Ivy's siblings came across the mental link between us —Kit with a wide, scared gaze, her mouth magically sealed shut, and Jon with the same startled expression, his arm curled protectively around Lizzie, who didn't look any better. Edward's cheeks were gaunt and big bags hung under his eyes, his hand gripping Kit's so hard, their knuckles had turned white, their nails digging into each other's skin.

Had they been transfixed this whole time? What was he doing to them? Where were they mentally? A thick scalding fury settled in my gut, the drive to protect my family nearly sending me on a warpath straight to him. I sensed his presence lingering over the horizon, and if I lowered the bridge surrounding my mental tower, perhaps I could end this now.

"Miri." Carter grabbed my hand, bringing my attention back to Faerie and the pandemonium about to erupt. The moment he touched me, my skin glowed brighter, hotter, more radiant than it had when we first woke up. "Do you see that?"

I nodded, the king's voice fading to the dark recesses of nothingness. "Let's go to the others."

He tugged me along behind him, weaving through the crowd to make our way to the platform. My heart raced as I dodged bodies in every direction. A fairy ran by carrying a child who cried in loud, fearful hollers while another bigger, brutish fairy barreled in front of us, nearly cutting us off. I gasped and circled him, dread lining my nerves as the king's energy crested on the hill behind us.

He was here...truly here...in Faerie.

Diana came out of the tent, likewise looking revitalized and glimmering with energy. Her long pale hair had been cleaned and braided behind her head, and her dress had returned to its pre-amnesia decadence. Pale transparent mist poured off her, equally terrifying and powerful as the king's. Poppy and a few others appeared out of the tent next, the changeling now even taller than when I'd last seen her a few hours ago. She looked like a teenager, her face fuller and longer, her body resembling more of a woman's than a girl's. I had a million questions but didn't ask them, only returned my attention to the queen.

"Well," she said, glancing around at us and straightening her broad shoulders. "What are we waiting for?" Then she walked down the steps to the ground, gesturing for us to follow her.

The crowd parted for us as we approached, Poppy immediately behind the queen, the four of us behind her, and Siobhan trailing with her lovers. Diana led us through the forest, over the winding path that led out of Faerie. I recognized it from the last time we were here, but the familiarity did nothing to ease the dread in my stomach.

Eventually, we made our way to the ruins, the same decaying building where my spouses and I made an oath to each other four years ago. Heavens, how much we had changed since then. Seeing the ivy-covered stone structure lit a warmth in my chest, reminding me of the emerald mist from last night.

Just as we rounded the corner, the entrance to Faerie came into view, that shimmering veil between the human realm and the fairy. The battle maidens stood facing the king on one side in long, sprawling lines, the *Fianna* on the other. Both were dressed for battle, their armor shimmering in the dawn sunlight, their weapons poised to strike, their shields at the ready.

He was alone, his arms crossed, an indignant smirk on his lips. His long obsidian hair now reached the middle of his chest, brushed back behind his ears. His beard had grown out too, but remained as black as the rest of him. Dark tendrils swirled out of his hands, scooping up and over us, blocking out the hazy blush of Faerie at dawn. He vibrated with chaotic energy, almost as powerful as he'd been the last time he'd come sweeping down that hill, but nowhere near as controlled. He seemed to be cracking at the seams.

"Friends, fairies, countrymen, lend me your ears." Hands held up on either side of him, he stalked down the rolling green grass toward the armies, now more lush and vibrant than when we'd arrived. How long had we been in that tent? How long had it taken for the king to break his way into Faerie? How long had he been standing here waiting for us?

"We once were brethren," Alberich continued. "We once were on the same side."

Metal clinked as the soldiers prepared themselves for battle, shifting into formation. The sight startled me, and I didn't see how one man...one king of fairies could stand against them. I grabbed Ivy's hand and straightened, reminding myself we were safe inside my mental tower. The king couldn't corrupt me here. He couldn't reach me. We were stronger together.

"There is no need for violence today." Alberich almost stumbled over his words when his gaze landed on Finn, Donnelly, and Siobhan, who had moved to the right of the queen. Instead, he refocused on the fairies filing in behind us and the battalions on either side, the entire population of Faerie now united against him.

My cousin and the rest of his abductees stood mindlessly next to him. Like the guards at Kensington when he'd attacked, their eyes were completely dark, the whites and irises gone to swirling pitch and smoke.

Siobhan moved to the other side of Diana, perhaps to make a show of a more balanced force, but it caused me to separate hands with Ivy. I lamented the loss but still held Carter's on my other side, his fingers squeezing mine to let me know he was still with me.

"Ah, Diana." Alberich stared at his wife with a devilish smirk on his full pink lips. "I see you've come to your...*right mind.*" He chuckled softly, but I seethed with rage.

It was the first time I'd seen him since I'd remembered he'd done something vile to me, and I trembled as I struggled to stay in my spot. I wanted to gather the strength from the woods surrounding us and choke him to death for violating me. I wanted vengeance for the hell he'd put me through, for taking Edward and the others, for messing with Diana's mind in the first place.

He didn't deserve forgiveness. He may not want violence today, but I thirsted for his demise in a way I'd never known before.

"Alberich," Diana said, "have you come to apologize?"

He twisted his features into an incredulous scowl before barking out a laugh and clapping. "Apologize? Whatever for? Trying to protect my own?" Alberich glanced around at the bystanders, former members of his *Fianna* and peerage alike, and opened his hands as if to suggest he meant them no harm. "Look at the damage that has been done since we allowed their kind in." He pointed over the hill, toward the entrance of Faerie. "Have you seen what they did each other? When left uncontrolled, they revert to wild animals."

"That's not true," Ivy cut in. "You did this to them. You did this to all of us."

Diana held up a hand, shushing Ivy, who gave the queen a side eye but didn't argue.

"My love," Diana said, shaking her head with a soft smile. "Can we not find common ground?"

Poppy chose that moment to move around Diana, opposite Siobhan, and grab her hand. Alberich focused on the changeling, his dark eyes even more villainous now that the object of his ire had shown herself.

"We can, my love," he snarled, "if you rid yourself of that *thing*."

Poppy winced and ducked her head, squeezing her free hand into a fist.

He stood to the side, showing the diminishing remains of the veil. It had been rotting when we'd come through on Beltane, but now, it hummed with a fraction of the same power I'd come to associate with it. If we didn't act soon, we might not make it out of Faerie.

"There is the door," Alberich said, holding out a hand in a dismissive gesture. "Look at it. So weak. So volatile. Just like them. It won't last much longer. Send them through it. Send all the humans through it, and we can go back to how things used to be."

Sure, Poppy had made mistakes, and I'd be the first to say she couldn't be trusted, but that didn't mean she was *unhuman*. She wasn't a *thing*; she was a person. We all were. We didn't deserve this type of treatment, no matter what had happened in the past.

I reached into my pocket, squeezing the ruby dust as Lex's plan from last night churned in the back of my mind. Alberich deserved a taste of his own punishment. He'd messed with my mind since I was a child, he'd made Diana forget her entire life, he'd used Poppy and nearly killed her. Now, I planned to do the same. The elemental magic buried in its molecules hummed through my blood. I could manipulate it if I wanted. Ivy had given me the spell.

"That is not an option." Diana straightened her shoulders, folding her hands in front of her, setting her jaw in a tense clench.

"Well, that is unfortunate." Alberich's gaze drifted to the battle maidens before narrowing on the *Fianna*. "And this show of strength is meant to...what? Intimidate me?"

Siobhan straightened, jutting her chin out defiantly.

"Do you think me so weak that I could not just—" The king flicked his hand like swatting a fly and half of the battle maidens slumped to the ground, their eyes gone obsidian, their bodies limp.

"No!" Siobhan called, taking a step forward before Diana held up a hand to hold her back. Alberich cut his hand the other way and a third of the *Fianna* did the same. This angered Finn, who squared his jaw and tightened his grip on his sword.

"My lady," Finn murmured. "Give the order."

Instead, Diana shook her head and tsked her teeth. "Charades, my darling. Come now. We are surely past this. There is no need to enthrall our own."

"Traitors, the lot of them." Alberich snarled before narrowing his eyes on me again. *"Little Thistle."* His sinister voice filled my head, taking me back to that night. *"We had so much fun. Don't you remember?"*

Flashes of his memories came next, ones where he held my wrists by my head and shoved himself inside me. I writhed and moaned and arched into the touch like I enjoyed it, like I wanted more. I'd been dreaming about Carter. I'd thought he was my star-crossed lover.

Holding back a sob, I visualized myself behind my castle tower again, forcing those wretched images out of my head, forcing him to retreat.

"Miri," came a feminine voice from my right. Ivy was still standing there with me, holding my hand in my head, if no longer in reality. I squeezed tighter, holding Carter's palm even harder. *"Miri, hang on to us. He can't hurt you anymore."*

I moved past the point of agony and straight into flaming rage.

How dare he take from us like that? How dare he violate me with no repercussions?

"It seems we are at an impasse." Alberich's lips pulled into a cruel smile, his gaze drifting to Ivy and Lex.

A tense moment passed, the anticipation so thick that it nearly electrified the air. Wisps of darkness licked at my face, rolling over my curls in a soft caress. I shook it off, grimacing against the icy fingers that tickled down my spine. I hated it, almost as much as I hated him.

Then, two things happened in quick succession.

Ivy called, "Miri!" and reached out for my hand. I turned to her just as a white blast flew out of the queen. The force hit me square in the chest, knocking me back, and just before I landed, I focused on Diana and Alberich lifting into the air like two fallen angels hellbent on destroying everything in their path.

21

CARTER

Hitting the ground on my back hurt, knocking all the air out of my lungs, and when I finally got my muscles to work again, I gasped and scrambled to my feet. I gaped at the sight in front of me, my mind almost unable to understand it.

Diana and Alberich hovered thirty feet in the air, their magic twisting together like the clouds in a hurricane, creating a force field around them that stretched as far as I could see in either direction. Dark tendrils swirled with the queen's pale counterparts, engulfing the ruins and the ground between them. A loud roaring sound whipped through the atmosphere, blowing the trees against each other, the crisp Faerie air hitting me in the face. If I couldn't see this, I'd swear a helicopter had landed right in front of me. But no, this was two pissed-off royal fairies taking it out on each other on their most hallowed ground.

The rest of the fairies had been blasted as far away as us, and now they pushed to their feet, their eyes as black as the others. But they weren't going for the circle of chaos, no. They were turning on each other. Clangs of metal from crashing swords echoed over the wind, and I moved out of the way of two fairies who had tackled another to the ground.

He'd entranced them all. He'd put them under some spell that made them fight among themselves.

The bastard!

We were the only ones left standing, the only ones in our right mind. I didn't know why he wasn't able to manipulate us the way he'd done to the others. If he tried, it didn't work. Perhaps the queen was protecting us. Or perhaps it was our magic shielding the effects of his. I thought back to Siobhan's insistence that it had to be us, that we would be the ones to end it. Now I understood what she meant.

But Ivy and Lex were on the *other* side of the whirlwind, and we'd either have to go around it or through it to get to them. I found Miri on the ground near me, scrambling on her hands and knees like she was looking for something. I kneeled next to her, grabbing her shoulders to try to pull her to her feet.

"No!" She shoved me away. "Help me find it!"

"Find what?" I held her face up to mine, cupping her chin so I could wipe the blood off her cheek. She must have hit her head when she fell, but it wasn't too serious. "Miri, we have to get to Ivy and Lex."

She said something back to me, but I couldn't hear it over the sounds of soldiers and royalty tearing each other apart. Miri kept searching, her features draped in alternating shadows and bright lights, making me feel like I was in some fucked-up rave.

"Miri!" I shouted again.

She found whatever she'd been trying to get and sagged in relief before pushing to her feet and showing me the bag containing the ruby dust.

"Come on, Romeo." She leaned in closer to my ear so I would hear what she said next. "Just like Lex said. We can do it." Miri glanced back at the swirling nightmare of magic in the distance, Lex and Ivy on the other side of the shield...on the other side of the veil. Ivy's features contorted into confusion while Lex talked at her with his hands, probably also trying to figure out how to get through.

The screams of the battling fairies around me grew louder, drawing my attention. Some of them tried to enter the force field, and the strength of it ripped them to pieces. Another one ran for it straight on and disintegrated the moment he crossed through. A few of the enthralled soldiers on the ground got caught up in it, exploding into dust.

When the rest of the bystanders realized they couldn't get inside or go around it, the front line backed up, but the storm grew bigger. They pushed into the human realm to keep from getting caught in it, others retreating farther into Faerie. The longer we waited, the more overwhelming their combined power became, and if we did nothing, it would eventually take over. How much damage could it do?

"We have to get to the other side," I said, tugging Miri over to the edge of the spiraling magic, the crackling energy nearly sending me back into the crowd with the rest of the fairies, but I squeezed her hand tighter and focused on Lex and Ivy.

"We can't get in." Miri stopped and winced, looking at the fairies that were still risking their lives to join the fight. "We have to throw it at him from here."

I couldn't explain how I knew this was the right thing to do, only that luck had been on my side this far, and it wouldn't abandon me now. I remembered that green mist last night, the one created out of our love for each other, the one that grew exponentially with each confession of adoration.

If they're like us, we're like them.

I visualized that emerald energy like a shield, like I could wrap it around my body, around the bodies of my lovers. It would protect us, it would give us strength. That was why it was still within us, why we still glowed with it. It flowed out of the center of my chest, coating my skin like armor before cascading to Miri behind me.

"Don't let go, okay?" I shouted at her.

She nodded, but I had no idea if she heard me. The thunderous boom of crashing energy might have blocked it out.

I pushed my other hand into the explosive mist, now twirling more violently around the two royals locked in its embrace. When I didn't lose an arm or disappear completely, I pushed in farther and the strength of the forest-green magic held, allowing me to take a step.

Then another. And another. The weight of their fight bore down on me from either side, suffocating in its intensity, like I'd suddenly been dragged thousands of miles below sea level. The pressure ached, pulsing and throbbing against my skin while I walked. It took eons to get through to the other side, and even then, the roaring did not stop. My hand clamped around Miri's, yanking her into the eye of the cyclone so hard, she tripped on the edge and stumbled into me. I caught her, my knees locking in place as I glanced around.

From inside, the sight was even more mesmerizing. Each royal's power had hit the other and launched skyward, arching over the middle to create a dome. Gale-force winds ripped around me, chapping my cheeks and making my eyes water, but I gave myself one heartbeat to admire its raw primal beauty. I had never seen such magnificence, and despite the dire circumstances, I believed I never would again.

"We need to get them," Miri said, our combined attention going to Ivy and Lex, who were still trying to get through the force field. We couldn't do this without them. We were stronger when we were together. We needed them to finish this. Their emerald shield did not radiate as powerfully as it did with me and Miri. I needed to help them. I needed to reach through the magic and tug them both inside with us.

"This way!" I pulled her over to our spouses, too focused on getting to them to realize Miri was scrambling for the ruby dust and chanting something too low for me to hear.

Ivy's fingertips were so close to the middle, so close to breaking the barrier. I dug deep for more of the power we'd generated between us, feeding the extension of it through my arm into my hand. I pushed against the fairy magic, knowing only I could do it, only I could rip it apart.

The pressure ached like a thousand splinters sliding into my skin, piercing my bones, but I kept going. We needed Lex and Ivy. *I* needed them.

"Ivy!" Her name came from the depths of my soul, as if by calling it out, I could will myself to get to them faster.

"Carter!" Her cry rattled through me, urging me on. I thought of all the times I'd called her Weeds, all the times I'd taken her and kissed her like our lives depended on it. I thought of my night with Lex in London, and the tiny moments in college when we'd stared at each other from across the room and *wanted.* Memories of California flashed through me, when Miri and I had shared our heartbreak and spilled our secrets like we'd found our twin flame in each other. The details of every time the four of us had loved and lost and loved again came barreling to the forefront, and all that we'd survived hit me next. I used that raw emotion brewing in my chest to shove the rest of the way to Ivy, finally wrapping my fingers around her wrist.

Once I had her, the vibrancy of their shared connection flowed through me, energizing what I'd just conjured, amplifying it to such an extreme that I yanked them through the wall with hardly any effort.

"*We have to stop them,*" Ivy said telepathically. "*Where's the ruby dust?*"

"*Miri's got it.*" Lex held up his free hand to shield his eyes from the queen's bright fury. "*Where'd she go?*"

"Miri!" I shouted, realizing the connection with her had been broken. While I worked to get to our spouses, she'd disentangled her hand from mine, the emerald energy thinning as it stretched between us. The ruby dust had fallen to sparkling nothing at my feet and Miri now hovered in the air just like the king and queen, a dark sword made out of the king's mist spearing through her chest.

"You thought you could use my magic against me?" Alberich's

voice amplified the pounding of my heart, my brain struggling to rationalize what I was seeing. "Little Thistle, I am so disappointed in you."

The sword withdrew, and Miri dropped to the ground like a limp fish. My chest clenched so hard, I thought I might throw up. Falling to my knees, I ignored the blood dripping from her mouth and nose, wiping it off so that I could see if she was okay.

"Miri!" I pulled her into my arms, ignoring Ivy's screams and Lex's panicked questions as they kneeled on either side of me. The fairy storm went on, loud and chaotic, drowning out all other sounds in my mind, all except the agony of watching my best friend, my lover, my spouse...my Juliet...get mortally wounded in front of me. "It's okay," I murmured, staring down into her wide, scared eyes while she sputtered to talk.

"Miri, no," Ivy said, gripping her hands. "No, no, no."

"You stupid woman." Lex growled, putting his hands on Miri's chest, trying to staunch the wound, but it was no use. "Why did you do that?"

Miri coughed and tried to say something, but the words died on her lips as she took one final breath and let it out on a wet sigh.

"I love you," I said, leaning down to press my lips to hers. "I love you, I love you, I love you."

When I glanced up, Ivy held her hands to her tear-stained cheeks, her eyes wide with horror. Lex's face had gone pale and his hands were covered up to the elbows in Miri's blood. I, too, had crimson all over my chest and arms and down the front of my pants.

I couldn't believe it. How had this happened? There wasn't supposed to be a sacrifice. I knew it in my bones. My luck told me so. It had never steered me wrong before, and I didn't believe it would now. This shouldn't have happened...This couldn't be real...

Unless...

I glanced up at the two royals, still duking it out four stories above us. The king had proven himself capable of fucking with people's minds, making them think things that weren't true, making them live inside their heads while he did whatever he wanted. Look at what he'd done to the battle maidens, to the *Fianna*.

What if this was all in my head? What if this was a dream or a fake vision planted there by the worst creature to ever walk either realm?

I pushed to my feet and wiped the tears from my face, apathetic to the smears of Miri's lifeblood that I left there. Walking to the place just under the king, I stared up at his vile, rotten form and willed that emerald energy back to me.

"Carter!" Ivy shouted, trying to run after me, but it was already too late.

I stuck my hand into the barrier again, grabbing at the dark mist with my own emerald energy, using our love and the power it gave us to bring him down.

Enough of this, now!

ENOUGH!

I bellowed the word in my head as I pushed our magic into the shield, screaming as it ripped from me in a devastating and all-consuming fury. Every molecule in my body burst into flames, and I wanted to pull my hand back to make it end, but no.

It wasn't real. None of this was real.

Once upon a time, I had made a promise to Miri that I would be the one to help her distinguish reality from her dreams. Now, I couldn't tell myself, and she was gone. I'd been forced to watch her die, and if I didn't do this, if I stopped now, I'd have to watch all of them die.

A sledgehammer hit me in the back, amplifying the anguish in my chest, radiating through to the other side.

I looked down to find a bright sword sticking out of my heart, matching the one that had been shoved inside Miri, obsidian and gleaming with my blood.

As I took a step back and turned to face Ivy, warm metallic liquid coughing up the back of my throat, I learned the horrifying truth.

This *was* very real...and we were going to lose.

22

LEX

My chest exploded into a thousand pinpricks of misery when Miri went down, but seeing Carter go shortly after her sent rage curling through my veins.

This isn't supposed to happen.

"No!" Ivy scrambled to Carter's limp form, but I didn't need to see him to know what had happened. The king had murdered two people I loved. I kneeled next to Ivy and grabbed Carter's hand, watching as the light drained from his brilliant indigo stare.

Those eyes had gazed up at me so many times with eternal warmth and sunshine. Without Carter Scott and Miriam Stuart in the world, there was no such thing as sunshine anymore. There was no air, no oxygen, nothing, and no one. I simply could not exist without these two people in my life.

How could she let this happen?!

The queen had said it would be my choice, my decision.

What the fuck is this?

Hot, angry tears spilled over my cheeks, and I watched as Ivy held Carter in her lap, rocking him back and forth while gut-wrenching sobs poured out of her. Miri's body lay lifeless and pale a few feet away, the permanent blush on her cheeks now faded to a waxy pallor. The spiraling white and black clouds twisted around us faster, more violently, urging on the storm brewing inside me.

"Give in to me, Alberich," Diana said. "Stop this madness."

"Look at what you've done, Diana!" His voice came louder and angrier, almost demonic in its metallic pitch. "Look at the carnage you've wrought! This is your doing."

Watching this maniacal motherfucker gut two of my beloveds hit me in the stomach, ripping apart my insides, a physical thing that nearly had me collapsing on that grass. But I had to keep going. We were supposed to be the strongest when we were together, but that didn't matter anymore. There was no more together. *Until the end.* That had been our promise.

This *was* the end.

I had loved Miri and Carter as dearly as I could for as long as I could, and now I would follow them wherever they had gone. Pushing to my feet, I wheeled on the queen, sparks of this newfound green energy licking off me in thick waves, tingling through the ends of my fingers, crackling with each step I took.

I couldn't manipulate it like Miri, and I couldn't wield it the way Carter had to pull us through. Up until last night, I didn't even know such a thing was possible. We were human. We weren't meant to have magic like this, but fuck it. *When in Rome, am I right?* And if these two assholes thought they could just kill my spouses with no repercussions, they had another fucking thing coming.

I stalked across that field like a villain out of a horror movie, covered in blood, stuffing my pathetic emotions deep down inside of my chest like I'd done for all of my pathetic life. I willed that icy exterior to cascade over me, cooling my rage so that I could think more clearly.

I had to get me and Ivy out of this. I had to fix it somehow.

I found Poppy squatting by a rock inside the vortex, her hands over her ears, a silent scream on her lips. A million things raced through my mind all at once. I could force her to take me back in time so I could prevent the king from taking my loved ones. I could make her teleport me to Siobhan, Donnelly, and Finn for help. But I landed on the worst option, the one that would reveal the monster in me.

I found an axe on the ground, perhaps dropped there by one of the *Fianna* during the initial blast, and I picked it up, closing the distance between Poppy and me with a few strides. Wrapping my fingers around her arm, I yanked her up and put the blade of my axe to her throat, staring up at the queen.

"Lex, no!" Poppy sagged in my hold, trying to get away from me, struggling against the weapon at her neck. I tightened my grip on her.

All of this mess started because of her, because of what she could do. We were right not to trust her. I lost Miri because of her. I lost Carter because of her. I would probably die because of her.

No.

"Diana!" I shouted, willing my magic around me, sucking up whatever remained of that green essence. "Diana!" My voice came out more mechanical that time, sounding like the king with its deep, sinister tones. "Stop this now, or I swear to all the fucking Gods, I will kill this changeling in front of you."

Alberich laughed, and the sound skated down my spine with a mix of horror and vindication.

"You see," he sneered. "Humans are all the same. Violent. Unpredictable. Do it, Alexei. Do it."

"Is this who you are? Murdering an innocent child in front of its adopted mother?" Diana's voice echoed inside my head while she spoke out loud to her husband. "Do not overlook your part in this, Alberich. All would be well if you would accept my terms."

"Accept mine," Alberich spat back. "It's time we reconcile, Diana. It's time we made peace."

"Bring them back," I said to Diana. *"Heal them, and I'll do whatever you want."*

"Lex!" Ivy's voice came from somewhere behind me, distant and overshadowed by the rush of my blood and Poppy's screams.

"Heal them?" Diana's high-pitched cackle was damn near insulting. *"Even I cannot bring back the dead."*

The lie hit me in the gut so hard and fast, it nearly knocked the wind out of me. Either she could do it or...they weren't dead. A spark of hope lit deep down inside, and I almost let Poppy go. But no, I had the leverage. Diana couldn't hold me off, fight her husband, and save Poppy at the same time.

"Don't lie to me, you fucking bitch!" The words spewed out of my lips like an avalanche from my personal stores of ice-cold fury. *"Tell me the truth! Can you bring them back?"* I said this last part through our mental connection, unwilling to let Ivy in on my plans.

"Come now, Alexei," Alberich taunted, using his magic to lash wisps of darkness out at both of us, but Diana blocked those with her corresponding white tendrils. "I took them from you. If you want them back, you must make a deal with me."

"You know what that requires," Diana chided, her tone patronizing and opportunistic. In our prior conversation, she'd said I was her counterpart, that she almost didn't let me go the first time we'd met. Whatever she saw in me had prompted her advice about this battle. In the end, it would be me who decided the outcome. *And here it is.*

She flashed mental images of the rest of my life at her side, living in Faerie as one of her consorts. She showed me what *their* life would be like, how Carter would father children with both Miri and Ivy, how they'd live at the cabin part-time and at Aberdeen the rest of the year. They'd grow old together, they'd die together, and I would miss it because I'd given myself to the fairy queen to ensure it happened. It wasn't what I originally had in mind, but if it meant Miri and Carter would survive, if it meant Ivy got to have a life with them... Fuck it. There were worse ways to go.

Reluctance squeezed my lungs as I refused to admit...perhaps I had been wrong. Perhaps there was a fate. Perhaps there was a destiny. The queen had known. Carter and Siobhan had known. I'd been the stubborn idiot that refused to admit it. But now, I no longer could. I had to reconcile what I knew about my existence with how it had all been wrong. *This…This* was the truth.

"I accept." I said the words and tossed Poppy to the ground, glancing over my shoulder when I heard the rush of inhale from Miri first and then from Carter.

They weren't lying on the ground, lifeless and rigid. They hadn't been stabbed; they weren't even dead. They pushed to their feet, completely revived and functional. I sighed, the weight of their loss lifting off my chest as I inhaled.

But my relief was short-lived.

"What did you do?" Ivy shoved my shoulders, her tearful eyes even more sorrowful. "What did you do?!"

"What I had to." I glared at her, steeling my jaw as I prepared myself for her challenge. We didn't have time for her to act like a pig-headed twat. We needed to move. The vortex had grown while we were fucking around, tearing up trees and decimating the ancient ruins. It had expanded past the veil, now encompassing parts of the human realm. *My* realm.

"You're a fucking idiot!" Ivy banged her fists on my chest, nearly knocking the wind out of me. "How could you do that?"

Carter ran over to us, his hand in Miri's, both of them as lucid and clear-headed as they were before any of this.

"What happened?" Miri shook her head.

"Did we…Did we die?" Carter's eyes searched mine for the truth, but there was no time to explain. Ivy knew what I'd done, pain echoed out of her eyes, squeezing my heart with desperation.

"Diana," Alberich taunted, tsking his teeth at her. "That's cheating."

"You forget your place, Alberich." Diana's commanding voice filled the space, cutting off any reply and reminding me we still had business left to handle. Just because I'd signed my soul over to the devil didn't mean we were out of the woods yet. The walls around us were nearly opaque now, and the other fairies had long since faded from view. "Look at you! Look at the monster you've become!"

They continued to bicker, but I'd lost my patience for this farce. It stopped being cute four years ago, and now, I was done with this fairy-tale bullshit.

23

IVY

Somewhere between my spouses dying and Lex accepting a demented deal with the fairy queen, reality seemed to slow down. By the time I realized Lex had an axe to Poppy's throat, my feet weren't moving fast enough. I couldn't get to him. I couldn't stop whatever he'd done that had brought Carter and Miri back.

This whole thing had been botched from the beginning, and now that we were standing in the center of it, I needed to finish it. My mind raced, all of the information we'd been told coming back to me.

"They can be stopped," Lex said, holding my gaze. "We have to do this together."

"The ruby dust didn't work." Miri shook her head, grabbing my hand on one side and Lex's on the other. Carter took the spot next to me, slipping his big palm into my own, and once the four of us were connected...*finally* connected...the energy flowed between us, bright and magnificent and omnipotent.

Carter's warmth cascaded up my arm, into my heart, and Miri's delicate blossoming frost came next, complementing the avalanche of Lex's ice-coated interior. All of it steamed against my raging inferno of iron turned to steel, radiating out of us in a massive

211

display of emeralds and jades and forest greens, all the colors of the woods at Midsummer.

It reminded me of everything we'd been through together, all the moments when our love had saved us.

"Alberich, please my darling," Diana roared, the wisps of her magic dwindling as his took over, strangling her energy, dimming its glory. "Please, remember us at our best."

That sparked a memory. I'd already sent the king away once at my wedding, when I'd claimed Mount Vernon as my own and demanded he leave. I'd been able to connect with his mind and access a part of him that he'd long since forgotten. I closed my eyes and saw it there, shimmering out of the depths of his being.

"*I have an idea,*" I said inside my spouses' heads, shoving my way further into their minds than I'd been before. Lex accepted me immediately, probably because I'd been there so many times, and Miri and Carter relented shortly after that. Their emotions rushed through me like a whirlwind of tangy panic and adrenaline-laced fear, but I used that as fuel.

I willed the green energy around us, the magic of Midsummer that had gifted us with the power to be here in the first place. I imagined the four of us standing inside Miri's castle walls, our fortress, our safe haven, holding hands with an unbreakable grip. We were wrapped together by more than skin and bone, our magic kept us permanently linked. Nothing and no one could separate us again, and as long as we were together, we were immortal. Alberich's dark swords couldn't penetrate our emerald shield or our stony foundation. We were forged in the fires of our love for each other, in the depths of our undeniable vow.

Only once I had Carter's support and Miri's acceptance, only once I knew Lex wouldn't fight me, only then did I lower the shield to the connection I'd forged with the king. His dark fury rushed at me, twisting and obsidian like the mist he threw at the queen, but it bounced off us, disintegrating into nothingness at our feet.

I surged forward.

He resisted, throwing up a thick mental cloud of magic. Its tension weighed us down and suffocated us despite how strong our walls had become. But I pushed through, using all the strength I had to shove inside.

My brain splintered, and a sharp dagger of pressure sliced through the center of my forehead, but I held Carter and Miri's hands tighter, using the energy they offered to ignore that pain, ignore it all, just keep fighting him, just keep going.

He was weaker than the last time I'd tried to crack through his mind, so the barrier between us vanished much quicker than I remembered, almost like he wanted me there. I didn't waste the opportunity. I rifled through his memories like a spider, twisting through his timeline faster than I had before.

Walking through the veil, knowing Diana would meet me there—

Toying with Ivette's siblings, entering their minds to make them believe whatever I wanted, planting scenes for them to play out—

Meeting with Poppy, going back in time, dark tendrils wrapping around the bow of a sailboat, screams dying in water as Marcus drowned—

The ache in my chest echoed in Lex's, and I gritted my teeth to go deeper, further back, past the time he'd spent in the human realm, past the fight with Diana in the first place. There was something hidden here, something he'd locked away a long time ago. I focused on the queen.

Her white light burst through the darkness, and suddenly, we were catapulted into her memories as well. Back before time and space, back before the war with the humans, back when they were young.

He had been beautiful, his jaw clean shaven, his eyes not yet so angry and soulless. He had once used his magic for creation, for breathing life into the planet and the world around him. Together with Diana, they'd built everything we'd ever known of Faerie. They'd created their community, and eventually, the one that had been destroyed when humans decimated their populations.

In this particular memory, they sat in front of a fireplace inside a small home with stone walls and uneven wooden planks for floors. They'd bathed in the same water we had at Midsummer and drank from the same enchanted wine, letting their most vulnerable emotions run wild between them. And now, they'd returned to their home to celebrate the evening in peace.

"I'll love you forever, Diana," he had told her, lifting her hands to his mouth so he could kiss every knuckle.

"I'll love you, too, Alberich." She leaned in to connect their mouths, and the flutter in his heart had nearly made him gasp. In all his years wandering this dreaded existence, he had never considered that he might feel this way about someone, that he might find his one true love and feel so completely consumed by her.

"Marry me," he said, leaning back to meet her gaze. She had looked so much younger then, but still as gorgeous and resplendent as she was today. "Be my queen. Share my magic with me, share my soul."

She smiled, and her eyes shimmered with tears as she nodded. "Yes. Yes, my love. Yes."

"Until the end," he'd whispered.

"Until the end," she'd replied.

He kissed her, his heart overwhelmed with pure, undiluted joy. He loved her so thoroughly, so deeply, he believed there would never come a moment when they would find themselves on opposite sides of a war, much less over a human child.

Once upon a time, Alberich had been compassionate and loving. He'd been gentle to everything—Diana, humans, other fairies. He had an affectionate heart.

Present-day Alberich balked against the memory, trying to shove us out of his mind by forcing his worst memories to the forefront.

Holding Miri down while she struggled and screamed, manipulating her mind to make her believe she liked it.

Relishing in the sounds of Marcus's dying gurgle.

Watching as Miri's parents took their last breaths, knowing he could do something to stop it but choosing not to.

That was all it took to draw out that vengeful side of Miri. I sensed what she planned to do before she did it, and I couldn't think of a reason to stop her.

"Do it," Carter said telepathically, confirming luck was on our side.

"Ivette," Alberich teased, "do you think you can make me sentimental? Do you think I could be that easily fooled?"

Miri pulled on the magic to gather the ruby dust, but I kept my focus on distracting the king, ignoring the shimmy through our bond as it vibrated with resonance, with the same thing that gave us our gifts.

"No," I said inside his mind, inside all of our minds. *"But you are a fool all the same."*

Alberich gasped as the ruby dust hit him in the face, bewildering him, perverting the connection between our minds as I slammed the stone walls back up. I knew then what I had to do, what I should have done from the very second Miri called for the ruby dust. Lex's ability to identify a lie surged through us, saying the king was bluffing and had been this whole time. Carter's luck clenched inside our souls, seeming to shout that it was the right moment, that we needed to make our play *now*. It had taken all four of our gifts to do this. I channeled that energy into my next words.

"Suffer in solitude, suffer in silence, only then will you know the pain you have caused."

The spell landed on the king like a sledgehammer, and the storm around us dissipated, drifting away on the wind. Alberich dropped to the earth as the sun shone through the clouds, illuminating the destruction of Faerie in the bright light of midday. Holding onto my spouses, I pulled on their love for me, their love for our love, and I drew that power deep inside me.

The king pushed to his feet and looked up at us with bewilderment in his eyes, his mouth hanging open, his hair windswept around him. Diana lowered to the ground gracefully, her radiance dimmed for how much she had fought, but still holding that intelligence that made her the queen.

She opened her mouth to speak, but I'd heard enough.

This fairy-tale nightmare had to end, and no matter what she had to say, I didn't care.

"All of Faerie, hear me now." My voice dropped several octaves as my words echoed over the space, sounding like they came from the depths of my soul. Warm, sticky liquid dribbled down my cheeks and over my lips, tasting like copper, and I realized my eyes and nose were bleeding from the exertion. I pushed harder. "I am Ivette Washington, and the human realm is *mine*. I claim it as my own, and so long as my blood lives, you are not welcome. Be gone from this realm. Be gone, now, and never return."

The weight of the spell tore off out of me, potent and overwhelming, sucking the rest of the magic from our connection. It flowed from my molecules in thick emerald waves, pulsing with the rage and fury that had been building inside me for four years. This had been only a game for them, a grand nothing in the vastness of their eons, but for me, it had screwed with every aspect of my life.

This is the sacrifice. Blocking them out would mean losing Siobhan, Finn, and Donnelly. We would never see them again—never see *Poppy* again. Anyone stuck on that side would forever be in Faerie, and whoever was on the human side would never see Faerie again. But it had to be this way. As I said the words, the rightness of this moment settled in every molecule.

I met Siobhan's soulful brown eyes, a huge grin on her face. She mouthed the words, "Well done," before she faded away. Finn and Donnelly soon faded as well, the rest of Faerie dimming while I pulsed with our magic, casting every last bit of it out of us, pushing them into their realm to deal with their mess.

The veil disappeared. It closed permanently.

Then, with the relief that came with winning a long-earned

battle, I dropped to my knees, planted my fingers in the dirt, and passed out.

24

LEX

What the fuck?

That was the first thing I thought when I woke up.

What the actual fuck?

The sun hit me square in the eyes, and a blinding, splitting headache shot straight through to the other side. I winced, squinting as Ivy's ginger hair came into focus. My arm was draped over her waist and my fingers intertwined with a heavy palm that felt like Carter's on the other side, their foreheads touching. Miri had an arm over Carter's ribs and her hand was latched on to Ivy's.

Fucking hell.

Everything hurt. People say they feel like they got hit by a train the morning after doing hard drugs, but I really did. Every nerve ending I had screamed when I moved. I disentangled my hand from Carter's and sat up, running my palms over my face to try to figure out where I was or what we'd taken.

Ecstasy, maybe? A shit ton of cocaine? My head pounded like the comedown from a serotonin overdose. I'd probably feel like hell for another twelve hours.

Wait...

No.

This was a memory. I'd already been here. I'd already done this. I reached for my pants, grabbing my pack of cigarettes to light one as I scooted myself so I leaned back against the mossy stone walls. We were in the ruins, the same run-down, decaying structure where we'd spent a night and a day under the influence of fairy magic. Judging by how much my body ached, I might say we'd done that again.

Flashes of the last few hours raced through my brain.

The battle with the fairy king and queen.

Watching Carter and Miri die right in front of me.

Hearing Ivy's anguished cries.

Making the deal with the queen to bring them back.

Knowing, deep down, only I could make that sacrifice and go through with it.

"Shit," Ivy said, groaning as she rolled over. "What time is it?"

Carter stretched, kissed Ivy on the mouth, and ran his hands over Miri's arm, rolling so he could give her a peck on her nose. "Maybe nine, maybe ten? Judging by the sun."

"This is a memory," I said, causing all three of them to look at me.

"What?" Ivy scrunched her eyebrows together. "What do you mean?"

"*Make your goodbyes,*" came Diana's voice, seemingly on the wind. "*Alexei must stay.*"

"Stay?" Miri sat up and winced, running her hands over her face.

"What is that supposed to mean?" Carter gaped, shifting his wide, terrified eyes to meet mine. "Why do you have to stay?"

"Oh, no," Miri's sorrowful tone split my chest in two. "Alexei, my prince, what did you do?"

Ivy's burning steel gaze turned to me, nearly incinerating me where I sat. I inhaled deeper on my cigarette, praying for the nicotine to soothe the desperation rising in my chest. Everything in me wanted to lie to them, to keep one last secret for myself, but I couldn't do that. This was the last time I'd ever see them again, and I didn't want to spend a moment being dishonest.

"You two were dead," I said, blinking back the tears that threatened to spill over. My chest burned, my heart throbbed, and when I looked into Ivy's eyes, I saw echoes of my own pain reflected back at me. "I did what any of us would have done."

"What?" Carter pushed to his feet, reaching for his gym shorts to put them on and slide them up his long legs. "What's going on?"

"I gave myself to the queen in exchange for your lives." Finishing my smoke, I stabbed it out and rose to my feet, likewise getting dressed, though it didn't matter anymore. They had seen me naked a thousand times, and this was in our heads. Any second, we'd wake up on that wretched battlefield—bruised, broken, and alone.

No one said anything, only stared at me with heartache pouring out of their souls while they processed this information.

"For how long?" Miri's voice sounded weak but hopeful.

I didn't answer because I honestly didn't know. That wasn't part of the agreement, but I assumed indefinitely. Or...until I could find a way to get out of it. Something banged around in the back of my mind, urging me to pay more attention, but at that moment, all I wanted to do was relish in these last few moments with them. I didn't know how much longer we had, and I couldn't waste a second.

"You didn't have to do that." Ivy's voice cracked when she spoke. "You shouldn't have done that."

"It's too late, X," I said. "It's already done."

She closed her eyes, big, angry tears spilling down her cheeks while that beautiful flush crept up her neck and into her face. I watched the X appear over her pulse, delightful in how it still rattled right through me.

"I will come for you," she said, grabbing the back of my neck to bring our foreheads together. "I won't stop coming for you."

My stomach churned as I imagined Ivy, old and gray, hunched

over her desk, researching lore to figure out how to bring me back. "Don't be ridiculous. The veil is closed. You ended it yourself."

"No," she insisted.

"Listen to me," I continued, yearning for more time to tell her everything I'd always left unsaid between us. I settled on the most important. "Don't spend your life looking for me, okay? You go back to DC. You marry Miri and Carter. You pop out a bunch of little meathead gingers."

"Lex, stop," Ivy said through a broken sob.

"Don't let your mother have control over you ever again. You're stronger than her. You live your own life, understand?"

Ivy shook her head and kissed me, hard and deep. "Didn't you hear me? I'm not going to let the fairy queen have you. I claimed you first. You're mine."

"X, I knew what I was doing when I made the deal." I disentangled myself from her and stepped back, giving her one last kiss. "This is about me and Diana. Not you, not any of you."

Ivy reluctantly hugged herself, backing away so that Miri could rush into my arms, wrapping hers around my waist, pulling me close to her. Flowers and gardenia at midnight flooded my senses, and I inhaled her floral scent, praying I never forgot it. She sobbed into my chest, holding me tighter, digging her nails into my back. "It was supposed to be me, you bloody idiot."

"No, Princess." I put my hands on either side of her chin and tilted her face up to mine, leaning down to press my lips against hers. "It was going to be me from the beginning."

The man I'd been in this memory, the man of four years ago, he would have given anything to trade spots with his brother. The twenty-two-year-old version of Lex Fairfax would have laid his life down a thousand times if it meant that Marcus had gotten to live, gotten to be the one that married Ivy. In the four years since, I'd found a love and devotion that few ever got to experience...and I had it times three. It was worth the sacrifice. Now, I understood true adoration on a fundamental, unconditional level, and given the chance, I would have lived it all over again just to make the same choice.

"Please don't let some antiquated idea of family loyalty keep you from your dreams." I kissed the top of Miri's head, drifting down to her soft, perfect mouth when she looked up at me. "You deserve to be happy, so be happy."

"How am I supposed to do that without you?" Miri stepped back, wrapping her arms around Ivy's waist and tucking her head under the ginger's chin. I sighed, knowing they would find strength in each other.

I turned to Carter, who had his hands on his hips, staring at me with bloodshot eyes, wet streaks running down his cheeks.

"No," he said.

"Yes." I held my arms out. "Get in here. Tell me you love me."

"There isn't supposed to be a sacrifice," he said. "We are supposed to go home together. You—" His voice broke and he cleared his throat to try to hide it. "You made me a promise."

I nodded and rubbed the back of my neck, knowing I wouldn't be able to hold up my end of it after all. "I hope you can forgive me, Chicago. I did save your life."

"My life?" Carter let out a sardonic laugh and hung his head. "What is my life without you in it? What are any of our lives without you?"

"You'll have each other." It was hardly a consolation. If it had been any of them, if it were me on the other end of this, I wouldn't drop it. I'd fight harder than Ivy. I'd find some way to get the queen to transfer the deal to me instead.

"What about the gift, huh?" Carter sneered. "We can't be apart."

"We blew our load on the big guy," I said. "The gift is gone."

"How do you know that?" Ivy's choked tone nearly buckled my knees.

"We said until the end." I forced myself to take a deep breath, to steady the pounding in my heart. "This is the end."

"No," Ivy cut in. "Stop saying that. I claimed the realm and everyone in it. I claimed you. You belong to me."

I smiled, warmth settling in my gut to hear her say that. If the Ivy from this memory could see her now, she'd be pink with disbelief. I snickered to myself at the thought, but a sudden tension in my gut interrupted my sentiment. We were almost out of time. Diana had come to take me, and these were literally my last fucking words to them. I had to make them good.

"Carter, you made me a promise, too. Don't forget it."

My physical body stirred, and I was seconds away from opening my eyes to a foreign realm with fairies I barely knew. I memorized the way they looked and how I felt at that moment, with nothing but deep, abiding affection for these three amazing humans.

"I love you all. And for the love of fucking God, take care of each other, yeah?"

Perhaps sensing it was almost time, Carter rushed toward me, pulling me into his arms with a deep kiss on my lips. I inhaled his woodsy sandalwood scent, letting the softness of his lips yank me under.

I closed my eyes on that deep shade of indigo, and when I opened them again, I was alone.

25
MIRI

I woke in the forest. My entire body ached. The joints in my fingers and toes cracked as I sat up and glanced around, hoping to find Lex on the other side of me, hoping our farewell hadn't been real.

But I only found Carter and Ivy huddled together about a meter away. She kneeled on the ground, leaning into his shoulder while they both sobbed.

"I can't believe he did this," she said. "There has to be a way back. There has to be a way to get to him."

I shoved my fingers into the dirt, closing my eyes and willing the life energy of the plants around me to grow, but they didn't respond. I listened for the trees, praying I might hear their whispers, but nothing came. Only the sounds of my spouses' tears and my own racing heart echoed through my mind. Lex, of course, had been right. Our connection to fairy magic had faded away, and whether that was because we'd cast ourselves out or because we'd spent it on the fairy king, I'd never know.

Pushing onto my knees, I crawled to Ivy and took her hands. The rush of connection that usually came from touching my wife was noticeably absent, and when I looked down at our joined palms, the scars were gone.

Our physical manifestation of the oath we'd taken, *Until the end,* had disappeared. In its place was clear, unblemished skin.

I grabbed Ivy's face, holding her cheeks so I could stare into her eyes. "It's over, my love. He wanted it this way. We need to go home."

"We can't leave him, Miri." She scrunched her eyebrows and narrowed her steel gaze. "We need to go back."

I would have sat there and argued with her for the rest of eternity if that was what it took, but footsteps cut through our anguish, and a familiar voice made me stand up.

"You all right, little coz?" Edward rushed toward me, throwing his arms around my shoulders to pull me into a big hug. "Bleeding Christ, have I got a proper story to tell you."

Jon and Kit walked a few paces behind him, their faces lighting up when they saw Ivy. The three Washington siblings hugged, and Lizzie leaped into Carter's arms, crying while she hugged her big brother.

"Fucking hell." Edward put me down and stepped back to run his hands over my face. "You look like shite."

His ginger hair stood on end around his head, caked with almost as much mud and grime as was on his face. His emerald eyes shimmered with emotion, making his golden-tanned skin even more blush.

"You look like you've spent too much time in the bogs." I brushed a piece of grass off his face, and his lips broke into a smile. For half a heartbeat, I'd forgotten what we'd lost. I'd forgotten my prince of darkness had given himself up so that we could have this reunion.

"There has to be another veil," Ivy said, returning my focus to the present. "Between all of us, we can find it. We can go through it and—"

"Ivy, you claimed the entire human realm and everyone in it," Carter said. "That includes the other veils, too."

She looked crestfallen but resolute, her defiant chin jutting out as a rebuke to Carter's logic.

"Let's regroup, okay?" I said. "We'll go back to our room and—"

"No," Ivy said, glancing in the direction of where the entrance to Faerie had once stood. "No, he wouldn't stop looking for me, and I won't stop looking for him."

Carter and I exchanged worried glances, but it was Kit who finally broke through to her.

"Hey, hey, hey." She grabbed Ivy's face and rubbed her thumbs over her cheeks. "We'll find him, okay? I promise. But we're exhausted now, and we can't pour from an empty cup. We need rest."

"Diana won't hurt him," I added. "Remember, she said we were honored guests. She'll keep him safe until we can save him. Siobhan, Finn, Donnelly...they'll protect him."

Ivy didn't like it, and honestly, I didn't either. But I didn't see how we had another choice.

With our hearts heavy, we returned to Killwater, only to discover the town repaired to the way it had been before Beltane. People bustled around, completing their business like they weren't just in the woods devouring each other a day ago. When we charged our cellphones, we realized we had been gone for two months. Today was Midsummer, and that seemed appropriate given that was when all of this started. It had to end where it began.

We went back to the same bed-and-breakfast we'd stayed in the last two times we'd been here. Bill and Keely were surprised to see us but welcomed us all the same.

"You look like you've been through hell and back again," Bill said, handing us keys to a few rooms.

"Something like that," Carter quipped, taking one before handing the others to Edward and Kit to sort out.

"Will there be a Midsummer celebration tonight?" Ivy asked. "Out in the woods?"

I knew where her mind was going. She thought we could go back and try to find the fairy realm that way.

Bill glanced between us, perhaps seeing more than our appearance, and raised his eyebrows. "By the looks of ya, I'd say your days out in the woods are over. Wouldn't you agree?"

Ivy did not, and perhaps I'd always been a romantic at heart because I wanted to believe my gut feeling was wrong. I wanted to think we'd go back into the forest and find fairies dancing around bonfires with flowers in their hair and ambrosia on their lips.

But we didn't. After a day of fitful rest and passionate deliberation, we snuck into the forest at twilight, the peach haze of the darkening sky not nearly as vibrant or beautiful as I remembered from four years ago. We wandered our tired, achy limbs down the trail that led to the valley, and my heart raced when I heard drums in the distance.

Maybe we'll get lucky. Maybe all is not lost.

We crested the hill, but we did not see large flames raging in the distance. There were no fairies and barely any townsfolk, only a small gathering huddled around a tiny campfire. No more than thirty people sang and chanted, banging on tiny drums as they recited their ancient hymns. But there was no magic in the air. No one handed us bouquets and condoms and wine. Compared to four years ago, this hardly ranked as a party, much less a celebration the way we'd known it.

"No," Ivy murmured before running down the hill. "No. This isn't right. This isn't—"

My heart sank because I knew Faerie and everyone in it were gone forever. There would be no Midsummer festival, never again.

"Weeds," Carter said, taking off after our wife, but I stood there with my arms wrapped around my midsection, struggling to pull air into my lungs.

Some of the locals called to Ivy as she burst through the middle of their ceremony, but she didn't stop to talk to them. She took off into the woods in the same direction as we'd headed on Midsummer and Samhain. But I knew what she'd find.

There was nothing here for us. There was no Lex, no Siobhan, no fairy queen to bargain with.

My prince of darkness was truly gone, and I slumped in the grass to cry.

"You deserve to be happy. So be happy."

How was I supposed to do that without him? Perhaps the gift was gone, but my love for him started long before that. Memories of the first time I'd met Lex floated to the front of my mind, when he'd been an eighteen-year-old blue blood with a chip on his shoulder and everything to prove. He'd want to give the finger to the world, and in his own way, I supposed he'd never stopped doing that...not even now.

Sometime later, Carter and Ivy found me, tears staining their cheeks, eyes red and swollen.

"It's not there," Ivy said as she kneeled in front of me, her voice hoarse and cracked. "The veil is gone."

"I know, my love." I grabbed her face to kiss her, but even in our despair, I sensed the end approaching. We could spend our lives searching these woods and never have anything to show for it. If we did that, Lex's sacrifice would be a waste. He didn't want that.

We went back to our room, but we didn't have much to say. What *was* there to say? We'd each lost a love of our life, and while we still had each other, it wasn't the same without our king.

WE STAYED in Killwater as long as we could. Kit, Lizzie, Jon, and Edward went home, but my beloveds and I threw ourselves into research. Ivy held her mother off by simply not answering the phone, and Carter had figured out how to circumvent the rest of his tour.

Edward made my excuses to our grandmother, but over the last few days, she'd gotten quite insistent that I return to Kensington presently.

I sat in the Killwater College library, staring at Ivy while she flipped through pages of some dusty old tome. She hadn't showered in days, her hair fraying out at all angles from a messy bun on the back of her head. She never slept. She barely ate. She'd lost weight in the four weeks since Midsummer, and she didn't have it to lose at the beginning. This wasn't because of a magical separation like Solstice. No, this was from losing Lex...her counterpart...her companion since birth. Not that I could blame her. It was all I could do to bring myself to get out of bed every morning.

But I couldn't go on like this. *We* couldn't go on like this.

"Here," Ivy said, pointing to tiny words that had long since faded to time. "To bestow her gratitude is to show her favor. A kindness done is a kindness earned."

"What do you think it means?" Carter ran a hand over his face and took a sip of coffee. He, too, looked terrible. Bags hung under his eyes, and his hair had grown unkempt. He'd also hardly slept in days, and when he did, he'd wake up shouting for our husband like his nightmares were worse than reality. If he dreamed about Lex, I imagined they were. At least in unconsciousness, they were reunited. In this reality, Lex was a gaping hole in our hearts that would never heal, never scar over, never go away.

We were hardly taking care of ourselves. How in the world did we think we would find him like this? We were running on fumes.

"Don't spend your life looking for me, okay?"

His voice haunted me. I heard it on repeat in my head. I heard it on the wind, when the warmth of the sun faded into the chill of the moon and the nighttime animals made themselves vocal. My prince of darkness had wanted us to move on. He'd wanted us to be happy.

We weren't happy.

And what exactly were we looking for? A way into a realm we had permanently shut off? We could search until we were dead and never find anything substantial. To most of the world, fairies were myth. Legends. Bloody hell, we had researched for two years between Midsummer and Samhain, and it wasn't until Siobhan showed up that we understood anything at all.

We were so utterly fucked and rolling in denial. But to stop would admit defeat, and Ivy had never been defeated by anyone. She wouldn't stop now, and she'd drag both Carter and me down with her if she had to.

"I think it means that the queen only gives her thanks when she knows she owes the other person something," Ivy said. "To show her favor."

"It could mean favor as in favorite," Carter said, scratching his stubble. He hadn't shaved in weeks, and even if I liked a man with facial hair, I'd never known Carter to have any. It showed a careless-ness he'd never before exuded. We were stretched at the seams.

"Or it could mean favor as in...owing someone a favor," Ivy said, hope filling her voice.

I scoffed and shook my head, letting out a sad laugh. Both of them looked at me.

"What?" Ivy said, raising her eyebrows in disbelief.

"This is pointless, my darling," I said, slamming my book closed. "All of this is pointless."

"How so?" Her eyes turned molten, equal parts furious and wounded. "Do you think trying to get Lex back is pointless? That his sacrifice for us was pointless?"

She was goading me. She wanted me to fight back, to argue with her the way Lex would have. But I didn't have the energy. We weren't complete without him, and it was time we stopped trying to be. There we were, on the wrong side of a war that had nothing to do with us. We'd ended it for humankind, and given I'd reset the king to his default setting, I suspected we wouldn't have to deal with him again.

That was the end, and there was nothing more to fix. I had died and come back to life, and because of that, we'd never see Lex again. That type of magic always required a sacrifice, all the lore had been quite sure about that. I didn't remember dying. I barely remembered being stabbed through the chest, which made me question my life in ways I'd never considered before. I'd spend the rest of my breathing days trying to unravel it.

But I'd never do that if I never moved on. It hurt me to think about it, but I *had* been thinking about it for days...maybe longer. We were wasting our time here. Lex would never be free from the fairy queen unless she wanted him to be, and we'd never get into Faerie again.

"Okay, enough for today," Carter said, shutting his book before grabbing Ivy's hand. "Let's go back to Bill's. It's getting late. We could use some sleep."

But none of us slept very well that night. In the weeks since Midsummer, we barely talked unless it was about finding Lex, and I just...I hurt too much to do it again the next day and the day after that and on and on until forever.

I couldn't do it anymore.

I knew what I had to do, even if it killed us, even if it made them so angry with me that they never wanted to see me again. Perhaps that would be best. Perhaps they were a bad habit. Cold turkey had always been my favorite way to quit.

Better make it quick.

"I have to go home now." My heart ached to say it, but I saw no other way. I had wanted to stay with them, I'd wanted to throw my royal title away for my beloveds. I'd even decided that was what I planned to do before all of this. But now...now we were broken and worse yet, there were no pieces of us to put back together. What we used to have simply died out there on that battlefield.

"Don't do this, Miri." Carter sighed and brushed a finger under his puffy eye. "Not after everything we've been through. We need each other, maybe more now than we ever did. You're just tired. We'll regroup tomorrow and—"

"No. Enough of this." I took a deep breath and whispered a quiet, "I'm sorry, Ivy, but Lex didn't want this for you. He didn't want this for any of us."

"Don't talk about him like he's dead." Her voice broke as she said the words.

"He's been gone for weeks," I said. "If he could come back to us, he would have done it by now."

"There's got to be a way—"

"Stop doing this to yourself, my love." I brushed the back of my knuckles down her cheek, wiping away a tear. "Enough now. Enough."

No one said anything after that. Ivy rolled onto her other side and cried herself to sleep. Carter clenched his eyes shut and breathed through sobs until Ivy's whimpers softened into slow, deep breaths. And I got up.

After everything we'd been through, after all we'd already done for each other, I couldn't bear to say yet another goodbye. So after I dressed and gathered my things, I stood at the doorway to take one last look at them, knowing in my bones this was right.

Ivy's steel gaze crept open just as I turned to leave, glaring at me from her spot on the edge of the bed. She didn't move to stop me, nor did she open her mouth to tell me to stay. It wouldn't matter if she did. Though I loved her more than life itself, I needed time. I needed space.

I wanted to tell her I loved her, that I would never forget her, but even those words would fall flat. What was love, after all, compared to what we'd been through? What was love but chemicals and hormones designed to trick people into caring, only to have the rug pulled out from under them? What was a broken heart compared to duty and honor?

What the four of us had surpassed a silly, stupid thing like love years ago. We were the same soul existing in four bodies, and now that a quarter of us was gone, our combined life force was a leaking sieve with no plug to save it, least of all for a spoiled princess who'd already had her life planned out for her.

I might as well return to my sullen castle and live out my remaining days as peacefully as I could. So, with all of that weighing heavily on me, I turned to the door, opened it, and left my soul in Killwater with the two people who would always own it and the prince who'd sacrificed it all to make sure they could.

ACT V

If we shadows have offended,
Think but this, and all is mended,
That you have but slumbered here
While these visions did appear.
-Puck, Act V, Scene II

26

MIRI
SIX WEEKS LATER

"Why didn't you tell me this when it happened?" Edward crossed his legs and took another sip of tea, his bright green eyes narrowing suspiciously at me from across the table. I'd hired a private jet to take me back to England, and now we sat in my rooms at Kensington for our daily afternoon tea.

After we disappeared together for nearly three months, Gran had been loathe to let either of us out of her sight again. Edward had officially moved into the rooms next to mine, and now that I could finally talk about Killwater without sobbing, I had agreed to tell him the entire story. I'd started with meeting Ivy at boarding school and confessed all of it, right up until Edward had been taken the day of the Washington-Fairfax wedding.

He had listened, promising to tell me what he had experienced while his mind had been taken over by the king.

"Would you have believed me?" I took a drink of my chamomile and smiled, watching as he squinted in deep concentration.

"No, I suppose not—not until I'd lived the experience myself." He sighed and shook his head. "Honestly, Miri, don't you think you're being a tad ridiculous?"

I scoffed and balked at the suggestion. "How so?"

"It's obvious you miss them terribly."

"Bleeding hell, not this again."

"Yes, this again." Edward reached across the table to take my hand, squeezing my palm in solidarity. "You can't marry the prince of Monaco."

"Well, it's entirely too late for that, isn't it?" The wedding had been set for two weeks from now, and there would be no delaying it any longer. Because I'd run off so many times, the prince had gotten impatient with my flightiness. Now, he insisted on having my name attached to his as soon as possible. I didn't have a choice. I never had.

I'd be the royal princess consort of Monaco in a fortnight, and damn the consequences.

It didn't matter that I closed my eyes and all I thought about was them. It didn't matter that they haunted my dreams, and every night, I was back at those ruins with Lex, Ivy, and Carter. I loved them, I did, but this was about more than love. This was about duty and honor and—

Bloody hell.

Even I didn't believe my propaganda anymore. Compared to dying and coming back to life, none of this mattered. Compared to losing Lex, this was a trivial game. Hell, I even missed Poppy. She'd betrayed us at the end and sold our family members to the king for her own purposes, but I had loved her. The loss of her amplified what had already been there.

I thought again about the fury in Ivy's gaze when I left, how angry she'd been when I turned to go. She wouldn't want me back. Not now. Not after I left them the way I had.

No. No, it was the right thing to do. I couldn't go on like that. Lex didn't want us to. He wanted us to be happy.

At times like this, when I questioned every decision I'd ever made, I could almost hear his snide, sarcastic voice whispering, *Are you happy? Does all this make you happy?*

I feared the answer was no and always would be for as long as I stayed away from my beloveds.

"Please, distract me," I said, cutting off that line of thought. "You were going to tell me about your experience."

"Oh...uh." Edward's cheeks turned an uncharacteristic shade of rosy pink, the tips of his ears damn near crimson. "There's not much to tell, I'm afraid."

I narrowed my eyes at that. "You were under the king's mind control for nearly two weeks. Surely, there's something."

"It was like...an alternate reality. Like we were living as normal people."

"We?"

"Katherine and me." Edward cleared his throat and took another sip of tea, distinctly avoiding my gaze.

"Katherine?"

"Kit," he corrected. "Though, I much prefer her full name."

"I didn't realize you had opinions about her name." I raised my eyebrows at him.

"Miri"—Edward ran his fingers over his forehead and scowled, glancing out the window to the gardens below—"we were living together for quite some time."

Uh-oh. That sounded ominous.

"How long?"

He winced before looking back at me. "I can't be sure."

"What do you mean you were living together?"

Edward's lost expression reminded me of when we were children and his first dog had passed away from old age. He seemed scared and unsure, devoid of his usual confident swagger. "We were room-mates, I suppose."

"And?"

He opened his mouth, struggling to find the words, and before he could say anything more, the doors to my sitting room opened and a steward walked through to announce a visitor.

"Her Royal Highness Elizabeth, the queen consort of England." He bowed before standing aside so Gran could push her way through.

"Oh my dears, my dears," she said, giving me a gentle smile as she walked closer. "I've just heard the most wonderful news."

"Oh?" I raised my eyebrows, expecting celebrity gossip or word from Edward's elder brother on his annual world tour.

Gran looked at me with her bright blue gaze, curling her lips into an excited smile. "Yes, Reginald has decided to arrive early. He'll be here the day after tomorrow."

"Oh." I loathed this type of update the most.

"Don't be so glum," she said. "Your marriage will be the highlight of the summer. Classically impromptu. We'll do it in Aberdeen to give it a vintage ambiance."

She meant secret. After the gossip surrounding Ivy and me, she didn't want to make it seem like Reginald was my cover-up, though that was precisely what he would be.

I hardly cared about being the princess of Monaco or my upcoming nuptials. If it weren't for everything else that came with it, the place among my family and a chance to restore my father's name, I would have taken Carter up on all the times he'd asked me to move to the US and marry him instead.

Of course, that ceased to be a possibility when I left. I hadn't heard from either of them in weeks, but I preferred it this way. The separation didn't chafe like it used to. I didn't lack for sleep nor did I waste away like some invalid on death's doorstep. The magic had truly left us, but with it went my last bit of hope. I no longer enjoyed the sunrise. I found no pleasure in decadent foods. I no longer found anything joyful about the world around me. At night, when I was my most lonesome, I stared at the moon and swore I heard my prince of darkness calling out to me. I'd become pathetic, and I had no desire to change it.

Likewise, Edward had turned equally somber and morose. Since we'd been home, he hadn't gone out to his usual nighttime haunts, nor had he paraded his retinue of slags through his rooms. We had both been irrevocably altered by what had happened on Beltane, and nothing Gran could throw at either of us would make much impact.

"Thank you, Gran," I managed when she'd stopped rambling and looked at me for a response.

"Do try to cheer up before he arrives, yes?" She sighed and pinched my cheeks the way women used to do when trying to add color to their faces. "No one wants to marry a corpse."

Edward snickered, causing Gran to snap her attention his way.

"And you," she said, narrowing her piercing gaze. "Have you made up with the duchess of Hanover?"

He groaned and rolled his eyes. "Granny, please."

"Don't destroy this match, Edward." She tsked her teeth at him, reminding me of all the times we'd gotten into trouble as children. "It took a great deal to get her parents to agree, especially after all of your...*indiscretions.*"

"I am perfectly capable of finding my own bride, thank you."

"Then why have you not done so?" She raised her eyebrows.

Edward made a weak attempt at an excuse by gesturing vaguely to me and waving his hand around. "I've been caring for my little cousin, you know? She's a bit more work than she looks."

"Tut!" Gran shook her head and took a deep breath. "You'll be married by the end of next year. End of discussion." She was still muttering about her ungrateful grandchildren after she'd waltzed through the room back into the hallway. The steward shut the door behind her, and I glanced at my cousin with a thousand questions on the tip of my tongue.

"Have you talked to Katherine since—" Since you woke up in the Irish forest? Since you came out of a never-ending dream? Since you stopped being trapped by the king of fairies?

"No." He shook his head. "What is there to say? It wouldn't work out between us."

"Well, that's not very optimistic, is it?"

"Hmm." He sat his teacup down and put his elbows on the table, a very ungentlemanly thing to do, but it gave him the advantage when he leaned in and narrowed his brilliant hunter-green gaze on me. "You're the one to talk. When was the last time you spoke to your wife or your husband?"

I scoffed. "I'm not married. Not yet, anyway." The words tasted vile in my mouth after all these years of saying I'd been wed to three people at the same time. But I wasn't. I didn't have the scars on my hands. I didn't have the gift. Whatever we'd done on Beltane had reversed the magical tie that bound us together. Now, Carter and Ivy could be together untethered, and I'd marry Reginald just like I always should have.

"Miriam," Edward said, a rumble in his deep tone informing me of his great displeasure with my behavior. "Do you hear yourself?"

"Edward, I'm fine."

He snorted out a laugh. "Fine? Yes, you're so fine that all you do is mope around this bloody castle like Henry VIII's ghost. Will I find you in the showers next?"

Laughter bubbled up my chest and over my lips, and I shoved his shoulders while I tried not to cry. "Hush!"

"Will I see you lurking under the maid's mattresses, trying to lick their feet?"

Hysterics took me over, and for the first time in months, I found myself grateful for one thing. If I had to have a kindred spirit stuck in this royal hellhole with me, I was overjoyed it was Edward.

Perhaps he had a point. Perhaps I'd been too emotional the day I left them. Perhaps going with no contact had been more separation than necessary. Perhaps I'd made a terrible mistake, and now I'd come too far down the rabbit hole to fix it.

I would have to marry Reginald, if only to save my pride.

"You deserve to be happy. So be happy."

Lex wouldn't have wanted this for me. He wanted me to go

home, to live the rest of my life with Carter and Ivy. That was what he sacrificed himself for.

Was I besmirching Lex's memory by marrying Reginald and leaving the others?

I didn't know. And Lex wasn't here, so who cared? Carter and Ivy would have each other, and me...I would let them.

27

CARTER

"Seriously, Carter," Lizzie said. I could practically see her eyes rolling through the phone. "I'm fine. Mom's fine. Everyone's fine."

I wanted to believe her, but being kidnapped by a maniacal fairy king and put under his enchantment for however long would fuck anyone up. She wouldn't talk about it, only to say that she and Jon had spent the time in the same mental capacity, and she needed space to process it. I wasn't sure what that meant, but Jon wouldn't speak of it, either. I figured it probably wasn't my business.

"You keep saying that word," I teased, "but I'm starting to question if you know what it means."

"I have to go." She sounded...well...*fine*. "I'll call you tomorrow."

"All right, Lizzie Bizzie."

She chuckled softly. "Stop calling me that. Love you, big brother."

"Love you." I hung up and pursed my lips, staring out the window of the penthouse apartment we'd rented on the outskirts of DC. The lights from downtown twinkled in the distance, the monuments to Ivy's ancestors bright against the night sky.

I listened to Weeds rumbling around in her office opposite our primary bedroom and hung my head, knowing I'd have to physically go get her to make her eat. How had Lex done this for so long—watched as she withered away, stood idly by while she worked herself to nothing?

She hadn't wanted to go back to the house she'd shared with Lex, and I couldn't blame her. There were too many memories there, too many long nights and longer mornings.

We'd stayed in Killwater for only a day after Miri left, but other than that one passage about the queen's favor, we didn't find anything helpful. Lex was gone. Miri was gone. And we were broken.

So we came home.

A few days after arriving in the States, I'd called my agent to announce the end of my filming career, and after everything I'd told her about my twisted, fucked-up backstory, she had agreed I needed some R & R. I wasn't sure if I'd ever go back to the industry or if I ever wanted to.

Now, a full six weeks later, the entire world knew. We had disappeared for three months, only to come back without Lex Fairfax and no explanation as to what had happened. The media wanted answers, his family had threatened to press charges, and all we could say was no comment.

How were we supposed to tell the truth?

Ivy's chief of staff, Giana, had advised us to keep our mouths shut until Lex returned, and that was what we did. Weeds agreed to a remote re-entry at Congress, I put my career on hiatus, and we hid here together, rarely venturing outside.

Trying to continue with life did not heal the huge hole in my heart where Lex and Miri used to be. She didn't even say goodbye, and that broke me more than anything else she'd ever done.

She was my best friend, and this absence hurt more than the last.

Neither Ivy nor I could speak about it, so we didn't.

We woke up. She went to her office for fourteen hours, and I played housewife until she eventually emerged to eat. We tried to fuck, decided we couldn't, and ultimately passed out together in front of the television. Once, a long time ago, I'd imagined a life with her similar to this. I imagined our last names smushed together in matrimony, a white picket fence with a golden retriever barking in the yard, and two-point-five little Washington kids running around.

Four years ago, I thought I hadn't been good enough for her. I thought I needed to prove myself. I'd been a fucking idiot. Fortunately, I had literal luck on my side or I might never have made it this far. And now that I was here, I didn't even enjoy it.

Because the young man who had envisioned his life with Ivy had always imagined Lex and Miri in that scenario. Before things were romantic, they had been our neighbors, the ones that came over on the weekends for burgers and babysat our kids when we needed a date night. And after Midsummer, after we decided we all loved each other, I couldn't stomach thinking about a future home without them in it.

Now I faced that reality every time I woke up, and nothing seemed worth it. What good was sliding inside Ivy without Lex there to comment on it? What pleasure was there in taking her mouth without Miri pressing sweet kisses into mine? What thrill was there in getting out of bed when Lex wouldn't be downstairs with coffee or Miri wasn't around to make breakfast or Ivy had no motivation to smile, much less go about her routine?

I missed both of them. I missed our nights together. And when I searched my heart, I even missed Poppy. She had become a surrogate daughter, almost a little sister, and now I'd never see her again. I'd never get to reconcile what she'd done or hear her apologies. She'd been a member of our family, and now she too left an aching chasm in my soul.

"Weeds," I said one night at our dinner table, pouring her a glass of wine as she ate her chicken parmesan in silence. At her nickname, she glanced up at me with lifeless eyes. They were perpetually swollen these days, red with tears for all that we'd been through, all that we'd lost. "You need to stop this."

She didn't say anything, just stared at me and grabbed her glass to take a long drink. "You, too?" She scoffed and shook her head. "How can you both just give up on him...on *us?*"

"I died and came back to life." The experience had been harrowing, and I'd only just now started to peel back the layers on how that fucked me up. I couldn't remember anything after being stabbed in the chest, and the philosophical implications of that sent me into an existential crisis every time I thought about it. But I knew one thing for certain, one thing that would guide the rest of my existence. "Life is too short to waste away in this house searching for someone who doesn't want to be found."

"I'm not wasting away. I'm trying to fix this."

"Lex is gone," I said, stammering while I spoke. "He's on the other side of the realm, and there is no way to get to him, not unless the queen lets him out of his deal. There's nothing to fix."

She shook her head. "No, I refuse to believe that. Poppy must be able to help. Perhaps Siobhan could create a new ring or—"

I cleared my throat, channeling my inner Lex when I said, "Poppy is gone. Siobhan is gone. We are still here." *I* was still here, and I needed her.

"Carter, I can't live without him. I—" She put her elbows on the table and dug her palms into her eyes. "—I cannot exist in a world that does not include him."

Unable to resist her, I reached across the table to grab her hand, tugging it so she'd rise and come to me. When she settled in my lap, I wrapped my arms around her waist and leaned her against my chest, tucking her head under my chin.

"He's my oldest friend in the world," she sobbed. "We've been together since we were infants."

"I know." I kissed her forehead, the pain inside my chest expanding to include hers. At times like these, I wished we still had our gifts. I wished she could tunnel into my mind and give me this torture, give it all to me and I would bear it for both of us. I had long ago faced the reality that I wasn't enough for Ivy Washington and I never would be. She needed the antagonism that Lex brought her. She needed Miri's feminine softness. So did I.

I used to love that about our unconventional marriage, and now I hated it. If I could be enough for her, just this once, I'd do whatever I could to ease her torment.

"How could I have let this happen?" She cried into my chest, wrapping her fingers tightly around my shirt. "How could I have left him there?"

"You have to stop blaming yourself." I twisted her so she was facing me, my hands on either side of her cheeks. "The king and queen did this to us. Lex didn't have a choice. None of us did."

"I could have fought harder."

"You nearly died," I said. "I did die. We gave it everything we had."

She fell silent after that, and a few moments later, her soft snores told me she'd fallen asleep.

Thank fucking Lord. She hadn't had a good night's sleep since... well...Solstice, perhaps. Or maybe even before that. Honestly, neither had I.

Scooping my arms under her legs, I carried her down the hallway to our massive bed, burying her under the covers before grabbing the pack of cigarettes off the nightstand and walking to the balcony. Biting one between my teeth, I lit it and closed my eyes as I relished the taste and smell. It reminded me so much of him, it brought tears to my eyes.

I stared at the moon, inhaling the death stick while I prayed to whatever deity might take pity on me.

"Please help us," I said. "If there's a way to bring him back, to bring them both back, please tell me what I need to do."

I waited to feel that churning in my gut, the one that told me which cards to pick in a poker game and which direction to go in the dark. I yearned to find that telltale luck that had saved my ass so many times. When nothing came, I made a sad laugh and sighed.

I used to hate the curse, and I would have done anything to get rid of it. I didn't want to be marked, and I definitely didn't want to be a part of some screwed-up fairy tale. But now that it was gone, I missed it. It had become a part of me, like my kidney or my liver, and I had a gaping hole where it used to be, not just because of Lex and Miri.

We had been changed and then changed back, and the return to normalcy sucked. I just didn't understand. The last thing my luck ever told me was that there would be no sacrifice, that the queen had been messing with Lex. I had been so sure we'd end up together, that all four of us would grow old and gray just like Lex described.

I grieved my lost husband as much as both of my wives, and given the chance, I would trade all of this for one more day of what we had.

A familiar crack echoed through the night, and I turned to glance inside. Ivy still slept, too lost to the real world to have heard. But I did, and I'd recognize that noise anywhere. I walked out of the bedroom and down the hallway to the living room, glancing around.

"Poppy?" I called out, taking a slow, deep breath to calm my racing heart. She'd been in Faerie when the veil closed, but she had control over space and time. If she could teleport wherever she wanted, perhaps she could go in between the realms. "Is that you?"

No answer, but the churning in my gut said I wasn't alone. The hairs on the back of my neck stood on end, goose bumps racing down my arms and the backs of my legs. I remembered the prophecy about her, the one Ashley told us about at Samhain.

"She would use this gift to bring peace to the realms and reunite the humans and fairies."

Was this what they meant? Would she reunite us now after everything had gone to hell?

"Poppy?" I tried again, walking out into the dining room and kitchen. Still nothing. I froze, training my ears in the dark, and I could have sworn I heard a quiet inhale before another loud zap echoed into the night.

Then she was gone.

28

IVY

"As you can see, everything's been roped off for the royal wedding tomorrow," said the talking head on the television. "And this is no normal royal wedding. There will be no grand parade and no horse-drawn carriages."

"That's right, Sidney," said the co-anchor. "Princess Miriam has always enjoyed her privacy, and after the allegations about her and Representative Washington, she intends to keep her marriage to the prince of Monaco closely guarded."

A sharp slice cut right through my chest, making my eyes burn. Sure, they'd been hurting since I'd woken up on my pile of books this morning, but hearing that Miri planned to marry that guy agonized me more than anything else ever could.

I should have tried to call her. I should have done anything except hide away in my apartment like I did. But every nerve in my body had been flayed open, and the exposure left me a crumpled mess on the ground. I had barely been able to tolerate her absence the first time. How she'd left again only made me seethe with injustice.

This was not the way it was supposed to work out.

Siobhan had promised that if we made it through the battle unharmed, she would ensure we got home safely. Where was the truth in that? She had lied. They all lied.

"Ivy?" Kit's voice came from behind me, and I quickly turned the television off before smiling at her. She walked to stand next to me and sighed, wrapping an arm over my shoulder. "You need to stop torturing yourself."

We had been invited to a family brunch this morning, which was just a fancy way of saying we'd have to run the Washington-Fairfax gauntlet and make nice faces until our cheeks hurt. Kellan and Anna wanted an update on their son, understandably, and I had run out of things to tell them. Yes, I was still in contact with him, and yes, he was still alive somewhere in the world, but no, he wouldn't take their calls. All fabrications, of course, but what else was I supposed to say?

"She shouldn't be marrying him," I told Kit. "She should be here with me...with us."

Kit stared at me with those ice-blue eyes, now even more alarming after everything that had happened. Neither she nor Jon would talk about their time under the king's madness, but she had admitted it felt longer than it had been.

"I'm not poly, and I don't understand a lot of what happened to us, but even I can admit, you four belong together." Kit pursed her lips. "Want me to hack her phone? Find her location?"

"No." I clenched my eyes shut and swallowed the burn. "No more. Let it be."

Carter had convinced me to stop searching for Lex, but even my promise to do that had been an exaggeration. I still kept a running log of things to research in a hidden notepad on my phone, and when I had the time, I went through all of Lex's old notes from the first time we'd been trying to break into Faerie. I was so sure that if I kept at it, eventually I would find something...*anything*...that would lead me to him.

He wouldn't have wanted that. He'd told me to live my life, to marry and have kids and forget about him, to not let Evelyn control me anymore. But that wasn't who I was. The least I could do was argue with him from the human realm and convince him he was wrong one more time.

Maybe I even lamented the way things had ended with Poppy. I'd loved her, too, once upon a time. The thought of never seeing either of them again pierced my soul and left me half the person I once was.

Kit grabbed my hand and led me back to the patio, where our families sat around the breakfast table. Jon, Abigail, Kellan, and Anna sat on one side, my father and mother at the ends, with me, Kit, and Henry on the other. Literally, the entire family...except for Lex.

His empty seat screamed with his absence, reminding me how I'd left him in Faerie, how I hadn't done enough to fight for him. I could have brought Carter today. He'd offered to come, but I wouldn't subject him to this lunacy. Lex and I had no choice; we were born into it. But I had sworn to protect Carter from the fallout.

"Now that you're back," Mother said, her icy gaze zeroing in on me, "we must work to improve your brand."

I didn't answer, just let her carry on with her rambling, as if any of it mattered. My brand, the Washington legacy, a Congress so full of bureaucracy, nothing would ever get done. My Green initiative had failed, and now my reputation was so far in the gutter, I would be lucky to get anything through in the upcoming session.

I looked again at Lex's empty seat next to me, wondering how long they would let me get away with saying he was still in Fuji before they sent Uncle Dmitri to track me down and remind me how they handled people who lost their Romanov princes.

"Ivy, you must renew your attempts at the Green Deal," Kellan said. "I have a few priorities I'd like you to add this time around."

I nearly groaned at the reminder to keep fighting the good fight. Hidden away in our apartment, I could forget the rest of the world existed. I could forget that I'd been elected to office, that I lived the life of America's Sweetheart. Lex and I were a power couple, our names synonymous with US royalty. I couldn't just start walking around with Carter Scott, acting like the last four years of engagement to Lex hadn't happened.

"Why not?" said the tiny voice in the back of my mind that had started to sound depressingly like my long-lost archnemesis. *"You're stronger than her. You live your own life."*

"Okay," I said, too exhausted to fight anymore. When would this end? When would I be able to relax?

I glanced down the table at my mother, who smiled around her mimosa, her hair having long ago turned gray, the wrinkles around her face hinting at how hard being the president rode the person who held the title. Kellan, likewise, looked ten years older than he was, nearly two decades older than he had just four years ago.

Once again, I wondered—would that be me one day? Would I find myself sitting around the brunch table, planning out the lives of my children with such little care for their opinions about it? Would I create an environment where my family hid everything from me for fear of retaliation? Would I mess with their technology to keep them away from people I didn't like or publicize lewd photos of them to ensure they did what I wanted?

No, I would *never* be her. I never wanted to be her.

"Once Lex confirms his return to the States, we'll reschedule your wedding," Evelyn went on. "The sooner the better. We wouldn't want another scandal, would we?" She gave me a playful wink, but I seethed with frustration. It was her fault we had the photo leak in the first place. It was her fault that my spouses and I had lost so much time together.

So much for my outburst at our wedding. She'd pretended the whole thing hadn't happened, that I hadn't gone ripping through her mind on a rampage worthy of Dr. Charles Xavier. Maybe it embarrassed her, or maybe she thought she'd imagined the whole thing. Either way, it had been brushed under a rug and never discussed, much like every other skeleton in our closet.

"And what of Jon's upcoming engagement?" My father gestured to my brother across the table, who raised his eyebrows and nearly choked on the piece of egg he'd stuffed into his mouth.

"My...uh...what?" Jon looked between Mother and Father, glancing briefly at me before back down at his plate. He grabbed the napkin to wipe his mouth and took a quick drink of champagne.

"Oh, that's right." Evelyn's eyes glittered while she spoke. "We've struck a bargain with the Fitzgeralds. You'll marry the youngest girl. What's her name?"

Jon balked as I struggled to swallow the rage boiling up the back of my throat.

"She's supposed to be my fiancée, and you don't remember her name?" Jon shifted in his seat, gaze landing on me and Kit. "I thought we agreed the rest of the Washington children were allowed to pick their partners."

"Hmm." Mother's eyes narrowed on my brother. "Do you think that's wise, considering the *women* you've been known to date?" She said the word like Jon had been hanging out with rats instead of human beings.

"I don't know what you mean." He shook his head, narrowing his eyes. "If you're insinuating something, be out with it."

"Krista Karina? Heather McCall? B-rated actresses at best."

"Well, they can't all be Carter Scott." Jon's quip wasn't aimed at me, but I choked on a laugh, regardless. Look at what had become of us, and compared to what Jon, Kit, and I had just been through, none of their political games were worth it.

"Enough," my mother cut in. "I don't understand where this is coming from. You've known this was happening since you were born. This is the price we pay to live the life we have."

The price we pay...

She'd been spouting that nonsense since we were children, and likely even before that. When would I have paid my dues? What would be enough for her, for the world? Having her do this to me and

Lex was one thing, but I wouldn't stand here while she lined up my siblings and ruined their lives one after the other.

I didn't want that. I didn't want *this*. None of it. Suddenly, the pageantry and opulence seemed old, tired, and unnecessary. This place wasn't warm like our cabin. It wouldn't keep its occupants safe through the long winter nights nor stand to resist an evil fairy king. I may have come from her body, but I didn't want to be a part of her world any longer.

Nothing in my life had ever been more clear to me.

Jon opened his mouth to respond, but I caught his gaze and shook my head, using an ancient form of sibling communication to tell him to keep his mouth shut: a glare and a grimace.

He sighed, grabbed his champagne, and chugged the rest of it while a plan started to form in the back of my mind.

I STARED at the place on my palm where my oath used to be, remembering each curve of the scars, each tiny bump of marred flesh. In so many ways, I wished it was still there. I wished Lex was still with us, that I hadn't left him to be the queen's plaything. But most importantly, I wished I had done anything at all to keep Miri from walking out the door.

In eight hours, I'd lose her forever, and that hurt so damned bad, I struggled to breathe. Once upon a time, I'd made her a promise to never let her leave me again. I'd sworn I'd fight for her when she couldn't, when she thought she didn't deserve us. Perhaps I had let this go on long enough. Perhaps I ought to call her bluff.

"Are you ready?" My chief of staff, Giana, raised her eyebrows and crossed her arms, her wide brown eyes raking over me from head to toe and back up again. Compared to this time a few weeks ago, I looked the part of Representative Washington. I'd stuffed my feet into the designer pumps and I'd slipped on the expensive suit jacket. I'd even pulled up my politician mask, shoving my desperation so far down inside me, even I wasn't sure the last few weeks had happened.

Now, I had to give a press conference about my wedding, Lex's absence, and what I planned to do about the rumors of my sabbatical. Giana had prepared my speech, claiming that Lex was still on our honeymoon, that we planned to go forward with the wedding as soon as possible, and I'd return to the office on Monday morning. Short. Sweet. To the point.

Except reading the various drafts sent thick, gaping despondency straight through my chest, and it hadn't let up since I'd agreed to this fiasco.

"Sure." I nodded and followed her out of the green room and down the hallway, straightening my blouse as I took a slow, deep breath, exhaling through my nose.

Don't think about Miri. Don't think about Lex. Don't think about Carter.

Even though that last person was waiting for me in the SUV out back, thinking about him would inevitably lead to the other two, and then the chasm in my chest would open so wide, I'd have difficulty containing it again.

"You remember your prepared responses, right?" Giana narrowed her brilliant gaze at me, and I nodded. "Good. After the time limit, I'll get you out of here as soon as possible."

The stage manager gestured to the podium, holding their hand out to guide me between the curtains. Cameras flashed as soon as I appeared, blinding me as I made my way to the center and faced the swarm of journalists in front of me. They shouted questions, one on top of the other, making it difficult to hear. I caught things like "Lex's location" and "Miri's wedding" and "are the rumors true about Carter Scott?"

I swallowed down the lump forming in my throat, visions of our life together flashing through my imagination. Miri's beautiful mahogany gaze shimmered in the sunlight, flecks of gold and honey mixed with chestnut complementing the same tones in her curly hair. I thought of the way Lex used to hold me down and smack me around, and how we'd laugh at the marks afterward. I thought of Carter in the car, of his dedication to us, to me...his unshakable loyalty.

We were supposed to be unbreakable. We were supposed to be together in the end.

I opened my mouth to talk, reading the first few lines on the teleprompter.

"Thank you all for coming today. At least the weather's held up." The audience laughed, and I smiled, trying to seal up the cracks in my politician's mask. I read the lines as they appeared, reciting the bullshit that had been written for me, the lies that explained why we'd delayed the wedding again and what I planned to do about it. "Once we have a firm date, you'll be the first to know. With some of the names in this room, you'll probably know before I do."

Another round of laughter added insulation to my crumbling foundation, the chips in my fragile glass armor spider-webbing in every direction. I hated the words I was saying. I hated being up here. I always had. Closing my eyes, I took a deep breath and searched my mind for Lex, for any remains of his energy. We had been connected once, and even if I'd loathed it at first, I had grown to need it. Without it, I didn't know how to live. I didn't know how to exist.

I felt like that seventeen-year-old version of myself, facing Marcus's death and realizing I couldn't do any of this alone. None of it mattered. None of *this* mattered.

That younger version of me rose inside, the one that had blushed the first time Miri kissed her, the one that had run into Carter's arms when he called her his favorite girl, the one that had secretly loved Lex Fairfax her entire life. She wanted to hide away from the world, to hide away from all of these sycophants that sucked the life out of her and her family.

What would she think of me?

How would she react if she knew I saved the world from a fairy king at the expense of Lex? What would she do if she knew I'd gotten up here to lie to the world and carry on like nothing happened?

It all seemed so...insignificant.

"I intend to return to the office on Monday morning," the teleprompter read, and I knew I had to say the words, but they weighed a ton. My stomach churned at the thought of walking back into the Capitol, of facing all the maniacs that lived to make my life a nightmare. I'd tried so damned hard, and I just...didn't want it anymore.

I didn't want it anymore.

Fuck, perhaps I had never wanted it. This was *my mother's* dream, and I didn't let her control my life.

Those words...they made my shoulders soft. They eased the tension in my chest and evaporated the clenching in my gut.

"I intend to return—" I murmured, more to myself than anyone else.

Could I return? Could I finish what I'd started?

"Representative Washington," someone said, clearly taking advantage of the silence in my pause. "Princess Miriam is getting married in only a few hours? Any comment on that?"

I had a million comments, but none of them mattered, either. Nothing mattered. Only my loved ones. Only being happy and joyful, and none of this had ever brought me joy. Not being in front of the cameras. Not answering their questions. Not being a part of *the* Washington family.

I took a deep breath and thought of Lex's last words to me.

"You live your own life, understand?"

"Yes," I said, more to the version of him in my head than to the audience, but they took my affirmative statement to mean I had a comment. When I opened my eyes, they hung on my every word.

I had spent twenty-six years crafting this mask for myself, putting it on every day for *their* amusement because I'd been told I *had* to. I couldn't be in love with Miri because my mother said I couldn't, because I was supposed to marry Lex and play the part of Ivy Washington, America's Favorite Political Animal.

But this version of me, the one that had defeated a fairy king and lived with the wreckage of what little I had to show for it, had more backbone than any of the previous iterations. Ivy 2.0 was going to live her own damned life.

"Miri and I..." I paused, taking one last deep breath before pulling the pin from this grenade. "We've been in love with each other since boarding school. I've loved Lex Fairfax since before I could remember, and all three of us love Carter Scott more than anything else in this world." The collective audience gasped. "I know the perverted stories you will spin with what little information I'm willing to give you, but I love the three of them. And they love me. And I would argue that the world needs more of that, not less." Somewhere across town, my mother's jaw was on the ground. My ancestors were rolling in their graves.

Good.

I was doing things my way from now on. I would stay in Congress, but only so that I could keep fighting on *my* terms. These vultures couldn't have anything I wasn't willing to give them.

"I've gotta go."

Questions hurdled at me faster than I could hear them, but it was too late. My heart had been set free. My conscience weighed nothing for the first time in my life. I walked off the stage to an astounded Giana, her eyes the size of entire planets.

"What did you do?" she said, grabbing my shoulders.

"I'm sorry for the added stress I've just caused you," I said. "But I'm not keeping them a secret anymore. We can spin this however you want. I'm tired of hiding."

She balked like I'd slapped her, blinking a few times before grabbing my shoulders and staring me dead in the eyes.

"Do you know what you've done?" she said.

"Not a fucking clue," I replied with an enormous smile. "But it feels great."

"You're out of your mind." Giana laughed and pulled me into a big hug. "You have to get to that wedding before she says I do."

I nodded and held her tighter. "Thank you, Giana. For everything."

"Ugh, your mother is going to kill both of us."

"I don't care." And I meant it with every part of my being.

I'm going to get my girl.

29

LEX

It wasn't all fairy wine and wild bloody orgies in Faerie. After Miri and Ivy sent the ruby dust careening into the fairy king, he woke up with his factory default settings, and the queen's council argued for the next few hours over what they should do about it. The battle maidens and the *Fianna* came out of their stupor like nothing had ever happened, and the ones that had been wounded in the fight were miraculously healed, maybe from the queen's magic, though she would never admit as much.

With the veil permanently closed, the angry, maniacal version of him technically was no longer a threat, but he'd found a way through before, and he'd do it again. Because of that, Finn and his *Fianna* urged caution.

I sat in the queen's royal library tent, searching through ancient tomes for anything that might help me get home. Of course, half this shit was in a language I couldn't read or understand, so I spent most of my time chasing my tail.

After I'd woken up near the ruins, Siobhan and Donnelly had taken pity on me and brought me back to their lodgings until I could find my own. But I didn't plan on staying that long. I had agreed to this deal to save my beloveds. I didn't want to be here.

Something Diana had said when we'd returned to Faerie and greeted her audience, something in the way she had worded it, stuck out to me at the time. She'd been very deliberate, and she'd kept her focus on me while she muttered her Faero-Gaelic incantation afterward.

"I owe you my thanks," she'd said, and I wondered if her thanks meant something more tangible than pretty syllables.

Every day was the same. I woke up at dawn, ate before the others got out of bed, and headed to the library, where I sat and researched until my eyes burned. Occasionally, Donnelly would join me, gaze narrowed while he lurked in the corner and reluctantly translated whatever I found. Most days, I reminded myself of Ivy, like we were stuck in that cabin in the woods, trying to figure out how to kill an immortal fairy king. At night, when I couldn't hold my head up anymore, I dragged my sorry ass back to their tent and passed out before they started fucking.

I'd only had to walk in on that once to know I didn't want to be there when it happened again.

I missed my spouses too much, and watching their intimacy had me aching for my own. Fucking fairies. Fucking prophecies. Fucking human realm that had to be so damned far out of my reach, I had no idea how I'd ever get there again.

This went on for a week. And finally, when the three of them couldn't stand my bullshit any longer, they found me hunched over a book I couldn't read, flipping through pictures I barely understood.

"See, I told you." Donnelly looked smug as he crossed his arms, walking into the tent with muffled footsteps. Of the three, he prided himself on being the most stealthy, and honestly, the way he silently crept around had scared the hell out of me on more than one occasion. "The fucking library."

"Alexei...Mate..." Siobhan shook her head and sighed as she came closer. "You can't hole yourself up in here for the rest of eternity."

I took a deep breath and leaned back in my seat, rubbing my palms over my eyes before reaching into my pocket for my remaining two cigarettes. I'd been saving them for a special occasion, but if something had brought the three of them here, then I figured I might as well brace myself.

"I saved the world," I said, taking a long drag and relishing the buzz that came with it. "I can do whatever I want."

"Hmm." Siobhan scowled as she grabbed the chair directly across from me, flipped it around, and sat, resting her elbows on the back rung.

"What brings you to the library?" I raised my eyebrows and gestured around. "Looking for a book on fairy sex magic? I think I saw a good one over—"

"Don't be a prick," Finn said, lowering his massive body into the chair next to Siobhan.

I laughed and tapped ash into the crystal tray at the center of the table, ignoring the threat in his tone. "What can I do for you three?"

Siobhan's dark eyes dropped to the books in between us. "What're ya reading?"

I cleared my throat and shifted my hips, trying not to look as obvious as I felt. But she probably saw right through me, so what was the point of lying? "A loophole."

"You think the queen's that sloppy?" Finn blew out a disbelieving breath. "That deal was binding. Forever."

"Figured that much out for myself, surprisingly." I took another long drag and blew out the smoke, returning my attention to the old leather skin in front of me before flipping a page. I expected them to get up and walk away, but when all three continued to stare, I lifted my eyes back to them. "What?"

Finn shook his head and pinched the bridge of his nose. "Gods, he's thick."

"You're not thinking back far enough." Siobhan tsked her teeth and stood, giving me one last disappointed sigh before turning to walk away. Finn's eyes glittered as he watched her go, eventually rising himself to stalk after her. Donnelly stayed behind, leaning back in his seat while studying me.

I didn't know if he planned to stay to help me translate or if he was doing his weird silent-but-deadly hunter shit, so I started to go back to my research, but he cleared his throat and drew my attention again.

"Ya know," he finally said, "you'd get a lot further by asking around rather than holing yourself up in here, looking at books you can't understand."

Donnelly rarely talked, so when he did, I paid attention. This was more advice than he'd given me in days.

"Okay," I said, stabbing out my cigarette butt. "How do I get out of the deal I made with the queen?"

"You can't." Donnelly shook his head and tilted it to the side. "But perhaps you could ask a different question."

My shattered heart crumbled further, slicing open the insides of my lungs, tearing through my rib cage. "How do I get back to my realm?"

He took a deep breath and curled his lips into a devilish smile, his eyes glimmering. "You're getting warmer. Ask a different question."

"Why would you help me?" We'd never been particularly close, and I certainly hadn't had much to say to him since I'd been trapped into staying here.

"Like you said, you saved the world. You saved all of us. Why shouldn't you be rewarded?" Donnelly's bright blue gaze shimmered with amusement. "Alas, the queen has forbidden any of us from outright telling you what to do. You are an honored guest. But, if you were to maybe *ask* the right question, I might be permitted to give you the right answer."

I paused and considered this. I believed his reasoning and his motivation. I even believed the queen would forbid any of them from offering help. She wanted me to be her little prize, her beautiful human counterpart. But Siobhan, Donnelly, and Finn had gone out of their way to help us before. Perhaps Donnelly would do it again.

"Is there a way for me to get back to my realm?"

His smile widened. "Yes."

"Does it involve the fairy queen?"

He chuckled and clapped. "There ya go. That's using your upstairs brain, yeah?"

"How? Tell me. Please."

"I'll tell you a story." He hummed and looked at the pack of cigarettes resting on the table between us, crossing his hands in his lap. "For a price."

I groaned and rolled my eyes, running my hands over my face and back through my hair. "Just like a fucking fairy. Fine. What do you want?"

"You give me that last cigarette, and I'll tell you how I evaded the Ghost of Agincourt."

I sighed, exhausted by all of this shit. I'd been over it since Siobhan gave us the curse four years ago, and now, I almost begged Donnelly to stab me in the face just so it would end. Deciding he likely had the best intentions at heart, I grabbed the pack and tossed it across the table to him, sending the lighter over next.

"I take it we have an accord?"

"Yes. I gave you the cigarette. Tell me your fairy tale."

He grinned and lit it, inhaling deeply on my last bit of humanity before blowing the smoke out in a thick, sultry breath. "Once upon a time, the king was not so opposed to humans. He used to casually enter the human realm and mingle with royalty. He'd dress up in their human clothes and attend their human events, and even pass out gifts to anyone who, in his opinion, needed his magical assistance. As you might imagine, Alberich got into quite the scandal when the peerage found him dallying in a princess's bed." Donnelly leaned back in the chair and put his feet on the table, crossing them at the ankle while he smoked and regaled his memory.

"They tortured him for weeks before I found him." He shook his head and tapped ash on the floor, taking another long drag. "He was practically in pieces."

I grimaced, imagining it, but then I shook my head, confused. "I thought the fairy king was immortal."

"Hmm." Donnelly nodded. "That doesn't mean he can't be hurt. And by that point, he'd been out of Faerie so long, his magic had grown weak. It couldn't protect him."

"So what happened?"

"I brought him home, took him to my house on that side of the realm. It wasn't much, certainly wasn't fit for the king. Between Siobhan and I, we nursed him back to health." Donnelly took a long inhale on the smoke before putting his feet back on the ground and sitting upright so he could stab it out in the crystal. "When we brought him back to Faerie, in near-perfect condition, he stood on the platform and proclaimed he owed us his thanks." Donnelly repeated the same Faero-Gaelic passage that Diana had muttered on the stage the day we'd returned her home safely. A jolt of sheer excitement shot down the center of my chest. "Which essentially means the same thing...except for one tiny detail. The Faero-Gaelic word for thanks has its roots in the same word for favor." He repeated the sounds, pronouncing each one slowly and phonetically.

I froze, my spine straightening, as I finally understood the point of Donnelly's story. The queen had stood up in front of her entire population, stared at me, and proudly proclaimed that she owed me a favor. I knew then what I had to do. Donnelly had been right. I couldn't break the deal...but Diana owed me a favor, and maybe I could persuade her into a new one.

"Fucking hell." Tears burned at the corners of my eyes before I could blink them back. I cleared my throat and reached across the table to grab his hand, squeezing it in a show of gratitude. "Thank you, Donnelly."

He snorted. "Don't you want to know how the story ends?"

I waved my hand in a gesture for him to go on.

"Nearly a hundred years later, I was the one who had been

captured on the human side. By this point, the king had gone mad and been cursed to stay in Faerie, but…" He twisted his lips into a curious smile. "With fairy magic, a favor is a favor. A gift is given so that a gift may be received. My magic called to his, despite our distance, despite the different realms, and he sent Finn to find me."

I struggled to understand the implications of this. What exactly was he trying to say? That I could get out of Faerie? That the queen's magic would extend across the realms? "But I thought the veil to the human realm was closed. I thought no one could ever back there?"

At that, Donnelly leaned in close and narrowed his brilliant blue eyes. "Aren't you glad you know someone who can travel through space and time?"

"May I have a word with your lady?" I raised an eyebrow at Poppy, who sat outside Diana's tent like the world's most unassuming bodyguard, sharpening the blade of her knife on a rock. She'd grown up completely now, her form that of a woman. Sure, she looked about twenty, with big brown eyes and long pale blond hair, but I'd seen her catapult through time and take people to the top of the Sphinx. Poppy may not have lived up to her prophecy in the end, but that didn't mean she was inconsequential.

"What do you want?" She narrowed her eyes, seemingly both suspicious and disappointed to see me.

"I need to talk to her."

Poppy put down her weapon with a sigh and stood, crossing her arms over her chest. "The only reason I haven't gutted you yet is because you risked your life to save Carter."

"Yeah, and how'd that work out for me?" I raised my eyebrows. "Stuck here for eternity with the likes of you."

She sneered.

"Who's there, my child?" came a voice from inside, followed by several giggles in different tones. The white tent flaps pushed aside before the queen emerged, raking her bright eyes over me before curling her mouth into a grin.

"Alexei," she purred, running the back of her fingers down the side of my face. She looked amazing, her skin radiating the same power and grace I always associated with her, a far cry from the feral, confused woman my uncle had delivered to me before my wedding. "How are you faring in your new circumstances?"

I nodded, stepping back as she pulled her pristine white robes around her shoulders and came closer. Behind her, the king stepped out of the tent, his hair now cropped short to his head and his beard completely shaven. He had a light in his eyes that I'd never seen before, and as his grin grew larger, I realized they were a beautiful shade of dark brown, almost like Miri's.

"I'm well, thank you." I glanced between them—their matted hair, their flushed cheeks, their swollen lips. They'd been catching up for days now, and from the looks of it, they hadn't stopped. Not that I blamed them. Once I got home, I planned to tie all three of my spouses to our bed and take them for a fucking week. "I see you two are reacquainted."

Alberich's grin deepened. "He is quite beautiful. How do we know Alexei?"

"That's a long story, dear." Diana returned her gaze to me, now much kinder than it had been the last time I'd tried to make a deal with her. Alberich had spent a week learning how to speak multiple languages again, but the queen made no effort to remove the ruby dust from his head. Somewhere deep down inside, that maniacal version of the king still existed. He sat in a tent inside his mind wherever Ivy had locked him away. Instead of retrieving him to heal him, the queen had simply allowed it to continue.

Whether it was retribution for what he'd done to her or that Ivy's magic was irreversible, I didn't know. Nor did I care. That motherfucker had raped Miri and tormented Ivy for months. He was lucky amnesia was all he got. If it were up to me, I'd have already sunk a sword into his heart and torn it out to eat it in front of him.

"What can we do for you, Alexei?" Diana's warm voice brought me back to my request, but something in her eyes made me pause. A playfulness flitted just behind them, making me wonder if she already suspected why I was there.

I continued nonetheless. "When you lost your memory—"

"You lost your memory?" Alberich gasped and turned to Diana. "You poor thing."

"It's okay, love. All over now." Diana smiled and patted his cheek before returning to me. "Please continue."

"When you lost your memory, I took care of you. I brought you back to Faerie, back to your right mind."

Diana's smile widened, her eyes glittering with unshed emotion. "Yes, you did."

"You announced to the entire population that you owed me your thanks." I cleared my throat and put my hands behind my back, straightening my shoulders as I prepared to deliver my ask.

"Yes, I did." Diana moved to the chair at the edge of the platform, her proverbial throne, and sat, sprawling her arms out to either side and crossing her legs at the knee. "And?"

"I would like to cash in on that favor."

"What...favor?" She deepened her grin, pausing to let the request fall between us, the tension growing damn near stifling. Like that, she fit the role of the queen. She could be nothing else. No one in the world held as much power as she did in that one moment. Not even when Alberich took his seat next to her, crossing his legs and leaning into his wife with adoration in his gaze.

"I may have only been here a few days, but I've learned enough about fairies to know you choose your words carefully...especially you, Diana, queen of the fae." I steadied my gaze on her, wishing I had my gift again, willing the pit in my gut to form should she lie. "You wouldn't proclaim to owe anyone anything unless you meant it...unless you wanted them to use it."

"Ahh, I see." Seated in the rays of morning sunlight like this, her skin glowed, damn near iridescent, as the conversation continued. "You've been talking to Donnelly."

"Hmm." I neither confirmed nor denied her accusation. I wouldn't have my informant getting in trouble if this all worked out.

"And what is it you believe I owe you?" She raised an impeccable eyebrow at my presumptuous attitude.

"I want to return to my realm," I started. "I want to spend the rest of my life with my spouses." A list poured out of me, tedious and specific as fuck. I didn't want her making any assumptions for me, filling in any gaps with her own devious plans. This went on for longer than I thought it would, but I needed her to understand that I was tired of being fucked around. It was time for this story to end already, for me to begin the one I should be living.

When I was done, she nodded, seeming to deliberate over every single word. Finally, she leaned forward and held up a finger, waving it toward me like she wanted me to come forward.

Heart pounding and trying to hide it, I forced my shaking legs to move. Between the two of them, they could make my body explode into a million little pieces and I wouldn't be able to stop them. No one in Faerie would either, and without my spouses, I was so woefully weak.

She stilled when I got within arm's reach, only lowering her voice so that our conversation stayed between the three of us.

"What about our deal, Alexei? I saved two lives. You owe me at least one."

"Are you not living it?" I gestured around to her life of luxury. "I could have left you in a Russian shithole. I could have thrown you to the worst of the human realm. Here you sit. On your throne. With your...*husband*." The urge to call him a psycho piece of shit rattled through me, but I managed to choke it down.

Alberich gasped again, this time furrowing his eyebrows and twisting his lips into a snarl. "How dare you speak to my wife like—"

"Shh, it's all right, my love." Diana leaned back in her seat, eyes focused on me with both challenge and trepidation. She liked that I'd come to this conclusion, but she couldn't just *let* me out of our arrangement, not without losing face in front of the fairies. If she conceded this to me, then she'd have to concede to everyone, and where would it end?

"Magic like that comes at a cost." She took a deep breath and let it out slowly, as if there were all the time in the world. For her, there was. For me, my spouses aged weeks every second that I stayed here. "I cannot break the deal."

"That's not what I'm asking." I dug my argumentative feet in, knowing this was the right way to go. If Carter were here, he would have said his luck was speaking to him. "I want you to return the favor you owe me. I want you to send me home. A gift for a gift."

Alberich's jaw dropped, and Diana curled the ends of her lips into a pleased smile.

"The old words," she said, nodding. "Even if I could agree to this, the veil is closed. Ivette has claimed the human realm. None of us may enter."

I looked at Poppy, who up until this moment, had stayed quiet and still on the other end of the platform. Now, she crossed her arms and squared her jaw at me.

"No," she said, glaring at me with daggers in her eyes. "He can rot."

"Hmm." Diana held up a hand as if there was nothing she could do. "So it is. The child will not accommodate your request."

"Why not?" I raised my eyebrows. "Don't you think you owe me, too, you little monster? My uncle housed you for years. Carter kept you safe from the…" I cut myself off from saying fairy king, lest this new version of amnesia Alberich suddenly have a flashback to his alter ego. "You know he's upset without me. You know Ivy is, too. You know they want me back. They probably miss you, too."

She clenched her hands into fists and stood straighter, not daring to look away. "You held an axe to my throat. You threatened to kill me."

"You kidnapped my family and took the villain back in time to kill my brother." I reminded myself to keep my tone calm and level. Arguing about who was most evil when we both were in the top ten didn't make sense. "I think we're square."

"Come now, Poppy," Diana said, breaking up our argument. "Would it even be possible? Are you able to travel between realms?"

Poppy pursed her lips and took a deep inhale before giving us a solemn nod. "I've already done it."

My heart dropped into my gut.

This. This was why Siobhan and Donnelly came to me now, rather than immediately after the deal had been made. There would be no sense in suggesting I get out of this arrangement if there wasn't a way back into the human realm. Poppy must have told Siobhan, who would undoubtedly have told Finn and Donnelly.

"Poppy." Diana tsked her teeth in a chastising tone. "You should confide these things in me. How can I make sound decisions if I do not know what my children are doing?"

"Yes, my lady." Poppy gave her a small curtsy before walking to stand next to me. "Do you want me to take him back to the others?"

Rather than answering, Diana turned to her husband. "What do you think, my love?"

"I don't like the way he talks to you." Alberich pouted. "You should send him wherever he wants to go, so I don't have to see him again."

The queen made a delicate laughing noise and pushed to her feet, gliding toward me. Her white robes flowed behind her, a blond halo of hair floating around her head. She looked like an angel, and in that moment, I wasn't sure if she offered salvation or death. Neither would have surprised me.

"Oh, Alexei." She shook her head and ran the back of her fingers down my cheek, dropping her gaze to my lips before glancing back up at my eyes. "What a tragedy it is to let you go. I had hoped to have you for many moons to come."

The enormous weight that had suffocated me since I saw Carter and Miri drop evaporated. I was going home. Finally. After all this time.

"All my requests will be granted?"

Diana chuckled, grabbed my face, and leaned in to kiss me. Before I could ponder her response, Poppy's small hand slipped into mine and the world went dark.

30
MIRI

It was a sham marriage.

I knew it. The whole bloody world would know it soon. Ivy had confessed earlier, and rather than respond, I'd gone ahead with my wedding. That should have been answer enough, but the media was relentless, after all.

I didn't care.

I made this decision, knowing it was the best for everyone involved. After all that's happened, it was the only way this could end. In this fairy tale, the princess had to save herself.

I stared at my reflection in the mirror, memorizing the details in the lacing on the ivory dress. My hair fell in soft ringlets around my face, and my makeup had been done so elegantly, I had to squint to make sure I was still me. Underneath it all, I knew I still looked like rubbish. I likely would for the rest of my life if I had to live without my beloveds.

That wouldn't last long. Rubbing my thumb over the place on my hand where there used to be scars, I went back to the night this started.

"Until the end," we'd promised each other.

273

The end had come and gone, and we were still separated. I ignored the surge of agony in my heart as Lex's dark chuckle echoed through my mind, combining with Carter's blinding smile and Ivy's incinerating stare.

How I loved them. How I screwed up our happily ever after.

Stop that, I chided myself. I did what I had to do, and now it was over. Now, I moved on.

"Miriam, darling," Gran said, floating into the room with her arms open wide. Her smile stretched across her face, practically eerie in how much she forced it. If I didn't know better, I'd suspect she was a robot or perhaps an alien hiding in a convincing meat suit.

I turned and tried to grin, blinking back the tears forming in the corners of my eyes. "Hello, Gran."

"Well, now what's that frown?" She clutched her purse tighter, taking another step toward me. "The prince of Monaco is a fine choice, better than any I had, by far."

"You love Pop." I scowled, recounting the thousands of times she'd admitted it to being an affair of the heart between them.

"Yes, but that came later, darling." She sighed. "You'll understand what I mean in a few years."

I hated how she talked down to me, as if I was incapable of understanding what love meant on my own. Unfortunately, I knew what it was to sacrifice everything for the people I adored. I knew how it felt to be the one person standing in the way of a villain destroying everything I'd ever known. Was that not love? I clutched myself tighter, wincing against the stab in my chest.

"The sooner we get this all squared away, the better." Gran shook her head. "Honestly, Miriam. You'll thank me one day." She patted my cheek with her gloved hand before turning toward my waiting family.

I should be celebrating this day with the loves of my life. I should be walking down the aisle to someone I adored, someone who had been there the night I consummated my real marriage, the one that filled my soul with so much joy. But no, that wasn't in the princess's story, either. The princess married a prince and popped out a bunch of other little royals to carry on the traditions.

It didn't matter that my heart was breaking. It didn't matter that I'd rather swim through lava before marrying this ancient wanker. I carried the weight of the generations before me, and I'd never be able to break free.

It hurt too much to think of Ivy and Carter without also thinking of Lex and what he'd done to save us. I remembered Ivy's scorching stare the night I'd left. It told me I could never go back to them. Not anymore.

"Your Highness," the wedding planner called, refocusing my attention. "It's time."

Swallowing down bile, I nodded and forced my shoulders back, raising my chin. I'd done heroic things. I'd saved the world twice. I could do a silly thing like get married.

Just smile. Just get through it.

Forcing the grin on my face, I followed the wedding planner through the dark stone hallways of the tiny cathedral. Once the prince learned I was capable of disappearing for weeks on end, he demanded a quick, private ceremony to tie me down. I had agreed because I could do nothing else. My hands had been tied by heartbreak and centuries of tradition. I had loved and lost and now, nothing mattered anymore.

"Are we ready?" Edward held out his elbow for me. I gave him a hesitant nod, turning to look down the short aisle. My grandparents stood to one side, matching grins of pride on their faces. Reginald, the prince of Monaco, stood next to the minister in his gleaming black suit, his eyes soft and warm with appreciation. Rancid anxiety churned in my gut, but I choked it back.

"Last chance to run," Edward whispered, raising an eyebrow. "I've got the escape car out back."

"Ha ha," I said, taking a deep breath to slow my racing heart. "Very funny." The organ blared to life and the cameramen on either side swiveled the lenses to me.

This is it. No going back now.

"I'm serious," Edward whispered. "You don't have to do this."

"Yes, I do." I sighed, clenching his arm tighter. "This is the only option."

"No, it's not." He glanced around, shifting uncomfortably. "This is a raft of horseshite, and you know it. I know it. Fuck, even Gran knows it. She doesn't want to admit it."

"Not the point." We hadn't even started walking down the aisle yet and my pulse beat so hard, I could barely hear myself think, let alone plot an escape. What the hell was he saying?

"Little coz," Edward's voice echoed with the years of endearment between us. I'd never had siblings, but the closest in relationship would be him. "There is nothing in this life worth more sacrifice than true love, and it's not with this old man."

I furrowed my brows. Who the hell was this and what had he done with my cousin? I'd never heard Edward talk like that before. The man despised monogamous relationships more than I did.

"I saw the way you are together, the four of you. It was always meant to be that way." He shook his head and pursed his lips, looking around at this charade while we waited for the bridal march to begin. "This is a joke, and someday, you won't find it funny."

"You're the one to talk." I balked. "I'm surprised you even made it. No orgies close enough, is it?"

He held my hand tighter. "Make your taunts. It only proves I'm right."

"What am I supposed to do?" I gestured to the cameras and photographers and family members. It wasn't a typical royal wedding with thousands of guests, but Gran wouldn't have let this happen without getting some press. The official story was that the prince and I had fallen in love months ago, but waited to make it official until we could have a small ceremony at the cathedral in Aberdeen. I'd never been a public person, so it fit well enough even if I hated everything about it.

"Well, at this point, you've got to make a scene." Edward

shrugged, brushing a hand back through his ginger hair. "Object to your own wedding. Tell the entire world your heart truly belongs to Ivy Washington. Let the chaos fly."

I rolled my eyes and ran my fingers over my forehead. "That *would* be your advice."

The opening notes came from the organ, marking the point we'd have to start walking. Edward held my hand tight while my entire body shook, each step bringing me closer to my fate. Gran widened her smile, and Prince Reginald straightened his spine, running his hand down over his suit.

"Miriam," he said, holding out a hand when I got close enough.

I turned to Edward, who kissed me on the cheek, whispering a quick, "The safeword is lemon tart," before winking and placing my fingers in Reginald's waiting palm.

"Who presents this woman for marriage?" the minister said.

"I do," Edward announced. "On behalf of God, the United Kingdom and its commonwealth, and her family."

"Thank you," Reginald said, guiding me closer to the minister. He gave me a gentle smile, the creasing skin around his eyes reminding me again of our age difference. This wouldn't be a love match, and the first time he put his hands on me, I'd truly have to close my eyes and think of England. The idea made me retch, but in my chest, a hollow hole throbbed that had once been my heart. Absent such a vital organ, nothing in the world made sense.

The doors to the chapel flew open, a gust of hot summer wind whipping my hair around my face.

"I object!" said the intruder.

My heart dropped to my ankles.

Down at the end of the aisle stood my wife, all five-foot-seven inches of her in Jimmy Choos and a power suit. Her wild ginger hair hung around her head in a frayed mess, indicating how rushed she'd been to get here. She must have come right from the press conference. Behind her, Carter stood with hope glowing in his eyes, and on either side of him were two bodyguards that must have helped her get this far.

They'd come for me.

"Miriam Stuart, duchess of Aberdeen…I forbid you to marry anyone else." Ivy stalked forward, her chin held high, rendering all the journalists and family in attendance speechless. My bodyguards moved toward her, Reginald's and Gran's joining in.

"What is the meaning of this?" Gran snapped.

"Fucking finally," Edward said, rolling his eyes.

"Grab her!" one guard shouted while one of Ivy's guards joined in with, "Touch her, and I'll snap your neck, buddy."

"Stop," I said, the desperate word shoving out of some place deep in my gut. "Just…stop."

All bodies turned toward me, the guards pausing to see what I would do.

"Let her through." I nodded, tears burning the corners of my eyes as I dropped Reginald's hand and turned to face her.

"My love?" Reginald said. "Miriam? Do you know these people?"

I ignored him in favor of watching my wife move through the crowd toward me like some kind of Amazonian queen come to rescue her princess. She'd never been more beautiful, and I realized I'd never been more in love with her.

"Miri," she said when she reached me, running the backs of her fingers down my cheek in a tender caress. Her steel eyes shimmered with unshed tears, and her voice coated my skin in velvet, reminding me of all the times she'd whispered it in the throes of lovemaking. "You can't do this. You know you can't."

I took a deep breath, fighting the sob that threatened to tear out of my throat.

"I love you," she continued. "I've loved you since the moment I met you, and now the whole world knows."

"Miriam," Gran tried to cut in. "This is preposterous, and hardly the place."

I ignored that, too, tuning it all out. She'd come for me, as she promised she would all those years ago. And that ache inside, the place where my heart once occupied, gave a half-hearted pulse. I missed Lex, I truly did. But was my grief worth separating myself from the only people who had ever truly loved me? Or was I rash in assuming we couldn't grieve together, that we couldn't *love* together? Ivy and Carter's adoration poured into me like an avalanche, and I let it take me. I let her have me. I *wanted* her to have me, even if it meant suffering through losing Lex together.

"Miri, please come home," Ivy said, cupping my face and pressing her forehead to mine. "I'll do whatever you want, be what-ever you want. I'll marry you if that's what it takes."

Visions of walking down the aisle to Ivy dressed in a white suit echoed through my mind, and my stomach lurched. I had never considered the possibility that she and I could go public, that it wouldn't be her and Lex or her and Carter...but her and me. Us. All of us.

"Do you realize what you've done?" I whispered, clenching my eyes shut as tears streaked down my cheeks.

"I know," Ivy said. "I know, it's a PR nightmare, but...I don't care." She pulled back so she could look down at me and wipe the tears away, gentleness and determination radiating out of her stare. "I want you, Miri. I want the dream Lex told us about. Don't you want it, too?"

The mention of our former lover split me right down the middle, cracking open my bleeding soul. I *did* want that with a desperation I could barely describe. Sobs raced up the back of my throat, squeezing my lungs.

"After all we did," she went on. "After all we've done for them, don't we deserve a choice? Don't we get a say in our own lives?"

I couldn't deny her, not anymore. The thought of rejecting Ivy publicly and returning to my arranged marriage made me want to curl up into a ball and weep. But what she described, running away and living our lives together despite the public scrutiny, well, that made me weightless.

Why shouldn't I have it? I'd suffered at the hands of a fairy king. I'd defeated him with his own magic. I'd sacrificed my prince of darkness for this realm.

I'd been a stupid, stupid girl. Again.

"Okay," I finally said, the word coming out in a whisper.

She smiled the most radiant grin and leaned in to kiss me, right there in front of God, my grandparents, and the rest of the world. Unable to resist her, I deepened the kiss while most of the audience gasped or applauded. When we broke away, I caught the melting metal in her eyes, burning affection, just for me. Then she grabbed my hand and raced down the aisle to the protests of the king and queen of England and the old creep I'd been engaged to.

"Miriam, you can't do this!" Gran shouted. "Miriam, stop this instant!"

But we didn't. I jumped into Carter's arms, pressing my mouth to his in a blatant display of possession and love.

"Hiya Juliet," he whispered.

"Hiya Romeo." I couldn't contain my grin. I'd wasted so much time. Why did I ever think that leaving them could have been an option? No one dared love me as much as them. No one ever could.

"Ready to go home?"

I nodded and Ivy leaned in to kiss Carter next, turning back to give the world a single-finger salute before shoving open the thick, heavy doors and walking out onto the street. A crowd had gathered behind metal blockades, keeping them at a distance. Despite that, there could be no hiding this, especially not after the public display we'd put on in there.

I stopped when I recognized the tall familiar figure waiting outside our escape vehicle.

"No," Carter murmured, dropping my grip.

"Lex?" Ivy's hands shook nearly as hard as her voice.

"My prince!" I sprang toward him, picking up my wedding gown to run faster. He looked the same as when we'd left him, beautiful and cut from marble like a Renaissance sculpture, and my heart dropped down to my ankles. I had missed him so fucking much.

"How?" Ivy ran toward us. "How is this possible?"

Lex grinned and opened the back door of the SUV, nodding inside. Cameras flashed around us, the crowd calling out questions and cries for clarification, but we ignored it all. Lex kissed me before I climbed in, following that up by pulling Carter in for another desperate embrace. Finally, Ivy wrapped her arms around our king of darkness and pressed her lips to his.

"Get in the vehicle, X. I'm taking you all home." His hazel eyes twinkled with the love he had for us, especially his X.

She smiled and got in next to me.

Sure, the media would have a field day with this, but I didn't care. What was anyone going to do to us that hadn't already been done? Kill our brand? Hack our phones?

I dared anyone to try. We had survived so much worse.

The kings and queens of yore couldn't control us anymore.

We were truly free.

IVY

"By the power vested in me by the Commonwealth of Virginia, I now declare you married." Carter grinned and closed his folder, gesturing between Miri and me.

The tiny audience applauded as I stepped closer to my wife, cupping her jaw before leaning down to press a tender kiss to her lips. She grinned against me, opening her mouth wide enough for me to tease her with my tongue.

"I love you, Miri," I murmured, pulling back long enough to meet her gaze before leaning in for another gentle embrace.

"I love you, Ivy," she replied and turned to face our witnesses. My siblings had come to watch us tie the knot as had her cousin, Edward, who currently held our sleeping son, Donnelly. My mother had refused, no surprise.

"This is outrageous," she'd said. "An absolute waste of your privilege."

It had been two years since we'd announced our relationship to the world, but she still didn't understand. She couldn't control what

I did anymore, and I wouldn't let her. I hadn't resigned from Congress, much to the chagrin of my more conservative colleagues. But the queer community embraced us, and with their support, my public image bounced back enough for me to win re-election. I was the preferred candidate for the Senate in two years. As for my mother, I'd done what Lex had told me to do before leaving us for Faerie. I now lived my life for me. I'd taken her plan and ripped it apart on live television.

First, I wanted to make good on my promise to my wife. When I'd barged in on her fake wedding to Reginald whatever-the-fuck-his-name-is from Monaco, I'd told her I would marry her if it came to it. That I wanted to be the one who brought her into my family, who made her mine.

It had taken two years, but finally, I was making an honest woman out of us both.

"All right," I said, turning to Carter and taking the folder from him. "Your turn."

He took a deep breath and held his hand out to Lex, who stood next to me, my "best man." Now, I traded spots with Carter, and Miri became Carter's matron of honor, and we started the ceremony over again. Sure, maybe it was cheesy that we held a double wedding, but after much deliberation, we couldn't figure out a better option. It was only for silly legal purposes since polyamorous marriages weren't technically allowed in our society. *Yet.* But that was another thing I planned to change with my newfound sense of empowerment.

The public had a lot to learn, and we could be role models for that ideal future.

Miri had to get married to inherit her father's fame and fortune, something that had taken a year's worth of pleading with the king of England to accomplish. But in his eyes, neither Carter nor Lex were suitable options.

Me, on the other hand...well, I had the name and the formal background, and four of my direct ancestors had been president. My genetics made up for my gender and nationality, and once Miri became pregnant with Donnelly, there was only one solution—put me on the birth certificate and silence the deliberation about which man in our union was the baby's father. Sure, the world would still speculate, but it no longer mattered. Any baby that came out of my body would be Miri's, and any baby that came out of hers would be mine. End of story.

I repeated the same vows that both Miri and I made, waiting for Lex and Carter to echo the sentiments before proclaiming them married in the eyes of Virginia and all the human realm.

Then, it was over. Our closest friends and family gathered around us, kissing and hugging my spouses.

"Holy Hell, I thought this day would never come," Kit said, rolling her big ice-blue eyes.

"Don't forget you still owe me twenty bucks for calling the couples." Jon nudged her in the shoulder with his, and I swallowed back the retorts I had about my siblings betting on which ones of us would get married.

"Jon, be nice." Lizzie shook her head and wrapped her arms around her big brother, who pulled her into a hug.

"I think someone needs a nappy change." Edward grimaced and held the miniature version of himself out to anyone who would take him.

"Oh, I'll do it," Carter's mom said, her grin stretching from ear to ear. Renee had recently moved to Virginia to be closer to her grand-child (and any future ones). Out of all our parents, she'd handled the news the best, which had surprised none of us. She'd likely seen this coming four years ago.

"No, that's okay. Thank you, Renee. I can do it," I insisted as Edward handed Donnelly to me, pretending to retch, and after catching a whiff of my son, I figured it was urgent. But as I kissed his ginger head and turned to the bathroom, I thought I saw chestnut hair and a tattooed shoulder with vines twisting around the upper arm. I walked to the end of the church sanctuary and glanced back and forth in the dark hallway.

"Hello?" I called, seeing no one. "Siobhan? Is that you?"

Donnelly let out a whine and gripped my white jacket with his chubby fingers, and despite the sneaking suspicion we were among fairies again, I took my son to the bathroom so I could use the changing table.

In the two years since we closed the veil, there were moments when I thought I heard Siobhan reaching out to me mentally or times when I'd wake up in the middle of the night certain I'd been running from Alberich or Diana in my dreams. But then I'd try to enter Lex's head or talk to Carter telepathically, and nothing happened.

It's over, I reminded myself. *We're done and it's over.*

"The gift is gone, right, my little bug?" I cleaned Donnelly and refreshed his diaper before picking him up to take him back to our family. Even though he'd come out of Miri's body and looked more like Carter the older he got, he'd become most attached to me. I was the only one who could get him to go to sleep when he had colic, and when he got scared, I was the one he searched for first. "When do you think we should tell them about your little sibling, huh?"

He grinned up at me with his silly smile and I kissed his face, thankful yet again that it had all worked out the way I wanted it to. While we didn't know who Donnelly's father was, and we never wanted to find out for certain, I did know who had impregnated me. I was just over twelve weeks along, which would be the time when Miri and Carter went to Scotland for a month, just the two of them. Lex and I had torn the house apart...and now I faced the consequences.

I laughed to myself at what the sixteen-year-old version of me would think—married to Miri, pregnant with Lex's baby, certain to fuck all of them tonight. Her brain would explode, but I wouldn't have changed anything about my story if it ended this way every single time.

My heart had never been so full, and I swore to protect it. Any deities, fairies, or media monsters that came for us would have to go through me first.

I was Ivy Fucking Washington, and I had finally claimed my life for myself.

I intended to keep it.

CARTER

My mom had taken our kid for a sleepover, leaving the four of us to spend our official wedding night in our cabin, far away from the prying eyes of the rest of the world. After the way the Washingtons, the Fairfaxes, and the Stuarts had treated my spouses, I thanked my lucky stars my family had always been accepting of whatever I chose to do with my life. They wanted me to be happy, and after seeing the way I interacted with my spouses, Mom needed no more convincing. She would have been just as thrilled if I'd married Miri or Ivy that day, but I understood why the girls had chosen to do what they did. Which left me with my moody, broody DC, not that he was a consolation. The opposite, in fact.

He stood at the end of the bed with an arm draped over Ivy's shoulders, leaning into our ginger-haired wife with mischief echoing behind his eyes. They'd spent the better part of the last hour undressing Miri and me as slowly as possible, now whispering in cahoots over what would happen next.

"Do you remember that night in Faerie?" Lex said, eyes glittering, lips curling into a smirk.

My heart pounded behind my ribs as I recalled the same look echoing out of Miri's eyes on the night in question. It felt like ages ago, despite only being twenty-four-ish months. Our princess and I had held them down and taken them how we wanted, knowing it might be the last time we ever did.

"I do," Ivy said, refocusing her attention on me, steel gaze burning with retribution.

"How about a little payback?" Lex smiled like a wolf with a rabbit between its teeth, amping up my anticipation as Ivy crawled over my prone form, her white lingerie hiding all the best parts of her. My cock twitched as Miri turned in to me, biting my earlobe before pressing up to kiss Ivy. Our queen allowed it for a moment before pushing Miri back down next to me, sitting back on my pelvis, rubbing her laced cunt right over my sensitive flesh.

Fuck, they'd been at us for an hour—biting, licking, demanding we do the same to each other. I didn't know how much more of this I could take. Lex handed something to her, and when the jingles of the metal clasps on her strap-on rang out through the air, I shivered with anticipation, my balls clenching at what would come next.

"Oh, look at that," Ivy said as she tightened the straps. "Are you excited for me to fuck you?"

"Yes," I said quickly, damn near embarrassing myself.

Lex laughed and climbed on top of Miri, mirroring Ivy's pose, and leaned down so he could press his lips to hers. "Don't worry, Princess. You're going to get fucked good and proper, too."

She smiled. "I certainly hope so."

Then, they did. Ivy held one of my legs over her shoulder, lubed up her rainbow-colored dildo, and fucked me until I couldn't remember my name. I came all over both of us twice, much quicker than I would admit to anyone else, and when Ivy took off the strap to crawl on top of my face, I noticed a softness around her cheeks and a heaviness in her breasts that hadn't been there a few weeks ago.

Is she pregnant?

I ignored that for the sake of making her come, and then they switched places so Lex could have his way with me before we came up for air.

"God, I'll never get tired of fucking your ass, Chicago." Lex inhaled his cigarette and let it out on a sigh.

I chuckled and rolled to throw an arm over his waist, pushing my head up on my hand and bending my elbow so I could look to Ivy and Miri on the other side of him, cuddling against each other and giggling at whatever Ivy had whispered to my Juliet. She turned to face us, catching my gaze and holding it for a second before shifting to Lex so she could lean in and kiss him. When she glanced back at me again, I raised an eyebrow to suggest I knew what she was hiding.

"What?" she said, furrowing her brows.

"How far along are you?" I smiled as the flush crept up her neck and made the X on her neck.

Miri gasped and Lex sat up straighter, whipping his attention to his former fiancée. "Seriously?"

Ivy nodded and grinned down at him. "It was the time we spent here when Miri and Carter were in Scotland."

Lex smiled harder, his eyes glimmering with the joy he must have felt, the same happiness echoing in my chest. A younger version of me might have been jealous that Ivy's first child would be with Lex, but the one in that bed with them only knew true elation. This was what we wanted. This was what we fought so hard to get. I loved these three humans more than I'd ever loved anyone, and if I got to spend the rest of my life proving that to them, I would.

After I left *Fractured Crowns*, I dedicated my life to LGBTIA+ outreach programs in the greater Washington, DC area. While we might have been shunned in political high society after the news of our affair first went public, our own community opened their arms in welcome. Eventually, the more liberally minded politicians came around, choosing to enmesh their brands with the radical one we had created. We were the most famous queer poly couple in the world, and I wanted to use that platform to make sure no one else ever had to deal with the shit we did. Our children would only be more proof that these types of family structures worked, that our house was full of love and devotion to each other.

"I hope it's a strong-headed ginger," Miri said, leaning in to kiss Ivy.

Ivy wrapped her arms around her and pulled her in closer. "I hope it's a hazel-eyed nightmare. I need someone else to give Lex a run for his money."

Lex laughed and I hugged him closer, and when I fell asleep that night, I realized I never needed the fairy gift. I became the luckiest motherfucker to ever live the day the four of us met in that college cafeteria, and I'd go on that way for the rest of my life.

LEX

I couldn't sleep, so I went downstairs to grab a drink and stood out on the balcony, basking in the full moon's glow. The sounds of the June nightlife echoed around me, cicadas and crickets desperate to make their presence known. Warm, humid air coated my skin and I moaned as I relished the feeling.

The weather in Faerie was weird. It never stormed, and the days could go on forever, making the moon seem even more unattainable. But fuck it...I'd gotten what I wanted. I had my spouses and my kid and another one on the way.

But something didn't quite feel right. When I first returned, I told myself it didn't matter. The queen had fulfilled every other part of my request down to the minute. Poppy had dropped me off outside the church where Ivy had absconded with the prince of Monaco's bride, and Carter had nearly fainted when he saw me. I was living my life. I had gotten out of it all unscathed.

Except...when I stared down at my palm where the proof of my oath to my beloveds used to be, an aching chasm opened in my chest. The queen had restored me to them, but left a chunk of us missing. I remembered how deeply the four of us connected the night before the battle at Beltane, how our union had created a tangible energy that we used to defeat the most powerful fairies in Faerie. I used to be a walking-talking lie detector, for fuck's sake.

Perhaps this was better. Wasn't this what we said we wanted? Normalcy? For things to go back to the way they were before we wandered into those woods on that ill-fated Midsummer? Then why did it feel like I was being suffocated by the mundaneness of my new reality?

Trying not to break down into a full existential crisis, I lit a cigarette and let it out with a soft sigh, telling myself I needed to cut this filthy habit. I didn't smoke around Donnelly, and now that we were having another child, the opportunities to destroy my lungs were dwindling.

Footsteps behind me brought my head up before warm, tender arms circled me, a soft kiss pressing into the center of my shoulder blades.

Ivy.

"What are you doing awake?" I murmured, stabbing out the smoke so she didn't accidentally inhale it.

"Wondering what you're doing." She trailed pecks across my shoulders, soft and sweet, much more civilized than I was used to from her.

"I couldn't sleep." Turning in her hold, I wrapped my arms around her shoulders and brought her in for a hug, inhaling her vanilla scent as deeply as I could.

"What's on your mind?" Ivy twisted her head so she rested her chin on my sternum and looked up at me with a grin.

Nostalgia overwhelmed me, and my thoughts went to much younger versions of us standing in a loft in Georgetown, just figuring out our powers for the first time. She'd entered my head and felt my emotions for the entirety of our lives together.

"Remember how you used to be afraid what we had wasn't real?" I kissed her temple, squeezing her tighter when her muscles relaxed against me. "That I would go back to hating you once the gift went away."

She hummed an affirmative noise. "Yes, I remember."

I dropped my hand to her belly, rubbing the spot where she carried my child...*our* child. "All these years later and pregnant with a Fairfax heir, how do you feel now?"

"My inner teenager is screaming in mortification." She grinned as I laughed, touching my forehead to hers. "But I'm happy with how our life turned out. Aren't you?"

I nodded, but that sense of missing something rose again, like the last puzzle piece hadn't pushed into place yet, like it was just over the horizon, taunting us with being out of reach.

What are we missing?

"What's wrong, Lucifer?" Ivy rubbed my cheek, forcing me to look her in the eyes. "Are you letting regrets eat at you?"

"No, I just—Don't you miss it? Don't you miss the gift and the connection and being able to pick through people's minds?"

She sighed and licked her lips, drawing my gaze to her perfect mouth. "Sometimes. But if that means I lose any of you or have to fight a fairy king again, I'd rather live without it."

Taking a deep inhale, I let her reassurance sink into my skin and tried to adopt that attitude. We had survived. That was supposed to be enough. I had sacrificed my life with them to save them. Shouldn't I be grateful that Diana had sent me back here at all?

Once, long ago, I wished I *had* died instead of my brother, and now I had a family of my own. It was my dream become a reality, my true north, the one vision that kept me going all these years. It was everything I'd ever wanted. It should have been enough.

"I thought I saw Siobhan at the wedding today." She pursed her lips and glanced out toward the woods, almost as if she could will our fairy friends to appear out of the tree line like they once had. "I took Donnelly to change and I could have sworn she was there. I called out for her, but she didn't answer."

"What do you think it means?" I held her tighter, needing her strength as much as she needed mine.

Ivy shook her head. "That I've been working too hard and the pregnancy hormones are starting to fuck with me."

I chuckled, still delighted with her sense of humor after all these years. "Do you think you'll crave chocolate ice cream and sauerkraut like our princess?"

"Ugh." She stepped back and shook her head, pretending to gag. "Don't remind me."

I opened my mouth to tease her about Carter's breeding kink, but stopped when our spouses appeared behind us.

"It's time," Miri said, moonlight twinkling in her eyes, a hint of mischief on her lips.

"Time?" Ivy furrowed her brows and stepped away from me, glancing at Carter. "Time for what?"

Our husband shrugged. "She woke me up and told me to get moving."

"Trust me," Miri said, holding a basket in one hand as she descended the stairs and walked toward the trees.

"Juliet," Carter said, toting after her like a lost puppy. "Where are you going?"

"Just come along," she said. "I've got an idea."

I glanced at Ivy, who raised her eyebrows and followed. Against most of the logical thoughts telling me not to wander into the forest in the middle of the night on Midsummer, I turned and went with them.

MIRI

It was not a sham marriage.

We were in love, all of us, all together. We were always meant to be a four.

The world looked at a relationship like ours and judged us for it, but I no longer cared what they thought. I couldn't, not when my wife brought out the fire in me, not when one of my husbands lived in the darkness and the other was as blinding as endless sunshine.

I'd been having dreams about this for months. The woods had been calling me, reaching out to me however they could. So many times, I had ventured out here and shoved my fingers into the dirt, praying I'd vibrate with that same vitality the plants had once used to communicate. I'd close my eyes and reach out with my senses to dead air.

Ivy hadn't been able to get inside our minds anymore. Lex tried to get the truth out of his clients, but the words held no magic. Carter's luck had finally run out.

A part of me, perhaps the part that had always had a special connection to the trees, lamented what we'd lost…what we'd given up so that we could win. But in my darkest moments, I'd admit I'd do it all again if it brought me the same life.

The tears. The heartache. The threat of a terrible, irreversible loss only to know unimaginable joy.

Until the end, we'd once promised. *Until the end* had been branded on our hands for four years.

The end had come and gone and we'd survived.

All of us. All four of us. Here to bring in the new day.

"What if the lust hits us again?" Ivy said. "What if we get stuck out here?"

"We're not expected anywhere for a few days," I said. "It'll be okay."

Ivy took a deep breath and nodded, sinking to her knees in the grass before opening the bag we'd brought with us. Ivy grabbed the candles and put them on the ground as I sat down next to her to light them. I grabbed the scissors to rip off a piece of my long white dress before handing them to Carter to do the same to his white T-shirt. Lex cut off a strip of his matching shirt and handed it to me as Ivy sliced through her dress for a scrap of the same.

Once I had the four pieces of linen, I tied them together into a tight knot and held my hand out in the middle, overtop of the open flame. I grabbed the ceremonial knife that had been sanitized before coming out here and made a tiny incision in my palm, right over where the words had once shined bright against my alabaster skin. Crimson blood bubbled over the cut, and I watched as my spouses did the same to their hands before placing them over mine. Ivy gripped my palm and Carter lay his on top of hers. Lex went under me, holding all of us up with his indomitable strength, truly the king of our world, the gravity around which all of us spun.

I wrapped the fabric around our combined embrace, over and under and over again until Ivy helped me knot it on top.

Blood dripped from Carter and Ivy over my hand and down onto Lex's, combining each of us, mixing our life force. Ivy's fire soothed Lex's ice and emboldened Carter's autumn chill. And each of them complemented the sunny frost of my springtime spirit. We were always meant to be a four, and after everything that happened, I thanked God that had not changed.

"Okay," I said, glancing at each one of them before returning my attention to our embrace. "Here goes nothing." I cleared my throat and went first. "I vow to love you. All of you. I will honor and cherish you and treat you with respect." I winked at Ivy when she smiled, clearly recognizing the words from the first time we'd made this promise, all those Midsummers ago. "I will never betray you. I will never hold you back from your dreams or each other. I promise honesty. From today until the end."

Lex went next, reciting nearly the same words over again, followed by Carter and Ivy, who both struggled to get through the whole thing without breaking into tears.

"I know I say this all the time," I continued, giving their combined hands an endearing squeeze. "But thank you for forgiving me. I haven't made it easy to love me, but you do. And I can never be as grateful as I should be."

"Miri," Ivy said, wiping away a tear with her free hand. "I told you. I'll always take you however I can get you. There's nothing to forgive."

"If anyone is difficult to love, it's me, Princess," Lex said.

"We deserve each other," Carter added. "In all the ways possible."

"It's time," came a voice on the wind, a whisper that made the hair on my arms stand on end.

I gasped as a sharp burning pain sliced through the center of my palm, sucking in air as it ached and throbbed. Lex winced and Ivy groaned, each one pulling away from our handfast.

"Fucking hell!" Ivy said, grabbing her aching hand with her free one.

I watched it happen this time, staring in amazement as the letters burned into my skin.

Until the end.

The vow we made to each other six years ago in Killwater woods was now etched bright and brilliant on my palm.

"It worked," Ivy murmured, her eyes glimmering with wonder and anticipation.

"It fucking worked," Lex said, running his hands back through his hair. "It's back. Lie to me. Say you hate me."

"Come see," the trees called again.

"I hate you, Lucifer," Ivy said. "I've always hated you."

Lex winced and curled his lips into a smile. "Liar."

Carter laughed and held his uninjured hand out to Ivy. "Try to get in my head. Go on! See how hot I think you're gonna be when you get all swollen with our baby."

Ivy took his hand, but I already knew the truth. Our gifts had returned to us. My dreams had been right.

"They're coming," the trees said. I didn't know who or what they meant, only that I needed to stand to greet our new guests. I glanced

around, exhilaration filling me when the heavy rustling of under-growth announced multiple visitors.

"What is that?" Lex said.

"Who's here?" Carter called.

I didn't know what we would find in the woods, but whatever it was, we were together. We could face it as long as we were a four. Gone were the days of insecurity or questioning when they would leave me. Gone was thinking I could protect them by staying away.

I loved our little family, and once I'd dug in my heels and pressed the issue, my grandparents relented. It had taken time, but they had started to recognize Donnelly as a member of their family, if not yet a part of the royal household. But I knew they would come around to all of it. Even if they didn't, I no longer placed such emphasis on their opinion. The only family I needed was the one I had with these three humans.

The strength in that knowledge had me standing firm, gripping Lex's fingers on one side and Ivy's on the other, her free hand in Carter's.

But when the visitors broke through the tree line, relief lifted the weight off my chest.

Siobhan walked ahead with a fully grown Poppy standing next to her, now almost the same height as our fairy friend.

"Poppy?" Carter called in disbelief.

The changeling raced toward my husband and threw her arms around his neck, pulling him in for a hug. He laughed and held her, spinning her around in his embrace. Then she went to Ivy, holding her arms out. I thought my wife might turn her away, but she didn't. She hugged Poppy like an old friend, tears in her eyes and a smile on her lips. I likewise greeted our adopted daughter with a grin.

"What is this?" Ivy said, turning to Siobhan. "I thought you were banned from this realm. I claimed it as my own."

"Aye, you did," Siobhan said with a nod. "I told you Poppy was special. She's the key, and she always has been."

"Are you staying?" Carter asked. "Are you home for good?"

"For a while," Poppy said. "We have a lot to catch up on."

"And we have the rest of our lives to do it," I said, joy swelling in my torso that we'd all been reunited and things had worked out the way they were meant to. In this fairy tale, the princess wasn't rescued by a knight in shining armor or a king who had faced a dragon or a queen with an axe to grind. Instead, I was saved by all three, and now, I knew how to stand on my own. No one and nothing could separate us again.

Like Lex had said all those years ago, I deserved to be happy. So I would be.

SHREW
TEASER

What, with my tongue in your tail?
Nay, come again, Good Kate; I am a gentleman.
-Petruchio, Act II, Scene I

"Does it feel good?" I asked, dragging my tongue along the underside of his cock, a small swell of pride shooting through my stomach when he rolled his head back.

"God, yes," he groaned, tunneling his hands through his hair. "You're such a good fucking girl."

I kissed the velvet skin on his shaft, working up and down again, knowing he liked it this way the most.

"How much do you love it, sir?" I squeezed his balls before dipping his cock back into my mouth, slowly allowing it to slide to the back of my throat.

"More than you could possibly imagine." He buried his fingers in my long dark hair, fisting handfuls as he guided my head the way he wanted. I loved this the most, when he took control, when he made me purr in a way only he could. "My little kitten. My precious cub."

Fuck, that turned me on more. All these years I had walked this planet and no one had ever made me as wet as him. No one had ever come close. Pressure built between my legs and I dug two fingers into my clit, trying to alleviate it.

"Uh, uh, uh," he said, slowing his pace while he tsked his teeth, chiding me. "Don't you dare touch that pussy, love. That's mine to play with. Mine to have and to hold, forever and ever."

I whined, letting his cock go with a loud *pop* that had his hips bucking off the cushioned seat.

"We're not married," I said. "Not really."

He ran the back of his fingers down the side of my cheek. "Just like we're not fucking, not really."

I took a deep breath and glanced at the scene he'd chosen for us. We were in his grandfather's throne room, or at least, I thought we were. I hadn't gone to London with my parents any of the times they'd visited, so I couldn't be sure. But he'd told me about this fantasy in one of our lifetimes, how he liked to bring people back to the palace and sit on his family's ancestral throne and skull fuck whoever would let him. In this case, he liked doing it to me because of what it said to his grandparents.

What did it matter?

This wasn't real. None of this was real. Not even my feelings for him. They, too, were manufactured by the world's biggest villain— Alberich, the fairy king. My heart clenched and I blinked back tears.

I thought I had loved him, once upon a time. I thought I had loved him and married him over and over again for a hundred years. But no...that was a fiction built for me by a monster from a nightmare.

I didn't have a choice in loving Prince Edward, Duke of Sussex, nor did I have a choice in connecting to his mind every single night and living out these deliciously vile fantasies with him.

But alas, there I remained.

"*Kit,*" someone called from the real world, and I glanced up at Edward's green eyes one last time before blinking back to existence. "Kit," came the voice again.

I focused my gaze on my much younger sister, Abigail. "What?"

"Are you okay?" She squinted at me. "You were calling out some random dude's name in your sleep."

Ahh, hell.

"I'm fine. What do you want?" I didn't talk about my time spent under the fairy king's spell. Aside from my siblings, who would believe me? It wasn't like being abducted by the fairies was a modern-day occurrence, if it ever was, and almost no one on the planet could relate to feeling mentally seven hundred years old while being in a twenty-four-year-old body.

"It's Mother," she said, her steel eyes swimming with torment while she wrung her hands. "I need your help."

WANT MORE?

Thank you for reading *Beltane* and the entire Midsummer Series, and if you enjoyed it, please leave a review on Goodreads, Amazon, and/or anywhere else you get your books. Not only do they help other readers, but the algorithm uses reviews to promote and categorize the book.

If you want more of the *Midsummer* world, I have a novella featuring Siobhan, Finn, and Donnelly. It's a 13k short that takes place before *Midsummer*.

If you're interested, please follow this link: https://books.jenadoyle.com/WeWildThings

Thanks again. Keep reading for more on how I adapted the play and how I feel about Shakespeare.

Acknowledgments

Dear Reader,

That's a wrap on my *Midsummer Night's Dream* redux. Thank you so much for sticking with it *until the end*. I hope you fell as much in love with these characters as I have, and be sure to subscribe to my newsletter to find out about *Shrew* when it's ready. Right now, it's feeling like two books about Kit and Edward, tentatively titled *Shrew* and *Tamed*. After that, I have plans for a Jon book and an Abigail book, but more about that later.

I'm often asked why I decided to adapt this play and how I went about it. If you don't know the major plot points of the original storyline, it goes a little something like this:

- Hermia is in love with Lysander, but her father betroths her to Demetrius.
- Hermia's best friend, Helena, is dating Demetrius until he unceremoniously dumps her because of the engagement.
- Hermia rebels against her father's wishes and runs into the woods with Lysander.
- Helena, hoping to win Demetrius back, tells him what Hermia did, so he takes off to find his fiancée.
- Distraught that this did not win back the love of her life and determined to take it out on Hermia, Helena goes after all three.
- Enter the fairies, stage left.

- King Oberon and Queen Titania are in a pissing match over a changeling child who each wants to keep for themselves.
- As is often the way with fairies, King Oberon can't resist meddling with our four lovers when they cross his path.
- He sends his henchman, Puck, to give a love potion to Demetrius so he falls in love with Helena.
- Puck accidentally gives it to Lysander, realizes his mistake, and gives it to Demetrius without removing it from Lysander.
- For a brief time, the two men scorn Hermia in favor of Helena, who thinks they're playing a cruel joke on her.
- By the end of the play, Puck removes the fairy potion from Lysander so he can marry Hermia.
- Demetrius doesn't get the same treatment, and he marries Helena under the illusion that he's in love with her. (The real plot is far more complex than this, I am paraphrasing for brevity. If you want to know more, google that shit.)
- And then they all live happily ever after... *or do they?*

Every time I read the original work, I'm left thinking...poor fucking Demetrius. Ya' know? Just because he's a jerk doesn't mean he deserves to be under a fairy curse forever.

Some have argued that Demetrius deserves it for breaking it off with Helena, but what *about* Helena? Does she deserve to live a lie for the sake of karmic revenge on Demetrius?

Maybe this is a play about feminism and sticking a middle finger to the traditional patriarchal bullshit that is matrimony. Hermia and Helena get to have their desired partner in a time when women were offered little choice if none at all. Does this mean that Demetrius plays the feminine role, that he must marry who was chosen *for him* because he was so willing to marry for lands and titles at the beginning?

Where is his consent? Would Helena have made the same choice if she knew he was only doing it because of Oberon's influence? Why do Lysander and Hermia get what they want and the other two just get what's left? And if we take away Demetrius's choice to marry Helena, since he did so under the guise of the fairy potion, then none of them truly have consent. Helena can not consensually marry Demetrius, as she does not know he is still under the fairy potion. Hermia and Lysander can not consensually marry each other since Demetrius does not remember that he objects to it in the first place.

This is to say nothing of the homoerotic undertones between Helena and Hermia from the beginning. It is easy to take the position that Helena is truly jealous of *Lysander,* not Hermia. There is good evidence in the play to suggest this, especially if we consider that Shakespeare might have been a woman (or that one author of the combined Shakespeare might have been a woman. More on this in a second.)

I tried to play with those themes in all of the *Midsummer* books. Ivy is my Hermia, Lex is my Demetrius, Carter is my Lysander, and Miri is my Helena. None of them have a choice because Lex and Ivy never did. I've made the homoerotic undertones between all of them blatantly obvious and painfully part of the plot. It's more angsty and fun that way.

I also wanted to play with the literary criticism of Hermia and Helena being interchangeable. Their names are very similar. They grew up together so we can assume they must have come from similar backgrounds. This is why I've made Ivy our American princess and Miri our British princess. They initially become friends (and lovers) because of this similarity. They know each other on a level that cis-het presenting men simply can not and never will understand.

I loved the idea of keeping the double marriage at the end, but I couldn't pick a man for each Princess. Would it be *technically* accurate for Ivy to end up with Carter and Lex to end up with Miri? Yes. But the play is about couples switching and then switching back, thus proving the mercurial and trivial nature of love and marriage in the first place. Even though we are compelled to do it, marriage itself is a sham, a farce, and sometimes a trap. Let us not forget that matrimony as we know it today was created as a means for a man to "possess" a woman's body so that he could be sure any children she birthed were his. (The agricultural revolution ruined everything.) It was important to me that the women kept their bodily autonomy. Any children of Ivy's are Miri's. Any children of Miri's are Ivy's. End of story.

As for Poppy... Ah yes, my sweet changeling child. Another part of the original play that irritated me was that the child is never seen on stage. Many variations have added him almost as a prop piece, seen in the background but never really contributing to his own sovereignty. In the play, he's the reason the Queen and the King are fighting to begin with. But what does the changeling want? Does he want to stay with the Queen? Or would he prefer to go with the King? Or maybe the changeling just wanted to find what remained of his human family and forget the fairies altogether? I wanted to give my changeling more agency, to make them a fully developed character capable of their own choices. Say what you will about Poppy, but she's always playing her own game, and we will see her again.

For the sake of my health and magic, I will not speak ill of the fairies, only to say that I always hated how the King turned Bottom into a donkey and made the Queen fall in love with him. It's meant to be funny, and I guess to a Renaissance audience, it must have been. But when the spell is broken, the Queen submits to the King, gives him the changeling, and says she was wrong to defy him in the first place. Fuck all that noise. The Queen of the Fae (as I know her in my witchy woo woo shit) would have handed the King's ass to him on a silver platter. So when our lovers turned the curse back on him, I wanted him to get a taste of his own medicine. I hope you agree.

Finally, a note about authorship: If you ask me, Shakespeare was written by a lot of different people — Edward de Vere, Emilia Bassano, Ben Johnson, Christopher Marlowe, and probably a few others that have been lost to history. The playwright "William Shakespeare" was an amalgamation of several different authors who kept their identities secret for one reason or another. (i.e. belonging to the peerage, being a woman, being unable to find notoriety on their own, etc.) It was certainly NOT William Shaksper from Stratford-Upon-Avon, who could barely spell his own name much less write several infamous and deeply complex plays. No, I will not take questions on this, even if I cannot prove it (though many have tried). I know it to be true in my heart and in my gut. It's the only thing that has ever made sense to me about the topic.

This is why I say that yes — Shakespeare was a man. And a woman. And straight. And gay. And rich. And poor. And English. And Italian. And Christian. And Jewish. Like the plays themselves, Shakespeare was rife with contradictions and plagued by pervasive undertones we can only guess at. And that has only made the works better.

There are a lot of people I have to thank for helping me through this. Most importantly, my loving partner and best friend in the whole wide world, Mr. Doyle. His support has been incredible, and he is always willing to walk by my side on whatever road I choose. I love you so very much.

To my shadow work circle - Amethyst, Nae, Willow, and Becca. Thank you for supporting me, guiding me, and listening to me vent. Thank you for reading my stories and loving them. Thank you for everything. Old ladies today, old ladies tomorrow, old ladies forever. (That's going on the survey.)

To my beta readers - Leslie, Maggie, Shannon, Jenn, and Sarah. You made this story what it is. Without your input, it would have been so much different and likely worse. Thank you for suffering through the muck with me.

To my editors - Misha and Kimberly. Thank you for being on my team. It's been a hell of a ride and I appreciate every correction.

To my ARC readers - Your early acceptance and hype of these books has meant so much. Thank you for finding me, and thank you for sticking it out with me.

To Freya - When I first started writing this book, I was in the darkest chapter of my life. You reached out to me, gave me hope, and told me not to fuck it up. I try every day to live up to that. I hope I make you proud. Thank you for being there for me. I am honored to call myself one of yours.

And finally, to you, dear reader. Our lovers have been through it, and you've been there every step of the way. I want you to know something — if you are queer, if you are non-het, if you are poly, if you have ever been "othered" in your life, you are valid. You are worthy and deserving of love. *I love you.* I probably don't know you and I likely never will, but if you are reading this, I am reaching out through the vastness of time and space and words and I love you. You are a part of my queer family. Don't ever let anyone take your power. You owe yourself that.

Until the end.

Cheers!

-Jena

ALSO BY JENA DOYLE

<u>MIDSUMMER</u>

We Wild Things (Prequel Novella)

Midsummer

Samhain

Solstice

Beltane

<u>STEEL ROSES MC</u>

They Called Him Saint (Prequel Novella)

Crimson Chaos

Savage Saint

Oleander Oaths

Mischief Mayhem

Ruthless Reign

<u>ROYAL BASTARDS MC: HELENA, MT</u>

Blood and Whiskey

Blood and Magic

www.ingramcontent.com/pod-product-compliance
Lightning Source LLC
Chambersburg PA
CBHW030146310726
48970CB00005B/1610